Nowhere to Hide

The tape kept running and then a voice, speaking softly and slightly distorted by the maximum volume of the small tape recorder.

"This is the voice of Tenterallah, the Army of God. I speak for Abu Beka.

"The Holy War has started. With their latest atrocities in Puerto Rico and their savage assaults on our sacred soldiers in New York and Rome, the forces of Satan in the West have once again shown that they cannot be permitted to live. Those responsible for these savage attacks upon Islam will pay the supreme price for their evil. That is the promise of Tenterallah, the Army of God, and we warn all the nations of the world: Either stand with us or you stand with Satan. If you choose to do Satan's work, none of you shall be safe.

"From this moment on, we carry the fight to the enemy's heartland, the United States. Lives will be forfeit because holy justice is on our side. God is great!"

BLOCKBUSTER FICTION FROM PINNACLE BOOKS!

THE FINAL VOYAGE OF THE S.S.N. SKATE   (17-157, $3.95)
by Stephen Cassell
The "leper" of the U.S. Pacific Fleet, SSN 578 nuclear attack sub
SKATE, has one final mission to perform—an impossible act of
piracy that will pit the underwater deathtrap and its inexperienced
crew against the combined might of the Soviet Navy's finest!

QUEENS GATE RECKONING   (17-164, $3.95)
by Lewis Purdue
Only a wounded CIA operative and a defecting Soviet ballerina
stand in the way of a vast consortium of treason that speeds toward the hour of mankind's ultimate reckoning! From the best-
selling author of THE LINZ TESTAMENT.

FAREWELL TO RUSSIA   (17-165, $4.50)
by Richard Hugo
A KGB agent must race against time to infiltrate the confines of
U.S. nuclear technology after a terrifying accident threatens to
unleash unmitigated devastation!

THE NICODEMUS CODE   (17-133, $3.95)
by Graham N. Smith and Donna Smith
A two-thousand-year-old parchment has been unearthed, un-
leashing a terrifying conspiracy unlike any the world has previ-
ously known, one that threatens the life of the Pope himself, and
the ultimate destruction of Christianity!

*Available wherever paperbacks are sold, or order direct from the
Publisher. Send cover price plus 50¢ per copy for mailing and
handling to Pinnacle Books, Dept.17-333, 475 Park Avenue
South, New York, N.Y. 10016. Residents of New York, New Jer-
sey and Pennsylvania must include sales tax. DO NOT SEND
CASH.*

WARREN MURPHY

Scorpion's Dance

PINNACLE BOOKS
WINDSOR PUBLISHING CORP.

PINNACLE BOOKS

are published by

Windsor Publishing Corp.
475 Park Avenue South
New York, NY 10016

Copyright © 1990 by Warren Murphy

First printing: April, 1990

Printed in the United States of America

For Andy McCabe, Bob Meier,
Bob Gallagher, Al and Shirlee Neumaier,
Hank and Erika Holzer . . .
Friends All.

And Always For Molly Cochran.

PROLOGUE

Maria Barsotti shifted the sleeping child in her arms, trying to get comfortable, but no matter what airline it was or what they said in their commercials to grab your money, airplane seats were never big enough for comfort.

Maybe up in the first class section, and she had thought for a moment about the family flying first class, but then she found out that first class seats would cost twice as much and quickly settled for the family fare tourist package.

And it wouldn't have been so bad, she thought, except that the roar of the jet's engines on takeoff had frightened Cara and she had screamed until Maria had to take her from the next seat, hold her in her lap, and comfort her.

Nick had offered to help, but he had his hands full with the other two across the aisle. Both Teresa and Nick Junior were full of questions, and their father delighted in answering them. Nick had not seen them for three months because he had financed this vacation trip back to their old hometown in Italy by working for three months on a hurry-up roadbuilding project in Alabama, far away from their home in the New Jersey suburbs.

Imagine. Auntie Irena one hundred years old. And still working, still taking in sewing, still straining her eyes. So much for the Russians and their yogurt, Maria Barsotti thought. Auntie Irena had never even heard of yogurt. She said her only health secret was Chianti, the stronger the better, at least four glasses a day. She said red wine fortified the blood, and maybe she was right. Every day, it seemed, some doctor somewhere was announcing in the paper that some old wives' tale about how to live long was really true. Cod liver oil. Chicken soup. Why not Chianti?

Maria shifted the baby around to the empty seat next to her, smiled at Nick, and shut her eyes, hoping to catch a nap.

Nick grinned back at her and watched her eyes close. Even with her face relaxed and even without her pixie smile, Maria still did not look thirty-two. Maybe twenty-two. Lots of his friends, heavy equipment operators like himself, whistled at her and teased him about robbing the cradle.

"What?" Nick turned to look at Nick Junior, ten years old, but still wide-eyed with wonder about the flight, about Italy, about the grandparents he'd never seen, about everything.

"Dad, do they have Pizza Huts in Rome?"

Nick laughed. "Probably not," he said. "But don't worry. There's pizza everywhere. We always had it at home."

"At home?" Nick Junior said. "You mean, like homemade?" Obviously he had never heard of such a

8

thing. Pizza came from a parlor or a hut or a freezer.

"Dummy." Teresa poked her younger brother with the assurance of a twelve-year-old who knew everything. "Pizza was invented in Italy. Everybody knows that. So was pasta."

"Oh." Nick Junior shrank down in his seat. He always felt so dumb. Nick put an arm around him and said, "Teresa's right about the pizza, but not the pasta. Let me tell you about Marco Polo. . . ."

Coming down the aisle, a tall brunette slowed down to look the children over. They were really cute, she thought, almost in the league with her two kids back home in New York City. What were they doing now, she wondered. Having dinner with Hannah, her former mother-in-law? Or perhaps Joel "the king" had even deigned to stop by and take his children out to dinner.

As Sarah Huddlestein got to her seat, she wavered slightly and a stewardess asked her if she felt all right. The correct answer would have been no, but instead Sarah said, "I'm fine. But I'd love some club soda."

"Sure thing," the stewardess said with a perfect plastic smile, and sashayed back down the aisle of the aircraft while the man in the seat across from Sarah leaned out toward the aisle to watch the stewardess's undulating walk.

Sarah brought her seat forward and dropped the tray down in front of her. Maybe the club soda would help the nausea, but she didn't really think so. Of all the stupid times to get pregnant. She had found out exactly seven hours earlier when the doctor's office had called Saks Fifth Avenue and Sarah was practically out the door to catch the flight to Rome. It had not really sunk in until she was in the cab on her way to JFK.

Well, she would just have to put the nausea and the pregnancy out of her mind for a while. This was her first buying trip to Italy, and she had to make good. The store planned a tribute to Italy for the Christmas season, and the evening gowns she bought had to be more glamorous and more Italian-looking than anyone else's in the city.

She looked up into the smooth, unlined face of the stewardess, who said "There you go" as she swooped the club soda past Sarah's nose and brought it to a safe landing on the tray. "Thanks," Sarah murmured, but the stewardess was already undulating away again and the man across the aisle was ogling again. Would he keep that up the entire flight? Obviously a married man. Probably a married salesman.

She felt her cheeks color as she remembered that the father of her unborn child was also a married salesman. Did they have abortion clinics in Rome? *Of course not, you twit, Italy is a Catholic country.* One more reason to postpone a decision, and Sarah knew there would be postponement after postponement until finally an abortion was out of the question. The trouble was that she loved being pregnant, loved giving birth, loved babies. But would Saks Fifth Avenue love this unwed mother? Maybe she could con them into putting her in a window display with a star over her head. After all, that's what Christmas was all about. Sarah smiled softly at her own joke and told herself she would make out somehow. She always did.

He *was* a married salesman and he shifted his attention to the dark-haired woman across the aisle smiling to herself. Maybe, Tom Waldor told himself, that was what he needed: someone closer to his own age of forty and someone who could smile at herself. But the stewardess had already accepted his dinner invitation after, he noted, she had checked out his eight-hundred-dollar suit, his diamond pinky ring, and his handmade glove-leather loafers. Probably the pickings this flight weren't too good in the first class section for her to have to settle for somebody back in the tourist cabin. Well, no problem. He would take her out—what was her name anyway? . . . Ginny. He would take Ginny out and get her so liquored up that she didn't even notice the crummy hotel room with the rusty plumbing in the closet-size bathroom. Hey, he told himself. Eat, drink, and be merry, because your wife's three thousand miles away.

The pilot announced over the loudspeaker that he was preparing for landing. The no smoking light flashed on. Two minutes later it was followed with the warning to fasten seat belts, and Ginny announced that passengers should make sure their snack trays were secured and their seat backs were in an upright position.

Cara Barsotti woke up wailing as Maria fastened her seat belt around the four-year-old. "Shh, shh,

11

angel, we'll soon be on land again. Everything will be okay." Cara seemed to understand that and quietly examined her mother through her tears. Maria fastened her own seat belt more tightly and put her arm around the child's shoulders. "Soon, baby, soon."

Nick had the other two children strapped in and, as always, reached across the aisle to take Maria's hand.

Sarah Huddlestein had already fastened her belt. She took a quick look at her appointment book. She knew it by heart but kept worrying that she might not leave her hotel early enough in the morning to get to the unfamiliar streets. She should have stopped at Barnes and Noble to buy a street map.

Tom Waldor shut his eyes in prayer. He was not a religious man, but aboard an aircraft he became as devout as Billy Graham.

"I don't see what you see in the older guys," the other stewardess, Pamela, whispered to Ginny as they both fastened their belts in the utility seats in the rear of the plane.

Ginny's plastic smile became a real one. "You know what they say," she whispered back. "Because older men are so grateful."

Pamela snorted. "You've got it backward. That's what they say about old women and young men."

"So, when I'm old I'll go for young men. If I keep adding to the little nest egg, I'll be able to afford them."

"And *then* I guess you'll be grateful," Pamela said.

Ginny winked. "No. They'll still be the grateful ones."

The landing at Leonardo da Vinci Airport was smooth, and the plane glided effortlessly toward the terminal. As usual, even before Ginny and Pamela could unbuckle themselves, there were people in the aisles, collecting their overhead bags, jostling each other as if being first off the plane were a contest. Some, however, like Maria and Nick Barsotti, were content to wait.

Finally, all had disembarked and were waiting for clearance through customs. The Barsottis had arranged for a rental car because Nick hoped that he and Maria would be able to stash the kids with their grandparents and spend a couple of days out in the countryside, alone together as sort of a second honeymoon.

Sarah Huddlestein and Tom Waldor were going to take the airport bus which stopped at their hotels. Ginny had hurriedly arranged with the salesman to meet him at a late-hours restaurant where the prices were high, the decor lush, and the strolling musicians filled in conversational gaps.

Struggling with baggage, the passengers and crew of Flight 606 from JFK were crossing the immense airport's oddly quiet reception area when the first two gays in the crowd, two men from New York's SoHo district stopped dead, causing a backup.

One of them cried out, "Oh, no. He's got a gun." He turned and tried to run.

He was the first one shot.

The crowd swung around, almost en masse, and saw more gunmen behind them. They all wore ski masks.

The survivors would remember forever the frozen seconds while the gunmen just took dead aim. They would remember, too, the smells of excrement and urine, perspiration, and the unforgettable metallic odor of blood running everywhere.

There were four gunmen and one woman. One terrorist was killed by a security guard whose wild shooting also injured an airport reservations clerk. Two of the gunmen were knocked unconscious by two passengers who were New York City policemen on vacation. The last two men got away.

Behind them, they left Maria Barsotti and her daughter Cara dead in a pool of blood. Nick Barsotti had been grazed with a bullet as he tried to throw his body over his two other children. Twelve-year-old Teresa Barsotti's stomach had been pulverized with bullets, and she lived only long enough to die in the arms of her brother, Nick Junior.

Ginny and Pamela, their eyes open but unseeing, lay side by side in death, as if they had been lovers.

Tom Waldor's last words were "What's happening?" He fell near the body of Sarah Huddlestein, whose unborn baby would be not even a memory in anyone's mind.

Besides the seven killed, twenty-four passengers aboard Flight 606 had been wounded by gunfire.

It tooks weeks to scrub the bloodstains from the airport's porous marble floors.

CHAPTER ONE

Within moments of the massacre at Da Vinci Airport, all hell broke loose at Questura-15 on the Via Svitale, the headquarters of the Pubblica Sicurezza, the public security police of Rome.

While officials there knew that the carabinieri, Italy's national police, would be taking over eventually, there was a chance that the city police could claim early jurisdiction and thereby have the glory of holding and questioning international terrorists, which might even mean a visit from the Pope. Captain Giorgio S. Luciano already planned to write a book about it — *Roman Slaughter* he would call it — and become the Italian Joseph Wambaugh.

Everyone with gold braid on sleeve, collar, or hat fled from headquarters for the airport, leaving behind a skeleton force to man the phones, collect messages, and to wonder why they, too, could not be at the scene of the crime. It would have been worth many drinks at the local trattoria to be able to report firsthand information on what the monster terrorists looked like, what they said, what they ate, and what cowards they really were.

A handsome blond officer sat at a desk and addressed a sergeant, who paced back and forth in his annoyance at being left behind.

"Sergeant, suppose another terrorist attack happens. Can we go to it?"

The sergeant glared at him before snapping, "This isn't a carnival, Venditio. This isn't one party after another that we're invited to. You have paperwork to do, I assume? If not, I could find you a broom."

Venditio ducked his head almost to his blotter and examined the stack of papers in front of him. When the telephone rang, he looked up at the sergeant, who glowered, indicating that he, as a sergeant, was not in the mood to pass the time of day with an ordinary report of an ordinary crime.

It was going to be one of those nights, Venditio thought with a sigh. It was always one of those nights. On the third ring, he answered the phone in a brisk voice: "Pubblica Sicurezza."

There was the sound of fumbling on the other end of the phone before the caller spoke.

"Do not ask my name. It is not important. I am a friend of the Tenterallah, the Islamic Army of God. Am I speaking to someone of importance?"

Venditio sat up bamboo straight, his muted blue eyes flashing as he cradled the phone between his chin and shoulder, found pad and pencil with one hand while the other flailed about in the air, trying to capture the sergeant's attention.

From the corner of his eye the sergeant saw the hand waving but ignored it. It was too much for Venditio. He covered the mouthpiece and bellowed,

"Sergeant! Trace this call! It's Tenterallah."

"Little fairy," the sergeant muttered, picking up another phone and doing what Venditio had told him to do. One could not take chances with anything, even if a well-worn asshole was the one giving the orders.

"Go ahead. I'm important enough to write it down," Venditio said into the phone, his voice assuming authority. The sergeant picked up the extension and held both phones, one to each ear, and his bushy eyebrows rose ceilingward as the caller talked. *Goddamn the little queer. He should have put me on the phone,* he thought.

The caller's voice seemed to come from a long distance away. It was muted and spoke in precise, polished, but obviously not native Italian. Later, the sergeant would say that Venditio had handled himself well because the boy pretended to have never heard of Tenterallah, the most infamous terrorist group in the world.

"Are you there?" Venditio said. "This must be a bad connection. I can hear nothing."

"The connection is fine. Stop your babbling and listen to me. I am from Tenterallah and I have a message from Abu Beka. Do not bother tracing this call, for I will be long gone. Abu Beka's message is this: This evening's events at Da Vinci Airport are just a beginning. There will be more deaths, for that is the only true way for the people to understand us and to learn we are right. Do not pity the people who died tonight; they are at peace, and that is all we seek — peace for the world, peace for Palestine, peace for freedom-loving peoples anywhere. And hear me

17

now. Free our captured brothers immediately or there will be reprisals and the blood will flow in the streets of Rome."

Venditio hugged the phone to his face and spoke, although he knew the line was dead. "But why did you kill children?"

The sergeant listened to his other phone, then banged it down in disgust. "Not long enough. We couldn't trace it. Goddamn filthy bastards. Venditio, stop your whining and type up that fucking conversation."

Venditio hung up the dead phone, but before he started typing, he crossed himself surreptitiously.

A short time later, the police brass returned to the station and Venditio was questioned by them, by the carabinieri, by several government officials, and finally by men in very expensive Italian suits who he assumed must be reporters for American television networks. Everything from his birthplace and date, his education, his family connections . . . all was filled out in triplicate. Venditio had never before had so much attention. He gloried in it and lovingly recounted how he had asked the terrorist, "But why did you kill children?"

After a few hours the important men all left and the not-so-important policemen crowded around the blond officer. "I felt like ripping out the phone and throwing it through the window," Venditio said. He said it so often that his fellow officers became bored listening to him.

Venditio asked where the two captured terrorists had been taken and again became the target of jokes. "Why?" asked a short, muscular policeman. "You looking for a date?"

Venditio blushed but persisted. "I just wanted to see what those bastards look like. The report that came in after the phone call said they looked like anybody."

"They look like anybody if anybody is a fucking Arab," one policeman said. "But you won't see them. The big guns from the carabinieri took them away to hide them."

"Why?" Venditio asked.

"There were Americans killed, almost a whole family wiped out, so the carabinieri hid them away so the Americans can't question them and try to get them extradited before we have a chance to try them for murder and cut their fucking throats."

"I hope we do," said Venditio, and this time there was no mockery and no laughter. All the other policemen wished for the same thing.

By the time the eleven P.M. news came on in New York City, most of the relatives and some friends of the people slain had been contacted and a few coerced into making statements for the cameras.

Hannah Huddlestein and her son Joel allowed a camera crew and Rupert Dillon from ABC-TV into Hannah's tacky apartment. The glare from the sofa's clear plastic cover infuriated the cameraman, but Hannah refused to let them remove it. "Sarah was a wonderful mother for our children," Joel Huddlestein said, even as he was calculating if the cost of raising two children was so much that he would have to give up his membership at the New York Racquet

19

Club.

Miriam Lopez-Luciano was sent by CBS to round up friends or relatives of the Barsotti family. The best she could do was stand in front of the small New Jersey house where they had lived and show viewers the front steps. "And here, little Cara and Teresa played. . . ." The head of CBS news watched the report and decided that Miriam's fat ass was cooked.

NBC did better. They found the wife of Tom Waldor, the married salesman, in a bar near her home on West 70th Street, trying to pick up a much younger man. When they told her the news, she clutched her heart and leaned on the young man. Somehow, the word got out that he was her son. He was drunk enough to agree to anything. Mrs. Waldor said that the tragic news had shattered her universe and asked "her son" to take her home immediately.

Correspondents all over the world kept trying to top each other with a new angle to the story, but the only one who succeeded was Ian Prince, a freelance TV journalist, who had an "in" with Muammar Kaddafi, Libya's leader.

Prince sold the interview to ABC which got it by satellite in time for use on Ted Koppel's *Nightline*. Kaddafi, eyes piercing, tight-lipped, read a statement in strained English: "Again, Tenterallah has acted in a most heroic way. The two martyrs who were arrested must be freed to continue their work for peace. The people in the airport this evening died for a just cause and are more important now than they ever would have been if they lived. Allah praise Tenterallah, the Army of God, and their good works."

20

Ted Koppel shook his head on television, trained his beagle eyes on the camera, and said, "On that sad note, we end this evening's broadcast."

The sky swam with stars. The full moon hung so low that it seemed to touch the trees in Fiumicino, a small city twenty miles west of Rome, on the shore of the Mediterranean.

Three men, wearing black clothes and black ski masks, sat patiently at the bottom of a vertical cliff that stretched above them for a full hundred feet. An occasional sturdy wave would splash up onshore around their feet and lap against the side of the small black rubber raft that had brought them there.

While the three men huddled close to the rock wall, it was not really necessary because even if it had been broad daylight, no one from above could have seen them without crawling out to the edge of the cliff. Since the house above the men had been built into the cliff and the stone wall of the first floor was almost directly flush with the face of the rock, it was virtually impossible.

The men had been sitting motionless for thirty minutes and none had spoken a word. There had been no need to speak; everything necessary had already been discussed. There was a contingency plan for everything. Including death.

Finally, one whispered in Arabic, "Fucking weathermen always lie."

"Shhhh," replied the leader of the group, but he understood the frustration. There was supposed to be rain tonight. But where was it? Where were the clouds that would cover their ascent? He would have to make a decision whether to proceed before the Italians had a chance to move the prisoners again. In a few hours it would be daylight, and they needed at least an hour to get in and get out.

Just as he began to say a silent prayer for the weather to cooperate, there it was! From far away a flash of lightning. The storm was traveling in from the Mediterranean. Now pray to God that it was in time.

In fifteen minutes the sky that had been so grandly lit was scattered with clouds. First the stars disappeared. Then the moon gave up and let itself be covered, and at the first drops of rain, the men moved quickly.

They lashed themselves together with ropes, and using mountain climbing gear designed for use in the Alps, slowly began to work their way in single file up the face of the rock. Aziz went first; the leader brought up the rear, and as they climbed, he reviewed again what he had learned about the villa. An exiled Mafia boss from the United States had built it for his mistress while his wife and five children lived in cramped quarters in Rome. The chief had bragged to his friends that his blond honey was his captive, his love slave, and she adored that life, but one night the Mafioso's chauffeur killed two guards and tossed the boss's body over the cliff. Then he and the blond honey had disappeared with the money from the villa's safe. When no one showed up to pay the taxes on the property, the villa was bought up covertly by the Italian government and used for secret meetings. Its location was ideal. Only one road led into the property, and it was impossible for anyone to scale the wall leading down to the sea. Or so the Italians thought. The leader of this mission knew that nothing was impossible for the right men.

At the top the men stopped, roped to the rocks, resting for a moment, and the leader examined the house. The closest balcony to them was illuminated by bright lights from the room behind it. Not good, the leader thought. He motioned the men to move left, and they eased over until they were thirty feet beneath another balcony. This one was dark and quiet.

This was the toughest part, the leader knew. Now one of his men would have to throw a rope fitted with a soft plastic grappling hook and attach it to the balcony. It would have been difficult enough under ordinary circumstances, but here, hanging on to a rock face as smooth as a windowpane, with rain pelting down on them, the three men knew that one small slip meant death for all of them.

He nodded to Aziz, who bought a little slack between himself and the rock and then tossed the weighted rope up over his head. It made a slicking noise through the air. There was a soft thud and then silence. The hook had caught the balcony's railing.

Aziz tested the rope with his weight. Without waiting for orders, he started up, hand over hand. The other two men followed quickly, and in ninety seconds they were on the darkened balcony. Their clothes were rain-soaked, but they were sweating with the effort of the climb and chilled by a wind that had suddenly gusted across the beach.

The double-louvered doors to the room were open,

23

but before the men could move, a light went on. The leader went to one side of the balcony hugging the house while his men went to the other side. There was only a few feet of wall between them and the stucco ring of the balcony.

From inside came two voices speaking Italian. "I'd better shut the doors before the rain soaks the carpet," said one, his voice growing louder as he came closer to the balcony.

"Fuck the carpet," said the other. "The fresh air feels good. If I'm going to get any sleep, I have to be able to breathe."

"All right, all right, but I'll close them a little anyway."

As the three men outside shrank away, the doors were closed.

"Okay, okay. Thanks. Now go upstairs and check on those fuckers and make sure they're paying attention."

"Christ, the Arabs are tied up. Where do you think they're going? To mass?"

"If they get away somehow, I'll be going to a mass. Your funeral mass. Now get out of here."

The other man laughed and the men outside heard the door to the room slamming shut.

The men on the balcony crouched, silently waiting. After a few moments there were snoring noises from inside that competed for attention with the still-far-off thunder. The leader gestured to his men that they were on the wrong floor and must go farther up.

Aziz gathered the hook and the rope and climbed up to the rim of the balcony rail which was uneven and only six inches wide. The leader closed his eyes

24

and said another small prayer.

The rope whistled again; the hook grabbed again. Aziz tied the free end of the rope to the balcony railing and then, like a mechanical monkey on a children's wind-up toy, he used his hands and feet to clamber up the slack rope. The other two men followed him. The louvered doors to the room were closed, but there was a dim light on inside. The leader stood on tiptoe and peered between the louvers and saw that one of the prisoners lay on the bed, his hands and feet tied. A guard sprawled in a chair, almost asleep.

The leader unsheathed a knife from his side and slid the blade through a sliver of space between the wooden doors. The old-fashioned hook latch lifted with ease, but a sudden gust of wind caught the doors and shoved them open.

"What!" the Italian guard cried, but that was all he was able to say before the leader was on him and knocked him unconscious with the heavy hilt of his commando knife.

The prisoner had not been asleep. Although only hours earlier he had killed and wounded a half dozen people from behind the anonymous cover of a ski mask, he now seemed frightened at these three masked apparitions in front of him. He shrank back on the bed until Aziz said softly, "Tenterallah."

The prisoner smiled and struggled to his feet. The leader cut the ropes on his hands and feet, and the prisoner said, "Abu Beka sent you."

Aziz nodded.

"Let me kill him," the prisoner said as he advanced on the sprawled unconscious body of the guard.

"No," the leader said in Arabic. "Abu Beka says they must know that your brothers have rescued you."

The prisoner looked astonished, but the leader's cold eyes stared at him from under the ski mask and finally the prisoner said, "Abu Beka be praised."

"And Allah," Aziz said. "Where is the other?"

The prisoner pointed to his left. "Down the hall," he said. "I saw them put him in a room there."

The leader went to the door, opened it slightly, and looked down a massive hallway. Tables and chairs took up some of the space and a Persian carpet with an intricate design ran the full forty-foot length. Ironic, he thought, that it would be Persian. Two carabinieri were in a deep conversation outside a door at the end of the hall.

He and Aziz slipped from the room and on silent feet moved down the heavy-piled rug. They were on the guards before they were even noticed. Identical choke holds silenced the guards and rendered them unconscious.

Waving back for the third man to bring the prisoner up from the other room, the leader stood outside the door and whispered in Italian, "Psst. Are you awake?" When there was no answer, he whispered again. Still silence, and he was satisfied that one of the men they had knocked out was the guard who was supposed to be on duty inside the room.

He opened the door and saw the frightened eyes of the second terrorist staring at him.

"Tenterallah," the leader whispered. "Allah akbar."

He stepped inside and cut the ropes holding the second prisoner. The prisoner threw his arms around him, hugged him, and kissed his cheek. But the leader turned away, cautioned all the men to absolute silence, and led the way toward the stairs.

There were supposed to be two guards outside the front door of the villa, but they had scurried inside to be out of the rain and were easily overpowered by the three men in the ski masks.

And then the five men went outside and raced through the pelting rain, down the driveway toward a truck the leader knew would be parked two blocks away.

Behind him, he heard one of the terrorists say, "Long live Abu Beka. Tell Allah we praise Him."

"Tell him yourself," the leader mumbled.

CHAPTER TWO

The worldwide shock at the terrorists' escape was easily as great as the shock of the airport massacre. Everyone knew that the rescue had been engineered by Abu Beka and the soldiers of his "Army of God."

But the press could not understand why the shadowy Beka had not issued a statement of celebration. Where was he? Why was Tenterallah keeping so low a profile?

The world press waited and in the absence of any additional hard news fell back on interviewing each other. They all seemed to share one opinion: that things could only get worse.

In the United States, President Prescott Walker held a news conference at which he angrily denounced the Italians for their refusal to turn the terrorists over to the United States for trial.

"If those madmen had been extradited here, as we requested, this could not have happened. But this does not mean it is all over. These cowardly assassins will be brought to justice. You can count on that. And we will also bring to justice Abu Beka and the other baby-killing monsters of his Tenterallah. There is no room in a civilized world for such savages."

The press yawned and reported that President Walker was talking tough again but revealed that their interviews of each other clearly disclosed that America had no workable plan for dealing with such terrorist acts. Some said the President's response was obviously just an attempt to provoke another incident so he would have an excuse to move more U.S. troops into the Middle East.

The Russian premier called a news conference to say that he had no comment on either the airport atrocity or the escape of the perpetrators. In Hollywood the Actors and Screenwriters' Sanity Organization criticized the United States for creating "so fascist a world that noble freedom fighters can make their message heard only by striking out at women and children," and a two-time Academy Award winner let it be known that she felt sorry for everyone, especially the wives of the terrorists, and she was looking for a screenplay about that very subject.

Again, the hardest news came from freelancer Ian Prince, who again sold Kaddafi's latest televised statement to *Nightline*. This time, Kaddafi's words were heard as news footage as the dead and wounded in the Rome airport were shown. "It is a time for celebration, for our brothers are free," Kaddafi said. "And I say to the satanic United States that it is time to eliminate their President and all others in power who do not understand that simple justice has been done."

For twenty-four hours the press speculated on the escape and still did not hear one word from Tenterallah. One American newswoman in Paris asked her boss, "Why do you suppose they didn't kill the Italian guards who were watching the terrorists? That's not like them."

Her boss said, "Don't worry about it, dear," and assigned her to cover a fashion show while mentally noting that she seemed to lack the intellectual acuity to be an international correspondent.

And still Abu Beka was silent.

Fifty miles from Rome, in the small village of Santa Anna, Nunciata Lombardo awoke well before dawn. Today it was her turn to replenish the flowers around the village's only notable attraction: a marble statue of Mary holding the infant Jesus. Some said that the statue in the village square had been sculpted by Michelangelo, but experts disputed that, although the peaceful serene faces on the Pietà had some of the great artist's touches. Sometime in the eighteenth century a stone arch had been erected over the statue, to keep it from the worst of the unpredictable inland Italian weather.

Nunciata looked in on her sleeping children, smiled, and slipped out into her own backyard. While flowers had been planted around the border of the town square, she did not like to cut them, especially when her own roses were so much more beautiful. She hummed to herself in the spare light just before dawn as she snipped one large bloom after another, ignoring the thorns pricking the skin of her hands.

She carefully laid the flowers in a large basket

woven of meadow grass and then started toward the town square. If she timed it just right, she would arrive just as the first rays of the morning sun struck the faces of the statue, bathing them in heaven's golden light in what Nunciata always thought was a special gift from God to her.

But what was that?

Some feet?

Oh, Madonna, they're kicking you. Not only was the statue of Mary and the Babe swathed in gold but so were four feet . . . no, they were hooves . . . swaying in the morning breeze. Nunciata dropped the flowers and fell to her knees and screamed until most of the village awoke and ran to the square to help her.

"My God." A man crossed himself. Someone had hung a pair of dead pigs from the arch over the statue. He went around the archway to get a better look, for the pigs faced away from the sun.

He looked at the other men standing by him. Yes, it was two pigs. How disgusting. Who would play such a vile prank? Nunciata was still screaming. One man raced to his house only fifty feet away and brought back a ladder and a knife.

Nunciata screamed as he came back, "Yes, yes, cut them down. Get them away from my Lady."

Three other men held the ladder and the man climbed the ten feet to the top of the archway. Then a breeze came up and one of the pigs slowly rotated and through the slit of its throat something appeared.

A man's head.

The eyes bulged and a blackened swollen tongue hung from the open mouth like a half-blown-up

31

balloon. The man on the ladder almost lost his balance and felt faint for the first time in his life.

He closed his eyes, shook his head, and then, trying not to concentrate on what he was doing, he took a knife to the ropes holding up the pig carcasses.

When the pigskins were laid out on the cobblestones of the square, another man took his knife and cut open the stitches of the skins. There was a man inside each pigskin. Each man was naked; each had been shot through the heart.

When the women crowded forward to look at the naked bodies, the men ordered them all to go home. Nunciata Lombardo had to be carried.

Then the bodies were dragged into a local garage and covered until the priest and the carabinieri could come, which took minutes for the priest and an hour for the police.

By noon the news had flooded the world: the bodies of the two "rescued" terrorists had been found sewn into pigskins in the sleepy Italian village of Santa Anna.

Kaddafi this time did not wait for Ian Prince. He went on Libyan national television to accuse the United States of committing "this terrible atrocity."

President Walker would have no immediate comment, his press secretary said. The Russian premier later called a press conference to announce that he had no comment.

· The press reported that sewing the dead men in pigskins had been the vilest form of insult, since Muslims were supposed to avoid contact with that unclean animal. The press immediately attacked the killing of the two terrorists as a particularly vicious criminal act. Inside of six hours the three U.S. networks made it seem as if the two men had been the innocent victims of a Ku Klux Klan mugging.

The carabinieri waited twenty-four hours before releasing the news that messages had been tucked with the bodies into the pigskins. The Italian police said that they had been withholding the information so that if anyone called to claim responsibility for the killings, they would have a way of testing the claim. Actually, the notes were being analyzed in criminal laboratories for fingerprints, hair fragments, body fluids—anything that might tell something about those who wrote them. But there was nothing.

They had been typewritten on an ordinary Arabic typewriter, on heavy bond paper made in Egypt but sold widely throughout the Middle East.

One note read:

To the killers of babies and women: your turn in the pigskin is coming.

The other read:

You Tenterallah butchers have run out of time. Abu Beka, you are next.

No one knew who Abu Beka was.

No photograph of him existed; no tape recording of his voice.

The intelligence agencies of the world, even though his apprehension was topmost on their agendas, did not know what country he operated from and had not even a clue toward the location of the headquarters of his fanatical terrorist group, Tenterallah, the Army of God.

It was rumored that he had five hundred men under his command, ready to die at his order. He had led them since the late 1970s, and more than a thousand terrorist acts had been laid at his doorstep.

When he had first come to prominence, he had been lumped among the large number of Palestinian terrorists working in the Middle East, and the press, which liked easy labels, still referred to him that way.

But it was an opinion no longer shared in the highest echelons of antiterrorism experts. They noted that many of Tenterallah's attacks were now perpetrated against other Arabs, especially those who dared to speak out in favor of a moderate no-war approach to the region's problems. In the last year two Russian diplomats had been the target of Abu Beka's attacks. The most important thing experts noted was that Abu Beka's organization never attacked anybody associated with Iran. And this led many of them to the conclusion that instead of being a "Palestinian freedom fighter," as the Western press generally dubbed him, or a psychotic killer, as some world leaders felt, Abu Beka was instead a paid mercenary murderer in the employ of the government of Iran. But no one knew for sure.

Abu Beka translated as "father of struggle." His real name no one knew.

All that the West knew was that his messages were always transmitted the same way—by a telephone call originating in Paris to the home of the bureau chief of the International Press Association. The caller was always the same. He spoke in French. His voice was known to the IPA's bureau chief. He was not, he had explained many times, Abu Beka but merely his emissary.

The evening after the terrorists' bodies were found in the Italian village, he called the bureau chief again and read a terse statement in the name of Abu Beka.

"The brave men and women of the Tenterallah will not let these savage sacrilegious killings go unpunished. Beware our wrath."

CHAPTER THREE

"Look. You're in charge of sales in Great Britain. You tell *me* why they don't like our helicopters." Mark Donovan, president of Whirlaway, Inc., leaned back in his chair and cupped his hands behind his head. What he really wanted was to cut the nonsense, dance around the desk, and celebrate. But his secretary, Maggie Henson, was still in the room, searching the files for a land deed he had misplaced.

The man he had spoken to moved around on the seat of his chair until he found a position that seemed more comfortable before he answered.

"Well, old chap, I think it's an esthetic problem," he said in a dripping British accent.

"Esthetic? What's esthetic about a military helicopter? It's supposed to go up, down, front, back, side to side. It's supposed to be able to handle cannon and gun. Our helicopters do all that better than anybody else's. What esthetic?"

"Sorry, old sod. I just get the feeling that they don't like the way our craft looks."

"We'll paint it pink for the pansy bastards," Donovan said, then spun around. "Maggie darling, are you done yet?"

"I'm not your darling," the woman said, "and I'd be done if you'd remember where the hell you put that land deed."

"It's not important, sweetheart. It's just some highway or something." Donovan grinned impishly, knowing that his smile always brought out the motherly instinct in her, even though at forty, she was two years younger than he was.

"It's a defunct roadbed that could be rebuilt and save us thousands of shipping hours a month, moving supplies into the Pittsburgh plant," she snapped. "Honestly, Mark, sometimes I wonder how you got to be rich."

As she always did when chiding Donovan, Maggie angled her feet away from each other and raised her hands above her head. It had always amused Mark how someone so beautiful could occasionally look so awkward.

"Maggie, dearest heart, you have been responsible for all of it."

Maggie ran a hand through her already tousled, natural blond hair, and the laugh lines appeared around her ginger-brown eyes. "Then how about a raise?" she said.

Mark looked away from her and answered to the other man. "Listen to this, Tolly," he said. "She's already got maximum health and life insurance. She buys her clothes from a designer I know. She gets four weeks vacation a year, and she owns more company stock than I do, for Christ's sake."

"Skip the fringe benefits and give her more money," the man responded.

"Thank you, Tolly," Maggie said. "It's nice to know somebody around here appreciates me." She patted the man's shoulder and was surprised to feel him recoil slightly from her touch. Some people, she knew, didn't like to be touched, but she had always assumed that Tolly Peterson was one of those hail-and-farewell Brits who shook hands, touched, and hugged at every opportunity. *One never knows, does one,* she thought to herself and regretted the attempt at physical contact.

"We'll find the deed later," Donovan told her. "Now clear out. I've got to teach the English branch of the firm how to sell helicopters."

"Okay, okay," she said, and walked briskly from the office.

When the door had closed behind her, Donovan stood up from behind his desk, reached forward, grabbed Peterson's hand and shook it forcefully. A grin crossed his ruggedly handsome face.

"It's at times like this I wish I were still a drinking man," Donovan said. "But you can celebrate for the two of us." He walked to a well-stocked built-in bar at the side of the room and asked, over his shoulder, "Vodka?"

"If you don't have absinthe." Tolly Peterson stretched out his legs until they touched Donovan's walnut desk. He thought it interesting that the office had only the desk, a handful of chairs, and the bar. He had always thought that Americans did more entertaining in their offices. Still, the view from the office windows was magnificent. Once, a long time ago, he had seen a picture of the Chrysler Building in a magazine article on art deco and had thought then that the building looked foolish. But now that he spent so much time in it, he had come to think it beautiful. Peterson lit a cigarette, a French Gauloise, and puffed out strong blue-gray smoke.

Donovan handed him a glass of raw vodka without ice, sniffed Peterson's smoke, and said, "I don't suppose there's anything I can do to get you to switch to a milder brand, is there?"

"No. Or how do you say it, nope. These are closest to what I am accustomed to."

"Better watch it." Donovan went around the desk and sat down. "Don't drop the Colonel Blimp accent."

"Sorry, but it's just us folks now, ain't it?" Peterson said, putting on a broad Texas cowboy drawl, then checked his watch. "Almost time," he said.

"Okay. Lock the door."

Peterson started to rise, then sat back down. "You lock it. It's your door."

Donovan got up with a grunt. "Would it have helped if I had said please?"

"No."

"I thought not."

Donovan locked the door, came back to the desk, and with a key from his jacket pocket unlocked a desk drawer. As he took out a nondescript, old-fashioned black rotary-dial telephone, Peterson fastened his gaze on the instrument, put out his cigarette, lit another, and checked his watch again.

He said, "Five. Four. Three. Two. One. Zero."

39

And a small red light on the side of the telephone began to blink noiselessly.

Donovan picked it up before the ring was completed. "Yes, sir," he said. Then he listened. Then he laughed and said, "Thank you, sir," and hung up. As he did, he looked around the room. Both he and the other man had checked it for electronic bugs, but it was an instinct that would never die with either of them.

"So what did the President of the United States have to say?" Peterson asked.

"He said, 'Next time, sew Kaddafi into the goddamn pigskins with them.' "

"I'll drink to that," Peterson said, and hoisted up his vodka glass.

"And you, Comrade Petrov. Did you get a cheery phone call from the Premier of all the Russias?" Donovan asked. He was not expecting the stormy look that rushed over the other man's face.

"Peterson. Even in jest, Donovan. It's Peterson. It's too easy to make mistakes." The man downed his vodka and went to the bar for another.

"Sorry," Donovan said, rubbing his forehead with his eyes shut. When they opened again, there was a slight pinkness in the whites surrounding very deep blue irises. "I'm tired, I guess. It's a long time since I've done this."

"No excuses." Petrov shook his head. At five feet ten and 150 pounds, the Russian was five inches shorter than Donovan and fifty pounds lighter, but there was something snakelike and formidable about him. Perhaps, Donovan thought, it was that he had never seen the man really smile. Now Petrov was leaning against the counter of the bar, staring into the vodka as if it contained all the secrets of the universe.

Donovan leaned back again in his chair and ran a hand through his thick, dark brown hair. Petrov reminded him of a cross between a lightweight boxer and a street urchin. He was thin but muscular, his nose small but sharp, his mouth narrow and without humor although there were a hundred creases on either side of it, as if he had once smiled a lot. His skin was that transparent pale shade common to Russians; his hair was an ashy color and his eyes a cold yellowish-brown. He was nondescript enough to blend into a crowd, but if anyone took a close second look, Donovan thought, they would see that there was a hard, sinister quality about him.

Aware of Donovan's scrutiny and not enjoying it, Petrov raised his gaze from his glass and said, "In answer to your question, no, the Premier did not call. However, this morning a case of Stolichnaya was delivered to my apartment. The sender wished to remain anonymous." He looked up and attempted a small smile which involved only his lips. "So you tell me, which is better?"

"Make it a case of Scotch and I'm on your side," Donovan said. "In case I ever fall off the wagon."

"I'll put in your order." Donovan came toward the bar to get himself a fresh pack of cigarettes and Petrov moved back to his chair. He disliked standing near Donovan; it always made him feel small. What was it about Americans anyway that made so many of them grow so tall? Even Maggie Henson was tall, almost as tall as Petrov. But instead of the high

41

heels that Petrov liked on a woman, Maggie wore sneakers almost all the time in the office. It was a popular fad in the United States right now, but Petrov thought it looked stupid nonetheless. Today Maggie's sneakers had been shocking pink. Bizarre perhaps, but not nearly as stupid as Mark Donovan's necktie. Its background was dark blue, shot through with diagonal stripes of green, red, and gold, and Petrov recognized it as the regimental tie of the U.S. Army's 506th Paratroop Regiment. Petrov could recall from memory the design of more than a hundred regimental ties, and something in his professional soul recoiled at the thought of wearing such an advertisement of one's military background. It was a small thing, but people in his business were most usually tripped up by the small things—by a habit of speech, by using an old-fashioned military cigarette lighter. A professional never gave away anything he didn't have to and maybe that was one of the reasons he had been unable to get close to Donovan. Petrov was a professional; in his view Donovan was another well-meaning amateur, and amateurs got professionals killed.

The intercom buzzed an interruption of his thoughts, but Petrov gave no outward sign of having been startled. Donovan answered and Maggie's voice said good-humoredly, "Hey. How come the door's locked? I told Brian to go right in and he tried but . . . what are you guys doing anyway, making obscene calls?"

"Nah, just telling dirty stories. Too raunchy for your young ears. Send him in."

42

As he walked to unlock the door, Donovan heard a sound behind him and turned to see Petrov locking the private telephone back in the desk drawer. Another goof, Donovan thought, although this one would not have been too bad because Brian Cole was the only other person in the world, beside the President of the United States and the Premier of Russia, who knew what Donovan and Petrov were up to. Still, it wouldn't do for Maggie Henson to look into the room and see that telephone, so Petrov had been right again. Naturally. Maybe Mark Donovan was just too old and too rusty for this kind of business.

"Brian, come in." Donovan shook hands in the open doorway with Brian Cole and led him into the office, shutting the door before Maggie could follow.

Petrov came around from behind the desk, extended his hand, and said, "Good work."

While slight of build, the Russian had abnormally large hands and Brian Cole was surprised at the strength of the handshake. And even more surprised that any handshake had been offered at all.

"Thanks," Cole said, looking down at the shorter man. "It was a little hairy there for a while, but we got lucky."

"In our trade we live on luck," Petrov said, then dropped Brian's hand with almost as much decisiveness as he had used to shake it.

Brian Cole looked past him at Donovan. The two Americans had known each other since Vietnam, but after Mark had quit the service to start the helicopter company, Cole had gone into the Green

Berets. The two men had kept in touch, and Donovan knew how bored Cole had become when, with no war to fight anywhere, he had shuffled from one desk job to another. So when the President of the United States had summoned Donovan to talk about taking over this new secret assignment, Donovan's only stipulation was that he be allowed to hire Brian Cole.

They counted each other as best friends; they could talk to each other in unfinished sentences and send messages with their eyes, and for some reason that always seemed to irritate Petrov, so when he was around, they tried to correct that behavior.

Brian settled his big, rawboned body into a chair. His long blond hair curled around his shoulders. Swiftly and professionally he began his report on the mission, confident that he and his men had done the job right.

Petrov leaned against the bar, his arms crossed over his chest, listened intently, and when Brian was finished, asked, "Did you get anything out of them?"

"No," Brian admitted. *Damn the Russky for coming up with the only failure in the whole operation.* "First of all, they were nuts. Crazy zealots. And just henchmen. They didn't even know the names of the other gunmen at the airport. So after we strung their bodies up to dry, we hung around Santa Anna for a while, making believe we were newsmen, hoping that somebody would show up that we could trace to Abu Beka. But no such luck. And then the bastard's people called the International Press Association in Paris and we knew there was no point in hanging around anymore, so we split. I sent Aziz and Stanhope on to Paris to see if they can maybe figure out something about Abu's telephone messages."

Petrov lit his eighth cigarette in a row, pulled the full ashtray toward him, and contemplated Brian Cole with the intensity of a prison psychiatrist. "So we're no closer to Abu Beka than we were before," he said.

Cole met his gaze levelly as he shook his head. "But we got a rise out of him," he said.

Petrov examined his cigarette. "We could have done that by taking an advertisement in the *New York Times,*" he said.

Brian Cole seemed to bristle at the implied criticism, and Donovan glanced over at Petrov. "Lighten up," he said. "We both know we're in this for the long haul. We got a rise out of him once; we'll keep putting the pressure on him, and sooner or later he's going to make a mistake. And then we have him."

Petrov squashed his cigarette into the ashtray with an abrupt motion and said, "I hope it works that neatly."

"I'm open to suggestions," Donovan said.

"Just one thing comes to mind," Petrov said. "Do you think you could arrange with your French friends to put a tap on the IPA man's home phone in Paris? When Abu Beka's people call again, if we had it on tape, maybe it would help somehow."

"Consider it done," Donovan said.

During this exchange Cole had been glaring at Petrov, and the Russian now turned to him and said in a gentle voice, "I don't want you to think I was implying any criticism of your mission. You handled things exactly right. And yes, there are people who do not know anything and there are people who might know something but cannot be forced to talk. If you thought I was being critical of you, I was not." He paused, then said, "And now, if you'll excuse me, I'm late for an appointment."

Donovan said, "I thought we three would go to lunch. Maybe to celebrate."

"We don't really have all that much to celebrate," Petrov said, "And I'll have to beg off lunch. As I said, I have a prior engagement."

Without any further conversation he left the office.

Brian Cole looked at the door as it closed behind the slim Russian.

"Jesus," he said, "how do you put up with him? I know you think he's brilliant, but he doesn't have an ounce of fucking class." He mimicked Petrov's British accent. "We don't really have all that much to celebrate. Well, screw you, Russky."

Donovan laughed. "Class? I don't know about class. What I know is that he is the top of the line in his field, the best KGB agent in the business. The only way the Russian premier agreed to go along with this attack on Abu Beka was if Petrov were part of the deal. He carries weight."

Something in Donovan's face told Cole that he had had enough complaints for the day and Cole quickly said, "Okay, okay. But you agree? He is an insufferable bastard."

"I agree," Donovan said. "But you agree that he is the best in the world at what he does. He's got no

46

class? Well, what do you want, class or trust?"

"You trust him?"

"In this job I do," Donovan said. "So come on, let's get out of here, go get loaded and you can tell me how our real Brit, Will Stanhope, did on the mission. And Hafid Aziz too. They any good?"

"The best. I trust them with my life," Cole said warmly.

"Yeah, but do *they* have any class?"

"Compared to the one who just left here, they've got more in their armpits than he has in his whole body."

CHAPTER FOUR

Maggie Henson had looked up and smiled as Petrov came out of Donovan's office.

"Tolly," she said, "do you think they're going to be long in there? I have to find that property deed."

"Have no fear. You'll find it," Petrov said, careful to slip back into his good-old-boy accent.

"How are you so sure?" she asked.

He shrugged. "You have to to live up to your reputation. The way Donovan tells it, you're better at your job than any two others put together."

"Three," she corrected him, pushing her blond bangs back off her forehead and winking at him.

He winked back. "I'm off. Ta-ta and all that. They'll be done in there very soon too, I 'spect."

"Have a good one," she said. Maggie's eyes returned to her desk, but as soon as Petrov had left, she looked up and stared at the slowly closing door that led to the hall and the other offices of Whirlaway Inc. Something didn't quite ring true about Tolly Peterson, she thought. He sounded like this veddy-veddy Brit, but there was something cold and hard about him that didn't go with the accent, or the post as a helicopter salesman. And he had no more interest in helicopters than she had in chain saws. Oh, well. Maybe that was just his style. He didn't seem to have any interest in her either, and that was a little bit of a shame because he was the first man in a long time who made her heart beat a little faster whenever he was around. It might be all for the best; office romances usually turned out to be bummers.

Nice woman, Petrov thought as he rode down in the elevator. She seemed to respond to his good-old-English chum attitude. He knew he put it on a bit thick when he was around her, but Americans, he had found, were always most comfortable when someone lived up to . . . or down to . . . their expectations, and the only expectation he wanted to create in anyone was that good old Tolly Peterson was the nicest fellow you were liable to meet at the cricket match.

Donovan had told him that Maggie had led a hard life but it certainly didn't show. She had a sense of fun that peeked through and he thought fleetingly that at some other time, in some other circumstances . . . well, it was no use worrying about things like that. The time for romance had ended a long time ago in his life.

He hailed a cab and told the driver to take him to Eighth Avenue and Twenty-ninth Street. The cabbie kept up a nonstop conversation with himself all the way across town. Petrov ignored him and finally the driver retreated into silence.

Around the corner from his stop was El Fazid's Gardens. It was located on the ground floor of a run-down four-story building between a quick-copy shop and a Chinese laundry, and while it was on nobody's tour of New York City's best restaurants, it was heavily frequented by the city's large Arabic-speaking community.

Petrov paused inside the beaded curtains to let his eyes adjust to the dim lighting inside the main dining room. The walls were covered with brocade-looking vinyl and the floor with a nondescript linoleum that was wearing through in patches under the dining tables from the constant friction of people's feet.

Fazid, the owner, saw Petrov and approached him with a large smile, then salaamed flamboyantly to him. "Mr. Peterson," he said in a thick middle-eastern accent. "I have saved your table."

Petrov nodded, and as the dark-skinned man in the expensive Bill Blass suit showed him to his table, Petrov slipped a five-dollar bill into his hand and settled himself at the Formica table that was covered with a plastic tablecloth decorated with printed sketches of mosques and Arab princes on horseback.

The lunchtime crowd had thinned out and Petrov hoped he had not missed his favorite belly dancer, a bosomy blond housewife from Long Island. She had convinced herself that "Mr. Peterson" was a lonely rich man, ripe for the plucking, and spent most of the lunch hour at his table which afforded him an excellent cover while he kept an eye on the other people in El Fazid's. When you sat at a table with a half-clad belly dancer, people — especially men — had a way of not paying too much attention to you.

50

"Has Miss Geraldine performed yet?" he asked Fazid.

"No," Fazid said. "I would not let her on until you came." Later that would call for another five-dollar bill whether it was the truth or not. "The musicians are on their break now, and then Fatima and then Miss Geraldine."

"Thank you, Fazid," Petrov said, and nodded as the restaurateur left to see his other customers.

Petrov had spent three years under cover in the Middle East for the KGB, posing as an oil buyer from England. He not only was fluent in Arabic and could get along in a few other languages of the region, but he knew the customs and the protocol of Arabic society. However, at El Fazid's, he kept up the pretense of being a stupid tourist awed by Arabs and their culture. And if anybody wondered why he did not go to some of the raunchier topless and bottomless joints to ogle women, he made a pretense of being enraptured by the various lamb dishes that Fazid offered, even though in truth everything that was served on his plate tasted like boiled rat.

The two musicians—one of them a string player and the other, who had a box filled with a bewildering variety of flutes and horns, each of which seemed capable of producing only one note—came back to the bandstand and started playing. Moments later they were joined by Fatima, who appeared to have learned belly dancing at Minsky's. The music was not an authentic middle-eastern sound, but then, Fatima, who was now lying on the floor on her back, bumping and grinding to some invisible Priapus, was from Spanish Harlem.

Petrov's lamb and rice meal arrived just as Fatima worked herself into her highly erotic finale. Playing dumb tourist to the hilt, he concentrated on her, letting his food get cold, then signaled the waiter for a beer. It was Bud Lite instead of the excellent native beer brewed in Iran. But all that was done now on the q.t. because Iran's fanatic religious leaders disapproved of the consumption or manufacture of alcoholic beverages, and the small amount that was brewed was secretly shipped off to Turkey and none ever reached the United States.

If anyone had been watching the quiet, thin man in the corner, they would have been sure that Fatima had brought him almost to the peak of sexual ecstasy, because he sat mesmerized throughout her performance and then, when she was done, wolfed down his food as if he had only just realized it was there.

He was sipping the beer slowly when Miss Geraldine came out to dance. She looked automatically to Petrov's usual table in the corner and when she saw him, smiled warmly. She was wearing see-through harem pants and some sort of transparent gauzy veiled top, and a great deal of warm young skin was visible as she danced her way around the room, steadily inching closer to his table. As she expected, Petrov slid a ten-dollar bill into the elastic band below her navel. That was a sure sign that he would buy her champagne after her stint onstage. The man was really very sweet and generous, and Miss Geraldine already had the ten spot earmarked. It would go into the fund for the Cabbage Patch play set for her daughter, Susan, whose seventh birthday was coming up in a couple of months.

Suddenly the dancer realized Petrov's attention had drifted, and she danced her way toward the men who had just entered the room. She had seen them before, but they meant nothing to her; they looked like ordinary Arabs and all Arabs looked alike. Often people came into El Fazid's wearing the kaffiyeh headdress and traditional Arab robes, but these three men were bareheaded and wearing ordinary western suits.

She was annoyed, as they seemed to ignore her presence and sat at a table only eight feet from Petrov's.

The Russian swore to himself. He should not have had the vodka in Donovan's office, not before lunch, not on an empty stomach. What was that Yiddish word Americans liked to use? *Plotzed*. He had almost plotzed when he saw a familiar face enter the restaurant, and the dancer had noticed his reaction. *Very careless, Petrov,* he told himself. *That's how people get killed in our line of work.*

Geraldine danced back to him, ground her navel a little in his face, leaned over, and whispered, "Friends of yours?"

"You're my only friend here, Geraldine," Petrov said, thickening up the British accent so he sounded like a man on the verge of alcoholic stupor. He grinned at her and she smiled back lasciviously, gyrating closer and closer to his face, and he put another ten-dollar bill into her waistband and she twirled away and Petrov could see the men at the next table again.

He had never met any of them but he recognized a

53

face. It was Hussein Ayoub, and he was considered a top follower of Abu Beka. Ayoub was a Syrian who held some kind of nebulous position with that country's government, and while he had never personally been connected with any terrorist act, he was always available to serve as an apologist for Abu Beka and his murderous gang of thugs. The fact that Ayoub was in the United States, without any intelligence note having been made of the fact, was likely proof that he was traveling under a false passport.

True, in the photographs of him that Petrov had seen, Ayoub was wearing a moustache and full beard and now he was clean shaven, but there was no mistaking the craggy nose and the somewhat askew set of his eyes. The man always looked as if two artists had crafted his face, with neither one checking to see what the other was doing. One eye seemed a centimeter lower than the other and drooped at the corner while the other was normally rounded. Even his jaw seemed misaligned; one side angular and the other heavily jowled.

Ayoub was looking at a menu while the two men with him, obviously his bodyguards, kept busy glaring around the room. As their gaze reached him, Petrov drained his beer and waved his arm drunkenly over his head toward the waiter to order another. Then Petrov allowed his eyes to meet those of the two bodyguards.

"Hi-de-ho," Petrov said. "Howsh about a drink with me?"

The nearest bodyguard leaned over toward him and said without a smile and with a trace of an accent, "Sorry. We are Muslims. No alcohol."

"Almost enough reason to convert, isn't it?" Petrov said thickly, and then started braying loudly at his own joke. That brought over Fazid, who stood at his table and said, "Mr. Peterson, maybe it is time I brought you some good coffee."

"Okay," Petrov said, blinking as if he were having trouble focusing his eyes. "Okay. Coffee. And another beer too. All right?"

"Okay," Fazid said. "And I'll get Miss Geraldine for you too."

"Okay," Petrov said. He stared morosely into his empty beer glass as Fazid walked away. The restaurant owner stopped at the next table, and Petrov heard him tell the men in Arabic, "Don't worry about him. He can't drink. And he's in love."

From the corner of his eye Petrov saw Ayoub respond in his raspy voice. "Tell him to beat his woman," the man responded in Arabic. "Westerners never learn that."

All the men laughed, and as Fazid moved away, Petrov relaxed into what looked like a drunken stupor. Ayoub sipped some mucky Arabian coffee and said, "Some think it might have been Kaddafi."

"But why?" Petrov heard one of the bodyguards respond. "Why would he kill two of our brothers from Tenterallah? I thought he was our friend."

Ayoub said, "No one knows. But it is the kind of crazy thing he would do." Petrov could see the man thoughtfully shaking his head. "It is not like the westerners to kill our men in cold blood and then mutilate the corpses that way. The West is too soft for those kinds of acts."

They stopped talking as Fazid returned with coffee

55

and beer for Petrov and with a tray of appetizers for the three men. It was only when he left that they resumed talking with no more regard for Petrov than if he had been a bum on the street. Anglos never spoke Arabic.

"Kaddafi would have no reason to attack Tenterallah," the same bodyguard said stubbornly.

"Perhaps not," Ayoub agreed. "Or perhaps there is another player in the game."

Petrov looked up from his fresh beer as Geraldine joined him. She was now wearing a pair of blue jeans tight as the shell on an egg, and a T-shirt that clearly revealed her small dark brown nipples.

"Hi, Tolly," she said brightly. "I understand we're getting a little drunkie-poo."

Petrov shrugged a great drunken shrug. "Why not? Champagne for you?"

She nodded as she moved her chair closer to his and Petrov yelled across the room to the waiter, "Champagne for my honey."

Geraldine enjoyed the ritual of the popping cork and thought about telling her husband that she was going to stay over in New York that night at her friend Joyce's. It looked like that Tolly Peterson might be ready for plucking. Hell, if he were just good for half of what he had spent on this cheap bar champagne in the last month, it would be a big piece of change. And he wasn't bad-looking either. A little wimpy perhaps, but not brutish like those three gorillas at the next table. And they were nothing but animals with their propositions to her. What did they think she was?

She clinked her champagne glass with Petrov's and

the Russian sipped his, then put it down, rested his head on the table, and said, "Just a minute for a nap, sweets." He closed his eyes and heard Ayoub's deep voice clearly.

"If the United Nations passes such a resolution, we will have to retaliate."

The other bodyguard responded. "Pro-Zionist. Straight from Satan. Tenterallah must resist."

"Will it pass?" the first bodyguard said.

Ayoub said loudly, "I say it makes no difference. Even to consider it makes them enemies of ours. I say strike!" He pounded the table, and one of the plates flew to the floor. "Leave it," Ayoub ordered the waiter. "When we are gone, you may clean up. Now go away."

There was a long pause and then Ayoub's voice again, this time softer. "Perhaps we have discussed this enough here," he said. "We are surrounded by enemies in this evil land. So? How is your family?"

Petrov heard one of the bodyguards answer in great detail. He had five children and each one seemed smarter than the others. Eventually he chided the other bodyguard for not having had yet a passel of children to carry on the great work of Tenterallah.

No more was coming. Petrov knew that and he started to stir at the table, then opened his eyes, raised his head, and smiled at Geraldine. He toasted her with his champagne glass, then said he had to go to the men's room. Geraldine was halfway through the bottle of champagne and did not seem to care where Petrov went.

He locked the door behind him, then relieved himself at the urinal. He remembered graffiti he had seen in the men's room at JFK when he arrived in the United States. "You don't buy beer. You only rent it." He tried to sort out what he had just heard the three men talking about. What was it that the United Nations was doing that had Ayoub so upset? And what was he doing in the United States anyway?

Someone pounded on the door behind him and called out in Arabic, "You coming out of there soon?"

Petrov responded in English. "In just a moment." Then he washed his hands and left the men's room, brushing past the bodyguard in the narrow hallway.

It wasn't until he was again seated next to Geraldine that he realized he had responded to the question posed in Arabic. That could have been a mistake. The Arab bodyguard came back but Petrov could not see anything amiss from his expression.

Geraldine had almost finished the bottle of champagne, and now she put a hand onto Petrov's thigh and mumbled that her husband did not understand her. She yearned for a man who could understand her, she whispered in Petrov's ear. "Understand me. Thoroughly. That's the kind of understanding I need." She touched the inside of Petrov's ear with the tip of her tongue.

Petrov felt himself being aroused by her hand and then he saw the three men standing to leave at the other table. He removed the dancer's hand from his crotch and brought his face to Geraldine's and whispered back to her. "The next time I come in, I would like to understand you very thoroughly. But today I have an appointment."

She could not disguise the disappointment on her

face, and Petrov fished out his wallet and took a fifty-dollar bill from inside. "Pamper yourself until I can pamper you in person," he said. "Take a cab back to your home."

She thanked him and took the money, but of course she would go home by train. Two cups of El Fazid's thick coffee and she would be sober enough to walk the thirty miles home.

And next time maybe she would do more with this little Englishman, maybe even go to bed with him. And she would make it worth his while for all the money he had spent on her. And might yet spend in the future.

CHAPTER FIVE

The bright sun of the sweltering August day was like a knifeblade in Petrov's eyes as he stepped onto the sidewalk outside Fazid's.

He stopped to light a cigarette while his eyes scanned Twenty-ninth Street in both directions.

Nothing.

No one.

He walked casually toward Eight Avenue, and as he neared the corner, he saw one of the body-guards—the one who had banged on the bathroom door in the restaurant—pausing at a greengrocer's on the corner to feel the oranges.

Petrov felt a tingle in the pit of his stomach. No matter how many times he had done just this, tail someone, it never failed to draw some sort of visceral response from his body. *Maybe it was nature's way of telling you: Don't make any mistakes or you'll be dead*.

Nonchalantly, Petrov stopped to look into the window of Boffa's Bakery, home of Baby Watson cheesecake, whoever Baby Watson was. He was on the shady side of the street, and in the bakery window could clearly see the bodyguard fondling the fruit at the stand. Finally, the greengrocer came outside to stare at him and the bodyguard walked off, along the west side of Eighth Avenue, moving uptown at a stroller's pace.

Before following him, Petrov turned from the bakery window, lit another cigarette, and carefully surveyed the street in all directions. There was no sign of Ayoub or the other bodyguard. Perhaps it was what it appeared to be: Ayoub and the other man had left by car or cab, and this bodyguard was just out to take the air.

Perhaps. And perhaps not.

Petrov crossed the street and, from the other side of the street, followed the bodyguard down Eighth Avenue.

When the Arab neared the post office at Thirty-third Street, he ran across Eighth Avenue, nimbly avoiding traffic, and darted up the steps.

Petrov walked a little faster in that direction, automatically checking the side door above the multiple layers of stone steps. As usual, there was a rope across the side doors and a sign that read CLOSED. USE FRONT ENTRANCE.

Petrov had been in the huge post office building three times, sending presents home to Russia to his sister and her children, and every time all the doors to the building had been sealed off except the main front entrance.

He made himself comfortable on the steps with the hobos and the lunch picnickers, and after about five minutes the Arab exited, bounded down the stairs past Petrov, and walked rapidly down Thirty-third Street toward the Hudson River.

Petrov followed carefully as the Arab crossed Ninth Avenue and then Tenth. The sidewalks were fairly empty of pedestrians, but the traffic to the Lincoln Tunnel to New Jersey was piled up as usual.

Just before the Arab started walking south on Tenth, he glanced behind him, but Petrov somehow had sensed the move coming and darted behind a parked truck.

When he looked out again, the Arab was a block ahead on the other side of the street. Construction was under way there. A landfill on the old railroad yards and an abandoned railroad trestle built high on pilings snaked from one warehouse, across the street to a junction a quarter of the way down the block, then traveled on downtown as far as the eye could see, connecting warehouses and storage buildings that were old and dingy. Petrov was curious about why so much of the city's core structure had been allowed to deteriorate; he had read a book about the old days when the railroad was the lifeblood of New York City but here it had just been permitted to decay and the price was that the city was choked with auto and truck traffic from morning till night. Even Moscow was run with more sense than that.

Beside him, through the broken fence that was supposed to keep people away from the trestle, Petrov could see jungle growth that had defied the smoky, smoggy air. Trees stretched up to the sun and had grown past the trestle itself. Ivy strangled the pilings and there were even pale blue flowers that Petrov could not identify.

Before following the bodyguard down toward Eleventh Avenue, Petrov again looked behind him but no one was following him.

Still, he had an uneasy feeling about this. Where was the Arab going? Something inside his gut said that the man was leading Petrov somewhere. This was not just a stroll.

He put the thought quickly out of his mind. There was no reason to think any such thing, and getting jumpy was the second worst thing a working agent could do. The worst was being careless, and Petrov glanced around him again. At the corner of Eleventh he stood in a corner of a warehouse's loading dock. The piers were right ahead of him; he could smell the foul oily waters of the Hudson River.

He saw the Arab talking to two street prostitutes. So that was what this was all about. The Arab had ditched his lunch companions and then come here for a quicky dessert after Fazid's lunch.

As Petrov watched, the bodyguard seemed to make his choice: a small black girl who looked about twelve and who was wearing a bikini bathing suit, with a skirt wrap kept open to show her skinny, gawky legs, that looked curiously flamingo-like atop her stiletto heels.

The other hooker hip-swayed away to let the lovers make their deal. Petrov tried to anticipate where they might go. There were no hotels in this area, only parked trucks seemingly abandoned by humanity, and a few occasional automobiles that sped through the street as if it were a racetrack.

As the hooker and the bodyguard came back up the street, Petrov ducked under the loading dock. He could hear the young girl giggle as the two walked by him; she was holding on to the Arab's arm as if she were out on a high school date. Then the two of them crossed the street and walked out into the undergrowth below the trestle. Appropriate, Petrov thought. A little Garden of Eden for committing original sin. There might even be a stack of mattresses back there in the bushy growth.

Petrov crossed the street and edged up toward the trestle. A convenient dark doorway held a load of stinking black garbage bags. It would have been Petrov's first choice as a hiding place, but one of the bags moved and he saw a bum there sleeping off a cheap drunk.

The next doorway was empty. God, the street was quiet. The hum of the city went on and on all around it, but this area could have been struck by a bomb and, except for the noise of the explosion, no one would have noticed it.

Five minutes passed as Petrov waited for the two people to come back out of the brush. He lit a cigarette as he thought. Perhaps he could use this little romantic interlude as blackmail against the Arab bodyguard. Ayoub was a Muslim fanatic, and this Arab was the one who had talked about his wife and children back home. *No. It won't work. These people think all women are animals, good only for screwing. No one would even raise an eyebrow at the bodyguard's indiscretion.*

The hooker came out, ducking under the broken fence, brushing off her clothes, and then walking off on those impossible heels toward Eleventh Avenue again. Petrov watched and waited for the Arab. His cigarette went to stub and he lit another. *What is going on? Where is the Arab?*

Petrov thought of streetwalkers he had encountered. There was one in Algiers who had pulled a knife on him and would have stabbed him if he had not stabbed her first. She had thought him an easy mark and had planned to rob him of his money. Hookers everywhere were the same. So this little black child-hooker might have put a blade in the Arab's heart and shoved his money into her bathing suit.

He lit the next cigarette off the last one and puffed nervously. He would give it one more cigarette, and if the Arab had not made an appearance, he would go under the trestle to check it out.

He waited through the cigarette and five minutes more for good measure before he crossed the street and peered through the broken fence into the darkness under the trestle. But he saw nothing except weeds and rubble.

As he went through the fence, Petrov thought this might work to his advantage. If the Arab were wounded, Petrov would have a few questions for him to answer before calling for medical help. Of course, if the Arab were dead, then the game was over . . . but who would care?

It was darker than it had seemed from outside. Almost pitch black. How did these bloody bushes that were tearing at his skin survive without sunlight? He had heard once that if New York City were abandoned, it would take only twenty years for it to grow back to nature. And down there, obviously, the weeds were practicing, getting ready, waiting for the day when the people left.

He was about twenty feet into the area where he heard a light rustling in the bushes. A warning went off in his head; there was no breeze to rustle bushes. He started to turn to the sound but it was too late. Someone had a hammerlock around his neck and that someone's breath stank of Fazid's food stuck into cavities in his teeth.

"I've got him," a man's voice said in Arabic.

"Good. I was getting tired of waiting," came the answer, also in Arabic, and the bodyguard Petrov had been trailing stepped forward from behind a clump of bushes. But his face was just a blur to Petrov, who felt his breathing being cut off by the arm around his throat.

"You can let him go. He's not going anywhere."

The arm released Petrov's throat and the Russian was thrown forward against a dank, smelly piling. He was quickly patted down for a gun, but he had never carried one in the United States, especially since he was never supposed to let himself get into a position like this.

Petrov turned and asked in halting English, "What do you want? I don't have any money. . . ." The sentence ended on a cough as one of the men punched him in the abdomen.

Petrov gasped and moaned. "Oh, no. Don't hurt me."

"Speak in Arabic," the bodyguard he had tailed said. "You understood it well enough at Fazid's. Now, who are you and why are you following me?"

Petrov hesitated, and a sharp jab into his stomach punctuated a demand to "Answer me."

"Ooooh," Petrov groaned. "I was curious, that's all," he said in English. "I saw you and the tart, and I thought she had hurt you. Sliced you up. I was trying to help, that's all. Honestly." Even though these two probably would not recognize it, he was careful to talk with his deep British accent as he whined his answer.

"That's fine. But why were you following me in the first place?" the bodyguard demanded. He kicked Petrov in the left calf.

"No, no. Don't hurt me!" Petrov's mincing became more marked as he drew in great gasps of air, even while pretending to enjoy the pain. He turned to anchor his throbbing left leg against the gummy surface of the piling.

"I thought . . . well, I thought you were very good-looking. I thought . . . I thought you might like me."

"Me? You . . . you fucking faggot." The Arab paused and reached for his pocket. "I'm going to carve you like a roast goose."

Petrov pushed out from the piling with his left leg and planted the toe of his right shoe into the crotch of the man who had spoken. He stumbled back, into his companion, knocking him sideways, then fell to the ground, clutching his groin, moaning. The second Arab charged Petrov and wrapped his arms around Petrov's chest, trying to lift him from the ground. But Petrov's arms were free and like a cymbal player in an orchestra he clapped his hands together hard over the man's ears and the Arab cried out and lost his grasp. Petrov backed away, but the Arab recovered and drove a shoulder into him, bashing his head against the wooden piling. Petrov heard

67

rather than felt the sickening sound of bone meeting petrified wood. Just from instinct he coiled his right hand close to his chest, fingers extended, and then drove the hand forward into the Arab's windpipe. The man gurgled and while he fell, Petrov's left hand landed in exactly the same spot.

The other man, the bodyguard whom Petrov had been following, was getting slowly to his feet, reaching under his jacket where Petrov knew he must have a gun. Then the gun was out, in his hand, and rising slowly toward the Russian, who dove through the air, his arm raised in front of him. The point of his elbow smashed into the bridge of the Arab's nose, and even before the man fell backward, Petrov knew he had shoved the nose bone up into the brain. Blood came out of the Arab's mouth, oozing thick and dark onto the ground.

Petrov examined both men. Each was looking skyward with the stare of the dead. He had to get out of there before another hooker came back with a customer.

He frisked both men but neither carried a wallet or any identification that he could find. This was common practice among people who, if apprehended, did not want to be identified too easily. As he rose again, he wobbled on his feet and he could feel the sticky wetness of his own injury soaking the collar of his suit.

How was he going to get back home? Even in New York, a man walking the streets with a bleeding head was eventually going to attract some official attention. He found the answer in one of the Arab's pockets which contained the kaffiyah headdress and the akal headband. He donned the Arab scarf, wound it expertly about his head, and moved out of the brush into the street.

He doubted that Ayoub was anywhere around. He would have left his two bodyguards to check out the English drunk who understood Arabic. But there were no guarantees in this business. Time to leave.

The bushes scratched at him as if not wanting to let him leave the scene of his crime, but when he emerged from the growth, Petrov was as nonchalant as a tourist leaving a museum. Down the block he saw the two hookers approaching again and blew them a kiss. To hookers, all men looked alike.

Petrov walked purposefully to Tenth Avenue, carefully watching behind him to make sure no one was following. On Tenth he saw a bus and stumbled across the street to the bus stop. He let three chatting ladies get on first. Then he had difficult getting up the steep steps and knew that his head injury was worse than he had thought. He got to the back of the bus and stood in the stairwell until Thirty-fifth Street, when he got off, walked a block, then hailed a passing cab and gave him the address of the brownstone in Turtle Bay where Donovan had gotten him an apartment.

In front of his building once again, he looked around. The street seemed clear of anyone who might have been following him and he did not have the strength left to walk around the block to make sure.

His apartment was on the second floor, but the long flight of stairs seemed a mile long. How he was able to use his key to unlock the door and step inside, he never did remember, although later he would vaguely recall the floor of the foyer coming up to meet him.

CHAPTER SIX

When Mark Donovan heard Maggie's voice on the intercom saying that Tolly Peterson was holding for him, he detected a quaver in her usually lighthearted tone.

"Is something wrong?"

"I don't know," she replied. "He sounds peculiar."

"Okay." Donovan pushed the blinking button to pick up the call and said, "What's new?"

"Trouble," came the faint answer. "Come over here quickly, please."

"What . . . ?" But Donovan was talking to an empty line. He glanced at his watch, even as he was standing up to put on his seersucker jacket. Four o'clock. He should have put in three more hours of helicopter company work and then he had a fund-raising dinner to attend that night. *Damn the Russian.* It was a king-size pain to have him involved in this operation; Donovan felt that he and Brian Cole could have handled it alone just as efficiently. But after two Russian technicians were murdered in Syria by Abu Beka's organization, the Russian Premier

71

had been convinced by President Prescott Walker to join in the hunt for the shadowy terrorist. Donovan hadn't liked it then; he didn't like it now; but he knew that Russian cooperation provided the United States with a political cover it would not otherwise have had.

Even as he was thinking over the events that led to his meeting Petrov for the first time, Donovan was throwing on his jacket and preparing to go to the Russian's apartment. It must be something important, he knew. Petrov was not the type to cry wolf.

As he passed through her office, Donovan said, "Maggie, I've got to go out. I'll try to be back before you leave, but if not, here's your ticket to the benefit tonight. Cocktails at seven, a buffet after."

"I know," Maggie said. She wondered why Donovan seemed so nervous. "I thought I'd go home in a little while and take a long soak before getting dressed. We don't want Ancie to outshine me, do we?"

Donovan forced himself to grin. "Yuk-yuk. I have it on good authority that she's coming as a Christmas tree."

"Wearing nothing but tinsel, I'm sure," Maggie said. "I'll be understated in black. Anything wrong with our friend Jolly Tolly?"

"Nah. See you later."

Donovan hailed a cab outside the building and was at Petrov's brownstone a few minutes later.

The building had been a good choice, he thought as he buzzed the bell for the Russian's apartment. No doorman; no one to notice any comings or goings. Perhaps, he thought as the return buzzer answered and the front door clicked unlocked, it might not be a bad idea to hold their meetings here instead of in the office. Maggie Henson had seemed, lately, to be developing an inquisitiveness he wasn't too happy about. He would stake his life on her loyalty, but the best way to prevent leaks was to make sure that no one knew enough to leak about.

Bounding up the steps, he noticed how quiet the building was. Petrov's apartment took up the entire second floor and was the largest in the building which housed five others. No kids, no pets allowed. They were the only living creatures in New York without absolute, inalienable rights to urinate anywhere they wanted to.

Petrov opened the door before Donovan could knock. The Russian was white-faced, sweating, and his eyes kept drifting closed, then reopening through sheer willpower. He kept a towel pressed to the back of his head.

Without saying a word Donovan took the smaller man's arm, closed the hall door behind them, and helped Petrov down the long hallway to the front of the building. Massive bay windows padded with a bright yellow fabric were the focal point of the room that was furnished in white leather and wicker. A basket of flowers stood in the unused fireplace, but there were no touches of Petrov's personality in the room.

Donovan tried to steer the man to the white leather sofa, but Petrov mumbled, "No, blood." He brought down the towel and showed Donovan that it was soaked almost through. "Just keeps bleeding," he said.

"I've got to get you to a hospital," Donovan said.

"No. Too many questions. Can't think. Just concussion," Petrov said.

"Okay. Sit down. Fuck it," Donovan said, and pushed Petrov back onto the white leather sofa. "Sit there." He saw that Petrov's hands were shaking.

Petrov was probably right about its being a concussion, Donovan thought. He had seen a lot of them in Vietnam and had had a few himself. You had to learn not to panic at the blood because head wounds always bled like faucets. As he walked into the kitchen, he looked back and saw the Russian where Donovan had seated him, but his head was hanging limply forward, still trying to protect the white leather of the couch. It touched Donovan in an odd way; he would not have thought that a man like Petrov would even care about the furniture.

Donovan ripped the paper towel roll from the rack and brought it back into the living room. He removed the blood-soaked towel from Petrov's hands and dropped it onto a yellow throw rug, then wrapped a thick layer of paper towels around the head wound.

"Here. You hold this in place. I'll get a doctor."

He started for the telephone but hesitated as Petrov's eyes closed.

"Wake up," Donovan barked. "Petrov. Wake up! How many fingers am I holding up?"

Petrov blinked his eyes open. "Peterson," he corrected him. "Three."

"Peterson. Keep those eyes open." Donovan pressed a button on his wristwatch that activated a memory bank of phone numbers. He scrolled

74

through the numbers until he found the one he wanted, then dialed the phone.

"Dr. Milliken's office."

"Let me speak to the doctor, please."

"The doctor is with a patient. May I say who's calling?" the bored voice on the other end said.

"Mark Donovan. Tell him it's an emergency."

"I don't recognize your name, Mr. Donovan. Are you one of the doctor's patients?"

"Just get him. I said it's an emergency."

"The doctor doesn't like to be interrupted."

"Interrupt him or you're going to be a medical emergency yourself."

A moment later, a low and soothing male voice came onto the phone. "Nice to hear from you, Donovan. What's the problem?"

They had never met, but as Donovan sketched the injury with words, Milliken's responses were accurate and understanding. "I'll be right over," he said, and when Donovan gave him the address, he said, "Yes, I can find it."

Donovan hung up and mumbled to himself, "Well, sometimes the system works."

Petrov was stared at him with unseeing eyes.

"Okay, tovarich. We've got five minutes. Suppose you tell me what happened?"

Petrov forced the words out, and although his speech was slurred, Donovan was able to understand.

"And where are the bodies?"

"Twenty-seventh, near Eleventh. By the trestle," Petrov said.

"Okay. Now look. If it comes up, you were mugged. Let's see . . . the Thirty-third Street en-

75

trance to the Lexington Avenue subway. Two guys attacked you, took your money, and left your wallet. They got a hundred dollars. That's important. Everybody always asks what 'they' got. The guys were tall and black, but that's all you remember. Got it?"

"Why black?" Petrov managed. In Russia he had been told that all Americans hated blacks; he didn't like accusing the hated blacks of anything they hadn't done.

"Okay, not black. Fine with me. Two white guys, tall, long blond hair." Donovan kept talking, filling in Petrov's cover story even as he felt himself churning inside because the Russian had been going out on his own, every day to El Fazid's for lunch, taking chances that he should not have been taking.

"You're not going to report this to the police, are you?" Petrov asked.

"Not if we don't have to," Donovan said. "But I don't know much about this Dr. Milliken, so keep your story straight in case we need it."

"All right. But is very confusing," Petrov said.

"Speak English," Donovan snapped. "Not 'is very confusing.' You sound like a damn Russian. Peterson, remember?"

"Right. Peterson."

The doorbell sounded and Donovan went to the entrance to admit the doctor.

Milliken was short, fat, and all business. He examined Petrov's head wound cursorily and said he had to have X rays; the injury could be a skull fracture.

"A concussion," Petrov insisted stubbornly. He had turned the British accent on again, Donovan noted.

76

"You're probably right, but I wouldn't want to stake my life—or yours—on it. X rays," Milliken said. "And of course stitches."

Petrov looked at Donovan who nodded and asked, "Where can he go, Doctor?"

"I can get him right away into West Side Hospital," Milliken said. "I'd like him to stay overnight but he won't. But with luck and a clean bill of health, I can get him out by midnight, I think."

"Okay," Donovan said.

"For the records, they'll want to know how this happened," Milliken said.

"It was a mugging, Dr. Milliken, but for the sake of the records, can we just call it a fall at home?"

"Is it necessary?"

Donovan nodded. "Peterson is here on some quiet business for the British government. He'd rather not have it all over the papers, and a mugging means a police report, doesn't it?"

"A fall at home it is," Milliken said.

"And I'll take care of the bill," Donovan said.

"I'll have the hospital bill me," Milliken said. "And I'll pass it on to you."

"Thanks, Doctor."

"I'll take him over right now by cab," the physician responded, "and get everything under way. Will you be coming along?"

Petrov blinked. Suddenly he looked frail. "You don't have to be there, Mark."

"I've got an appointment tonight," Donovan said. "But I'll send Maggie over."

"I don't need anyone there," Petrov said again. "I'll be only a few hours." He looked around the living room, where he had spent so much time in the past two months. His own apartment in Moscow was a beat-up inefficiency with a kitchenette and rusty water in the bathroom. This place had a living room, dining room, complete kitchen, two bedrooms, and two baths, and when he first walked into it, it seemed like a motion picture set. It was decadent, of course, but he loved it. He regretted Donovan's using his yellow scatter rug to hold his bloody towels, for on cloudy days the rug had seemed like a pool of sunshine on his floor.

He had kept the apartment meticulously clean, allowing himself to clutter only the smaller bedroom, and that was taken up with all the books he had felt compelled to buy in New York.

He did not want to spend the night in the hospital.

"Maggie will come over and sit with you," Donovan said stubbornly. "You'll need someone to help you get back here anyway, and she'll jump at the chance not to have to go to that stuffy dinner tonight."

Petrov seemed too tired to argue; he thought for a moment, then nodded agreement.

As Milliken was helping Petrov to the door, Donovan said, "I appreciate this, Doctor."

"It's what I get paid for," Milliken said with a grin, and when the two men left, Donovan reflected on how well America was served by so many people who just did their jobs without asking a lot of questions. Milliken, he knew, did private work for the CIA. Like Donovan, he had been an intelligence officer, although in an earlier war, but he still regarded himself on call to his country.

Left alone in the yellow and white apartment, Donovan decided to take a moment to look around. He and Petrov had been together for almost two months now, but he still knew nothing personal about the man. Petrov, like Russia itself, was a riddle wrapped in an enigma, and maybe this apartment held some answers to the puzzle. He did not generally regard himself as a snoop, but he walked through the apartment, not touching things, just looking, thank you. In the smaller bedroom, past the master bedroom, he saw Petrov's collection of books. There were more than two hundred of them, he guessed, stacked all around the room. Not a bad collection for less than two months in the United States. Many of the books were open, with bookmarks noting the pages Petrov had read to. Half of them were what the trade called coffee-table books, big volumes, lavishly illustrated, and generally on topics that no one in his right mind cared the least little bit about. There were photographs of Hawaiian volcanos erupting. Another book was about the flowers and animals of Peru. There was the castles of Bavaria. An encyclopedia of animal life. Africa. Trains.

There were *Gray's Anatomy, New York Nightlife, Encyclopedia of Comedians* by Joe Franklin bought from a warehouse for $1.98. A book on snakes; another on Wisconsin. Eclectic choices, all over the board, as if Petrov had gone wild and raced through Manhattan's bookstores like a bibliophilic junkie, buying volumes by the pound.

It was, he supposed, a key to the inner Petrov, but for the life of him he could not see what door the key opened. He shook his head and went back into the living room. No television set. Wait. He found one inside a cabinet. He also found a current *TV Guide* in which Petrov had methodically circled the shows he wanted to be sure to watch. Apparently, he never missed the *Joe Franklin Show,* possibly the most insipid show Donovan had ever seen.

Donovan chuckled aloud. A Joe Franklin fan? Petrov? The man who had been known in Vietnam as "Molina," the Russian word for lightning? Would wonders never cease?

He decided to let himself feel a little guilty about what people in his hometown of Pittsburgh would call his "nebby-nosing." Then he decided that if the roles were reversed and Petrov were alone in Donovan's penthouse apartment over the East River, he would not only case the place but he'd probably install a wiretap and a couple of bugs. *Screw the Russky. Who cares?*

Donovan sat down on the white leather sofa and called Maggie Henson at home.

"Hey, how you doing?" she said. "I'm in my bubble bath."

"You're supposed to say, 'Wish you were here.' "

"Forget it, boss. After getting rejected for ten years, I can take a hint. I bathe alone. So what's on your alleged mind? I hope you're calling to say that I don't have to go to this windbag marathon tonight."

"Exactly correct," Donovan said.

"I changed my mind. Come on over and climb in the bath to celebrate."

"Don't get smart, I'll take you up on it. It's Peterson."

"Tolly? What's wrong?"

"He was mugged." Briefly, Donovan filled her in on the details of the fictitious mugging. "So he had to go for X rays, and if they let him out tonight, well, I thought it would be good if you were there. He'll need somebody to help him get home."

"Sounds good to me."

"If you get done early, you could still make it to the dinner," he said.

"Not on your life," Maggie said. "That barracuda who used to be your wife is all yours tonight."

"Don't remind me," Donovan said. "Look. I'll call you later to see how Tolly is."

"Okay. And you owe me one."

"I owe you more than one, dear heart," Donovan said, and hung up. Before leaving the apartment, he got a number from information and called New York City police headquarters.

"Homicide. Lieutenant Mendoza."

"Listen, Chico. My calendar just reminded me that this is be-kind-to-a-spick week. Can I buy you coffee? Or show you where there's an unlocked Cadillac with chrome hubcaps?"

"If I didn't know better, I would swear that this was the voice of Mark Donovan, millionaire playboy and tight-assed WASP."

"None other," Donovan said.

"Well, I hear from you every three years when you need something," Lieutenant Mendoza said. "What is it this time?"

"Nothing. I just want to buy you coffee," Donovan said. "You pick the spot."

"The beachfront restaurant at the Caribe Hilton in Puerto Rico."

"How 'bout someplace in fifteen minutes?" Donovan said.

"Julio's Saloon on West Twenty-sixth. You know it?"

"See you there," Donovan said.

The two men hung up simultaneously.

CHAPTER SEVEN

New York City Police Sergeant Robert Mendoza sat in Julio's the way a cop always sits in a tavern: at the far end of the bar, near the waitress's service station, so that nobody was able to sneak up behind him and he could watch everyone who came in the door.

He nursed a beer, wishing he could have a bourbon, but that was for after his tour ended at midnight, and it was not even six P.M. He reached for the peanut bowl, touched it, thought of his diverticulosis, and pushed it farther away from him. The smell of beans wafted through the air, and if it weren't for the runs they had begun giving him, he'd have told the doctors to go screw themselves. Beans. This place had the best, the hottest, the curled-toes variety of chili, and Mendoza wanted some the way a whore with a surly pimp wanted a trick.

The barmaid squeezed behind him to get some paper napkins for a table, rubbing against his body a little more than she had to, and Mendoza glanced over his shoulder and said, "Hey, Lillian. When you get a chance, how about a little chili on rice, no beans, and some yogurt."

"You got it, El Jefe," the pretty young Hispanic woman said, leaning her face in very close to his, "but chili with no beans ain't no chili."

He grinned and shook his head sadly. "When you get to be my age, you have to give up all the pleasures of life."

She took a deep breath and puffed out her bosom. *"All* the pleasures?" she asked.

"All but one," he said. "Come around and see me when you get to be eighteen and I won't get suspended for jumping your bones."

"You mean you didn't come in to see me?" Lillian said.

"Afraid not. Business," Mendoza said. "But I could probably be had."

The young woman giggled and walked away with the napkins, obviously aware of Mendoza's glance following her, because she swished her hips lasciviously. A good girl, Mendoza thought, and if she was lucky, she would find some nice guy with a steady job and get married and buy a nice house out in the burbs and raise nice healthy kids. And if she wasn't lucky, she'd get knocked up by some bum who'd vanish, leaving her with a baby and a lot of bills, and she'd work here until the day she dropped, getting harder and sourer, spending her days off visiting her son in some juvenile jail somewhere. Mendoza thought not; Lillian was going to be one of the lucky ones, and there was a young cop just on the job who might be the right sort for her. He made a mental note to bring the rookie down here

84

someday for lunch and to meet Lillian.

Mark Donovan walked through the double doors of the tavern and paused inside to look around. Mendoza waved to him and Donovan walked toward him, obviously self-conscious in his four-hundred-dollar jacket with all the trimmings. The handful of Hispanic men sitting at the bar turned to stare at the duded-up Yanqui.

As he neared Mendoza, the cop said, "Don't be embarrassed. You can't help it if you always look like a rich gringo."

"I beg your pardon?" Donovan said. "Are you addressing this Ivy League gentleman who never, ever talks to a person who has had a birthplace other than A-mer-i-ca?"

"We won't hold it against you," Mendoza said amiably, and Donovan slid onto the next stool. "You look as neat and trim as the day they shoved the silver spoon in your mouth," Mendoza said.

"You too, Bobby."

"What a liar. My ass is getting as big as a garbage pail. You know how tree rings go? Every year a new ring. Well, you can tell the age of us Latinos by measuring our asses. Why the hell do all of us get big butts?"

"It's so you don't slide off your burro," Donovan suggested.

"Oh. Well, thanks for explaining it to me. So what's on your mind?"

Donovan started to speak, then stopped as the waitress came with a plate for Mendoza.

"A booth might solve some problems," Donovan said.

"No problemo," Mendoza said. He told Lillian in swift Spanish to take the order into the back and to bring his friend a black coffee.

The two men followed her into the back and settled into a cracked red vinyl booth.

When the waitress left, Donovan said, "I have a hypothetical question for you."

"Hypothesize away," Mendoza said as he began eating. He remembered to chew even the rice as the doctors had said and not to wolf down anything but the yogurt.

Watching Mendoza eat, someone who did not understand him as well as Donovan might think he was paying only halfhearted attention to the conversation, but Donovan knew better.

"Suppose some law-abiding citizen knew where there were two bodies to be found. And suppose that law-abiding citizen told his favorite New York City policeman and vowed that he had nothing to do with the deaths. Now, would that policeman just take the information and run with it and not bother involving this law-abiding citizen in the matter?"

"It depends," Mendoza said through a mouthful of rice.

"On what?"

"Who's the law-abiding citizen?"

"Me," Donovan said.

"Then you didn't even have to bother to ask. I get anonymous phone calls all the time. I just got one telling me where to find two bodies. It's easy."

"Now, part two."

"With you WASPs, there's always a part two," Mendoza grumbled. "Go ahead."

86

"Would my favorite New York City policeman let me know what he turns up on these two stiffs? Confidentially, of course."

"What do you think your favorite policeman might turn up?" Mendoza asked.

"If I'm right, these guys will have a past history of being undesirable types of the Arab persuasion."

"Terrorists?" Mendoza asked, and put down his spoon.

Donovan nodded.

"The light dawns," Mendoza said, and pushed his plate away. "How did they hook you back into working for them?"

"They? Who?" Donovan smiled a crooked smile at his old friend.

"They. The ones who managed to hook you into an extra tour doing intelligence work in Vietnam," Mendoza said. "That's they who."

Donovan's face turned serious. "I think it's best if I told you none of your business," he said.

The two men stared at each other for a moment; then Mendoza nodded and said, "So, how's the family? You a grandfather yet?"

"Give me a break. Jeff's only fifteen and Chrissie's thirteen, so I got a way to go. Jeff's interested only in his damned computers anyway. He had to show me how to work the one in the office."

Mendoza laughed. "The younger generation. They're a lot smarter than we were. Bobby . . . shit, he hates that . . . Bob Junior is such a computer nut that he talks sometimes, I don't even know that it's English he's talking."

"How's he doing?" Donovan asked.

"The star of MIT," Mendoza said. "And by the way, did I ever thank you for that?"

"Only a thousand times," Donovan said. "Forget it."

"And Christine? She a smart one too?" Mendoza asked.

"I think so. But she's so beautiful nobody cares. She's got all her mother's looks but none of her faults, thank God."

"You ever think about . . ." Mendoza paused to finish his beer, then went on slowly, letting Donovan know that this was important. Donovan waited; there were certain rituals to be performed, even when sitting in a gin mill with an old, old friend who had saved your life a long time before. He sipped at the coffee. It was so raw it tasted as if it had been brewed in an earlier century.

"Did you ever think about . . . well, another baby?" Mendoza asked.

Donovan looked away, toward the big plate glass window that looked out onto the street. He felt the hand holding the coffee tremble a little. Mendoza could not know because Donovan had never told anyone about the scene with his ex-wife when she had come back from Europe five years before.

Donovan had been waiting for her after her six months away "to find herself"—whatever that meant—and now he wanted to get on with their marriage. Their two children were getting older and he couldn't change their diapers anymore or wipe their noses the way he had when they were young. God. He even loved the smell of baby powder, and although his wife had nannies all over the house, he had been the one, late at night, who would go into their rooms to soothe a cranky baby back into sleep.

So Ancie had come back from Europe, looking as lovely as ever. Her ash-blond hair was shoulder length and poker straight and her big cobalt eyes just stared at him when he suggested they have another child. And then she had laughed, a brittle brutal laugh and told him that she had gone to Europe to have an abortion. And for good measure, she had had her tubes tied. They would have no more children. Ever.

It was the beginning of the end. A year later they were divorced.

"Hey, buddy, I didn't mean to upset you," Mendoza said.

"What?" Donovan came to with a start. "Sorry. You reminded me of something. And yes, I've thought about having another baby if I find me the right woman. Why? You thinking about it?"

"Yup. Jenny is pregnant."

"That's wonderful," Donovan said. He reached over to slap Mendoza on the shoulder in congratulations but the policeman did not look in the mood for a celebration.

Finally, he said, "She says she wants an abortion."

"You can't," Donovan said. "She can't. You're Catholics."

Mendoza laughed. "You're naive, Mark. Catholics lead the parade in having abortions, and with her . . . well, she's forty now and the labor with Bobby, Bob Junior, was hard and she could probably get a therapeutic abortion."

"And what do you think?" Donovan asked.

89

"I want this baby," Mendoza said.

"I wish I knew what to say," Donovan said.

Mendoza shrugged; he did not know what to say either. It was the first time in more than twenty years of marriage that he and Jenny had been in serious disagreement. It wasn't like Donovan's marriage to that Ancie bitch. She had never even invited Jenny or him to the Donovan apartment, and on the few occasions when they had met, she had looked down her long nose at short, sweet, voluptuous Jenny with her clothes that were bought on sale at Mays.

And then, one day, out of the blue Ancie had called Mendoza at headquarters and asked him to meet her for lunch. He had gone, thinking it was a plan for a surprise birthday party for Donovan, but instead Ancie had tried to seduce him. She had wanted to go to a seedy hotel and "get it on." Her words. That he had considered it for even a second was a shame that Bob Mendoza would carry to his grave. Then he had laughed in her face and told her if she wanted to satisfy her craving for swarthy street types, she ought to go up to Spanish Harlem and swing a bag; there were a lot of guys up there who wouldn't mind scoring a tramp. He had never told Donovan about the incident; the divorce came a few months later and there wasn't any reason to mention it.

"You know," he said. "I think Jenny really wants the baby, but she thinks I'm only pretending to want it and she's trying to please me."

"You know the answer to that," Donovan said. "Talk about it. Talk about it a lot. Let her know

90

how you feel. Will it help if I talk to her?"

"Hey, you're my big gun. I'm saving you for the end. Jenny thinks you're God."

"Always knew that girl had good taste," Donovan said. He drained his cup. "I feel like I'm abandoning the ship here, but speaking of Ancie, I've got to go to one of her goddamn fund-raisers tonight. I'd rather sit and shmooze with you, but I promised."

"That's okay," Mendoza said. "I've got to go find a couple of bodies. Where would you suggest I look anyway?"

Donovan told him about the spot under the trestle way over on the West Side.

"And you can't tell me any more about it?" Mendoza said.

Donovan shook his head. He said, "You've got all my phone numbers. It's important I find out anything I can about these two stiffs."

Mendoza nodded and the two men shook hands. The policeman watched Donovan leave. Theirs was a good friendship; it did not require a lot of nursing to stay alive and well. Ah, what the hell. Maybe Jenny was serious about the abortion, but he would remind her that Donovan was a soft touch and would make sure the kid got into the best school. Mendoza knew his wife, knew what to expect. She would laugh her head off and say, "Mark thinks he owes you and I guess he does. But taking care of Bob Junior's education is enough. This kid, this one, is going to work her ass off to go to college. And after she's president of the United States, she can tell everyone she did it all on her own."

Mendoza loved that daydream. He had always

wanted a girl.

Maggie Henson, in jeans, pink sneakers, and a bright pink shirt, looked much younger than forty when she entered the West Side Hospital. She asked at the reception desk for Tolly Peterson's room.

"You must be Ms. Henson," the receptionist, a frazzled-looking woman with her hair in a tight bun, said sharply. "Dr. Milliken said to send you right up to the fifth floor."

For a moment her response made Maggie nervous.

"Is everything all right?" she asked.

The receptionist exercised her ultimate power, the ability to make nervous people more nervous. "You'll have to ask the doctor," she said crisply.

But everything was all right. She found Milliken standing near the nurses' station on the fifth floor and introduced herself and he said, "Our patient's all right and he wants to go home."

"That's why I'm here," she said.

"Not a minute too soon either," Milliken said. He led her down the corridor into a sunny room. It was seven o'clock, a time she should have been hanging on Donovan's arm at the antihunger benefit, trying to make Ancie the Bitch believe that they had a real romance going.

But this seemed like more fun, and Peterson seemed happy to see her. He was propped up against the pillows of the bed and appeared sallow compared to the white-bright of the hospital sheets, but the look of unalloyed pleasure that came over his face when he saw her made her think that the electric attraction she sometimes felt toward him might be reciprocated.

Or, maybe he was just eager to get out of there and would have smiled warmly at anyone who came to spring him.

"How you doing?" she asked. "You had us worried."

Petrov knew his grin must seem a little silly in these surroundings, but he *was* pleased to see Maggie. "Mugging," he said, remembering Donovan's well-rehearsed story. "They got one hundred and forty-two dollars. Two preppies."

"Sure. They needed the money for the next payment on their BMW," she said, then realized that Dr. Milliken was standing in the door of the room.

"Anything we should know or watch out for, Doctor?" she asked.

"No. Might be a little upchucks," he said. "But that's normal. Just ignore it and it'll stop. Buffered aspirin for the headache. That's about it."

Behind her, she could feel Tolly Peterson put his hand atop hers. She almost quivered from the surprise touch.

Milliken smiled at the woman and said, "Just make sure he slows down the activity for a day or two. No running marathons for at least a week."

Maggie nodded and Milliken left. He had the distinct impression that there was something going on between the two and he was nothing but in the way. He wondered for a moment what their relationships were with Mark Donovan, but then forced himself to put the question out of his mind. It was none of his business. That was how people stayed alive — by keeping out of things that were none of their business.

CHAPTER EIGHT

Donovan worked his way along the reception line in the main ballroom of the Plaza. After the governor's wife stood the mayor, who said that it was great to see Donovan again. Mark wanted to say, "Oh? And when was the last time?" but he restrained the impulse. WASP protocol to the hilt. Always.

And then he came to Ancie Bark Donovan, co-chairperson of the antihunger fund-raiser, and shook her hand formally and hoped she would just smile at him and let it go at that and then he could go off and find the bar and drink away the two obligatory hours of attendance.

But no such luck. Ancie held his hand firmly, leaned forward, and said softly, "Here stag tonight?" She paused and added, "Surely you could have found some high-priced trollop to join you. What about that so-called secretary of yours?"

"Too high-priced for me," Donovan said back through clenched teeth, matching her smile in wattage. "You gave me a liking for bargain-counter bimbos."

She released his hand as if it had suddenly become electrified, and for a moment, anger flashed across her model-perfect face. But just for a moment, and then she smiled broadly again and nodded over her shoulder to a much younger, insipid man standing behind her.

"I don't believe you've met my fiancé, Sir Reginald Durban." She batted her long false eyelashes at the man, and he stepped forward like an obedient house dog responding to his master's voice.

"Ah, yes," Donovan said. "Lord Dirtbag. I've heard of him."

The man smiled confusedly at both of them; then, because it was no doubt part of his training, he extended his hand toward Donovan, who grabbed it and squeezed the fingers tightly. Durban winced with pain but hung on while Mark examined him. Besides being slight, much shorter than Donovan, he possessed a long, narrow face and a long, narrow nose that rested on long, narrow lips. His eyes were tiny and a washed-out blue, and his blondish hair was thinning on top.

"So you're going to marry my ex-wife. Isn't that nice? Lady Ancie has such a nice ring to it. Now I'm really delighted that she didn't marry the flamenco dancer from Spanish Harlem. You're going to be a vast improvement over him, Lord Dirtbag."

"Mark!" Ancie was furiously tapping a gold-slippered foot. "You're going too far now."

"I thought you liked to let everyone go too far," Donovan said as he relinquished Durban's hand. He smiled at the other man. "Nice meeting you. You have my deepest sympathy."

He walked away and headed for the nearest service bar, set up in one of the corners in the rear of the room. He had not noticed anyone eavesdropping on his conversation, nor did he notice that he was followed to the bar. He ordered Perrier, wished it were Scotch, but took a large swallow anyway. Damn! Why was it Ancie always got under his skin? Love gone to hate in one easy lesson; and if it weren't for his two beautiful kids, he would have killed her by now. Strung her up by her lovely bleached ash-blond hair and tickled her to death with her fake eyelashes.

"Having a bad day?" the woman next to him asked.

Donovan had been vaguely aware of a presence there and had heard a woman's voice order a Wild Turkey and soda. Even though he knew she was speaking to him, he did not respond but just hunkered closer over his Perrier.

"Sorry," she said "I heard Queen Ancie say you were stag and thought I'd try to pick you up."

He glanced down at her. What he fixed on was her wildly curly mop of bright, brick-red hair. "I'm not in the mood," he grumbled.

"So I noticed," the woman said, turning to move away. But before she could leave the bar, a couple blocked her entrance. The woman said, "Tilda darling," and the man embraced her and the woman said, "Stop being such a letch, Harvey."

"Can't help it," Harvey said, squeezing the redhead harder. "She's always made me act like a dog in heat." He looked up and saw Donovan. "Mark! How the hell are you? Haven't seen you in a dog's age."

Mark turned then and greeted his old friends, the Gordons. He and Harvey had gone to Lehigh University together and he had been an usher at Harvey's wedding to Lily, right before Harvey had taken over his father's toy business. Harvey, who had never been known to keep his hands off anybody still breathing, hugged Donovan. Then Lily did the same.

Finally, she introduced him to the redheaded woman he had tried to shake off. "This is Tilda Matthews. You've heard of her, of course."

"Of course," he said lamely as he took the redhead's extended hand. And finally he took a good look at her. Besides the curly red hair, what he now saw was natural. She had the kind of large green eyes that reminded him of spring, and he felt an almost palpable surge of energy from her hand. "Of course I've heard of you," he said again.

"Of course *not*," Tilda Matthews said, and

smiled at Lily Gordon. "Just because you're a fan, Lily, you think everyone is."

"I couldn't believe that one today though," Lily giggled. "I love it. Kaddafi at a farm and the pigs all eyeing him. Where do you get such clever ideas?"

"Same place as everybody else." Tilda smiled with embarrassment, and there was a tinge of red glowing on her freckled cheeks. "The newspapers. Besides, that's what everyone was talking about."

Harvey looked professional as he rubbed his prematurely bald head. "But that's what Lily means. You create a funny scene out of a chaotic development. Don't you agree, Mark."

Donovan felt his jaw locking. He had forgotten that in social circles he would have to remain normal and spout stupid opinions, just like everyone else. And now they were all staring at him, including the redhead with the fabulous green eyes, who he had finally figured out must be a political cartoonist of some repute. Too bad. He had stopped looking at political cartoons right about the time they had all stopped being funny and started looking as if their political agenda was drawn up in the Kremlin.

"Perhaps," Tilda said, "he doesn't think much one way or the other."

Was she being insulting? Or merely trying to bridge an awkward gap? Either way, it annoyed Donovan and he growled, "Why don't you try making up something funny about the dead kids in the airport? How about little Nick Barsotti, Jr. Sure, I can see it now—a little Italian kid with a machine gun going off into the sunset to search for the killers of his family. You could dress him up like Sylvester Stallone in a Rambo headband and ammunition belt. It'd be a hoot. Everybody'd have a good laugh."

The blush on her face vanished and Tilda Matthews's skin turned white, making the freckles across the bridge of her nose stand out like brown spots on cauliflower. "Excuse me," she said quietly, "I think I'll see if Ancie needs any help collecting the pledges."

She walked quickly away and Harvey Gordon said, "That was pretty insufferable, old friend."

"Sorry," Mark said, and started to move away. "I'm feeling rather insufferable tonight."

Another bar in another alcove in the room was his next refuge. It was more crowded and most of the people were drinking champagne. The bright moving lights of the ballroom were giving Mark a headache, and the sparkling gowns of the women catching the reflected lights were becoming blurred. *Shit, I shouldn't have come. I should have stayed with Petrov.* And why hadn't he? Ordering another Perrier, he thought about that. Ancie again. If he hadn't come, she would have told everyone there was some horrible reason for his absence, AIDs or something. But why did he give a crap what Ancie thought or said or did?

"Mark love." Sadie Longshore approached him with open arms. Her chubby figure was covered with a pale blue sequined tent dress whose color matched exactly her pale-blue-rinsed hair. She barely came up to his chest, but the loving hug she tossed around him was strong and warm. Then she pushed him away and said, "You're always the most handsome man in any place. Especially in a tux. You've got to come with me sometime to the Food Emporium. The ladies would die, just die. Get me a martini, my girdle is killing me."

Mark laughed. "Does a martini loosen it?"

"No, but it kills the pain."

"I'll hurry, then." Mark was still grinning as he handed Sadie her drink. Something about her always brought out the good spirits in him, and if she hadn't been old enough to be his grandmother, and if she weren't married to his late father's best friend, this was the kind of woman he could spend his life with.

"Thanks. Could we sit for a minute? I forgot to mention my feet are killing me too."

They moved to one of the small tables against the wall. "How's business?" Sadie asked. "Wilton give you any new contracts?"

Wilton Longshore, Sadie's husband, was a United States senator and one who voted on defense contracts. He always seemed to be in Washington when Sadie was in New York and vice versa. Sadie referred to their marriage as the greatest traveling sideshow in the world. Since his own parents had died within a year of each other when Mark was twenty, the Longshores—old friends of the Donovans—had taken Mark under their wing. He loved them as if they were his real parents.

"Plenty of business," Mark admitted. Wilton Longshore so honored the memory of his old friend, Jeffrey Donovan, who had served with him in the United States Senate, that he had been instrumental in getting Mark involved in making helicopters back when Mark's business of making "fun planes" had been floundering.

"Good," Sadie said. She patted his hand; the diamonds on her wrist and fingers winked. "Are you a multimillionaire yet? And why aren't you married? Lord knows, those children need a better example of womanhood to look up to than you-know-who."

"They have you, their grandma, to look up to. You're enough woman for anybody."

"That's true," Sadie said seriously. Her face wrinkled around her bright eyes. "And I know you're a multimillionaire. The kids told me the last time we went to the zoo. Ach, my feet hurt that day. They also said you're not seeing anyone. Is this true?"

"This is true." Donovan put on a sad expression. "Not a single person."

"Well, darling, you're in luck." Sadie leaned

102

forward, almost whispering. "I've found the greatest girl for you. She's only thirty-five and looks much younger. And she's good-looking but not the kind you always have to worry about. And she has a great personality."

"And she limps only a little," Donovan said with a grin. He was a veteran of Sadie Longshore's matchmaking; her idea of a nice young thing usually was someone that Donovan started to say good-bye to on the hello.

"There she is. I see her." Sadie jumped to her feet, waving over her head. "Yoo-hoo. Yoo-hoo. Darling. Over here."

Mark looked up and said, "Oh, no. Sadie. Not that one. No."

"Too late." Sadie winked at him. "So what's the matter? You prejudiced against redheads?" She smiled at the approaching woman and said, "Tilda darling. I want you to meet Mark Donovan, a fabulously wealthy man who is also handsome, intelligent, and single."

"And rude, insulting, and insufferable," Tilda Matthews said.

"Well, nobody's perfect," Sadie said with a chuckle. "Anyway, that's why God made women. To iron out the minor kinks in the lesser gender. Mark dear. Get us a drink." She pushed him toward the bar even as she pulled a chair out from the table for the redhead to sit down.

Donovan did as he was told and the bartender

103

was unbearably quick about it, and before he knew it, Mark was carrying the two drinks back to the table. He sat down himself, then sighed.

It wasn't his night, especially with women. Carol Henson, Maggie's daughter, was zeroing in on his table. She was wearing Maggie's black dress, filling it out more on top than her mother ever could.

"Mark darling. There you are," she said brightly, leaning over to kiss him at the table. "Hello, Mrs. Longshore. How nice to see you again." And back to Mark. "Sorry I'm late, but I couldn't get a cab and . . . well, you know. Have you been looking for me?" Carol touched his cheek with a hand that had savagely painted red claws for fingernails.

"It's all right," Mark said, gritting his teeth. How could Maggie have gotten him into this? Carol looked beautiful, of course. She was as tall as her mother but with an even better figure. Her slanted blue eyes contrasted spectacularly with her coal-black hair. She had been trying to make it as a model, but Donovan knew why she was not successful. No respectable model agency wanted to deal with a druggie, even if she was gorgeous.

Donovan studied her. Stoned as always and chattering on as if she thought she was making sense. He removed her arm from his sleeve and settled her down at the table. "Would you like a soda or something?"

"A soda?" Carol laughed hysterically. "Isn't he silly? You're so silly. I'll have a Black Russian, of course. My usual. Mark always forgets." Carol leaned over toward Mrs. Longshore. "Isn't he silly? And who's the lady with the red hair?"

Sadie Longshore said sharply, "Don't you think you've had enough?"

"You know what they say, don't you? Nothing is ever enough. A Black Russian. Silly, why are you standing there like a giant black bird in your tuxedo? Black Bird, get me a Black Russian." She thought this hilariously funny and laughed hysterically again.

"We'll try some coffee," Donovan said.

"Oh, for Christ's sake." Carol stood up. She was angry, but not so much that she forgot to smooth the black dress that draped spectacularly over her figure. "Here I am, I race over just to see you, Mark sweetheart, and you treat me so mean. If you won't bring your date a drink, I'll get my own."

"Carol, you're not my date. Your mother was, but she couldn't make it and I don't know how you wound up here. So why not get a cab and go home?"

"A cab? You're going to put me in a cab?" Her face was twisted in anger, and then her features smoothed out. "Isn't that silly. Put me in a cab." She looked at Mrs. Longshore and Tilda. "Just because he's known me since I was in diapers, he still treats me like a baby. So silly, too, because he knows he really wants to sleep with me. Don't you, Mark?"

"I want you out of here," Donovan said. He grabbed her arm to escort her to the door, but Carol pulled loose and started away from the table.

"Well, you blew your chance," she said. "Somebody else will have to service me tonight. Mrs. Longshore, where's your husband?"

"Washington, darling. I'll give you his address. Please, take the next plane."

"I'll do that," Carol snapped. When she walked away across the ballroom, men turned to watch her, for she made the simple stroll seem like a sequence from a porno film.

Still standing, Mark sighed. "I'm really sorry."

Sadie Longshore downed her drink. "To quote our friend, don't be so silly. But before you sit down, please, another martini."

"I should go after her," Mark said, unmoving.

"No, you shouldn't. She's what now? Twenty-two or three? It's her business. And if you get her out of here, what next? She'll just go find trouble somewhere else. If she needs trouble, better she finds it here than out on the street somewhere."

Donovan stared at his old friend. What she said made sense. Sure, he could drag Carol back to the apartment she shared with Maggie, but he couldn't keep her there. Maggie had told him that Carol often disappeared for days on end, and when she did finally put in an appearance, she was so high on drugs that Maggie could not get out of her where she had been.

"But I do have to make a phone call," Donovan said.

Tilda Matthews rose. "Go ahead. I'll get Sadie her drink."

Donovan looked at her again. What was it Sadie had said? That she was thirty-five and looked young and that she was good-looking but not a smash? Some yes, some no. She did look younger than thirty-five; she had a gaminesque quality that belied those years. But she *was* smashing, with her wild red hair and luminous green eyes, set into an angular face with a short nose and huge mouth. And it was easy to miss that her figure was a showstopper too. The cowl neckline of her dress drooped low enough for Donovan to see the cleavage between her breasts. A slit up the side of her skirt showed long, shapely legs.

"You're staring," Tilda told him.

"I'm sorry. I just noticed you for the first time tonight."

"Well, it wasn't my fault," Tilda said. She smiled, showing remarkably white teeth that were even and shining in her large mouth. "Make your phone call. I'll get the drink."

"Thanks," Donovan said.

Donovan let the phone ring twelve times, but there was no answer at Petrov's apartment. It was, he saw, only a little after eight. Why had he thought it was late already? He would call again in twenty minutes. By then, unless something serious had happened, Maggie should have brought Petrov home from the hospital.

His heart was beating irregularly as he made his way back to the table. Tilda Matthews was sitting alone.

"Sadie said to tell you that she had to get home. How about if you and I pretend we'd never met before," she said.

Donovan sat down and extended his hand. "Hi, I'm Mark Donovan. You come here often?"

CHAPTER NINE

The telephone had kept ringing for a long time, but Maggie had been busy putting Tolly Peterson to bed and had decided to ignore it.

Most likely it was Mark, and he would call again. So no harm done. And maybe it was a girlfriend of Tolly's, some Manhattan bimbo taking advantage of the gentle Briton. Probably young . . . real young. And very blond. Bleached blond. And not real smart, but with a street savvy just shrewd enough to keep Tolly reaching for his wallet. She'd be a stewardess and share an apartment with three other stews and regale them with stories of the rich pigeon she had caught and how she was going to make him into her favorite dish: penniless squab. A bitch and obviously the wrong kind of woman for Peterson, so it served her right that Maggie hadn't answered the phone. If the little slut was any good at all, she would have been there herself in Tolly's time of need.

The whole script flashed through Maggie's mind as she sat on the sofa in the yellow and white living room and for the tenth time looked at the sheet of paper listing the danger signs to watch for in concussions. Of course, the telephone call had been Mark Donovan and of course he would call again.

She had brought Peterson home by cab and in the taxi he had leaned against her the way Carol used to when she was a child. It had brought out the motherly instinct in Maggie, the instinct that she thought had been killed and buried by Carol's absolute worthlessness as a daughter. But the love was still there though, and Maggie knew she would never abandon her child, even though it meant going through the hell she was going through now.

Tolly Peterson was another story. Would she always warm to men who were weaker than she was? And was it just because she felt the need to mother someone who would respond to her warmth and her concern? It never worked because then the men became too dependent, and while she liked mothering, the fact was that she wanted to be dependent on someone herself.

She put aside the list of concussion warnings and, to break the silence of the apartment, said aloud, "Don't suppose there's a bar around here anywhere, is there?"

She looked in one cabinet and found the television set, laughed at the selections Petrov had marked in his *TV Guide*, and tuned the set to an old spy movie. Maybe Peterson kept his liquor in the refrigerator, she thought, sure that as a typical bachelor he would have no ice, no wine, and no food.

She went past the lacquered table of the dining room, wondering if Peterson ever entertained, but the refrigerator was so full she was amazed. Gourmet cheeses from Zabar's crowded one shelf and there were farm-fresh vegetables. Several varieties of juices were on the top shelf along with four bottles of white wine. The freezer compartment held veal cutlets and pork chops and steak and microwave pizza.

She popped a small pizza in the microwave, then opened a bottle of wine and poured a large slug into a crystal glass she took from the dining room cupboard. "No place like home," she said aloud.

The spy movie had escalated into a disaster film by the time she was on her second glass of wine and nibbling the crusts of the small pizza. It was time to check on her patient: every two hours had been Dr. Milliken's orders. But before doing that, Maggie took her plate back to the kitchen. It had been so neat before she made her small mess that she wanted to clean it up.

Strange to be in someone else's apartment. Her own was a rent-stabilized flat in Greenwich Village, with two small bedrooms and a utility kitchen. But every time she thought she was making enough money to move—and Donovan was a very generous employer—rents all over the city increased and she decided to stay where she was. Donovan had offered to call friends, but by then Carol had been happy in her school. Maggie sighed. She should have moved. The Village had not been good for Carol at all. At one time it had been New York's refuge for artists, but in recent years it had become another high-rent district for drug freaks pretending to be artists.

Too late now to worry about it. She was saving her money and soon she would buy a large condominium on the East Side. Better late than never.

As she went down the hall to the master bedroom, she heard a delirious cry and began to run. Peterson was sitting up in bed, but not seeing her. He was yelling something that sounded like *Kakoi ya gavno! Kakoi ya gavno!*

Maggie hurried to the bed, took Tolly in her arms, and said, "Shhh, shhh. It's all right. Maggie's here. You're fine." She rocked him back and forth, giving him her warmth. Holding him tightly, her right hand moved softly to the stitches in the back of his head. No more blood, thank God. "Shhhh, shhhhh. It's all right. I'm here."

Peterson blinked. "Maggie. What are you doing here?" For a moment Maggie thought there was something odd about his voice, the way he spoke. And then he said, "Where am I?" and the British accent was so thick you could cut it with a knife.

"Home. You're home." Peterson looked around

at the king-size bed and then, with Maggie still holding him, he slumped back against the pillows. She cradled him in her arms but he was falling asleep.

"Don't. You have to stay awake for a moment. I have to check your temperature."

Tolly turned toward her, reached out, and held her body against his, then kissed her lips hungrily. His tongue caressed hers and she felt herself responding, but although her body wanted more, her mind stopped it and she pulled away.

"No, don't. You don't know what you're doing."

Tolly's eyes caught hers as she sat up, busily trying to smooth her rumpled blond hair. "I think I know quite well what I'm doing," he said.

"No, you don't," Maggie insisted. "I have to take your temperature."

He stuck his tongue out at her. "So take it."

Maggie smiled; it was a nice tongue, pink and healthy-looking and she wanted to put it back in her mouth. She looked at the thermometer, shook it down, and plopped it into Peterson's mouth.

He took it under his tongue but spoke around it. "If I do what you want, will you kiss me again?"

"Not if you have a fever," Maggie said. She took his hand and began to count his pulse. "And shut up."

His pulse was normal but the thermometer read 100 degrees even. "How do you feel?" she asked.

"I feel fine," he said, then reached over and gently cupped one of her breasts. "And you feel even finer."

"Don't," she said even as she closed her eyes, feeling the nipple hardening against his touch. "Don't. I mean it. You're in no condition."

In answer, he took her hand and placed it on his groin. Even through the light blanket he was so big and hard, she found her touch frozen for a moment before she pulled away. "No, not now." She backed off and smoothed her clothing. "You're a hell of a patient. If nursing is like this, no wonder there's a shortage. Go back to sleep now. I'll see you in two hours."

"I count the minutes, dear Maggie," Peterson said with a small smile. Then his eyes began to close.

Maggie stood watching him for a moment before going back to the living room and pouring herself another glass of wine. She stared unseeingly at the television set, but her mind was trying to remember what it was Peterson had called out in his sleep.

Something *ya gavno*. That meant something to her but what. *Gavno*. *Gavno*. She remembered. A long time ago she had dated a man who worked as a manager at a Russian restaurant in New York. Although he was an Italian from Jersey City, he had picked up some slang along the way. *Gavno* meant "shit" in Russian.

114

Now, why did a nice English laddie like Tolly Peterson swear in his sleep in Russian? She dozed off on the couch with the question still in her mind.

"Look, you've done enough. How about if I come over and spell you?" Donovan said. He hoped that Maggie would say no. Tilda Matthews was waiting outside the telephone booth. Both of them had agreed that it was kind of ghastly to pretend you were doing something about third world hunger and then scopping down a lobster tail buffet; so they were going out to eat.

"Nope," Maggie answered. "I'm here and I'm fine. Tolly is asleep right now, but I've got to wake him in fifteen minutes to take his temperature. Really, boss, I've got a handle on this."

"Okay. By the way, did you send Carol over here to take your place tonight?"

"Carol?" Maggie's voice revealed her surprise. "No, she was at the apartment when you and I talked earlier, and she knew I was supposed to meet you. You mean she took my place?"

"Well, tried to. She even wore your black dress."

"She behave?" Maggie asked.

Donovan hesitated. "She acted like we had a date. I couldn't do anything with her, and the last I saw of her she was circuiting around. Maybe I should go back inside and get her?"

"Not a chance." Maggie had known for years that Carol had a thing about Donovan and the young woman still had not outgrown it. "Don't worry about it. She'll be all right. Now, get off the phone before you wake my patient. See you tomorrow."

"All right," Donovan told the redheaded woman. "What kind of food would you like?"

Tilda Matthews pursed her lips and smiled at him. "Deli? Wolf's? A pastrami sandwich?"

"Be still, my heart," Donovan said. "My choice exactly. Are you trying to seduce me?"

"We could get it to go," Tilda said.

Maggie hung up the telephone and got up to check on Peterson again. *Gavno*. Why Russian curses? Was Tolly something other than the mild-mannered British helicopter salesman he pretended to be? Did Donovan know? Whirlaway Inc. did a lot of secret work for the U.S. Defense Department. Was it possible that they had a spy in their midst?

As quickly as the thought entered her mind, she discarded it. Tolly Peterson a spy? Idiotic. She had been watching too many bad spy movies on television.

It was more important to think of her daughter,

116

Carol. For Donovan to say that he hadn't been able to do anything with her led Maggie to fear the worst. She knew how out of control Carol could get at times, and she had the dismaying feeling that things were going to get worse with her. A lot worse.

At seventeen — five years younger than Carol was now — Maggie had made a mistake, one that had forced her strict fundamentalist parents to put her out of the house. And at age eighteen, in the Florence Crittendon Home for Unwed Mothers, Maggie had given birth to Carol. If she had given Carol up for adoption as everyone urged her to do, would Carol have turned out differently? Was this the original sin coming back to haunt the mother?

Tolly Peterson called out in his sleep and Maggie scrambled down the hall. This time she heard something that sounded like *Eop tvoi mat*. Russian again. Another curse? Maybe she really didn't want to know.

Petrov was dreaming. He was a small boy again in Odessa and his mother had engulfed him in her arms to soothe his troubles away. Maya was there too; Maya with her long, soft brown hair and large doe eyes, looking with worry at her older brother, who seemed to fear so much.

And then one day their mother was not there to

117

comfort them anymore and when Anatoly or Maya asked about their mother, they got a brutal slap or kick from their father and he would yell, *"Eop tvoi mat."* Screw your mother. "You are both pieces of shit. I don't believe that I'm your father. Say it, say it after me. 'What a piece of shit I am.' "

Maya always gave in first. She was less stubborn than her brother and, in many ways, more clever. It wasn't until Tolly was beaten and bleeding that he would give in and whimper *"Kakoi ya gavno."* What a piece of shit I am.

Gavno. There was that word again. Maggie leaned over the bed and soothed the fine brown hair from his creased face. God, Tolly looked like he was in such pain. Maybe it was time to call Dr. Milliken and ask for his help.

But suddenly Peterson sat straight up in bed, almost bumping into Maggie leaning over him. "Maggie. What are you doing here?"

He doesn't remember I was here before. Or maybe he would rather forget making a pass at me. Okay, either way, Maggie thought. She said, "I've been here a couple of hours. I brought you home from the hospital, remember?"

"Oh, yes. Oh, what a headache." Peterson sank back on the pillows. "I vaguely remember. A cab, right? How did you get me up the stairs?"

"The cabbie helped. Thanks to ten dollars."

"Did he undress me too?" Peterson asked.

"No. I asked him to but I think he thought we were a couple of perverts. So I got your pants off by myself." She paused. "Would you like something to eat? Soup or toast maybe? You threw up in the hospital so you're probably empty."

"Sure. I am hungry." Peterson sat up again and swung his feet over the side of the bed.

"No. Don't get up. I'll bring it in here," she said.

She left him sitting on the edge of the bed, but when she had warmed a can of mushroom soup and toasted some bread, Tolly, with a red robe wrapped around his body, walked into the kitchen and sat at the small table.

Maggie felt so motherly that she thought she might have to feed him, but his appetite was hearty and the color had begun to return to his face and he ate like a man intent on gaining weight.

"Watching television?" he asked her.

"Oh, some spy thing," Maggie said. She had forgotten to turn off the set, and the low murmur floated into the kitchen. "You know. One of those things where the good guys are wonderful macho Americans and the bad guys are disgusting Russians who kill women and babies and smile a lot."

"Stark realism, right?" Peterson said as he chewed carefully on his toast.

"Depends on what you think of Americans and Russians," Maggie said as she stood, taking away the soup bowl. "You want to watch it?"

"No. But I don't want to miss Joe Franklin," he said. "And how about a vodka?"

"Sorry," she said. "This is white wine. It's all I could find."

"You didn't look in the right place. The vodka's in the freezer."

"Frozen vodka?" she said.

"The only way to drink it without ice cubes watering it down," Peterson said.

"How's your head feel?" she asked.

"I feel fine now. I just needed that rest."

"Okay. Then I guess one little vodka won't hurt. Go inside. I'll bring it in."

He did as he was told, and when Maggie came into the living room holding the two glasses, he was seated in the center of the long couch. There was room for her on either side of him, but she put the glass down on the coffee table and sat in a white leather chair next to the sofa.

Peterson sipped his drink, sighed pleasurably, and then began punching the buttons on the television's remote control, apparently searching for a channel.

Maggie said, "Do we have to watch Joe Franklin?"

"You have a better suggestion?"

"*Casablanca*'s on," she said.

120

"What's that?" Peterson said, then winced when she gave him a quizzical look. "I haven't watched a lot of American telly before this," he said quickly. "Been too busy."

"Don't know how you could have missed this one. Bogart and Bergman. The best movie ever made."

"The best American movie every made," Peterson corrected her, and handed her the remote control. She found the right channel just as the movie was starting.

"This color is pretty pitiful," Peterson said after watching a few minutes of the film.

"Well, it was originally black and white, but they colorized it," she explained.

After about ten minutes Peterson was so caught up in the film he could see why Maggie had been surprised he was not familiar with it. She was watching him carefully too. Donovan would have to be warned that perhaps Petrov had blown his cover with her. Donovan . . . had Petrov told him about those Arabs sounding unhappy with the United Nations? He could not remember.

During a commercial Maggie went into the kitchen to make some microwave popcorn and Petrov made them both fresh drinks. Why couldn't he relax, he wondered. He would have to get her out of there. Even as he thought that, he looked at her standing in front of the microwave, her soft, rounded hips, her long legs encased in tight-fitting jeans, and he felt his body tingle. *No! Not with her.* Petrov took his sexual pleasure with prostitutes, with women he would never see again. He could not go through the shame of someone he cared about looking at his body . . . at the scars . . . at the mutilation.

He returned to the living room, and when Maggie brought in the bowl of popcorn, she did not return to her chair but set it between them on the white couch. It was dripping with butter, and when she handed him a napkin, their hands touched and he could feel his underwear bulging uncomfortably under his robe. He had to get rid of her. He had to. But he wanted her to stay.

The popcorn was finished and the movie was over and Maggie finally spoke. "Tolly. Do you remember kissing me?"

So that was it. With her question, the memory came back. They had kissed and he had guided her hand to his body. "Yes," he said. "It was wonderful but I acted like an ass. I'm sorry. It must have been my concussion."

"Oh, for God's sakes." Maggie was up in a fluid motion and then was in his arms. "I didn't mind," she said. She moved her mouth from his neck, up the side of his face to find his lips. His tongue met hers, his hands traveled her body.

And then Petrov tried to pull away but he could not; she was holding him too tightly and her lips were demanding more of his. *No, this is all wrong.*

"No, not now," he said. "You're feeling sorry for me and I can't stand that." It was a lame excuse and Maggie saw right through it.

"I'm not sorry for you. You've got a concussion; you're not a cripple."

Petrov felt a blinding rage flash through his mind. So totally the wrong thing to say. How could she know? No one knew that he was a cripple except some doctors in Russia. And the men who had made him a cripple and they no longer lived. "I think you'd better go, Maggie," he said, and his voice was cold. "I'd like to get some sleep."

Maggie pulled herself away from his arms and said, "Sure thing. I've been thrown out of better places." She could not hide the sarcasm in her voice. "See you around. You'll be all right?"

"I'll be fine."

She hung her purse over her shoulder and left. The apartment door slammed behind her and Petrov felt a heavy weight sink onto him. He had hurt her and himself.

But what else could I do? What else could I do?

CHAPTER TEN

As Tilda and Donovan started to leave the Plaza ballroom, they were confronted again by Lily and Harvey Gordon. Lily smiled patronizingly at them, as if their getting together had been the result only of her careful planning, but Harvey Gordon asked Donovan if he could talk to him a moment, and pulled him off to the side out of earshot of the two women.

Donovan was annoyed but stolidly silent. He wanted to get out of there with Tilda and go buy sandwiches and cole slaw and pickles and anything else she wanted and then get her up to his apartment fast before something happened to change the mood of the evening. He put on what Ancie used to call his patient listener's face. That particular expression had always made her furious, but it did not seem to register on Harvey Gordon at all.

"Mark," he said, "you know Carol . . . your secretary's daughter . . . is here tonight?"

"I know. How do you know her?"

"Everybody knows Carol," Gordon said. "She must have gone through Maggie's Rolodex at the office and called everybody you know looking for modeling jobs. I even hired her for one of my toy shows at the Coliseum. I thought you knew."

"I didn't, but it's not important," Donovan said. "It won't happen again."

Gordon shrugged. *"Nada,"* he said. "Not important."

"So what about Carol?" Donovan said.

"She's over at the bar hanging all over some underprivileged third world sleazeball from the United Nations."

Donovan was tightlipped. "First of all, I doubt that he's underprivileged. They send only the sons of millionaires over here. Second of all, why are you telling me this?"

"Well, you know how Carol is," Gordon said lamely.

"No. How is she?"

"Mark, she's a goddamn cokehead. You know that. I thought you might . . . well, I don't know, I thought you might want to try to keep her out of trouble. Never mind. Forget I said anything."

He looked crestfallen and Donovan put his big hand on Gordon's shoulder. "No . . . thanks, Harvey. Really, I appreciate it. I had a run-in with her earlier and I guess just hearing her name makes me a little testy. I'll see what I can do. Really, thanks." He said it more heartily than he felt it;

125

he just wished Harvey Gordon had left him the hell alone, but now he was stuck with Carol and her welfare.

The two men walked back to where Tilda Matthews was chatting with Mrs. Gordon, and Mark told the pretty redhead, "I have to go check on my secretary's daughter. Remember her?"

"Who could forget?" Tilda said with a grin. "I'll join you. You might need reinforcements."

At the bar across the room, Carol Henson was indeed leaning on a dark-skinned man, but he was definitely not underprivileged. Donovan thought if that man had ever missed a meal, it was because he'd spent the dinner hour at his Weight Watcher's meeting.

Carol's eyes seemed to have an artificial shine as she looked up at Donovan and said, "Mark dear. This is Raffi. I think I'm in love." She put her arm across the swarthy man's shoulder. She was as tall as he was.

"Good," Donovan said. "New York is for lovers."

The plump, dark-haired man disentangled himself from Carol's arm and bowed slightly. "You are this lady's father?" he said with a small bow.

"A friend of the family," Donovan said. "Carol, I'd like to talk to you a minute."

Tilda Matthews took the arm of the other man and led him off to the side. "Tell me about yourself," she said. "While our friends talk."

The man nodded and followed Tilda away.

Carol said, "Mark, she's taking him away. Now I'll never get married."

"Carol, you couldn't pass the physical for the marriage license," Donovan said.

"What are you talking about?" Carol asked, a hardening edge on her voice.

"Because you could start a fire with your eyes. Because you've been off in the ladies' room putting toot in your nose. And now maybe I think it's time for you to go home."

"You're always talking at me, Mark. Never talking to me. You're like a father, but you're not my father. Or are you? Have you been sticking it to your secretary? Is that where I came from? Let me tell you, Mark, it doesn't matter to me. I think incest is neat."

She was prattling on like a lunatic, Donovan thought. No wonder Harvey Gordon had been concerned. "No," he told her somberly. "I'm not your father."

"No, of course you're not," Carol said. "I don't have one. Haven't you heard, I'm Maggie's little bastard love child."

Donovan sat on the bar stool next to her and talked softly "Grow up, girl, and stop making up reasons to feel sorry for yourself."

"Girl?" she said. Her tone was at first angry, but then her expression softened into a smile. "Maybe it's you, Mark, making up reasons that

127

you won't fuck me. I'm not a little girl. I'm a woman, or hadn't you noticed?"

"It's hard to notice when you always act like a baby," Donovan said.

"Is this the way babies act?" she said, and put her hand between his legs.

Donovan stood up. "Stop that. I'll take you home now."

"No." Carol stood also. "I'm going to be Raffi's fifth wife or second wife or something. I'm going to go live in the desert." She snapped her fingers but missed. "Shit," she said, then called out, "Raffi, come and take me to the Casbah."

The pudgy man showed up next to Donovan. "Don't worry, sir," he said softly. "I will see her home safely."

Mark leaned against the bar, watching the man steer Carol toward the exit. Tilda was silent for a moment, watching also, then she tapped Donovan on the stomach. "Hey, don't feel bad. You did the best you could."

"I guess," Donovan said with a sigh, still looking after Carol. Then he smiled down at the redhead. "Are we still on for tonight?"

"Am I still starving?" she answered.

The weather had turned sullen, sticky with humidity, carrying the promise of rain the next day. Donovan held Tilda's hand as they walked toward Wolf's Deli. They did not speak much, and Donovan felt that Tilda was also thinking of Carol

Henson. Had that twit ruined everybody's night?

When they reached the restaurant, Donovan sensed that the easy road toward a one-night stand had been rained out. In truth, he did not mind that either. There might be something important happening between the two of them, and while that prospect frightened him a little, it also made him think about giving it a chance.

"Maybe we should sit down and eat here," he said as they stepped inside the deli's front door. Yes, this might be too important to leap in the sack amid greasy paper bags smelling of pickles and cole slaw.

Tilda looked at him thoughtfully. "I was thinking the same thing. Besides, they never give you hot peppers to go."

"Oh, is this one of your hangouts?" Donovan asked. He had to wait for his answer until a waiter showed them to a table. Then Tilda said, "You asked. Daniel and I come here a lot."

"Oh," Donovan said sourly. He was surprised at feeling a twinge of jealousy. "Good old Daniel."

"Yup. We usually eat here twice a week before we go turn in." She paused theatrically for effect and then chuckled when his face turned sullen. She clapped his right bicep with her left hand. "Daniel's my son, Mark."

"Oh." Despite trying, he could not help but grin. She had a son. She couldn't very well object to his two kids. Maybe this was really going to be one of those few rare matches made in heaven. "And where's Daniel tonight? With a sitter?" Or was he home with his dear old daddy? But why would Sadie Longshore have gone to so much trouble to put them together if Tilda was already spoken for?

"Hah," Tilda said. "No sitter. Not with a brother and sister-in-law living two blocks away. We're those lace-curtain Irish with a lot of family and nobody in the family pays for a baby-sitter if he can help it. Our pop would come off the line at J&L and wring our necks and—"

"Where?" Donovan interrupted.

"Where what?"

"Where J&L?" Donovan said.

"J&L Steel. Pittsburgh," she answered.

"I don't believe it," Donovan said.

"I must be missing something here," Tilda said. "Maybe you would enlighten me."

"You're from Pittsburgh," he said, and laughed.

"Lots of people are from Pittsburgh. Lots of people in New York are from Pittsburgh. I've told lots of people I'm from Pittsburgh, and no one ever laughed in my face before."

"Say something in Pittsburghese," Donovan said.

"Say someth . . . okay . . . 'Are yuns waiting on the buz to go donton? What'd yuns think of the Stiwwers' season?' . . . How's that?"

"Perfect. Absolutely perfect," Donovan said.

"The light dawns." Tilda stared at him.

"Donovan. And a friend of Sadie Longshore. Any relation to old Senator Donovan from Pittsburgh?"

"My father," Donovan said.

Tilda shook her head. "Small world," she said. "All the time we were growing up, my father would talk about yours. He said he was the only honest man in Washington and he kept trying to talk Kevin, one of my brothers, into going into politics."

"And did he?"

"In a way. He's a priest," she said with a grin. "Sean was supposed to be the priest, but he got waylaid by a sultry brunette with sleek thighs. . . ."

"Oh, those sleek thighs will do it every time," Donovan said.

"Yeah, well, not so sleek anymore. She and Sean have four point five kids. That's where Daniel is tonight."

"And you have to pick him up there?"

"No," she answered slowly. "But I do have some work to do, and besides, I, well, I think that maybe it would be nice if . . ."

"If we ate and I dropped you off in a cab and then I called you for a date?" Donovan suggested.

"All you guys from Pittsburgh give great telepathy," she said.

Later in the taxi, Donovan put his arm around

Tilda and she snuggled against him. For the first time in a long while, he felt content, until he remembered his earlier thought about her husband. Big Catholic family, one of them a priest, was it likely that she was divorced? But if she weren't would she be out running around with another man? He felt her left hand; there was no wedding ring.

He finally decided on a frontal assault. "You know all about Ancie, my ex," he said. "What about your husband?"

He felt her stiffen a little next to him. "My late husband," she said.

"Oh, I'm sorry," Donovan said, feeling like a mutt.

"Yeah. Us too," she said. "Tom Matthews. He had the biggest heart in the world and the weakest. He died when Daniel was a year old. You sort of reminded me of him. He was big like you and had the same wavy sort of hair. That's why I came over to cheer you up after Ancie got on your case tonight." She sighed and then said, "Now, shut up and kiss me," and Donovan did.

He let her out of the cab at the corner of Seventy-third Street and West End Avenue, clutching the piece of paper on which she had scrawled her name, address, and phone number. It was a crackling piece of good quality bristol from the miniature sketch pad she had carried in her purse. She had told him she did not have business cards

132

because she could never make up her mind what to say on them.

Her mouth, when he kissed her, had tasted sweet with an overtone of hot peppers and onions and he tasted her on his lips again. She was a lady but a woman, too, and . . .

"Where to, Mac?" the cabbie intruded on his thoughts.

Donovan started to give his address on Sutton Place, then changed his mind. It was only eleven-thirty and Bob Mendoza should be at his police desk now, catching up on paperwork. He told the driver to take him to the Midtown South police headquarters.

"Gringo! *Que pasa?*"

Mendoza was sitting in his third-floor office, his feet on the desk and leafing through a pile of papers. Without moving his feet he reached into a drawer to produce a plastic cup and handed it to Donovan. "Coffee's over there," he said. "And don't worry, the cup is clean. I washed it right after the drunk driver left his specimen in it."

"Very funny," Donovan said. He took the cup, poured himself some coffee, and sat on the other side of the desk from Mendoza.

"So how's it going?" Donovan said. "I was just in the neighborhood and thought I'd stop in to see if you had any interesting cases."

133

Mendoza reached over his head and pushed the door to the office shut as Donovan glanced around. They were in a basic cubicle, decorated with basic institutional cheap white paint that had turned to basic dirty gray. Four large metal file cabinets took up more space than the small wooden scarred desk. The only personal touch in the office was a picture of Jenny Mendoza, posing like a fifties cover girl, which had been blown up to poster size and attached to a calendar.

"You're one lousy spy," Mendoza said quietly.

"I'm not any kind of spy," Donovan said.

"Then what are you?"

Instead of answering, Donovan said, "Nice office you've got here."

"Hokay," Mendoza said. "I'll keep my questions to myself. The interesting thing I'm working on today is the bodies of two men found on the West Side. Mugging victims, it looks like. No wallets, no ID. But their coats had dry-cleaning tags in them, and we ran down the dry cleaner and our two victims were"—he paused to shuffle through the papers on his desk—"they were Jacques Boule and Ferdinand Deladier, but they didn't look like Frenchmen and we faxed their prints and morgue shots to Interpol and what do you know, Interpol says that the two guys were Arabs—but they don't have any other names on them except those phony French names—but the two were definitely Arabs and they were high-powered bodyguards of some

134

high-powered individual in the field of Arabian-type conflict, if you get my drift."

"Arabian type," Donovan mused aloud. He already know that. "The dry cleaner. He have an address on these two guys?"

"No. At least there wasn't any on the file tickets."

"Too bad. We didn't get too much, then," Donovan said.

Mendoza shrugged. "Well, maybe more than you think. They had their clothes cleaned two months ago, so we know they've been in the country at least that long. They had to live somewhere . . . maybe even work somewhere. We just have to dig."

"Nothing else from Interpol though, huh?"

"*Nada,* amigo. Now, is there anything you'd like to tell me?"

"I can't think of anything, Bobby. I think I heard it mentioned that the men spent some time at El Fazid's on Twenty-ninth Street."

"Well, your police department does believe in checking out all rumors in such tragic crimes," Mendoza said. "Your tax dollars at work. I don't suppose you've ever heard of a man called Ayoub, have you?"

Donovan crinkled his eyes. "I don't know. Maybe I read his name in the *Post* or someplace. Is he important?"

"Donovan . . . amigo . . ." Mendoza took his feet down from the desk and leaned forward.

135

"This is heavy duty stuff here. I wonder what am I involved in. And how far I am involved. I tell you, I would like to cover my ass."

"No." Donovan's tone became official; it sounded the way it had in Vietnam when he was giving orders. "Your ass will stay as clean as the season's first snow."

"I've heard of snowjobs before," Mendoza said.

"Bobby, let me put it to you this way. If you need it, I can have the President of the United States call anybody who starts to get on your case. Don't worry about it."

"The President is a busy man," Mendoza said.

"He'll make time," Donovan said.

Mendoza's eyes met his; they locked for a moment and the New York policeman said, "I go where you go . . . and all of that."

Donovan got to his feet. "Nice chatting with you, Bobby. If you look around El Fazid's, let me know if you see anyone interesting having a snack."

"You got it," Mendoza said.

"And no one knows anything," Donovan said, and immediately regretted it because Mendoza looked hurt.

"You didn't even have to say that," the policeman said.

"I know. I'm sorry. I'm just out of practice."

"Get back in shape fast. There are sharks out there," Mendoza said.

When Donovan got to his penthouse apartment, he took out the slip of paper that Tilda Matthews had given him. The name, address, and phone number were there, but so was a quick cartoon sketch of Tilda offering him a huge pickle. He grinned and picked up the phone immediately.

"Hi," he said when it was answered. "Pickle sandwich tomorrow? Noon? Central Park?"

"At the statue. I'll be wearing a hot pepper over my left ear."

CHAPTER ELEVEN

Anatoly Petrov was dreaming in Russian, although there was a warning constantly running through the fragmented images telling him he must not do that.

Maya, his sister, was there in the dreams, sometimes a little girl and other times all grown up in her astronaut's space suit and with her children gathered around her, all in little space suits too.

Then she was pleading with Petrov not to denounce their father, but he knew that dream was not true because they had plotted together to denounce him.

And then the scene switched to Odessa, and they were children, walking by the sea with their plain and thin mother who showed the strain of raising two children by herself without even enough money to feed them properly. Then they were at a dinner table, children still, and Maya and Petrov looked at the last soggy lump of overdone potato still sitting on a platter and when Maya had reached for it, Petrov had pulled her

138

hand away and gestured to leave it for their mother, who had not yet eaten.

And then their mother was gone and their father, the brute, was there, beating both of them, forcing Maya and Petrov to pledge allegiance to Beria, although they did not even know who Beria was. The food had been better then, but Mama was gone and when they asked about her, they were beaten. Then they found out that Papa had joined Beria's secret police and he himself had sent their mother away to a work camp. Papa made them report to him everything that went on in school each day and any gossip they might hear from neighbors or shopkeepers. Once Maya was beaten black and blue because she had nothing to report and then she remembered seeing an old American magazine in a neighbor's apartment. That was enough . . . the neighbor, an old man with relatives in the United States, vanished. And when that happened, Petrov refused to report to his father anymore, although it brought upon him continuous beatings, administered even more savagely by the father because he was offended that Petrov did not cry. Petrov never cried. He only waited.

And now the memories of those beatings flooded his dreams and Petrov woke himself by snapping his spine upward into a sitting position. The sheets of his bed showed the twistings and turnings of his night and his dreams — bunched in places and tangled in others. The fitted sheet had come loose from the bottom of the bed and his right foot was tangled in the elastic and he tried to kick free but only made it worse and his head seemed to be splitting in pieces.

Finally he seized all the covers and sheets and everything he could get into his hands and tossed them off the bed onto the floor. And then he was free, and he leaned back into the pillows.

They were wet. He had been crying during the night. The thought filled him with revulsion, and he forced the memory of the dreams from his mind and tried to remember what had happened to him yesterday and last night.

Maggie. Her face as she was leaving came back to him. It was another hurting memory, and perhaps it had sparked all those other hurting memories. He got out of the bed as if it were responsible for the painful feelings and felt a hammering pain in his hand. He remembered his stitches and gingerly touched the covering bandage on the back of his head with his fingertips. The gauze was dry; no bleeding. Good.

He stripped his pajamas off on the way to the bathroom, dropping them on the floor as he went. Inside the bathroom he stared at himself in the full-length mirror on the door. The bandage over his stitches was about two inches square and Petrov thought he could probably replace it with a Band-Aid and then use hair goop to plaster his fine beigeish hair down over the bald spot where they had shaved him. The alternative was to wear a hat, and while that might work outdoors, it presented problems whenever he came into a room. And, truth was, he hated hats.

His head was close to the mirror as he had been inspecting the bandage; now he just backed away slightly to examine his face. It looked the same as always, regular and pleasant but a canvas on which he could paint any mood he wished. He could mold it into the silly face of yesterday when he had acted as open as a pansy in a field; or he could make his visage hard and so unpleasant that he could frighten the people he looked at. Either face was an act, an act he was very good at, but his real face was just that . . . just another ordinary face.

He examined his body. There were a couple of small bruises under his ribs from yesterday's fight, but otherwise he seemed all right. His body was lean, without fat and with stringy but not lumpy muscles. He kept his body in fine tune with karate, but he had never lifted weights to try to pile up flashy flesh.

His chest was covered with wiry brown hair that ran lightly down his body to his genitals, where, on one side, it disappeared, replaced instead by a mass of scar tissue around the spot where his right testicle had once been. He had not cried that time either; he had only remembered and paid back.

141

Suddenly he turned away; the scars and his deformity, as always, sickened him. No, he could never explain to Maggie what had happened. And women always asked.

He showered and despite Dr. Milliken's orders not to, he shampooed his hair lightly to remove the few traces of blood still clumped in it. For a moment in the shower he felt woozy but leaned against the wall until the dizziness passed. He must remember to take things slow and easy today; concussions could be dangerous.

He dressed and then, before leaving the apartment, he fished around in a dresser drawer for a switchblade knife, which he stuck into his trouser pocket.

Donovan had told him not to go back to El Fazid's but he knew it was necessary. For one thing, showing up would help maintain his cover in case he had to return there later on; and more important, he would be able to tell if anyone had, in any way, connected him with the death of the two bodyguards. He did not expect to use the knife; in fact, if there was any trouble, he could simply call Donovan and wait for the cavalry to arrive. But still, the weapon felt good in his pocket.

It was twelve-thirty when he stepped out of the bright summer sunshine into El Fazid's. He knew the stitches did not show, but the back of his head felt as if it were being attacked by a squadron of baby electric eels; he could almost feel it buzzing.

Fazid greeted "Mr. Peterson" with his usual warmth and guided him to his usual table. They had the regular conversation about Miss Geraldine, and when Petrov's eyes adjusted to the light in the mostly empty room, he said, "Not very busy today, are you?"

Fazid nodded and his chubby chin almost landed on his sloping chest. "So sad. A death in the community and they ate lunch here yesterday so maybe some think I am cursed." He smiled to show that he was jesting, but Petrov said quickly, "They?" He tried to look shocked. "Surely you don't mean food poisoning. What did they eat? I ate here yesterday myself." The British accent was as thick as plum pudding.

"No, no," Fazid said. "It was not the food. Muggers. Two men were mugged."

Petrov feigned relief. "Fancy that," he said. "I suppose that's what you get for living in New York. I told my wife I think we should move back to Shropshire."

"But I thought your alliance with your wife was over," Fazid said.

Petrov aligned the silverware evenly and admitted quietly, "We made up last night and I may be going back to England. But please, don't tell Miss Geraldine. I plan to tell her myself. I thought that would be best. What do you think, old chap?"

"I think," Fazid said with a wink, "that I will be sorry to lose your business."

Detective Lieutenant Bob Mendoza sat in an unmarked police car a quarter of a block down the street from the entrance to El Fazid's. Sitting with him in the front seat was his partner, Sergeant Gas Sullivan. His New Yorker parents had been music buffs and had named their son Gilbert. They thought the name Gilbert Sullivan was charming; their son, when he grew up, thought it was stupid. He preferred to be called by his initials, G.S., but in the perverse way of policemen everywhere, the cops who worked with him had changed G.S. to Gas. And if they were angry with him, Gas Bag. That nickname suited him because Sullivan was shaped like a paper bag stuffed with pillows and he wheezed a lot when he exerted himself. His eyelids hooded over blue-gray eyes that always seemed to have trouble focusing on things. Skimpy eyebrows and thinning gray hair made him look older than his forty-eight years, and his bulby pink nose and ruddy cheeks gave him the impression of being a friendly, avuncular type. People trusted him instinctively, whether they were law-abiding citizens or the pimps and hookers and drug dealers that he spent most of his time among. He had more snitches working for him on

144

the street than any other homicide detective.

Gas glanced at his watch and said, "Any minute now. I told him not to stay too long."

Mendoza nodded. "How much money did you give him?"

"Enough for lunch. But he might have drunk it up instead."

"Thought he was sober."

Gas didn't answer. One of the things that few people knew about him was that he often collected drunks off the street and if he thought they could be helped, drove them over the bridge to Brooklyn to a men's social service center that specialized in alcohol counseling. The man they were discussing had been one of his prizes—a man who had turned himself into sewage and then back into a human being, thanks to Sullivan. It had taken two years, but the man was now going to A.A. meetings every single night and had taken a job as a cook at the rehab center.

"There he is," Sullivan said with a voice that sounded relieved. He took a small cigar out of his shirt pocket, got out of the car, and strolled along the street until the man came abreast of him.

"Hey, buddy, got a match?" he asked.

As the man leaned toward Sullivan, lighting the cigar, he said, "Hey, the food ain't bad. I got to talk to the chef. He ain't no Arab but he knows his way around the couscous."

"Stick a sock in it, Vince, and talk to me."

"You ever think about going on TV, Gas? You'd be good. You talk just like a cop." Vince winked at him. "Okay, okay. The place isn't crowded. The chef told me about the mugging and said them Arabs don't think it was a mugging at all. Said it was some kind of terrorists, maybe the same guys what did those Arabs in Italy. But it sounds like horseshit to me. Anyway, he didn't know nothing. I mean, really *know* anything."

"Okay. You did good," Sullivan said, and patted the other man's shoulder. "Give me the matches. We'll talk later."

"Wait a minute. There's this English guy in there that don't fit in. The chef says he has lunch there most days to googoo the belly dancers. He was there yesterday too," Vince said, and then turned and strolled away.

Sullivan got back in the car and said, "An English guy. That place isn't on many tourists' lists for New York high spots, is it?"

"Gas, there's no law against letting me know what you're talking about," Mendoza grunted. Sometimes Sullivan did run off at the mouth a little about how good his snitches were.

Sullivan's cigar was out and he relit it with the matches he got from Vince before he told Mendoza everything that the informer had told him.

"So, the buzz is that it's either malcontent in the ranks or it's those guys who like to make Ay-rabs into footballs," Sullivan said.

"And the English guy? Where does he fit in?"

"Beats me," Sullivan said.

"Let's see if we can find out," Mendoza said. He snatched the pack of matches from Sullivan's hand and stepped out of the car into the street.

Fazid knew policemen when he saw them, and he knew these were two cops who had just entered his restaurant.

"Afternoon, gentlemen. Table for two?" Suddenly Fazid's accent was pure Brooklyn. If he didn't sound like an Arab, it would be easier to deny knowing anything about the Arab community.

"No," Mendoza said, looking down at the man. Although he was not as tall as he would have liked to be, the police officer was taller than fat Fazid was.

"Excuse me," Fazid said. "What do you mean?"

"I mean this," Mendoza said. He flashed his gold badge at the restaurant keeper, and so did Sullivan. Then Mendoza handed forward the book of restaurant matches. "This was found on the body of a mugging victim yesterday. His buddy was dead, too, but I guess he didn't smoke."

"Few Arabs do smoke," Fazid said quickly, then stopped, knowing he had made a mistake.

"So they were Arabs, huh?" Mendoza came a few steps closer. "What else do you know about

147

them?"

Petrov had originally chosen his table in the dining room because it had an unrestricted view of the front door, and now he saw the interchange between the two men and Fazid. Like the restaurant owner, the Russian, too, could recognize policemen on sight and he guessed that they were putting some heat on Fazid because he looked very pale under the shaded overhead light just inside the entrance door.

Petrov had finished his lunch and was waiting for Geraldine to join him. He wondered if these policemen were there because they were contacts of Donovan's, but surely something strange was happening. Petrov had already noticed a small dark man who had come in, looking for a job, and spent a lot of time making small talk with the chef. That man had been too obvious, clearly checking out who was in the restaurant as he walked to and from the kitchen. And now these policemen.

Petrov pushed back from the small table and stopped a waiter.

"If Miss Geraldine comes out, tell her I'll be right back. Have to make a phone call. Give her anything she wants, my friend."

He went to the pay phone in the foyer of the restaurant. The men were ten feet away from him, standing near the small service bar, and the Russian fumbled in his pocket for change. Finally, he dropped a quarter into the phone and dialed the pay phone's own number which was written on the machine, under plastic, in the center of the dial.

When he got the busy signal, he turned slightly away from the two policemen and Fazid so they could not see what he was doing, then pressed the earpiece of the phone tightly against his cheekbone so the annoying squawk of the busy signal did not interfere with his ability to hear the conversation. In a mirror behind the small reservations podium, he could see the men quite clearly.

The darker-skinned policemen had handed Fazid two photographs.

"These men were here yesterday, is that right?"

Fazid looked at the photos and visibly blanched. They must have been morgue shots.

"Yes," the restaurant owner said.

Petrov said into the dead phone, "Thanks for answering, dearie. Let me speak to Mr. Johnson, please. This is Mr. Peterson." He paused and said, "Of course I'll wait. That's what I've been doing."

He heard the policeman say, "Who were they here with?"

Fazid said, "Another man. I never saw any of them before."

"Was he an Arab too?"

Fazid shrugged. "I suppose so. But they spoke English as I was seating them."

"And what did they talk about?"

"I didn't hear."

"This other man with them. Are you sure you never saw him before?"

"Never."

"Who paid the bill?"

"The third man," Fazid said.

"How?"

"What do you mean?"

"Big bills, small bills, American Express, how'd they pay the bill?"

He was fishing, Petrov knew, to see if there was a credit card receipt around. But there wasn't. Petrov had seen Ayoub pay the bill in cash.

"Paid in cash. No large bills. Maybe twenty-dollar bills. I don't remember," Fazid said.

"Have you ever heard the name Ayoub?"

Fazid hesitated a beat too long. It would have tipped Petrov off and he suspected it would tip off these two New York City cops—if they were New York City cops.

Fazid said, "No. The name is a new one to me."

Petrov saw the policeman look up toward the mirror, and he instantly glanced away and snapped on the phone, "What do you mean, he's still busy? Oh, bother. I'll call back. Thank you for nothing."

He pressed down the cutoff switch, then popped another quarter into the phone and again dialed the restaurant number. But this artifice was unnecessary, because the policemen put their photos away and left. Before they did, the dark one looked hard in the mirror at Petrov and for just a moment their eyes met. Petrov gave him an insipid twit's smile, then looked over to see Fazid walk heavily to the service bar, grab a huge white napkin, and towel his sweaty face.

"Something wrong, old bean?" Petrov said as he hung up the telephone. "You look a tad green about the gills."

"Nothing, nothing," Fazid said. "Excuse me, Mr. Peterson." He walked away and back into the kitchen and Petrov returned to his table.

His head was aching now; the desire to scratch at his stitches was almost unendurable. But first Miss Geraldine, to see if there was anything she knew.

She whizzed out from the back of the bandstand. All her heavy makeup was gone and her face looked clean and fresh, even in the room's dim light. She wore pants and some kind of silk blouse through which Petrov could see her large breasts, and the pain in his head was joined by one in his groin.

"Hello," she said. "Hope I didn't keep you waiting long," she said breathlessly. "You're late today."

"Miss Geraldine," Petrov said. He nodded approvingly at her outfit, but stopped her from joining him at the table. "Why don't we step out of this dreary place and give the rest of New York a chance to see how lovely you are."

The dancer glanced around and said, "Where's Fazid?"

"It seems he's had a visit from New York's finest," Petrov said softly.

"The cops?" Her eyes widened. "Hell, yes. Let's go somewhere for a drink."

Petrov left a twenty-dollar bill on the table, although he knew his lunch cost less than half that. It was one of the charms of playing a capitalist; you could leave a good tip without being labeled an oppressor of the downtrodden working poor.

Fazid did not reappear as they left, and Petrov was glad about that. As he walked down the street with Geraldine, he sniffed her heavy perfume. It was musky, an animal smell that he always found attractive. He paused on the street and asked her, "Where would you like to go for a drink?"

Over her shoulder he saw the two policemen sitting in an unmarked car. They were cops for sure, but there was something wrong. They had given up too easily, and he did not believe that was the normal procedure among American policemen. He memorized the license plate number of their car.

"There's a spot just around the corner," Geraldine said. "It's quiet and dark. The girls go there sometimes in the afternoon. Everybody

152

leaves you alone."

"Just the kind of place I'd like," Petrov said. He put his hand around her upper arm and let her lead the way to the cocktail lounge around the corner on Ninth Avenue.

It was so air-conditioned inside that it reminded Petrov of a Russian ice skating rink. Even though it was Friday afternoon, the place was empty, and Geraldine led him to a booth in the rear of the dimly lit room, then told him that there was no waitress and he would have to get their drinks from the bartender.

"And what would you like?" he asked.

"Surprise me," she said.

Petrov purchased a bottle of good New York champagne from the bored bartender, who seemed fascinated by watching someone win an automobile on television, then carried it and two wineglasses back to the table.

She was impressed by the sparkling wine, as she always was, and as Petrov saluted her with his glass, he broke the bad news that he would have to go back to England for a while on business.

She seemed crestfallen, and Petrov, sitting alongside her, took her hand in his and said, "Miss Geraldine . . . oh, this is . . . I must call you Geraldine."

"Gerry," she corrected him.

"Gerry darling, tell me. I can't leave the country without knowing if you'll be all right. I saw the

153

police today at the restaurant and I insist on knowing why. Fazid said there had been a killing right outside the place and I can't bear to think of you, all alone and defenseless. . . ."

He was really sweet, she thought. So kind and caring. She raised a hand to cut him off.

"It wasn't outside the restaurant, for heaven's sake," she said. "I'm safe there. I leave at two P.M. and take the train straight home. The mugging was all the way down by the docks, although I can't imagine what those men were doing there, for heaven's sakes."

"Did you know them well? The men who were murdered?" Petrov spoke softly, trying to show his deep concern.

Geraldine sputtered, "They've been in a couple of times before yesterday and they always give me the goose bumps, let me tell you. All three of them, marching around like the Ay-rab Mafia. Parading around with French names as if anyone would believe them. I mean, who do they think they're fooling, you know? And that one with the flat face whose eyes don't match?"

Petrov nodded encouragement; he was interested in what she might have to say about Ayoub.

"He's the worst." She paused so he could refill her wineglass.

"Why the worst?" Petrov asked.

"I bet he's a white slaver or something. French, my ass. He says his name's Pierre Dubois and he

154

told me he'd take me to Paris. Did you see him looking daggers at you yesterday?"

Petrov shook his head.

"Well, he was. Because I was sitting with you. And then he slipped Ronnie the cook a note and fifty dollars for me. Fifty dollars . . . do I look like that kind of whore?"

"You don't look like any kind of whore," Petrov said. He took her soft hand in his and choked back the fact that he had also given her fifty dollars the day before. "You look like an angel to me. What did his note say?"

"That there'd be two more fifties if I'd meet him for dinner. The Bon Soir. That's a place on the west side. Anyway, he said it would be his last night in town for a while, he'd be taking a sea voyage or something. He wanted to see me before he left."

"Tut! Did you keep the note?" Petrov kept the excitement out of his face. Again her wineglass was empty and he dallied over refilling it. For somebody who practiced so diligently, he thought, Miss Geraldine had absolutely no skill at drinking, and if he wasn't careful, he would have an unconscious woman on his hands.

"I threw it away and told Ronnie to give the money back, but he didn't, so we split the fifty today. I mean, what were we going to do, give it to Ay-rab relief?"

"I still worry about you," Petrov said, finally

155

refilling her glass.

"I'll be all right. I'll just miss you. When will you be back, Mr. Peterson?"

"Tolly," he corrected her. "I hope in the fall."

"I'll wait till then," she said, and looked at him flirtatiously over the rim of the glass.

"I should give you something as a going-away present," she said. "What would you like?"

"You mean besides you?" he said.

"Including me," she said.

"You," Petrov said. In the back of the room, in the closeness of the booth, her musk scent was almost overpowering. It seemed that he could eat it with a spoon, and he felt his body responding to her closeness.

"Okay," she said. The champagne had just hit her and tears over his departure started to well up in her eyes. "I'll miss you, Tolly."

"And I you," he said.

"I think I love you," she said.

"A pure love," he said. "Ours has been the purest. I have been honest with my wife and yet I've been allowed the pleasure of your company." It was all dreck, but he said it so feelingly that she cried some more.

"It's just like *The Prisoner of Zenda*," she said, sipping from her glass. "You see . . ."

She went through the whole story, and Petrov nodded at every plot development, but when she got to so-and-so giving such-and-such a red rose once a year in a public square, he almost laughed aloud. But he had given her dreck and she had responded with drivel. What did he expect? Poetry?

And then he got poetry of a sort as Geraldine slid her hand down the front of his trousers, felt his erection, and with practiced skill, opened the zipper of his pants.

"But I believe in physical love too," she said. "as long as it's not petty and cheap."

"So do I," Petrov said. He would not be either petty or cheap; he would give the young woman another hundred dollars, he thought, and slowly pushed her face down into his lap. Then he closed his eyes, leaned his head back, and thought of Maggie Henson.

CHAPTER TWELVE

Unlike Petrov, Mark Donovan had not dreamed and his sleep was deep and untroubled. He was well rested when he whistled his way into his office and found Maggie Henson slumping over her desk, staring at a piece of paper, looking for all the world like a lost child in a department store.

"Morning, Maggie. My, don't you look cheery."

"I've had better mornings," she said.

"How's Tolly? The patient recover?"

"He's fine," she said. "No danger."

"Then why the hangdog look?"

"Look, Mark, I'd rather not talk yet. Later. You take me to lunch, maybe?"

"It's a date," Donovan answered, and went into his own office. It wasn't like Maggie to be morose, so maybe something had happened last night with Petrov. But he would have to let Maggie tell it in her own good time.

Meanwhile, his own good mood was ruined and he would have to cancel lunch with Tilda Matthews. Maggie . . . and business came first right now.

In his personal telephone book, he wrote Tilda's number down in felt tip, indelible pen. He suspected she would not be the pencil-in, erase-later type. Then he punched out her number.

" 'Morning, I'm taking a survey on whether artists like being taken to lunch or dinner?"

"Dinner. Definitely dinner. I can eat more and I can bring home a doggie bag."

"For a dog or for Daniel?"

"How nice. You remembered his name."

"I remember everything, Pickles," Donovan said.

"Be still, my heart."

"Where?"

"Italian. Giambelli's."

"Be still, both our hearts. Which one?"

"The one at Thirty-ninth Street. Around seven-thirty? I'll be the one with a red carnation in her navel."

Click.

Donovan leaned back in his chair, his good mood restored. Giambelli's had always been one of his favorite restaurants, but Ancie would never go there because she thought that garlic was eaten only by the lower classes. He had never bothered to point out to her that her father was a degenerate alcoholic who could not hold down a job, even at the Bark candy company which was owned by the Bark family.

He remembered.

In a period of six months Mark Donovan had lost both his grandparents to the diseases of old age. He had stood in the graveyard alongside his father, Jeffrey Donovan, senior United States senator from Pennsylvania, and buried them in the green rolling hills outside Pittsburgh.

And then a year later, it had been Senator Donovan's turn. Always the giant, he had been driving home to Pittsburgh from Washington. He had always called the drive "a chip shot," but age had taken away wisdom in this instance and Jeffrey Donovan had fallen asleep at the wheel, run off the road, and died.

Mark sobbed at his father's death, alone at the grave site under a gray sky near the mansion that his grandfather had built.

It was then that Mark had enlisted in the Vietnam war his father had hated. The senator had called it "a political war that those meatheads won't let us win." It took a long time for Mark to figure out what had provoked his enlistment and he realized that it was defiance — not of his father, who had turned out to be right, but a general railing against the gods who had taken in a short span all the people he had loved the most.

Without his consciously trying, he was routed into intelligence work as the son of a former senator, and when he came home, like other soldiers, he was ignored or attacked for going to

160

Vietnam. He did not brood about it, though. He went to the mansion in Fox Chapel outside Pittsburgh and for a time, rattled around the lonely old house. Marie and Antoine, the long-time family servants, had tried to help, and it had been Antoine who had finally said, "Mr. Mark, you have to do something with your life. You are a pilot, so be a pilot. You must fly."

Mark found an old airstrip, bought a plane, and decided he did not like the way it handled. He rebuilt the plane inside and out and when he was done, he knew what it was that he was going to do with the rest of his life.

His first company was called Fun Planes, and it was struggling along when Donovan was invited to a fund-raiser for the Pittsburgh Opera Company. The fund-raiser was sponsored by the Bark family, old friends of Senator Donovan's, and Mark went for old times' sake.

Ancie took his ticket at the door. They talked and three days later Ancie Bark and Mark Donovan flew to Maryland on his private plane and were married in the heat of lust by a justice of the peace.

It was only after the wedding that he found out that Ancie had no money of her own and that her father was from the poor side of the Bark family. He also learned quickly that Ancie had been in training all these years, because she knew immediately how to spend like a rich man's wife.

161

He could have put up with that; he couldn't put up with her being the bitch of all time, a woman who sneered at everybody with less money than Donovan had, but who would lick the shoes of the richer, more powerful.

Three months after the wedding he knew it had been a mistake. But the kids came and they were wonderful and he plugged away at saving the marriage until finally there was nothing left to save.

He fell in love quickly, he told himself. He hoped that wasn't happening this time with Tilda Matthews.

He snapped himself out of his reverie and decided to telephone Dennis Hastings, a deputy ambassador to the United Nations. Hastings was an old friend of Donovan's father and he tried to remember the last time they had spoken. He supposed it had been when he and Ancie had taken their penthouse apartment in Manhattan, four years before their divorce. Hastings had been at their housewarming party.

Donovan shook his head. He should not have let so much time elapse. It would have made this call easier. Still, how did he know he was going to be back in his country's service?

He wondered for a moment if he should call Washington so the White House could let Hastings know he would be calling, but he finally decided not to. The less Hastings or anyone else knew, the better, and he trusted himself to be able to pull off the adoring young man turning to his mentor for advice and information.

"Mark, dear boy," Hastings erupted into the phone. "How long has it been? I ran into Sadie Longshore the other day and got an update, but Jesus, I felt old when I found out your kids are getting up there. I remember holding you on my knee."

There was a pause and then Hastings said, "So what can I do for you?"

Donovan had forgotten the old man's ability to cut through the crap.

"I'd like to talk some business with you," he said.

"Important?"

"I think so," Donovan said.

"I'm tied up for lunch. Coffee in my office in a half hour? Can you make that?"

"Yes."

"Done and done," Hastings said as he hung up.

"Yes, done and done," Mark said into the dead telephone as he replaced it on its base.

A close-up view of the United Nations complex on the East Side brought back to Donovan the memory of his father, Senator Jeffrey Donovan taking him by the hand shortly after the construction of the center, and escorting him on a tour.

163

"This is history, boy," his father had said. "New history, and the decisions made in here will affect us all for centuries." Then father and son, like two ordinary out-of-towners, had taken the guided tour of the complex, but young Mark had been more impressed by the blond guide in her snappy uniform, looking like a modern-day princess in a modern-day palace.

Donovan had no idea how to enter the building, so he went through the visitor's entrance, past a metal detector, and told the information clerk, "I'm supposed to see Deputy Ambassador Hastings in a few minutes and I haven't the faintest idea of where he is."

"No problem," a young black man said seriously, then asked his name. He dialed a phone and said, "A Mr. Mark Donovan here to see Deputy Hastings."

Mark wondered if he should have made up a title; mister sounded so pedestrian.

"Go out those doors over there to the next building, then stop at the security post for a badge," the black man told him, then turned away to tend to a young Japanese couple.

Several guards were milling about in the lobby of the main office skyscraper and it seemed to Donovan that they all paid a lot of attention to him as he walked in from outdoors. But after showing his driver's license, he was given a visitor's badge and sent, with an armed escort, up to the fifth floor, where a tailored and proper receptionist met him and guided him to Hastings's office which had a panoramic view of the East River. Donovan had always thought the river was nicer on the eyes than on the nose; up close and personal, it smelled like a sewer.

"Mark, my boy." Hastings got up and came around his massive mahogany desk to shake Donovan's hand. He said apologetically, "The view is better from upstairs, but it made me seasick."

"You? Seasick? I thought you were an old navy man in World War Two."

"Greatest desk job I ever had," Hastings said, and smiled, showing his well-made false teeth. "Well, sit down. God, I'd forgotten how tall you are. Strains my neck to look up at you."

Donovan sat on a leather chair opposite the desk behind which Hastings had hurriedly plopped himself. He could see that age had taken its toll on Dennis Hastings; the long-time diplomat was hunchbacked and looked frail, and Donovan reflected that if his father were still alive, he might look the same way.

"Desk job? That's not what my father said. He said you ran a battleship, made admiral, and won the Pacific war by yourself."

"Well, I guess allowing for a friend's exaggeration, there might be a grain of truth in that. Fact is, Mark, I just don't like being on high floors. If there's a blackout like there usually is in this damned city and I was up on twenty, I'd be stuck. Here I can just walk downstairs. To hell with it. So why the sudden need to see me? Do you have a problem I can help you with?"

This might be harder than Donovan had thought it would be. Not only had Hastings visibly aged, but the signs of arthritis were on his hands; a few swollen knuckles and a lump distorted his wrist bone. He must be well into his seventies, and did he really know anything anymore? Or was he just some old relic that the United States government kept on the job because they didn't know what else to do with him?

But there was nothing wrong with Hastings's eyes. They were still the eyes of the old crap-cutter.

"Spit it out, boy," he said.

"Okay, Dennis," Donovan said. "I'm not at liberty to tell you how I know this, but I've heard that some Arab members of the U.N. might be a little upset about something the U.N. is planning. I'd like to know what it's about and I'd rather not have to go through official channels."

Donovan was not prepared for the look of surprise that came over Hastings's face.

"How did you hear about that?" the old man snapped. "Where?"

"I really can't say right now," Donovan answered. There was a palpable tension in the air.

Then Hastings said, "You said you'd rather not go through official channels about this. Could you go through official channels if you had to?" Hastings asked.

Donovan nodded and Hastings paused a long time, measuring the younger man, obviously weighing his response.

Finally he said, "Okay, Senator Donovan's son. I trust this conversation is staying in this office."

"It goes without saying," Donovan answered.

Hastings nodded. "The situation," he said, "is this. I am heading up a secret committee which is writing a United Nations proclamation which will brand terrorists as enemies of the world. *All* the world, not just the West. It will recommend that interested governments work in concert to take whatever steps are necessary to deal with certain sociopaths who have a predilection for murder and mayhem in airports and other public places. In fact, the resolution would also approve the payment of certain funds for the actual elimination of said sociopaths from the world political scene."

"I'm hearing you right, Dennis? The U.N. might approve payments to informers and bounty hunters to get rid of terrorists?"

"Close enough," Hastings said.

"It'll never pass though, will it?" Donovan said.

Hastings showed his false teeth again in a large smile. "It might, Mark. Naturally, Iran would be against it, but you're dealing there with an outlaw state that has no credibility anyway. But there's a good chance that the other mideast States would go along, unless . . ."

"Unless what?" Donovan said.

"Unless word of it gets out prematurely. You see, Mark, if I can peddle it to each one of the Arab states, I can get every one of them to agree . . . sort of 'we'll go along if everybody else goes along.' But if it leaks, then somebody's going to have to blow his horn in the press and say what a terrible thing this is, and then everybody will have to jump on the bandwagon and lock themselves into positions to save face, and the thing is dead in the water. So that explains my concern about how you know about this. Let me ask you . . . was it in an Arab context that you heard of it?"

Donovan hesitated a moment, then nodded.

"Damn," Hastings said. "If it gets out too soon, it's dead."

"Then maybe I've done you a favor, too," Donovan said. "Maybe you can move up your timetable and get these Arab countries to approve the proclamation early."

"Almost impossible," Hastings said. "The General Assembly reopens in October. That looks like our timetable."

"I'm glad I don't have your problems," Donovan said.

Hastings grunted, looked at his watch, and said, "If there's nothing else?"

* * *

Downstairs, Donovan realized there was still an hour left before he would meet Maggie Henson for lunch, so on a whim, he walked up to the counter and bought a ticket for the United Nations tour.

He was told to wait until his ticket number was called and sat in a room with benches and plants, set in front of yet another booth, where a man and woman were calling out the tour numbers.

The guides had changed since the last tour he had taken with his father. Gone were the glamour girls of yesteryear. His guide was a young Englishman, who wrung his hands past various photo layouts and the huge mosaic done from a Norman Rockwell painting. His speech over the display of ruins from Hiroshima and Nagasaki was anti-American politics at its most ghastly and thickheaded and made Donovan want to throw up. Or at least to ask the twit if he had ever considered how many more lives would have been lost if America had had to grind out an island-by-island victory in the Pacific.

As the group went up the escalator to the third floor, Donovan noted another group—these apparently French-speaking—on their heels, and nervously the young Englishman speeded them up. The Trusteeship Council, whatever that was, was in session, so one of the meeting rooms was off limits to the group. At the second meeting room, they sat and the young man explained what the Security Council did.

Donovan was interested to note that civilians could buy tickets for the visitors' gallery and watch the Security Council at work. And why not? Some people liked to go to zoos.

The next room was the largest and most beautiful. Here the General Assembly met, but again they were hustled through quickly because the French guide was hot on their heels and his spiel was drowning out the poor young Englishman's speech. Again there was another large visitor's gallery, and then they were pushed outside and thrust onto separate small elevators which their guide explained would take them to the basement, where the gift shop, bookstore, and U.N. post office were located.

Donovan felt as if he should take the tour again; it had been a little empty for him, and he realized sadly that perhaps it was because the United Nations as an institution had failed to live up to the great promise that Donovan's father had seen in it. Instead, it had turned into a two-bit debating society where tinpot tyrants of the left got their chance to beat up on Uncle Sam with no fear of his hitting back.

Twice the guide had told them the whole complex was international territory. To Donovan's mind, farewell and good riddance. Who needed the thing?

He stopped in the gift shop and bought a Russian doll for his daughter, and a book describing computers around the world for his son.

Then he bought one more gift, a Noah's ark painted with the flag of the U.N., stuffed with tiny wooden animals hand-painted with the flags of member countries.

He hoped it was something a six-year-old boy would like.

CHAPTER THIRTEEN

With his mouth full of lobster salad, Donovan said, "So what was the matter with you this morning?"

Maggie Henson was picking at her lunch. "I don't suppose you'd believe a hangover," she said.

"I've seen you with a hangover. That wasn't a hangover."

Maggie nodded. "Okay." She waited a while, then said, "Do you think I'm old?"

"For an asparagus, you're old. For a mountain, you're young. For a woman, you're just right. What brings that to mind?"

"I don't know . . . anyway, our friend Tolly Peterson, there's something strange about him."

Donovan's senses sharpened, but he did not want to let Maggie know he was overly interested, so he merely shrugged and said, "Hey, there's something strange about everybody, Maggie. So what's strange about him?"

"Last night, when I was over there, he was asleep. And then he was crying out in Russian. In his sleep."

"Does that mean anything?" Donovan asked. "When I dream, I think I scream in rock-and-roll sometimes."

"Jerk," Maggie said. "No, I thought I read once that people dream in their first language. I thought that might make Tolly a Russian."

"What did he say in his sleep? Could you tell any of it?"

"Yeah, he said *shit* a lot," Maggie said.

"I don't think it means much," Donovan said. "You're talking about a guy with a concussion. He's liable to do something like that." He paused a moment. "You know, I think I heard him mention once that his mother was Russian. It might have been the first language he ever heard."

He looked at her, but her expression had not lightened.

"That's not really what's bugging you, is it?" he said. "What's the nonsense about being old?"

She looked down at her plate, then pushed it away from her. "I don't know. I sort of like Tolly, I guess, and he sort of doesn't like me. If you get my drift."

"You mean he didn't rape you or anything disgusting like that?"

"Nope. He even spurned my advances is the way I think they write it in romance books."

"Chalk it up to a concussion," Donovan said. "And why have you never made advances to me?"

"Because, my dear friend, you are my dear friend. And besides, it's never come up, if you'll pardon the expression. I think you and I are a lot alike, boss. We want the stars and twinkling and pizzazz. I've seen you ogle and I've seen you twitch, but I haven't seen you glazed with stardust."

"Take another look, Maggie," Donovan said.

She stared at him, at the familiar face with the hook of brown wavy hair that tumbled over it, the very very blue eyes, and the heavy brown eyebrows that could jump in anger or excitement. It was really an average face—an average handsome American face whose good looks could sell shoes or shirts or helicopters but today there was a happier look about the mouth, a cast of the lips that seemed to indicate a smile was coming even though no smile was called for.

"Uh-oh," Maggie said. "It looks like you've met a damsel in distress or a damsel in sex."

"Neither of the above. But a flaming redheaded beauty that I think I'm getting nuts about." And then Donovan was off and running, telling his long-time friend about Tilda Matthews.

There were many things about Donovan that Maggie loved: his sense of fun, his smarts, his friendship above all other friends, and his absolute willingness to confide in her the inner secrets of his romances and love life. She knew all about Ancie, everything, things he would never have ad-

174

mitted to anyone else, things he might even be ashamed of.

So she listened to his raving about Tilda with her fingers crossed under the table. *Please. Let this be the right one. The one who'll give instead of take.*

Later, back at her desk, she was still thinking about Tilda Matthews and hoping that she would not turn out to be another Ancie. Ancie had been just simply the bitch queen to end all bitch queens. After Jeff and Christine had gotten past babyhood and into more manageable ages and Mark's business had grown with government contracts, Ancie had insisted on the move from Pittsburgh to New York City. Mark had taken the office in the Chrysler Building while Ancie had tried to buy New York City. After decorating their fancy penthouse and playing at New York society, Fancy Ancie had said she had not quite found herself and wasn't quite happy. She decided that her great passion was collecting art and decided to go on an art-buying tour in Europe. She had not been very disappointed when Mark could not take time off to join her, and she had been gone six months . . . a whole goddamn half a year.

She came back with very few artworks but tons of new clothes and, to Maggie, the look of a woman who had traveled across Europe flat on her back. But there was no telling that to Mark. There was still stardust in his eyes.

It all ended one night a few weeks later when a bartender Maggie knew called her and told her to come get Mark. He had been missing from the office for two days, and when Maggie arrived, he was teetering on the edge of unconsciousness.

She got him into a back booth, pumped coffee into him, and by the end of the night had found out that while in Europe, Ancie had undergone an abortion, then had her tubes tied. Mark had wanted another baby, but there would be no more.

She stayed with him until his sorrow had turned to righteous anger and then had sent him home in a taxicab. Two hours later he turned up at Maggie's apartment with a suitcase in his hand. He had moved out. He slept on the couch that night, and the next morning told his lawyer to start the divorce.

Maggie had often wondered: if she had brought Mark Donovan into her bed that night, into her body, would the stardust have been there for them? Maybe, but she knew it wouldn't have lasted, because neither of them would ever have been able to swear that it wasn't just sympathy by Maggie, it wasn't just rebounding by Mark, and those possibilities would have hung over their relationship forever. She did not worry about it anymore. It was enough that their friendship endured. And if they were doomed to be two trains forever traveling on different tracks . . . well, at least friendship kept them traveling in the same direction and that was a lot more than many people had.

It was almost time to start closing her desk for the week when Maggie saw Tolly Peterson come through the door. He smiled at her and she said, "You look like the cat that ate the canary."

"More like the canary," he said, then brought his hands from behind his back and offered her a tidy bouquet of tiny pink tea roses, decorated with baby's breath. Petrov had chosen the pink on purpose; he had noted her preference for it.

"A peace offering," he said, "along with my apologies for last night. Put it down to having a knock on one of the hardest heads in the world."

"My apologies too," she said. "I don't know what came over me."

"Probably sympathy for the poor bewildered Brit," Peterson said, and Maggie thought, *Who screams in Russian in his sleep,* but said nothing.

"Still friends?" Peterson said.

Maggie nodded. "Friends," and shook the hand he formally extended.

"Is one friend allowed to invite another one to go out to dinner?" he said. "Say tomorrow night? Dinner and the movies?"

"Movie first," Maggie said. "Then dinner. The

answer's yes. *Pinocchio*'s playing around town. I'd like to see it again."

"I don't think I'm familiar with that film," he said.

"You'll like it," she said. "It's sort of your life story. Go right in. Mark's inside. I'll put these flowers in water."

Petrov paused at Mark's door and, with pleasure, watched her walk across the office. She was wearing those moronic gym shoes again, but the legs and buttocks were wonderful under her tight pink cotton skirt, and she moved with ease and grace as she took a small Oriental vase from the cupboard. He scooted inside the office before she turned and saw him ogling her.

"Afternoon. How's the wounded warrior?" Donovan asked.

"I'll survive," Petrov said.

"Do you know you dream in Russian?"

Petrov poured himself a vodka from the bar; instead of answering, he just raised an eyebrow quizzically.

Donovan nodded. "Maggie heard you when she was at your place last night. She knows only a few words of the language. You said *shit* a lot."

"I'll work on my dreams," Petrov said, and came back to sit in the chair facing Donovan and lit a cigarette. It was too bad, he thought, that there was always a tension between him and Donovan. The American had given him no reason for distrust and yet there was something hanging in the air that made it impossible for Petrov to open up to him. It was not just that he considered Donovan a dilettante playing at the world's most dangerous occupation. There was more, and even though he was not a creature of ideology, Petrov suspected it was because of the long cold war between their countries. Both he and Donovan had grown up in that era since World War II, and somehow it had seeped into their minds. It was unfortunate too. If Donovan had been a Russian, he would have been the sort of man Petrov sought out for friendship.

He could not know, looking at Donovan's open American face, that Donovan was thinking exactly the same thing and remembering something he had been told that Loyola, founder of the Jesuits, had said. "Give me a boy until he's five and he is ours." Once the poison of preordained positions got into someone's bloodstream, there was no antidote.

"I went to the United Nations today," Donovan said, "to check on what your Arabs were talking about yesterday."

Petrov nodded.

"I have a friend there. He told me that a resolution is being prepared to condemn terrorism."

"Sounds like a million other U.N. resolutions," Petrov said.

"Except this one for a change has some teeth. It authorizes the paying of rewards for information et cetera, et cetera."

"Bounty hunters?" Petrov said softly, and when Donovan nodded, the Russian grinned. "Well, that will surely get the pot bubbling, won't it?" He stubbed out his cigarette and lit another.

"And I've been on the telephone today with Washington," Donovan said. "There's no record of Hussein Ayoub being in the country. He's obviously traveling under a fake passport."

"Try Pierre Dubois," Petrov said.

"I beg your pardon?"

"I went back to El Fazid's today."

Donovan clapped his hand angrily on his desk. "Jesus, Petrov . . ."

"Peterson," the Russian corrected him again with a small smile. "And I know, you think it was too risky, but I had to go to see if my cover had been blown and to try to find out anything else I could. And I found out that Ayoub has been traveling under the name of Pierre Dubois. French name, just like his two late bodyguards. And he mentioned something to some woman about taking a sea voyage. He invited her along."

"What woman?" Donovan asked.

Petrov shrugged. "Just a dancer at El Fazid's. A person of no importance. But he was trying to bed her, I gather. He had asked her once to Paris and she turned him down. Then he asked her to meet with him at some West Side restaurant, the Bon Soir, so they could talk about her going on a cruise with him. But she didn't bite."

Petrov tapped out his cigarette. The Gauloises were too strong after all. His entire body was tired and his head ached, as if a horse were pawing ground atop his skull.

The flushed face that had tipped off Donovan's annoyance at what he thought was Petrov's recklessness receded, and the American said, "I guess it was right for you to go back there. No one is on to you?"

"Not that I could tell," Petrov said. "But while I was there two men came in, flashed badges, and questioned Fazid. They were waiting outside when I came out with the girl. Police, I suppose, but something about them just rubbed me the wrong way. I have their license number."

"What is it?" Donovan said, and wrote it down as Petrov recited it from memory. "You don't look too well. Maybe you should head home and get some rest. When does the doctor check your head again?"

"Tomorrow. Just for infection as long as I have no other symptoms," Petrov said. "I'll be fine. By the way, Fazid lied to the two men. He said that Ayoub had been in there only yesterday and not before, but the dancer told me they were off-and-on regulars over the past few months, but they generally stopped in in the evening. That's why I never saw them before."

"Okay. I'll check it out," Donovan said. "Mind if I ask you something?"

"Go ahead," Petrov said.

"Why did you start going to El Fazid's in the first place?"

"I checked with Russian intelligence. They told me that if an Arab terrorist was going to surface anywhere in New York, it would be in El Fazid's. So it seemed like a good idea to establish a presence there."

Donovan pursed his lips in annoyance. "How the hell can you find out things like that from Russian intelligence when I can't find it out from American intelligence?" he asked.

Petrov smiled slightly. "The tables would turn if we were in Moscow. There, the CIA knows all the hotbeds of sedition and anarchy. The KGB can't find its foot in its shoe."

"If you say so."

"I do," Petrov said.

Both men rose at the same time and looked at each other. It was the longest semi-friendly conversation they had had in two months. But all the moment did was to establish them as two men working together on the same job. Not as friends and not even as comrades. Just coworkers. The moment seemed to Donovan to call for a handshake, but he could not bring himself to offer one.

After Petrov left, Donovan called Lieutenant Mendoza at Midtown South.

"How's it going? Can you talk?"

"Slow but steady," Mendoza said. "What's on your mind?"

"A license plate," Donovan said. He read it off the notepad. "Can you check that out for me?"

Mendoza immediately asked, "Who gave you that number?"

"Somebody I'm working with," Donovan said. "Why?"

"You just gave me my own plate number," Mendoza said.

Donovan sighed. "I guess you were at El Fazid's today."

"And I guess you have informers," Mendoza retorted. "Yeah, I paid a call on El Fatso. Didn't get much."

For a moment Donovan considered telling Mendoza that El Fazid had lied to him and that the three Arabs had been in the restaurant a number of times, not just once. If Mendoza had been working on a real murder investigation, Donovan would have told him. But here he didn't want Mendoza to solve the case of the "two murdered Frenchmen." Because Petrov had killed them. All

183

he wanted Mendoza to do was to dig out anything he could about the Arabs . . . just to stir the pot. So he said nothing and into the momentary dead air Mendoza said, "It was the Englishman, right?"

"What Englishman?" Donovan said.

"There's an English guy who eats in there a lot. We saw him leaving with one of the belly dancers. He gave you the license plate number, right? He's your informer, right?"

"Not exactly," Donovan said. *"Exactly" is that he's not an informer; he's working side by side with me.*

"Well, could he be a murder suspect, then?" Mendoza said.

"Definitely not one you should suspect," Donovan said, trying to keep his tone light.

"All right," Mendoza said. "I'll forget about him."

"Please do. Any word on the two dead men?"

"Not yet. But I'm trying."

"Keep up the good work, Bobby," Donovan said. "Give my love to Jenny and the snotty kid."

"You got it, boss man."

CHAPTER FOURTEEN

Even junking up on aspirin did not permit Petrov to relax or to forget the throbbing pain in his skull. He watched *I Love Lucy* in black and white on late afternoon television, then *All in the Family* in color.

When he had first come to America two months earlier, he had thought he would immerse himself in the country by watching all the news programs, all the talk shows, all the special reports, but after one solid weekend binge of watching nothing but news shows, he had realized that the shows were identical in content to those being broadcast in the Soviet Union. They seemed to center around how the CIA was the source of all evil in the world and also how things were improving rapidly in every communist country in the world, including Cuba and Nicaragua, ignoring that both of them routinely sent the political opposition to prison and neither of them, since becoming a "people's paradise," could feed its own population anymore.

Petrov decided that he was not going to learn

anything about the United States by watching such nonsense and that was when he started weighting his viewing habits on the entertainment side of the scale. His favorite was *I Love Lucy*.

There was a slapstick humor in the Lucy show that he could appreciate; many Russian comics went in for slapstick. But he could not fathom why Archie Bunker's prejudicial, racist comments were supposed to be funny. He was surprised the Russians had never taken tapes of this show, done a Russian translation, and then aired them in the Soviet Union as anti-American propaganda.

Petrov sat slumped in the white chair in front of the television. Maybe his sense of humor was faulty and maybe he did not even have one. Such things were, he thought, passed on from generation to generation by genes. So maybe he had a chance. His mother had had a gentle smile and, he thought now, a sense of color and fun. The little house in Odessa had been decorated with cheap bright fabric and photos torn from Russian magazines. He remembered that the cloth books with the bright, happy faces of Russian children ended up on the walls too. And his mother had insisted that when Petrov and his sister, Maya, were through with their schoolwork they spent some time using vegetable dye to decorate worn fabric. He had not thought of that in a long time. It didn't seem to him to have much to do with his having a sense of humor. Then he dozed and when he awoke, a game show was on the television.

One of the questions was about Pinocchio, and Petrov thought how the Russians often accused Walt Disney of being the corruptor of American youth, filling their heads with candy-coated fantasies instead of showing them the bleak reality of the lives they would face as adults. There was no Walt Disney in Russia. There were children's books and children's films, but they were gray, instructive things, and chewing your lip was more fun than looking at them.

It must be the concussion that's doing this to me . . . making me remember so much and question so much. Or is it being in the United States? Is there something contagious about being in this country that causes you to doubt all your truths? Whence this mania for reexamination?

There were things in his life, Petrov knew, that best stayed unexamined. The murders, the blood, the betrayals, all the missions for Mother Russia, and it wouldn't do to ask just what good any of them had done. *Eyes straight ahead. Yessir. Stick to the matter at hand. Yessir. Be a good little robot. Yessiryessiryessiryessiryessir.*

His attention drifted back to the game show. No wonder Americans spent so much time in front of the television set. The tube was the great tranquilizer. Marx had called religion the opiate of the masses, but that was only because he had never

187

watched *Let's Make a Deal*.

The telephone jarred him when it rang.

Donovan said, "That license plate you got? Thought you'd like to know it belongs to a real cop. A friend of mine."

Petrov bristled. "You've been talking to him? You told him what we've been doing?"

"Hey, take it easy," Donovan sputtered. "I haven't told him anything I didn't have to and that means almost nothing. But I've got to keep contact with him. He can do things for us. Go places we can't. Ask questions we can't. What the hell's the matter with you anyway?"

"The matter is you didn't tell me about this cop. That's what the matter is. How would you feel if you were in my country and I pulled something like that on you?"

Donovan was not prepared to concede the point that easily.

"If we were in Russia," he said, "I'm sure I could trust you to use whatever resources you had to and I don't know that anything would be improved by your telling me about them. And, pal, horseshit. We don't even have to be in Russia. Here you are in New York, and for the last couple of months you've been doing undercover work without me even knowing about it. How the hell do you think I'd look if those two Arabs had killed you and left you in the weeds over on the West Side? What would I tell the Premier of all the Russias then."

Petrov hesitated. "Tell him the truth. Tell him you fucked up again."

Donovan laughed. "Jesus, you made a joke."

"I am very humorous at times," Petrov said stiffly. "You Americans don't have an exclusive on comedy, even though you act like you do."

"Sorry. I apologize. You're a regular Milton Berle. Talk to you later. Rest for the weekend."

When Donovan hung up, Petrov was smiling. It was an unnatural expression for him, but it felt kind of pleasant. He went into the bathroom and looked at himself. The smile was fading, but it had not yet left his eyes, and his face seemed kinder, gentler somehow.

"Grrrr." He growled in disgust at his image, fixed a scowl on his face again, and walked back out to the living room.

CHAPTER FIFTEEN

When Maggie Henson left at five P.M., Donovan locked the office door and started, finally, to look through the day's papers.

The death of the two "Frenchmen" had made it quietly to the back pages of the *New York Times*. Nothing spectacular about it there. Two men killed. Ho-hum. They had French names, but the French embassy did not know anything about them. No one knew anything about them.

The *Post* had done a little better on the story. It had used it on page five with a headline: FRENCH TOURISTS MURDERED, and a subhead that read: *Victims of hookers?* The story was a lot of splash and dash but with no more facts than the *Times* had. The *Daily News* was much the same, with an insert about crime in the city and an editorial about the need to get hookers off the street, all done very seriously, as if such an act were really a viable option; as if New York City were really still a viable city.

The *Newsday* story had one extra point in it.

Police were alleged to "think" that perhaps the two men were trying to make a drug buy and were murdered for their money.

That wasn't a bad thought, Donovan admitted to himself. Too bad Petrov hadn't been carrying drugs; he could have planted them on the corpses and thrown this story into the big yawning maw labeled "unsolved drug-related crimes in New York City."

He dozed for twenty minutes at his desk. Then he took a shower and shaved in the full bathroom of his office, before changing into a fresh shirt from the closetful he kept there.

He got to Giambelli's fifteen minutes early, took a seat at the bar, then remembered he had not looked at Tilda Matthews's cartoon that day in *Newsday*. After ordering a drink and leaving some cash on the bar, he went back outside and found a nearby newsstand. He bought a copy of *Newsday*, whipped open the paper, and found the cartoon on the editorial page. It was something reasonably innocuous about Massachusetts going bankrupt, but to Donovan that didn't seem terribly newsworthy. Massachusetts was always going bankrupt, and then, at the last moment, saving itself from bankruptcy by . . . big surprise . . . raising taxes. Why should anybody be surprised and why should anybody care? Massachusetts voters made a habit of electing politicians whose first, middle, and last solution to every problem was to throw more tax money at it. They deserved bankruptcy; they brought it on themselves. Probably Tilda's cartoon referred to something fresh in the news that he had not noticed; he'd get her to tell him about it.

Back inside the bar, it was only ten to seven and he read the paper while sipping his drink and then he felt his collar being lifted off the back of his neck and a breezy kiss being placed there.

"Hi, sailor. Buy a girl a drink?"

Tilda was wearing white, a knee-length skirt and a silk blouse and a wide red belt that showed off her narrow waist. He stood and eased her onto the bar stool next to him and nodded to the maître d' that they were ready to be seated whenever their table cleared.

He had wondered what they would do about small talk—Donovan was generally no good at it—but he needn't have worried because Tilda showed herself able to hold up both her and his end of a conversation and jump about, talking with sense on a bewildering array of topics.

Out on the street after dinner, Donovan was carrying the small shopping bag that held the gift from the United Nations.

"What's that?" Tilda asked as they stood on the corner. Neither of them seemed to know exactly how to proceed from that spot.

"I'll tell you what. You come up to my place and I'll show you," Donovan said as he hailed a cab.

Tilda pursed her lips. "I'd like to, but Daniel is with my brother again and I think I should go home just in case and . . . and . . . and . . ."

They were in the cab then, and with a small sigh Donovan gave the cab driver Tilda's address.

Unlike the professionally decorated high-tech sterility of his apartment, Tilda Matthews's apartment was clearly that of an artist and even more clearly, a place where human beings lived.

The furniture was simple, mostly wooden, but painted in varied colors like a rainbow. The couch had a wooden frame and each of the six cushions was a different color. Two chairs that must have spent some time being redwood on someone's porch were painted as blue backdrops for different colored cushions too. There were framed paintings and sketches on the walls, interspersed with drawings that Donovan assumed Tilda's boy, Daniel, had done. They were childish but cute and showed a recognizable talent.

But all the furniture in the room seemed to center on one painting from an artist he recognized: a Janet Fishman watercolor with a rainbow progression of vases and flowers from yellow through orange, then red and blue.

Tilda walked into the living room and handed him a soft drink. Hers looked like bourbon. They clicked glasses and sipped.

She explained: "Most of this stuff is early off-the-street that I picked up before I was able to buy the apartment. I can afford better now, but I think I'd rather wait until Daniel gets old enough to appreciate it. This way if he carves his initials in the couch, who cares."

"I was admiring the Fishman. You didn't get that off the street."

Tilda said, "Well, you've got to spend your money somewhere."

Donovan sat on the couch and Tilda bustled about the room, looking for ashtrays, finding coasters, acting for all the world as if she were hosting the monthly meeting of a church sodality.

"Hey, calm down," Donovan said. "Sit down." He patted the couch cushion next to him.

"I'm afraid to," she said.

"I don't bite," he said, and patted the couch again. As she sat down, he said, "Just what are you afraid of?"

"You. Me. What I feel for you. I haven't been involved with anyone for a long time . . . you know what I mean . . . and . . ."

Donovan laughed. "You're so out of practice you don't even know the jargon anymore. What you're supposed to talk about is whether or not you're 'sexually active.' Then you can pump me and find out whether or not I've got AIDS or scurvy or jungle rot."

"God, do I hate that phrase," Tilda said. "Sexually active. It sounds like something you'd get on a stock market report. 'The broad market was about forty percent sexually active today, but analysts were predicting fifty percent sexually active tomorrow.' Who the hell talks like that anyway? Sexually active."

"All your liberal friends," Donovan said as she leaned back on the couch and he put his arm around her shoulders.

She turned as if to protest, then paused and nodded. "You're probably right. At least that's who I always hear it from. My friends are jargoneers."

"I know. I was married to one," Donovan said, and squeezed her shoulder in a friendly way.

"So," she said, "well, I feel for you, Mark, and, well, so . . ."

"So you don't believe in one-night stands," he finished for her. "Does that help?"

"Yeah."

"Okay. Neither do I. Now, shut up and drink your bourbon. If there's anything I hate, it's a yappy woman."

They sat in silence in the dim room for a few minutes, and then Donovan said, "I was wondering where your drawing table is. Or do you work out at the newspaper office?"

"Not anymore, thank God. I used to commute, but now I work here." She waved a hand at the hall off the living room. "My bedroom is big enough to hold the drawing table, too, and I'm here to take Daniel to school and pick him up. So

195

it works out fine."

"I like his drawings," Donovan said, gesturing toward one of the childish pictures on the wall.

"Whoops. That's not his, that's mine," Tilda said. "He's a perfectionist and he won't let me hang up anything of his so I put up some of mine, sort of to shame him. My mother keeps everything I ever did. She's a sweetheart. I'd like you to meet her someday." She gulped her drink. "I didn't mean that the way it sounded."

"It just sounded like good sense and probably someday I will. I still have a house in Pittsburgh, you know." He got up and brought back the U.N. shopping bag, then held it out to Tilda. "I don't want you to get the wrong idea either, but I happened to be shopping for my kids today and saw this: It seemed like something a boy might like."

Tilda took out the ark and examined it and all the animal pieces carefully. "Boy, did you guess right," she said. "Daniel will love it. He loves little things and he's already a collector, this and that and shells and what have you." And she chatted for a few moments more, then her conversation seemed to run out of steam and she turned her face toward Donovan and leaned forward to kiss his lips.

Tilda was passionate and yielding, but then there were moments when she would pull back, rearrange her wild hair, take a sip of her drink, and start a conversation. Donovan loved it; it was old-fashioned necking and he had forgotten what it was like. Most of the women he had slept with since splitting from Ancie were from their same circle—a large number of them Ancie's close friends—and they knew full well when they went to Donovan's apartment that they were going to wind up in bed and they seemed only to be waiting for the invitation. There was no necking involved there. Only foreplay. Necking was sometimes an end in itself. Foreplay was what you did before you screwed. Different things.

Tilda was talking about her cartooning and how her editor was big with all these society events and that was why she went to them and how she had come to meet Ancie, whom she deeply detested and even more so now that she had met Donovan.

And she said to him, "And you. You make helicopters, I gather. You make them for war?"

Donovan sat up stiffly. "Yeah. And I make them for the Red Cross. And the ones that snatch people off the top of burning hotel buildings are mine too. And the ones that fly crippled kids to hospitals for emergency operations are mine too. Yeah. And some of them I make for the military."

There was a moment's silence and Tilda said, "God, that was stupid of me, wasn't it?"

"Not that it was stupid . . . it's just that it was so New York twerpy Greenpeace lefty folksinging political horseshit."

"Guess so, huh?" she said.

"Yup," he said.

She put her arms around his neck and pulled his face down to hers. "You sure have a lot of things to teach me, Mark Donovan."

Their lips met; they necked again and Donovan felt himself getting involved, deeply involved, and finally he pulled away and said, "Getting late, Tilda. Got to go."

She looked at him in a little surprise, then lowered her eyes and admitted, "Daniel always spends Friday night at my brother's house. I don't have to pick him up tonight."

Donovan patted her arm. "That's nice. But we'll have lots of time."

"Okay," she said softly, and followed him to the front door. There she said, "You don't have to go."

"A first date, remember?" Donovan said. "And no one-night stands, remember?"

He raised her chin and kissed her, then unlocked the door and walked out into the hall.

He felt somehow noble . . . noble and stupid . . . as he started down the hallway toward the elevator and heard the door close behind him. Before he could press the elevator button, he heard the door open again and turned. Tilda smiled at him.

"Mark," she said. "Come here."

He walked to her and she put her arms around

him and said, "It's after midnight. It's not our first night anymore."

"You sure about this?" he said softly, and Tilda reached down and touched him, then smiled up at him.

"We both are," she said.

CHAPTER SIXTEEN

Petrov had gone to a bookstore on Fifth Avenue after buying a pack of American Marlboros on Eighth Avenue. He had finally decided that the Gauloises were too strong for him or for any other human. *When in Rome, do as the Romans* etc. etc. So he would smoke American cigarettes; he would be a Marlboro man. Yup. Farewell, tovarich; howdy, podner.

He smoked while walking to the bookstore and the Marlboros had tasted pleasant and hadn't given him a headache. He liked walking around in New York. The pedestrians were far different from those in Moscow. In New York they seemed much more eager to get where they were going, but they were also more polite. He liked New Yorkers. They wore brighter clothes than the people in Russia, and he did not see repeat costumes as he would have on the streets of Moscow, where most department stores sold the same styles over and over again and everybody wound up looking more or less alike.

America was different. It was a young country and one that he had been raised to despise, but he was enjoying it nevertheless. He passed a black woman who was joking on the street with a white man as their children laughed with them. There was an elderly couple who walked along holding hands. They were shabbily dressed but they looked happy and he could not remember, once in his life, ever seeing any adults holding hands walking down the streets of Moscow.

There was an underside too. The friendless, the homeless, a woman, a man, here and there, hugging garbage to their bodies as if it were important . . . some junkies leaning into each other, chortling about their latest scores; one girl with festering bruises on her otherwise pretty face, sitting, resting on a stoop, talking aloud to no one. They had them in Russia too.

Petrov kept walking.

At the bookstore on Fifth Avenue, Petrov lost himself as usual perusing the remaindered books sold at huge discounts from list price. He loved American books. It was not that the books in Russia were not well done; they were, and in fact, were probably better printed than those in the United States. But most Russian books concentrated only on Russia or its satellite countries, while in New York there were books on everything—trains, helicopters, movies, Russian movies, Yugoslavian country homes—anything you could

201

ever want to know was for sale somewhere in an American bookstore.

He purchased a large illustrated book about Walt Disney's movies as a gift for Maggie Henson and then continued walking toward her apartment in Greenwich Village.

He was surprisingly nervous as he reached her address on Twelfth Street, so he walked up to Fifth Avenue and then back again. He realized what was bothering him: This was a date, and he had little experience with dates. In Moscow, even as a student, dates usually didn't happen. Groups happened, and then out of groups couples happened, but dates didn't often happen. And then, since his wound, he intentionally had not once "dated" any woman in whom he felt real interest, preferring instead to sublimate his drives in work and in duty and in more solitary pursuits, and when the sexual drive was on him, it was enough to satisfy it with prostitutes or tramps who were well paid—and well advised—to be silent.

It was still a few minutes until six P.M. He walked by the building once more.

Maggie Henson's feelings were as mixed as those of the man she knew as Tolly Peterson. She found the man physically exciting and with the exception of a few fleeting encounters from a nearby tavern, her sex life had been nonexistent.

But there was something about Tolly Peterson that didn't ring true; it wasn't just the screaming nightmares in Russian . . . there was an attitude about him, a feeling that she got that told her that Tolly Peterson wasn't what he pretended to be. But how he was different . . . or why . . . she didn't know.

Fine, Maggie, she told herself. *Let your imagination work overtime and you'll have him an ax murderer by the time he's here. Let it go, for Christ's sake, and make yourself a drink.*

She poured herself a light vodka with tonic and lime and walked around the apartment straightening up, trying to put Tolly out of her mind.

Carol. She thought about her daughter. She had not seen her since yesterday afternoon when she had apparently decided to take her mother's place at the Plaza fund-raiser. At lunch Mark had told her the whole ghastly story of her daughter's behavior and she had been brooding about it ever since. It seemed to her that Carol was going out of her way to try to get for herself the kind of life that Maggie had been stuck with, a life where you had no one but yourself.

Back in her hometown of Venture, Ohio, Maggie's life had not started out that way. The family was close and it was assumed that Maggie would turn out just like her mother . . . married young and raising a family.

But Maggie had gotten "in trouble" and her

203

religious parents couldn't deal with it. And before she knew it she was on her way out of town with no money and no hopes. God, and it was in the sixties too. It wasn't as if it had happened in the thirties when an unmarried pregnancy was a scarlet mark. This was 1967, and you would have thought her parents had grown up some by then. But no, their fundamentalism had no stretch in it, no give, and no forgiveness at all. Their religion turned out to be all platitude, no compassion.

Maggie had gotten on a bus and come to New York, then wound up in Greenwich Village, taken in by a commune of hippies who loved everybody and most of all a pregnant young woman.

Eventually the group she had joined left New York and headed for Massachusetts to found a cooperative farm, but Maggie had stayed behind with her baby. Another group watched Carol during the day while Maggie went to secretarial school. At nights she waitressed at a Nedick's on Eighth Street.

Once she had tried to explain it all to Carol, but her daughter had merely demanded, "Who is my father?"

And Maggie didn't have the heart to tell her only child that her father was a man now well into his sixties and a pillar of the church in Venture, Ohio.

And things had never been right between them, even after Maggie had landed the job with Mark

Donovan and slowly had become able to give Carol the better things in life. None of it had mattered.

She wasn't worried about Carol right now, at least not her physical safety. Her daughter was over twenty-one and often stayed out the whole night . . . or would go away for the weekend without bothering to tell Maggie. But this business of marrying some camel-jockey diplomat and going to the desert to live . . . well, who knew what was going on in her mind? And some small voice inside Maggie said, "Hope it's true. Maybe it would be the best thing for her. And for me."

The doorbell rang and when she opened the door, Tolly Peterson walked inside, holding the Walt Disney book in front of him as a gift to her, like a shy schoolboy. He smiled sheepishly and she thought he seemed larger than she had thought, and also more handsome.

She took the book and thanked him, then motioned him to a sofa seat.

"Vodka?" she said as she walked to the kitchen.

"Uhh. Scotch if you have it," Petrov said. He sat on the wide couch and looked around the room. He did not really like Scotch, but Maggie's assumption that he was a vodka drinker had provoked him. He had spoken Russian in his sleep the previous night. It made sense to forget about the vodka for an evening.

Maggie already had taken the vodka bottle out

of the freezer, but she shrugged, replaced it, and reached for the Scotch that was tucked under the counter.

"Rocks or straight?" she called.

Petrov remembered he was an Englishman and asked for it neat.

He thanked her profusely when she brought it, and then sat down at right angles to him and they clicked glasses.

"This is a nice apartment," he said.

"Thank you. You know, there are times when you don't sound British at all."

"It's all you Yanks," he said. "I can't help but pick up some of your inflections, I guess."

"Mark said you had a Russian mother." Maggie sipped her drink and Petrov fidgeted with his cigarettes and lighter.

"Yes, I did," he said. He looked around and found a crystal ashtray that looked as if it had never been used.

"How'd you wind up in England, then?"

"Mother ran away from Russia in the early thirties. I gather her parents were dutiful little Communists, but she was sick of it. She went to England . . . she was very beautiful . . . and worked as a model in some clothing shops. My father saw her there and that sort of was that."

Petrov was speaking in an easy, quiet way, spinning a tale that might be true of some other young couple in the thirties. "They were very young; he was nineteen; she was eighteen, but he managed to see her on the occasional trips home from public school and then from Oxford. When he was graduated, he announced his intention to marry her."

As he spoke, Maggie sat, seemingly mesmerized, sipping her drink. "By then England was preparing for war. His parents were Old Guard. War was fine. Russian émigrés were not. He was cut off. They married anyway and hoped their children would bridge the gap in the family. But it was only after my father was shipped out that my mother found herself pregnant."

"But you don't look old enough . . ." Maggie began.

"Not I. My older brother," Petrov said. He had to remember not to make this story too melodramatic or too theatrical. It was a good cover story, but it needed some dullness to be truly believable.

"So, anyway, my father was in the RAF but stationed near London and he got home often and Reggie was born first and then me in 1945. And then my father came home and he wasn't enough of a hero for his parents to forgive. Mother was now designing clothing and then she was pregnant with my sister, May, and Mother died in childbirth. Then my father died from drinking too much and the three of us, Reggie, May, and me were taken in by the grandparents in Shropshire. Reggie died in a hunting accident and now there are just May and me." He paused to sip his drink and to check Maggie, who asked, "Can I have one of your cigarettes?"

"I didn't know you smoked," he said. The ashtray was littered with ashes and butts. He had been chain-smoking while telling his story.

"Sometimes," Maggie said. She took a deep inhalation of smoke, let it out, and said, "Please go on."

"I feel as if I'm imposing. I shouldn't have started this," he said. "It all began with my Russian mother, didn't it? You know, she talked to me in Russian when I was a child. I guess sometimes, in my dreams, I must remember the things she said to me."

Maggie flicked her ash. If only he hadn't said that. It marred the romance of the tale of his life which might, she knew now, only be a tale. It was one thing to remember the things one's dear mother said to you. It was something else to keep recalling her screaming *gavno* — "shit" — at you. Unless the woman was a witch about toilet training, that was a little heavy talk for mother to loving son. Aaaah, what did she know? Maybe Russians didn't have any baby-talk equivalent for weewee and poopoo.

"I'd like to hear the rest of it," she said.

That was fine with Petrov. He sensed there was something that Maggie was thinking that she was not saying.

"Well, after Reggie's death, the grandparents took a lot more interest in me. After all, I was the only one to carry on the Peterson name. Right schools for May and me, right friends, and so forth. I guess they were trying to make up for their treatment of our parents, but I never did find out. We were never real close, and when May and I were in college, both grandparents died within a couple of weeks from a flu that induced pneumonia."

There. He had wrapped it up. He glanced at his watch. Only twenty minutes. Not bad for making up an entire group of lives and lies. He looked at Maggie as she stubbed out her cigarette and thought, *She almost buys it, but not quite. I'll have to find out why.*

"Now you're going to tell me your life story, correct?" he said.

"Sure," she said. "But while we're walking to the movie house. I don't want to miss the beginning where Pinocchio is still a puppet."

"I hear that's the best part," he said.

Pinocchio had been charming but silly, Petrov thought, but he made an attempt to share Maggie's enthusiasm for the children's picture and she in turn decided that since she had picked the film, he could pick the restaurant.

"Just so long as it's not Chinese," she said.

"It isn't," he said. He had that feeling again, that feeling that he wanted to tell her his whole history. She didn't like Chinese food. He wanted to tell her how she would come to like it. If she had been like him, in China when no North Americans were. When he was regarded as a Russian diplomat and treated to the best cuisine available in the country. Exquisite fish laid out, head and all, with people vying to see who would be the one to eat the eyes. Shrimp also served with heads on; a delicate dish of cat; enough Chinese wine to float a junk, strips of bird wing meat sizzled in a crackling hot oil.

That would make her like Chinese food. But there would be none of it tonight; they were going to the Bon Soir.

"You're quiet," she said.

"I was just surprised. I thought all you Americans loved Chinese food," he said.

"Only if we're Jewish," she said.

"Oh." He would have to check that out. It was something he had never heard of.

The restaurant was in the fifties on the ground floor of a seedy hotel. Although it had good food reviews from several newspapers taped into the window, the clippings were old, tattered, and yellow. When Petrov had first come to New York, he had picked up a whore on Eighth Avenue who thought that the restaurant was the height of elegance and he had taken her there, bought her dinner, and left her at the bar.

The restaurant was as he remembered it. There was sawdust on the floor, an old dingy curved bar, and plain tables in the back. The place smelled of stale beer and even though it was Friday night, the restaurant was almost empty and the bartender was languishing on a stool behind the bar, watching a baseball game on television.

Petrov and Maggie seated themselves in the back of the room and after five minutes were finally greeted by a male waiter, very young and very handsome, who said, *"Bonsoir, Madame et Monsieur."*

He smiled, showing them a lot of teeth and Petrov, in impeccable French, ordered two drinks and then asked what was good on the menu. With every word he uttered, the look of confusion grew on the young man's face, and when Petrov was done, the man said in English, "Jeez, don't talk in French. I only know how to say hello."

They negotiated again for their drinks, in English this time, and the waiter allowed as how the veal cutlets weren't bad so each ordered the veal.

"And buy the bartender a drink," Petrov said. "He looks as if he could use one."

The waiter nodded, and later the bartender caught Petrov's eye and saluted him with a beer bottle from which he was drinking. Petrov waved back.

The conversation throughout dinner was casual,

211

comfortable, and confidential, the kind of talk that two old friends could share easily. Maggie told about her childhood and her early days in New York as a single mother and how she had finally landed a good job with Mark Donovan. Petrov filled in the gaps in the chatter with long rambling reminiscences of his childhood in England. He was a high-class bridge player, a chess expert, and one of the outstanding intelligence officers in the KGB. The memory demanded both by his profession and his hobbies was phenomenal, and Petrov's filled the bill, so he felt absolutely secure about elaborating the most complicated tales for Maggie because he knew that once spoken, he would never forget them. A spy for twenty years and what he had to show for it was a memory so good that he could lie to anyone, even someone as nice as this American lady, and never catch himself in a trap.

It was between the dinner and the coffee-*cum*-cordial that Maggie finally excused herself to go to the ladies' room and Petrov went to the still-empty bar to talk to the bartender. He ordered a brandy straight up, and as the bartender poured it, said, "A guy I know comes in here sometimes. I was wondering if you'd seen him recently. Pierre Dubois?"

The bartender's face took on a sour look, as if he had just bitten into a mushy peach. "A couple of nights ago he was in."

"Do you think he'll be in tonight? I haven't seen him in a while."

"Nah, I don't think so. He a good friend of yours?"

The bartender put the drink in front of Petrov.

"No, I wouldn't call him a good friend. More like a business acquaintance. Truth is, I don't think much of him."

"Me neither. A big blowhard and a cheap bastard. Spends all his money on the hookers and never leaves a tip here, not even for the waiters."

Petrov nodded and sipped at the brandy which burned like fire going down his throat.

"You said you don't think he'll be in. How come?"

"He told one of the girls he was going on a sea voyage this week."

"Oh. He say where, do you know?"

The bartender shook his head. "A cruise, I think. But knowing Dubois, it'll be something cheap."

"He ever come in here with anybody?" Petrov asked.

"Sometimes, some greaseball, but he just sits around and doesn't say anything."

"Like a bodyguard, huh?"

"Exactly," the bartender said.

Petrov saw Maggie coming out of the bathroom and dropped a five-dollar bill on the bar as a tip.

"Thanks a lot."

"If he comes in, should I tell him you were here?"

Petrov shook his head. "No, I imagine I'll see him before you do," he said.

CHAPTER SEVENTEEN

She was going to take the man to bed. She knew that as they got out of the taxicab a few blocks away from her house and walked through the pleasant evening breeze toward her apartment building.

But when they came close to the building, Maggie Henson could see lights on upstairs. Carol was home. But in what condition? Maggie knew she did not want Tolly Peterson to meet her daughter, not just now, not under circumstances which Maggie could not control.

Her body must have reacted, however subtly, to the lights being on because Tolly Peterson, holding her arm as they waited to cross the street, said, "Is something the matter?"

"No, no," Maggie answered too quickly. "Nothing."

"Your lights are on," he said. "They weren't on when we left."

"My daughter's home," she said.

He walked up the stone steps with her to the entrance and she said, "Tolly, this has been a nice

215

night and I wish it didn't have to end so soon." Before he could answer anything, she said, "But I have to talk to Carol and spend some time with her. Can we do this again? Right away? Tomorrow night?"

"Certainly," he said. "You're sure everything's all right?"

"Yes." She hugged him at the top of the steps. She felt his body respond to her closeness, and she quickly turned away, opened the door with a key, and went inside.

Her apartment was in the rear at the end of the long hall. The door was unlocked and Maggie walked inside and then down the pretty hall, adorned with photos of herself and Carol in their early days in New York. She passed the bathroom which contained a giant old-fashioned claw-foot tub that had been such a source of merriment to them when they had moved in almost fifteen years before. The tub was so big that the two of them could splash around in it together and their nightly ritual had been to take a bubble bath together.

When had that stopped, Maggie wondered as she walked down the hall toward the silent bedrooms, sealed off behind closed doors. Probably when Carol's breasts had begun to bud.

That was the same time that Carol's surly nature began to blossom too. Maggie had tried to talk to her as in the old days, but more and more Carol had dealt with her from anger. Often she demanded

216

to know, "Who is my father?" as if knowing that just asking the question hurt her mother.

Maggie had left Venture, Ohio, far behind and she didn't want it to be in her life anymore, or in Carol's. She would not tell her daughter and the gulf between them widened and deepened.

The door to Carol's room was ajar and Maggie went in and saw her daughter lying on the bed. Her sleek dark hair wafted onto the white pillow and the warm blue eyes were open and staring blankly at the ceiling. Her makeup, kohl eyeliner and shadow, had smeared, and she looked like the hostess of a television horror show. Her long fingers and long hot-pink fingernails were clutching the pale pink blanket below her. She was still wearing Maggie's black dress which she had worn the previous night to Ancie's fund-raiser at the Plaza. A cigarette smoldered in the ashtray on the bedside table and Maggie went over to put it out, and could tell by the sweetish aroma that it was marijuana, a smell she was familiar with from her early days in the village. But she had stopped smoking grass when Carol was five because she thought it was no good for her daughter to have to inhale the smoke in the house. Maybe it was her fault; maybe she should have quit smoking pot earlier. Come to think of it, perhaps this wasn't even just grass. She took a whiff of the fat, uneven cigarette butt in her hand. No. It wasn't crack or anything else. Just grass.

217

Her daughter was stoned. She still had not responded to her mother's presence in the room and when Maggie said, "Carol, Carol," the younger woman just continued staring at the ceiling with completely unfocused eyes. But she seemed to be breathing normally. Was she in a coma?

"Carol, Carol, Carol." Maggie slapped her daughter's face lightly and finally the younger woman turned to her and smiled.

"Oh, hi, Mommy." Carol giggled and her eyes focused.

"What have you been taking?" Maggie leaned over the bed.

"Uh, a little of this and a little of that." She giggled again.

"I told you not to bring drugs into this house," Maggie snapped.

"What drugs?" Carol giggled again and sat up. "Oh, that." She saw the butt balanced in Maggie's open hand. "Whyn't you light up and we can share it. It's only grass."

"You know I don't do grass and I don't want you to either. What else have you been doing? And where have you been since yesterday?" Maggie sat heavily on the bed. She was good at mothering, she knew, but she had always had a terrible time scolding Carol. As a child Carol had cottoned to that fast, and when in the wrong, she would simply yell so loud back at her mother that Maggie always retreated.

218

"Mother." Carol scrambled off the bed, resisting any communication. She was wearing no bra and one of the spaghetti straps of her dress dropped down off her shoulder, baring her breast almost to the nipple. "I'm an adult and I'm free, white, and twenty-one and I can do anything I damn well please."

She pulled herself out of the black dress. Then bare-breasted and wearing only bikini panties, she stomped across the room to get a robe that was hanging behind her door. She put it on but not before Maggie saw a string of scratches crisscrossing her back and a black bruise, the size of a slice of bread, at the small of her back.

"Modeling is tough enough work without you picking at me all the time," Carol said.

"If you were out on a job," Maggie said, "what'd you get paid?"

Carol giggled again and said, "A lot." She came across the room, picked her black leather purse off the floor, and opened it. "Why, you probably want your half of the rent. Okay." She wet her lips and started counting from a pile of hundred-dollar bills. "One room in an apartment should come to . . . let's say, three hundred dollars."

Maggie saw Carol must have had a thousand dollars. "Where did you get so much money?"

Carol tossed the three hundred-dollar bills on the bed in front of her mother. "I told you, Mother, I was out on a modeling job. Some girl got sick and

I took her place. I didn't even have time to come home and change. I was out on the Island, modeling."

"Is that where you got those bruises on your back?" Maggie asked with tight lips.

"Those?" Carol threw her head back and hacked out a phony laugh. "I fell off a rock on the beach while I was wearing a bikini."

"Must have made it difficult for the photographers," Maggie said.

"They were done anyway," Carol said. Her eyes were lying. She said again, "I'm going to take a bath. I'm exhausted, Mommie dearest."

Maggie sat where she was for another few minutes until she heard the tap gushing water into the tub. Somehow she knew that things were worse than she had thought.

As Maggie got up from the bed to leave the room, Anatoly Petrov, who had silently sneaked into the apartment after Maggie just to be sure that everything was indeed all right, let himself back out into the hall and walked softly to the front door. He had heard the whole conversation, and while he felt sorry for Maggie, it was a family matter and she did not need any help from him.

Petrov had fallen asleep on his sofa watching a

late movie, and awoke as the first streaks of daylight were slipping in through his windows. There was a news report being broadcast on the television.

A ship had been hijacked in the Caribbean. It was a Spanish luxury liner, *Buena Suerte,* good luck, making a multi-island swing cruise throughout the areas and it had been taken over by terrorists. So far no ransom demands had been made by the terrorists. The TV announcer also recapped the hijacking at sea several years before of the Italian liner, the *Achille Lauro,* during which an American man had been killed. Only a few months later, his wife had succumbed to the cancer she had kept hidden from her husband.

"All in all, a tragic story," the announcer said, "and one which we don't want to see duplicated," and that told Petrov that they had no further information on the hijacking and he turned the television off.

Impatiently he punched out Donovan's home telephone number. No answer.

He replaced the phone on the cradle and it rang almost instantly.

"Petrov, this is Brian Cole. Where the hell is Donovan?"

"I don't know," Petrov said

"Have you heard the news? About the ship?" Cole asked.

"Just now," Petrov said. "I'm looking for Donovan. Where can we reach you?"

221

"He has the number," Cole said.

"But I don't," Petrov said coldly. "What is it?"

There was only a moment's hesitation and then Cole recited a telephone number in Manhattan.

"Thank you. I'll be back," Petrov said, and cut off the call.

He dialed Donovan again with no result, then called Maggie Henson's home number.

She answered in a voice filled with Saturday morning sleeping-in. "Hello. Who is it, please?"

"Maggie, it's Tolly. I need to reach Mark. Do you know where he is?"

"I . . . I have to think a minute. Is something wrong?"

"It's personal. Where might he be?"

"I don't know. Wait. He was with a woman last night. What's her name? Tilda Matthews. She lives up on the West Side."

"Do you have a phone number for her?" Petrov said.

"No."

"Do you know where I could find one?"

"No, yes. Are you home?"

"Yes," Petrov said.

"I'll call you right back."

Maggie, sharp and alert now, disconnected the call and Petrov hung up the telephone. He waited less than a minute and it rang again.

Maggie was on the line and gave him the number of the Matthews woman. "I got it from a friend of hers, Mrs. Longshore," Maggie said. "Is there anything you need me for, Tolly?" she asked with obvious concern.

"Not right now," he said honestly. "Thank you."

In the half light of the early dawn, Mark Donovan smiled and caressed the freckled shoulder of Tilda Matthews.

"I suppose we ought to get a little sleep," he said.

"I suppose," she said, and then leaned over to kiss him again and he felt her hand on him, stroking him, then guiding him into her body and it felt excruciatingly sweet until the telephone rang.

He was about to growl "Let it ring," but Tilda had already slid away from him and picked up the instrument. He realized she was the mother of a young child and would not let telephones ring while the boy was away from her.

She said, "Hello," listened for a moment, then handed the phone across to Donovan with a quizzical look on her face. "For you," she said. "Tolly Peterson?"

"And a good morning to you too, Tolly," Donovan said as he took the phone. Then he listened and Tilda could see his face draw serious, then he said simply, "At the office. Immediately."

He handed the telephone back to her and clambered out of bed toward his clothes which were laid neatly across the back of a chair.

"Is everything all right?" she asked.

"A business problem," Donovan said. "I have to take care of it right away."

"I see. Is this what you call wham, bam, thank you, ma'am?" she asked with a smile.

He grinned at her even as he continued to pull his trousers on. "You only say thank you, ma'am, when you're done," he said.

"And you're not done?"

"I don't know when I'll get back," he said. "But when I do, I'll show you I haven't even started."

CHAPTER EIGHTEEN

The *Buena Suerte* was steaming full ahead through the Caribbean and the passengers' hearts were filled with prayers that the ship engines would break down.

Most of them were still in the main dining room, still sitting in their evening clothes, still looking at the plates from the meal that had been served to them the night before.

It was a given that there was always food to waste at a shipboard dinner, and this one had been no exception. Less than half the food that had been set out had at first been consumed by the diners, but now every scrap of it was gone, picked at nervously through the night by people who were beginning to realize that their fun-in-the-sun vacation might be turning into a close-up look into the face of death.

They reacted in different ways to the announcement that the ship had been taken over—some with fear, some with anger. One fat woman, in pearls and a black jersey gown, was reduced to picking crumbs up from the tablecloth while she kept up a running conversation with herself about her deprived childhood.

Their captors who were posted at the main entrances to the big room did not seem to care if the passengers moved around the room so long as no one did it quickly and so long as they did not approach the guards, who were armed with assault weapons.

The dining room was oversized; it sat seven hundred people, and the multilighted crystal chandeliers had not been turned off even though the sun had now appeared and turned the display of gaily dressed passengers into a mockery.

There were, Violet Harmshaw Thorn counted, only three guards. One guarded the set of entry doors at one end of the room; the other two guarded the entrance on the other end, and the doors that led to the kitchen and to the wine rooms. Only three guards, she thought, but they were carrying what she thought of as Thompson guns.

Miss Thorn—she would have nothing to do with Ms. as a title even though the fact that she had never wed sometimes weighed heavily on her mind—had been a WAC during World War II and she knew the devastation of machine guns. However, her constant companion, the Right Honorable Gerald Quincy Dodson, kept suggesting that they rush the blighters.

Violet put a well-manicured and unspotted hand

on Gerald's knee and pointed out that they might be massacred in any escape attempt.

"So what, my girl, so what? Haven't we been through it all? Haven't we? So if they kill us now, so what? Is there something besides death that we haven't seen? Damn fools, all of us."

Violet leaned forward even more, her lavender gown sparkling in the sunlight that poured through the windows that ran down both sides of the large room. There was the flush of natural English beauty on her cheeks, although lately she had finally taken to putting a blond rinse into her wavy hair which was at last starting to gray.

"Don't be an ass, Gerald. We will sit here as we always do, above suspicion. We are always above suspicion and then if someone makes a mistake, we will do what we need do to survive. As we always have."

"Yes, my love." Gerald Quincy Dodson patted her hand. He had recruited her, the lovely young WAC, for the Home Office during World War II and he had told the Nazis that she was his link with Prime Minister Churchill's plans. Throughout the war, the two of them had fed the Nazis false information on British war plans from Singapore to the Dardanelles.

Violet had been engaged then to a young RAF officer, Bruce Trent, and he had returned from the war, very decorated, to his spy of a fiancée, and had never understood why she did not accord him

227

all the honors he thought were due to a conquering hero. Violet had decided never to see Gerald again and to live up to her responsibilities, but instead RAF Lieutenant (ret.) Bruce Trent had not been able to let go of World War II and spent his days and nights drinking in pub and club, talking about it, until one night he ran his Morris Minor off the road into a ditch and that was that.

For a long time Violet played the role of the woman who lost her love, but then she tired of it and began to wonder how good old Gerald was doing. Still it was only by chance that they met again, on a luxury liner to New York City, where Violet noticed that old Gerald had taken up a new profession, cheating at cards.

It turned out that Gerald's pension from the Home Office did not include the luxuries he was used to and hence, the life of crime. It was not without its dangers, he explained to Violet. As a single man traveling alone, he wound up in card games with other single men, many of them shrewd and some of them professional card players, and it took all his skill just to eke out a small profit.

"But, aaah, the opportunities for a couple. Bridge, for instance. With a partner I could make more money in a week of playing bridge with rich Americans than I can in a year at the poker tables. Simple, don't you know?"

"Gerald," Violet had said, "are you asking me to be your partner in crime?"

"Well, humph, I hadn't exactly thought of it in those terms, humph, humph."

"I accept," Violet said. He had taught her and she had gotten better than he at the simple little nuances and signals that made bridge such a simple game to cheat at. They spent their lives on one ship after another, partners from another war, friends and still lovers, because still—just as during the days of the war—Gerald might humph-humph a lot, but he could get it up and keep it up and Violet thought that this was really rather an important attribute in a man.

She was very happy with their partnership and their life and so now, when he was considering some sort of rash counterattack on these awful men with their greasy skin and dark eyes, she simply took his large hand in hers and gazed into his beady gray eyes, lifted an eyebrow, and said, "All in good time, Gerald, all in good time. We don't want to be casualties in a fruitless war, do we?"

Across the way from Violet and old Gerald was a newlywed couple. Sheila Argent Jeffers was an attorney, her husband a private investigator she had met when she hired him to research one of her cases. She had thought her client innocent; the private investigator, Patrick Jeffers, had proved him guilty beyond a doubt. She liked his rough, honest ways and one thing led to another and another led to bed and wed.

Sheila Jeffers looked at her new husband and said, "Do you think we ought to do something?"

Patrick Jeffers answered, "Yes, but not right now. We need a distraction."

"Hell," said Sheila. "If only they'd bring out some more food, Fatso over there would give us one." She nodded to the fat woman who was still picking up crumbs and talking to herself.

Her husband laughed. "You always do that to me. You look so prim and proper but you've got a street-smart eye."

Sheila grinned and showed an array of dimples in her angular face. "Like that? Try this! We need a distraction; I'll get up and take my clothes off."

"Now, there's a distraction if ever I heard one. You do that, then I'll do that, then we'll fuck right here and I'll yell 'one for the gipper.' And by then the guards will be so confused, they'll be easy pickings."

They both laughed, but then, with just a nod, each shared the knowledge that they would not sit there forever waiting for these thugs to act. They would do something on their own if they had to.

In the children's playroom several decks farther down in the ship, another wife was looking at her husband. He had been in Vietnam and had been through the horrors afterward, she knew. They were now in their late thirties, she was pregnant, and the guard who stood at the door of the playroom, watching them and thirty other adults and children, was reminding her husband of past guards—the ones who had stood over him in the Vietnamese prison camp.

Their other children, all four of them, had been subdued after the Arab guard had pushed one of them, the girl Jeanine. That is what her father always called her: "the girl, Jeanine." The other three were boys and intimidated by their father but not Jeanine. She was the oldest, now almost sixteen, and born when Milt was away in 'Nam. She was pretty with long black soft hair and slit eyes that were sort of gray; not like a black girl at all. Claudine wondered sometimes if Milt, who was very dark-skinned, ever wondered if Jeanine was not his child. But how could he? From the tilt of the nose to the wrinkling of the eyes, she looked just like him.

"I guess this trip wasn't such a good idea," Claudine said softly to her husband.

She had thought it would be. Milt had wanted to go to Africa, to search for his roots, and she had convinced him that the kids would vastly prefer a vacation voyage and not a safari. She had hoped it would help Milt get rid of some of his crazed revolutionary "oppressed-black-man" ideas. Or at least to see that not much was accomplished by talking against a system that had brought them more money, certainly, than any other black couple she knew. They had a home in Scarsdale, hard won but earned honestly. Claudine bit her tongue as she looked at her husband, who did not answer her. Nausea rose in her throat. Her time to deliver her next baby was growing close, she believed.

Milt, an investment broker, watched the guard carefully and then said to him, "You speak English?"

The Arab, whose skin was almost as dark as Milt's, nodded.

"So what's it all about?" Milt said. "Suppose you tell me what your beliefs are, man. I'm one of the oppressed myself, you know. We all are."

Claudine moved her heavy body, comforting Jeanine, and eyed her husband. If he turned up on the side of these awful people, she was going to leave him . . . once and for all, and let him fight his revolution by himself.

Brian Cole and Anatoly Petrov were waiting for Donovan when he arrived at the firm's office in the Chrysler Building.

A television set in the corner of the room was tuned to an all-news channel.

"What have we heard?" Donovan said as he settled in behind his desk. Petrov poured some murky leftover coffee from the urn in the office and put it in front of him without being asked and smiled at Donovan's obvious surprise at the gesture.

"Nothing new," Cole said. "The hijackers have the ship. There's navy planes in the neighborhood but the hijackers say they'll blow up the ship if anybody gets cute."

"Any demands yet?" Donovan asked.

"No. But they're talking about Arab liberation and shit," Cole said.

Donovan nodded and looked toward Petrov. "What do you think, Tolly?"

"I think we've found where Ayoub is," Petrov said. "For the last week he was talking about a sea voyage. This was it obviously. The bastard's in charge of the operation."

"Any idea of where they're going?" Donovan asked.

Petrov said, "They just showed a map on television. The ship's steaming around, but it's a good guess that they're heading toward Nicaragua. They probably figure they can hit harbor there and let the Sandinistas cover for them."

"It's a Spanish ship though, isn't it?" Donovan said. "I heard that on the radio coming up. Doesn't Nicaragua get along with Spain?"

"Yes," Petrov said, "but the ship left from New York. Almost all the passengers are American. As far as the Sandinistas are concerned, I think they'll regard it as an American ship."

"Fucking communist bastards," Cole said.

When Petrov just grinned, Donovan said, "Hey,

Brian. Don't forget. We've got one of them, too, and he's on our side."

Cole nodded reluctantly and said, "I can't reach Aziz or Will Stanhope. They're in Europe somewhere, and I don't know where."

"Forget them," Donovan said. "We won't have time for them. We're going to have to get charts of the ship, sailing charts, and some solid information on where the hijackers are. I'll get Washington on that. And I think we're going to have to get Elliott involved here."

Petrov looked puzzled and Cole said, "Christ. Elliott's got to be seventy going on ninety. What do you need him for?"

Donovan glanced up at the tall blond man. Elliott Pennington had been the man who first taught Donovan how to build helicopters. He now worked at the main assembly plant of Whirlybirds Inc. in Atlanta. "Because Elliott is still the best helicopter pilot alive," Donovan said. "And because he and I have been working on a helicopter with more moves than Madonna's ass. He's been testing it down there and he tells me it's ready, so we're going to use it."

"I'd feel better if you were flying it," Cole said.

"Yeah? Well, maybe, but the way I figure it, we've got just the three of us in this room with Stanhope and Aziz out of reach. So I think the three of us are going to be pretty busy. Tolly, can you dive?"

"Underwater work?" Petrov said.

234

When Donovan nodded, the Russian said, "Yes. I'm an expert."

Brian whistled softly, almost derisively, but Donovan ignored him. "Then we've got three of us who can get to this ship. Let's go." He picked up a telephone and said, "I'll charter a jet to get us to Georgia. Any dissent? Any debate?"

Brian Cole punched one big fist into the palm of the other and said, "Let's go get these bastards."

Donovan looked at Petrov, who said, "My sentiments exactly."

Elliott Pennington, as usual, had arisen at 5 A.M., and not being exactly thrilled with the TV news, went out to look at Maxine. He had chosen that name for the helicopter because his half-assed knowledge of high school Latin convinced him that Maxine meant superior, and also because he just liked to give aircraft women's names.

Lately there had been a few television shows featuring a helicopter with almost magical powers but none had really come close to Maxine. He was standing with his hand affectionately on the glass-fibered body of the craft when he heard the faint buzzing from inside that indicated that a telephone call was coming into the helicopter's on-board computer.

It was Mark Donovan, who simply told him, "Get Maxine ready. We're taking her on a long ride.

For our uncle. And you're flying."

Pennington grinned as he disconnected the call. He did not need to ask who "uncle" was. That was Uncle Sam, and Donovan was talking about doing some work for the government. Several months earlier he had explained to Pennington that upon occasion they might be called on to do some work that no one else would be allowed to know about.

"You mean you're back in the spy business," Pennington had said, and Donovan had grinned and said, "You're just a suspicious old man, Elliott."

Elliott thought of that conversation now as he started to jot notes onto a pilot's pad of things to do to make sure Maxine was ready for her maiden voyage. And the thought sneaked into his mind that maybe, just maybe, their flight today might have something to do with those news reports he had heard that morning.

Donovan, Cole, and a man introduced as Peterson joined him two hours later, and then there seemed like a lot of work to do—charts to collect and plans to study and equipment to buy and haul aboard Maxine—but it was done quickly and then Donovan said, "Anybody wants to take a nap, go ahead. We've got a couple of hours before we go."

Pennington looked at him quizzically and Donovan said, "Where we're going, we want to arrive at night."

CHAPTER NINETEEN

The sun was setting behind them as they came within fifty miles of the *Buena Suerte*. She was still steaming toward the coastline of Nicaragua, although her speed was now down to a stately six knots.

Donovan, in the large helicopter cockpit with Elliott Pennington, had spotted the ship on the radarscope a hundred miles earlier.

"What now, boss?" Pennington said.

"Swing around it so they can't see you and let's pick out an intercept spot about four miles ahead of it. That ought to give us time."

Pennington grunted and pushed the main throttle of the big chopper forward and it seemed to surge as it picked up speed and altitude. The old pilot skidded the craft around to the right and then set off on a course paralleling that of the ship.

"Just hope we don't meet none of our own flyboys out here," he said to Donovan.

"They've got blanket orders to engage no one," Donovan said briskly. "They'll leave us alone." He

237

watched as the position of the *Buena Suerte* changed on the radarscope as they moved, first alongside it, then past it.

Ten minutes later Pennington said, "Here we are, Mark." They had reached a position five miles ahead of the luxury liner. In forty minutes or so the big ship would pass beneath them.

"Okay. Just hold it here for a while," Donovan said. He called out, "Tolly."

Petrov, who was sitting in a small compartment behind them, leaned back and looked up toward Donovan. The Russian was impressed. He had never been in a helicopter so fast or large or so quiet.

"You pick up anything on those radios?" Donovan asked him.

Petrov took off the earphones and set them on a small metal counter in front of a bank of radios, then came up and squatted next to Donovan in the front of the aircraft.

"A little," Petrov said. "I've been monitoring all the radio nets. The best anyone can determine, there are six hijackers in all. There haven't been any passengers on deck, so they're all probably down in the main dining room. That's in the center of the ship, one deck down."

"Not in their rooms," Donovan said.

"No, there aren't enough hijackers to guard them all there."

"Okay."

"Two of the terrorists are on the bridge with the captain. They've been seen waving guns around."

"Any demands yet?"

"The usual," Petrov said blandly. "They want Israel to release all its Palestinian prisoners. They want an apology from the Italian government for permitting, what did they call it, the 'atrocities' in Rome. They say if they don't get an affirmative answer by midnight, they'll start killing passengers, one an hour until they do."

"So they're definitely Abu Beka's guys?" Donovan asked.

"I'd say so," Petrov answered.

Donovan nodded. "They've got a radio frequency open?"

"Yes. But they said they won't acknowledge any messages except one that says their demands are being met."

"Good. Okay, you stay up here with Elliott. You know what to do."

Petrov nodded and took Donovan's place in the padded helicopter seat and the American walked back to the middle of the giant craft, where Brian Cole, wearing a skindiver's wet suit, was busy inflating a small two-man rubber boat. He looked up at Donovan with a quizzical expression on his face.

Donovan grinned and said, "Looks like a nice evening for a swim."

239

It was dark now, but a bright moon still illuminated the cruise ship as its white hull moved slowly, majestically, through the dark Caribbean waters.

In the helicopter, still hovering a mile away from the ship's stern on the starboard side, Petrov could see on the radarscope the twin dots — one from the ship and the other from a small radar-triggering beacon attached to the rubber boat of Brian Cole and Mark Donovan — move slowly together and then merge into just one dot.

He clapped Elliott Pennington on the shoulder. "Move in closer," he said. "Just don't let the bastards shoot us down."

"Not a chance, fella," Pennington said. He did not know who this man was except that Donovan called him "Tolly," but he was impressed by his cool, all-business approach to their mission. Truth was Pennington was enjoying himself. He had not had this much fun since World War II.

Petrov opened the radio channel to the ship and began to speak in Arabic.

"We are friends. We mean you no harm. Our leader, Abu Beka, is aboard. Answer immediately."

The ship was traveling without its main deck lights on, but Cole and Donovan had no trouble picking up its outline when it came within a half mile of them. They steered their soundless electric-powered boat to intercept the ship, then came up along its starboard side. The smooth white side of the ship rose above them like a five-story building, but there was only thirty feet or so to reach the permanent structure to which the gangplanks were attached when the ship was in port.

As Cole kept the small power boat alongside the body of the ship, Donovan opened a waterproof bag stowed in the bottom of the rubber boat and pulled out an instrument that looked like a crossbow. But instead of shooting an arrow, there was a grappling hook attached to the end of the gun.

Donovan lifted the gun to his shoulder, sighted carefully, and fired. Noiselessly, trailing a length of thin nylon rope, the grappling hood shot up into the air. Its hook caught around one of the steel posts on the small boarding deck. Donovan gave the rope a hard jerk to make sure the hook had been tightly secured, then tied the other end of the rope to a rubber cleat on their small boat. He clapped Cole on the shoulder to let him know they were secure. Cole grinned at him, his teeth glistening brightly in the black greasepaint that coated his face.

Both men checked the weapons that were strapped around their bodies, then one after another began to climb up the nylon rope to the ship.

On the bridge, Hussein Ayoub—the man who was traveling as Pierre Dubois—and another of the hijackers listened to the voice crackling over the radio. Both men carried small Uzi automatic weapons.

The master of the ship, Captain Carlos Calderon, stood next to the ship's controls staring out at the sea ahead of them, as if oblivious to the message that had broken into the ship's radio silence. Next to him a young seaman manned the helm of the luxury liner.

The younger terrorist looked at Ayoub questioningly, and finally Ayoub walked to the radio, lifted the microphone, and said, "How do we know you are telling the truth?"

After a moment the voice crackled back.

"Because I know who you are, Pierre Dubois. Or should I say Ayoub?" The speaker was Petrov, but the static over the plane-to-ship radio was strong enough to muffle his tones and make it impossible to tell anything about the speaker except that his Arabic was flawless.

"Allah be praised," Ayoub said. "Can you land on the deck?"

"Yes," Petrov responded. "We will come down shortly. Assemble your troops for inspection. All power to Tenterallah."

Violet Harmshaw Thorn said to Gerald Quincy Dodson, "Something's up, luv."

They were sitting at the same dining table, but

two of the terrorists had left and the one remaining had ordered all the passengers to move to one end of the room.

"Move! Move!" he screamed, and waved his automatic rifle at the crowd.

Sheila and Patrick Jeffers got up from their table slowly and Sheila whispered to her private-detective husband, "I know you brought your best friend along."

The private detective's dark eyes narrowed and a small smile appeared on his face. "Never go anywhere without it," he said, and carefully showed her the small automatic cradled in his hand.

They wound up standing next to Violet and Gerald in the front line of the passengers, facing the lone remaining terrorist, and Violet also saw the gun in his hand.

She met Patrick's eyes quizzically, and he whispered to her, "I'm going to shoot this bastard," then added, as an embarrassed afterthought, "Ma'am."

Violet smiled and whispered back, "Blow his fucking brains out, young man."

In the playroom Claudine and Milt had been left with their children. The hijacker had locked the door behind him as he left. The other parents and children in the room seemed content to mill around aimlessly.

"I think we'll get out of this," Milt said. "These

guys and I have a lot in common."

Claudine spat in his face and went to one of the toy cabinets to try to find a tool to pry the door open.

Brian Cole and Donovan crouched on the top step of the gangplank and Donovan used a small portable radio to call the helicopter.

"Is it working?" he asked.

"I hope so," Petrov said laconically. "I've ordered them all on deck. You aboard?"

"Midships," Donovan said.

"Stay put. You may see them soon."

Gerald and Violet were moving away from the young private detective, working their way slowly along the front of the crowd, trying not to be noticed by the young terrorist who was standing twenty feet in front of them, nervously swinging the barrel of his gun back and forth.

"I guess the old lady didn't want to be near the action," Patrick told his wife. "They're fleeing."

"I'm not so sure," his wife said just as Violet let out a scream, clutched her chest, and fell to the floor.

The terrorist froze in position, then came a few steps closer to her, his gun barrel pointed steadily at the old Englishwoman.

At that moment Patrick Jeffers stepped forward from the crowd and put one shot through the terrorist's temple. The man dropped like a rock; his gun thudded harmlessly on the wooden floor next to him.

"Good shooting, young man," Violet called out as she clambered to her feet.

Patrick handed her the pistol, picked up the guard's automatic rifle, and ran forward to lock the dining room doors from the inside.

A cheer went up from the almost five hundred passengers, and Patrick turned and called out, "Okay, everybody stay low and stay away from those windows. Lady, you keep an eye on that back door and don't be afraid to shoot if anyone comes back."

Gerald took the small automatic from Violet's hand and said, "You've already had enough exercise for one day, darling. Leave it to me."

"Of course, Gerald," Violet said.

The shot was heard by the two terrorists who had just left the dining room, and one of them went back to check on what had happened while the other continued up to the main deck.

The shot was also heard by Cole and Donovan, who looked at each other for a moment before Donovan said, "You take care of things here." Then Donovan slipped onto the deck, toward the nearest bulkhead, and went running down the steps to the dining room, where Petrov had guessed most of the hostages were being held.

The terrorist who had been guarding the play-room and the other one from the dining room came up onto the deck. They were met there by the young pockmarked man from inside the captain's bridge.

Ayoub chose to stay behind on the bridge, just to make sure the captain did not try anything.

Suddenly the helicopter, looming large and gray, came toward the ship out of the night sky.

The three terrorists backed away from it as it hovered over the section of deck used as an outside dance floor. It was only ten feet above the deck, floating, its thirty-foot-long rotors kicking up small twisters of wind above the wooden floor.

Ayoub came to the door of the bridge and kept a gun on the captain, while craning his neck, trying to see the helicopter landing, but his view was obscured by the ship's superstructure.

As the three terrorists watched from the deck below, a sliding door opened in the side of the aircraft, and a man jumped out and hit the deck below the plane.

And then the man did not move.

The lone hijacker pounded on the door to the

dining room with the butt of his gun but got no response.

Angrily, he swore, and then ripped off a string of fire at the door lock. The sound reverberated inside the enclosed compartment.

The door lock broke loose and the terrorist kicked the door open. He saw the crowd of people huddled on the floor at the other end of the dining room. Then he saw Patrick Jeffers pointing an automatic rifle at him.

He never saw Mark Donovan, who jumped down the last flight of stairs to the dining room deck, saw the terrorist in the doorway lifting his gun, and took the man down with a spray of bullets through the man's back.

The man dropped his gun and fell.

Donovan ran to the door and then called inside in English, "Everybody okay in there?"

Jeffers yelled back. "We're all right. Who are you?"

"We're the good guys. Everything's under control, but you just stay put there."

As he ran back upstairs toward the top deck he heard a roar of cheering behind him.

The three terrorists on the deck ran over to where the man who had jumped from the helicopter lay still and unmoving. The big plane still whirred only a dozen feet over their heads.

They turned over the man's body and saw that it was not a man at all. It was a headless dummy, men's clothing stuffed with rags and paper.

On the chest was a sign printed crudely in Arabic. It read:

SURRENDER NOW, ARAB SWINE. ALL IS LOST!

The terrorists screamed, then looked up and raised their weapons to fire at the helicopter which was already moving away from them.

But before they could fire, Brian Cole raised himself off the first step of the gangplank and took down all four of them with a single burst from his automatic weapon.

From inside the bridge Ayoub yelled, "Men. Report to me. Report!"

Thirty seconds had passed. Donovan and Cole crouched against the bulkhead outside the side entrance to the bridge. Ayoub was still inside, his gun still trained on Captain Calderon. The young seaman inside was hunched over the controls, not even looking, as if trying by ignoring it to put himself far away from the madness that was going on aboard their ship.

The helicopter, Maxine, was hovering a hundred

feet away on the other side of the vessel.

"Mexican standoff," Cole whispered to Donovan.

"Horseshit," Donovan said. "No ties allowed. We didn't come this far to wind up kissing our sister."

As he slowly rose from his crouching position, he said, "If anything goes wrong, plug that bastard and get out of here. But my body goes with you, understand?"

"You got it, Captain," Cole said.

Ayoub saw the tall man with the soot-blackened face stand up and come into the door on the other side of the bridge. An automatic pistol in his hand was aimed at Ayoub's face. The Arab threw his arm around the captain and yanked him back toward him. His own gun came up next to the captain's chin.

Then he spoke to Donovan. "We seem to be at an impasse here, sir. You shoot and I shoot the captain. Are you willing to pay that price?"

"Do you have any suggestions?" Donovan said. The tip of his gun did not waver; it was still pointed at Ayoub.

Ayoub glanced around nervously. What *could* he do? His men were probably dead, his scheme in shambles around him. The best he could hope for was to use the captain as a hostage and get these people to fly him in their helicopter to a safe port in nearby Nicaragua.

He was concentrating too hard. Behind him, he did not hear the helicopter as it turned its motor into a newly engineered mode for semi-silent flying and moved closer to the ship. But he felt the breeze as its rotors drew close and the big chopper hovered only ten feet above the door to the bridge. Before he could turn it was too late.

Anatoly Petrov had jumped feetfirst from the aircraft to land on the thin sliver of deck outside the bridge. As Ayoub turned to look, the heel of Petrov's hand shot forward and smashed into his nose. There was a sound like glass breaking as the bone separated and was driven back and up into Ayoub's brain.

The gun fell from his hand; the Arab teetered and then dropped to the floor.

Captain Calderon pulled free and looked down at the dead man. Donovan looked down at him, too, and snarled, "Shit."

Petrov, his face also blackened, stepped inside the door and said, "Sorry. Seemed like a good idea at the time."

Cole ran into the bridge. "Time to leave, I think."

Donovan said to the captain, "How many were there, Captain?"

"Six, I think."

"Then we got all of them."

He and Cole hoisted up the body of Ayoub and carried it outside. They slipped a rope around the man's torso, under his shoulders, and then clipped

250

it to a hook on one of the ropes dangling from the helicopter's open bay door. Each man grabbed a rope and as Captain Calderon watched, the helicopter's motors roared to noisy life again and the big gray plane swooped away, dangling the three men and the corpse below it.

In just a few seconds they had vanished into the nighttime sky.

CHAPTER TWENTY

The next morning, the body of Hussein Ayoub, sewn into a pigskin, was found hanging in a public square just on the edge of the Old City of San Juan in Puerto Rico.

A hand-lettered sign pinned to his chest read: SO DIE ALL THE TERRORIST BEASTS.

The press of the world was in a furor, but the only hard information that the government of Spain could release was that the rescue was effected by troops arriving aboard an unmarked helicopter. No one knew where the helicopter came from or who owned it. American warplanes had been tracking it after the rescue, but it had dropped down to wave height over the ocean and managed to skip under the tracking planes' radar.

The identity of the rescuers was unknown although the Spanish government made Captain Carlos Calderon, skipper of the cruise ship, available for a press conference in which he said that the men spoke both English and Arabic and had announced that they had been sent by Abu Beka, the well-known terrorist leader of the Tenterallah.

Passengers aboard the ship were of no more help, since they had not seen any of the rescuers. Violet Harmshaw Thorn said that she was thinking of writing her memoirs and would tell the whole story there. Gerald Quincy Dodson made sure to mention that he frequently cruised the Caribbean in similar ships and anybody who wanted to talk about the hijacking could look him up.

Patrick Jeffers, who had shot the terrorist holding hostages in the main dining room, was regarded as a hero who might have saved hundreds of lives, but when he returned to New York City later, the police department said it was considering lifting his pistol permit for unauthorized use of a weapon and one TV station instantly called him another Bernhard Goetz. His wife said she would defend him and make New York City's government look like a pack of cretins, and City Hall backed down and dropped the charge.

Maggie Henson followed all the news on one of the Sunday morning television shows and when they talked about the enormous mystery helicopter that had aided in the rescue, she gasped aloud, "Oh, my God. Maxine."

"What, Mommie dearest?" Carol Henson asked, looking up from the Sunday *Times* fashion section. She was making an effort this day to be especially good. She thought, despite her mother's opinion, that she was in no way hooked on drugs and she was going to make it through this day. Certainly the Quaalude she had taken an hour before would help her through the dry spell.

"Nothing," Maggie said. "Just thinking out loud."

"Maxine. Isn't that the name of the new helicopter you and Mark are so excited about?"

All Carol was trying to do was to take an interest in her mother's work, to placate her a little. Carol wasn't ready to be evicted until she had a place to go. And she wasn't yet ready to move in with Raffi either, even though she found his sexual practices very exciting and he had enough money for everybody.

"Mommy?"

"I didn't say anything," Maggie Henson snapped, and changed the channel.

Carol screwed up her pretty face. She hadn't been listening to the news . . . it was so boring, always the same thing . . . but now some of what was being talked about came back to her. Mark and his new chopper, Maxine? Daring rescue by helicopter? No. That didn't make any sense. Carol went back to the paper but somehow couldn't concentrate.

Later that morning a dozen red roses were delivered to Tilda Matthews. The card said simply "Thank you, ma'am."

CHAPTER TWENTY-ONE

Maggie Henson got into the office shortly after eight A.M. After her daughter had gone to bed, she had spent the night watching Cable News Network, but while they had spent the night covering the story of the rescue aboard the *Buena Suerte*, much of it had been conjecture and analysis. Hard news was in short supply, but the one indisputable fact was that a group of commandos, origin unknown, had reached the plane in a huge unmarked helicopter, had killed the terrorists, freed the passengers and crew and flown away, all in a matter of minutes, taking one of the hijackers with them. The best anyone could tell was that there were only three commandos.

Three. Mark, Tolly Peterson, and Brian Cole? Was it possible? Maggie found it too incredible to put any faith in, but there was still the fact that Donovan had been missing for the weekend and the helicopter sounded like Maxine, the super-secret military craft that Whirlaway Inc. had been working on.

255

At six A.M., for the sixth time since the first news bulletin on the rescue, she had dialed Mark Donovan's apartment, and for the sixth time she got his answering machine and hung up angrily without leaving a message.

She had finally pulled herself away from the television set long enough to shower and dress for work, but just as she was getting ready to leave the apartment, CNN had a news bulletin. The body of one of the hijackers had been found, sewn into a pigskin, in a municipal square in a small village on the northern coast of Puerto Rico. She watched for a few minutes but there was only the bulletin, and she snapped off the television and went to the office.

Now she was at her desk and she told herself, "You're crazy," and somehow her suspicions did seem crazy now that she was back in her familiar, comfortable office. For Mark to have been involved would have meant that he . . . and Tolly too . . . had killed people, and that just sounded too far-fetched for her to believe a moment. True, she had heard stories about Donovan and his heroic record in Vietnam. But killing terrorists? That seemed like a little too much.

But where had Donovan been? In all the years she had worked for him, he had always been only a telephone call away. In Pittsburgh or Atlanta or Europe or the Far East, she had always known where to reach him. And again the doubts crept back into her mind.

She tuned the radio on her desk to an all-news station, then opened the container of delicatessen coffee she had brought upstairs with her. She winced as droplets of the black mud splashed from the container cover onto the back of her hand, grumbled under her breath, and took a bottle of vodka from her bottom desk drawer.

She had the bottle poised over the coffee cup when she realized there was no room in the cup for the shot. Impatiently, she emptied out a cup of pencils onto the blotter of her desk, poured out a couple of inches of coffee, and replaced it in the original container with vodka.

"Hard night, Maggie?" She looked up to see Mark Donovan standing in her doorway, cocking an eyebrow in her direction. His blue eyes were clear and direct. "A little hair of the dog what bit you?"

"I'd like to bite your throat," she said stiffly. "And this," she said as she recapped the bottle and shoved it back into the desk drawer, "is my own personal business, thank you."

"Well, paaaardon me."

"You're not pardoned," she said. Maggie took a sip, shuddered as the combination went past her throat and into her stomach, and said, "And besides, you're the one who's driving me to drink. Where the hell have you been all night?"

"If I told you, you'd have no respect for me," Donovan said with a small grin.

He started to walk into his office and Maggie

257

said, "I thought you had gone fishing."

"I hate fishing," he said.

"For terrorists," she said, looking at him over the rim of her coffee cup.

"Maggie," Donovan said slowly. "Go to work." He went into his office, and Maggie poured some more vodka into her coffee container.

She had just finished the cup and her head was starting to hurt when Tolly Peterson arrived at the office.

"Hi-de-ho," he said. "Don't you look like the sun-drenched maiden this morning?"

She looked at him sourly for a long moment, then said, "Will you take me to dinner tonight?"

"My pleasure. Seven o'clock?"

She nodded, and he said, "The master in?"

"Yes. And will you please tell him I'm taking the rest of the day off."

"Sure thing," he said. "Are you feeling all right?"

"Nothing a little sleep won't cure. I'll expect you at seven." He nodded again and went into Donovan's office.

CHAPTER TWENTY-TWO

When Hafid Aziz had been a child of five in Tehran, his father had become involved with the Fedayeen Islam and had enthusiastically supported the Ayatollah Khomeini's first attempt to overthrow the shah.

The trouble with the elder Aziz was not just his judgment. He had been a failure. And now that he was grown, Aziz realized that was one of the reasons his father had become active in the Fedayeen. Guerrilla movements, popular liberation fronts, attracted more than their share of incompetents because they gave the incompetent something to hide behind. Their members were not poor because they were stupid or lazy or dirt ignorant; no, it was "they" who were responsible for their subjugation . . . "they" being anybody in any position of power.

So it was foreordained that "they" would capture his father. His companions were too smart to make themselves known, but his father liked to show off by holding meetings of the revolutionary cell in his own home . . . just to prove that he was a big, important man. That was more important to him than the obvious corollary fact that the Savak, the shah's secret police, were certainly watching him.

There had been many meetings in their home that ended with Aziz's mother wringing her hands and crying with fear. Their home had been humble; their father a ne'er-do-well who had tried and failed at many jobs and then had stopped trying. So it was not too surprising that he had not succeeded as a planner of rebellion either.

Aziz had been there the day his father had been hauled outside and executed against the wall of the shabby frame house. His mother and Aziz watched; only the chickens and his father screamed. His mother turned her face away; Aziz just stared.

For he knew something the others in their tiny little village enclave did not know. They all assumed that the Savak was the killer of the elder Aziz, but the young boy knew better. He recognized in the masked death squad a man named Neghassi, whom he had seen his father with many times, and although he was young, Aziz knew what had happened.

The revolutionaries had decided that his father was too dangerous to their cause to live. So they had killed him and blamed his death on the shah's hated Savak. The revolutionaries had declared his father a martyr of the revolution. Neghassi, the would-be friend, had read a proclamation. Aziz turned his face away during the ceremonies.

Soon after his mother had died and Aziz had been forced to beg in the streets. He was finally "adopted" by a traveling Egyptian businessman with much money and a penchant for sex with young boys. Aziz tried to ignore it; it was better than starvation; at least he would live long enough to find Neghassi and kill him.

When the Ayatollah and his crazies finally took over Iran, Neghassi had become one of the leaders of a new and even more brutal secret police organization whose job it was to deal with the international terrorist movement. Among the few in the West who knew more than was contained in the morning's headlines, Neghassi was believed to have recruited Abu Beka and set up his group as Iran's final secret army.

He was the force behind Abu Beka in the early days; together they had masterminded the attack in Spain which killed the publisher of an anti-Khomeini exile newspaper. They were responsible for the hijacking of a Kuwaiti Airways jet to Tehran and the bombing that killed two hundred marines at the U.S. Embassy annex in Beirut.

At that time Aziz did not care about Abu Beka; he cared about Neghassi, and his time came one hot summer's night in Iran when the terrorist leader had been in a nightclub—a secret club where only high officials were allowed to congregate because drinking was "officially" outlawed by the Khomeini regime—and had gone to the bathroom. A waiter stood there, at a sink, washing his hands, and when Neghassi stood in front of the urinal, the young waiter slipped up behind him and whispered in his ear: "This is for my father, Agdar Aziz," and slit his throat from ear to ear.

Aziz fled through a window, was spirited out of the country, and after a few months back in Egypt left the country to join the growing number of mercenaries who traveled around the world, fighting the private little wars that were too dirty or too small for regular armies to fight. Except Aziz did not do it for the money; his aim was to fight terrorists wherever he found them, no matter what disguise their governments took. He fought against the Sandinistas in Nicaragua and against the African National Congress. He was in Cambodia fighting against first the Khmer Rouge and later against the North Vietnamese.

It was there that he met Will Stanhope, another mercenary but one who truly was in it for the money, and Stanhope had introduced him to Brian Cole in a drunken all-night orgy in a Laotian whorehouse.

He had been at loose ends when Cole contacted him in Mexico a few months before with an offer to fight against the Ayatollah's bully boys; he had quickly accepted and had also rounded up Will Stanhope.

Aziz never asked about it, but he suspected strongly that he and Stanhope were working for some government somewhere, even though Cole had told them that the money for their missions was coming from private sources. He would have thought less of Brian Cole if the American had told him the truth. There was no need for Aziz or Stanhope to know; what they did not know could not hurt someone else.

After they had disposed of the terrorists from the attack on the Da Vinci Airport in Rome, Aziz and Stanhope had gone right to Paris to try to intercept, if they could, the next message from Abu Beka and perhaps trace it to its source. But they had arrived too late; Abu Beka already had called the International Press Association bureau chief to threaten revenge for the slayings of his men.

In the small apartment he occupied with Stanhope on the outskirts of Paris, Aziz received by post a packet of information from Brian Cole. It included all that was known — precious little — about Abu Beka and what sketchy details were known about his telephone messages to the bureau chief of the International Press Association.

Stanhope, a small but wiry Brit with bristling mustache, was content to await further orders from Cole and spent his time wandering Paris at night. His lust for women seemed insatiable; he explained once to Aziz with a wry smile: "God created Frenchwomen for only one purpose, my friend. To be tupped. I am busy doing God's work."

"Only one purpose?" Aziz said.

263

"Exactly. French girls are the only babies born in the world who come out of their mother's womb with their legs spread. They stay that way for life. It's a shame you're missing out, Aziz. It's all Frenchwomen are good for."

"And French*men?*" Aziz asked.

Stanhope shook his head. "They are good for nothing," he said. "I don't know what God's purpose was in making them, unless it was to give the Germans moving targets for rifle practice every generation or so."

So Stanhope wandered the city while Aziz pored over the reports from Cole and eventually by worrying it to death, like a small dog with a large bone, he finally found something significant in the mass of papers.

It was a tiny thing, small and insignificant enough to be overlooked by anyone, but the more he thought about it, the more Aziz thought it might be important.

The reports said that the bureau chief of the International Press Association lived with his wife and a full-time housekeeper in a large apartment in the First Arrondissement, one of the finer sections of Paris. He had neither an answering service nor an answering machine. His hours at the office were unpredictable; often he worked late into the night while at other times he was on almost a banker's schedule, leaving early in the morning, returning in late afternoon like clockwork.

Yet the calls he received from Abu Beka's spokesman always came within an hour after he returned home from the office. He had never been called at the office; and, so far as anyone could determine, Abu Beka's spokesman had never called his home and hung up when the newsman's wife or housekeeper had answered. At least, neither of them could remember any such hangup calls, they had told investigators.

The importance of all these seemingly unimportant facts jumped into Aziz's mind one evening as he was lying on his small bed, thinking, filling the room with smoke from his vile Egyptian cigarettes.

How was it possible to be certain that the calls always came when the newsman had just returned home? It meant, to Aziz, that he was followed home from his office, and when they were sure he was there, the calls were made.

Why wait an hour, then? Why not call him within minutes of his stepping inside the door?

He tried to visualize what would happen. The editor left his office and drove home. He had his own car; that was in the reports. Somebody followed him to make sure he was going home. Who? Certainly not the man who had set himself up as Abu Beka's spokesman; that would be too dangerous. Instead, it would be an underling, some henchman who knew very little or, for reasons of zealotry, would say nothing even if apprehended.

The editor went into his home and the man

tailing him drove off somewhere to meet his boss—Abu Beka's spokesman—who then called the editor.

That would explain the timing; why it took an hour after the newsman was home for his phone to ring.

Aziz thought about it some more. There was something wrong with that scenario. What was it?

He lit another cigarette and poured himself a cup of the granular Turkish coffee that he kept warm on the back burner of the stove.

He sat at the table and looked again at the reports.

No, he thought. From the time the tail left the newsman at his home and the time the telephone call was made, an hour usually elapsed. But in that hour anything could have happened. A news editor's life was not one wrapped up in a firm schedule. At least once, in the dozen or so times he had been called by Abu Beka's spokesman, he must have had to go right out again after coming home. Perhaps his office had called. Perhaps his wife had sent him to the bakery for rolls or to the vintners for a bottle of grape. And yet he had always been home when the telephone calls came.

He read through the reports which listed, as well as could be remembered, the dates and times of the calls. Sure. There it was. One night he had come home from the office and been home for almost an hour, and then had gone out to buy himself some cigarettes. He had been gone, in all, about a half hour. Minutes after he returned home the telephone rang with a call from Abu Beka's man.

It was clear, and Aziz pounded his fist on the table triumphantly. The telephone caller was able to see whether the editor was at home or not. Aziz was sure. Certain. He was certain that it went this way:

The tail followed the editor home and then called his boss to tell him that. Then the boss, Abu Beka's spokesman, drove to near the editor's house, where he met his henchman, who told him whether or not the editor was still inside. And then the telephone call was made. And if the editor *had* gone out, the spokesman would wait until he returned before making the call.

He must call from a phone within sighting distance of the editor's house.

A pay phone.

Aziz could feel his heart pounding faster inside his chest. He wanted to wait to tell Stanhope what he had deduced. He didn't want to wait. He had to wait. He couldn't wait.

He drained the dregs of his coffee, stuffed his cigarette pack into his pocket, and went out into the Paris night.

A long, expensive cab ride took him to the editor's house. The cab ride would have been even more expensive, as the French driver thought he had a foreigner to fleece, but Aziz snapped at him in perfect colloquial French: "I don't want a fucking tour of the city. Take me where I'm going and cut the side trips."

Found out, the cab driver just smiled sheepishly but then settled down to take Aziz where he wanted to go.

After the Egyptian got out on the street a block away from the editor's house, his heart seemed to sink a little. This was Paris. There were no pay phones on the street. Paris had telephone centers where someone usually went to make a telephone call.

Feeling like a fool, feeling as if he had spent days chewing over reports for no good reason at all, Aziz walked slowly down the street in the direction of the editor's home.

And then he found it. He passed a small neighborhood tavern whose banks of small paned windows overlooked the street. He glanced inside and saw, in the back, an American-style old-fashioned telephone booth.

Instinctively he knew he had found it. But to be sure, he walked around the block several times in each direction. He found no public phone anywhere else within sighting distance of the editor's home.

He was sure that tavern was where the phone calls came from. *Les Fées Altérées*. The Thirsty Fairies. What the hell kind of name was that for a café?

Was it even possible that the tavern was the headquarters of Abu Beka's operation in France?

Aziz went inside and ordered a glass of wine. It did not seem likely. The bartender was a grizzled old Frenchman, a retired seaman most likely from the looks of the tattoos on his bare arms. The patrons were also beret-wearing Frenchmen, blue-collar workingmen by the looks of them, sitting enjoying a Saturday evening away from the wife and children.

As he sipped his wine at the bar, he noticed the certificate of ownership on the wall behind the cash register; it gave the name of a Frenchwoman as the proprietor of the establishment.

He doubted that the place served as anything more than a phone location.

He drank his wine and then another and then another in a silent celebration with himself, and then went outside and caught another cab back to his apartment.

It was almost dawn the following Monday morning when Brian Cole awoke Aziz from a sound sleep with a telephone call. Will Stanhope was not back at the apartment yet; he had called Aziz the night before and told him he had found the prize of the world, a Frenchwoman who seemed to bathe regularly, and he was spending the night with her. He would be back in the morning.

When the telephone rang, Aziz thought it was Stanhope calling to tell him he was in love and

269

going to elope to Monte Carlo, but it was Cole instead.

"Sorry to blitz you out of bed like this, but have you seen the newspapers?" Cole asked without preface.

"I turned in early last night," Aziz said.

"Well, there was a ship hijacked over the weekend. Some small crew of commandos freed the ship and strung up the hijackers in pigskins," Cole said.

Aziz was silent for a moment. He resented having missed the mission, but then he remembered that the telephone might be tapped and he said only, "I'm sure the free world is grateful to those brave men. Anybody know who they were?"

"No. Apparently their identity is still secret," Cole said. "At any rate, I think it might trigger a telephone call to the news media."

"I think it might also," Aziz said. "And I have a lead on that."

"Good," Cole said. "Anything you can tell me?"

"I think I know where the phone call is being made from," Aziz said.

"Good work. Keep in touch. I'll be waiting for your report," Cole said.

"You'll hear from me one way or the other."

"Let's hope it's not 'the other,'" Cole said as he hung up.

CHAPTER TWENTY-THREE

The bureau chief of the International Press Association left his office in the traffic-choked heart of Paris and picked up his car at a nearby parking garage.

Aziz was parked in a car across the street from the garage, and when the newsman's Renault left the garage, Aziz waited a few seconds and then pulled in several cars behind him.

It took him only a few minutes to spot the tail. There was a small black Italian sedan following in their wake, clinging grimly to the two other cars as the bureau chief expertly made his way through the narrow, twisting streets of the city.

It wouldn't do to be found out, Aziz thought, so he pulled off to the side of the road as if parking and let the black sedan move ahead of him. After a couple of other cars had gotten between them, he pulled back out in traffic and followed the other cars.

There was no doubt that the black sedan was following the bureau chief, and when the news editor pulled into the garage in his building, the black car drove on and parked a block away. Aziz had parked at the end of the bureau chief's block, and now he saw the man who had been in the black sedan walking back along the street. He was a swarthy man, dark-skinned, with a raggy, dark mustache, and Aziz felt gratified that he had been right. The man walked into the neighborhood tavern across the street from the editor's house.

Nothing to do now but wait.

Inside Les Fées Altérées, Will Stanhope sat at a table near the telephone booth. He was uncharacteristically dressed in a brown suit and was busy playing the part of the British tourist buffooning his way through a strange land.

Since Frenchmen were well known to be pleasant to anyone who might buy them a drink, he had no shortage of companions at his table, broad red-faced men from the bar who insulted the crazy Brit to one another in gutter French, not knowing that Stanhope spoke the language expertly.

Stanhope smiled, poured wine from a large jug into the glasses of three men at the table, and hoisted his own glass in a toast.

"Up your money-grubbing asses," he said in English.

The men smiled and sucked up their free drinks.

"And your metered mother's," Stanhope added

with a big farmboy grin.

The men smiled and drank some more.

The swarthy man came into the bar and walked directly to the old-fashioned phone booth in the back of the room. Will just glanced at him, then looked away. The man entered the booth and pulled the door shut tight behind him and Will depressed the button on the small tape recorder in the pocket of his jacket which hung casually from the back of his chair. A wire led from the tape recorder around the back of the phone booth, where Will had stuck a sensitive microphone, built into a suction cup, to the wood. He leaned against the booth as if overtaken by an attack of alcoholic stupor, but could not hear any conversation from inside. He glanced at his watch and noted the exact time. It was six-fourteen.

Stanhope could still hear nothing from the booth and he suspected that the middle easterner who was making the phone call probably did not have to say anything. His signal that the editor was home was no doubt just to dial a number, ring once, hang up, and call again.

Sure enough, a moment later the swarthy man left the phone booth and found a seat at the end of the bar which commanded a view of the window and the IPA bureau chief's home across the street.

Stanhope filled up the glasses at his table again, hoisted his glass in a toast, and saluted the men at the table: "In your wife's mercenary mouth," he said with a grin.

The second man walked down the street to the tavern. He was dressed like a French workingman in an open-necked shirt and wide-legged pants, but his skin was dark, his hair curly black, his lips full. Aziz put his age at forty, give or take a few years.

When the man entered the tavern, Aziz checked his watch. Six-fifty. The news editor had been home for about forty-five minutes.

Still holding drunken court at the rear table, Stanhope saw the second Arab enter the tavern. He glanced at the other swarthy man who was still seated at the end of the bar, watching the house across the street. The swarthy man nodded; and as the newcomer walked to the phone booth in the back, the other drained his glass of wine and left.

They should have had more men, Stanhope thought. Both he and Aziz would be following the newly arrived man, but if they had thought this through, they would have had another warm body around somewhere to follow the man who had just left. Stanhope did not like putting all his eggs in one basket.

When the man entered the telephone booth, Stanhope looked at his watch. Six fifty-one exactly. They had a tap on the telephone of the International Press Association man. It would be easy enough to check later to make sure that the newsman had received his call from Abu Beka's spokesman at exactly this time. If he did, it was a lock. They had the man. Stanhope reached into his pocket and turned on the small tape recorder again as the doors to the telephone booth closed tightly.

Five minutes after he entered, the full-lipped man with the black curly hair came back outside the tavern.

Aziz saw him standing on the sidewalk in front of the building. The man appeared to be casually lighting a cigarette, but Aziz knew that he was taking the opportunity to look up and down the street to see if anyone was watching him. Aziz slumped down behind the wheel of the car so he was not visible from the man's viewpoint.

Back inside the tavern, Stanhope suddenly got to his feet, reached into his pocket, and tossed a crumpled-up wad of franc notes onto the table, among the four Frenchmen who had been drinking with him.

"The idiot is leaving," one of the Frenchmen mumbled sadly under his breath.

"Not too soon either. He is such a buffoon I would surely have struck him," another said, also in French.

"Have to leave now, old friends," Stanhope said

275

in Lord Haw-Haw English. "This tip is for the bartender, although I know you savages will steal it the moment my back is turned." He smiled all around at the men. "It has truly been my pleasure. My regards to your wives when they finish their shifts at the cathouse."

The men, uncomprehending, smiled back at him, and Stanhope walked slowly across the room toward the door. Through the tavern's big windows he could see that the Arab had moved away down the block. Stanhope paused to light a cigarette, then stepped outside. To his left he saw the back of the man, seventy-five feet away, walking toward the corner.

He glanced to his right, nodded to Aziz in the car, crossed to the other side of the street, then turned left to follow the man down the street.

When the man turned the corner, Stanhope walked more quickly so he would not lose sight of him. He saw the man get into a small red sedan with French license tags. The motor started and the man pulled out into the road and started off. Stanhope jumped into the middle of the street to wave to Aziz to drive up quickly, but his partner was already coming down the block and Stanhope clambered quickly into the car.

"Down that way. He's in a red Fiat," he said.

Aziz grunted and sped off. He wanted to get close enough to be able to read the other driver's license plate. That way, if they lost him in the early evening traffic, at least they would have a chance of running him to ground again.

"What happened to the other wog?" Stanhope asked.

"He walked off in the other direction," Aziz said. "I decided to stay here with this one. We should have had another man with us."

"My thought exactly," Stanhope said. "But no sense worrying about it now. Just don't lose this bloke."

Aziz had already gotten close to the red car. There were no vehicles between them and he spoke aloud the other car's license number.

"BEI-574. Remember it if we get separated."

"BEI-574," Stanhope repeated.

"Did you get the tape recording?" Aziz asked.

"Right here," Stanhope said. He reached into his pocket, took out the small tape recorder, and rewound the tape to the beginning.

He depressed the play button. As he expected, the first Arab into the booth had merely dialed a number, let it ring, then dialed it again. They could hear clearly the first two dialings, separated by a few seconds.

"It's an old type rotary phone. I don't know if we can figure out the number he called from this tape."

"Save it," Aziz said. "The new laboratories can do anything. We'll let Brian figure it out."

The tape kept running and then a voice, speaking softly and slightly distorted by the maximum volume of the small tape recorder, spoke out in French.

Both men spoke French fluently; neither had a need to translate as the soft voice filled the car.

"This is the voice of Tenterallah, the Army of God. I speak for Abu Beka."

They could not hear anything from the other end of the conversation, from the mouth of the newsman the Arab had called.

The voice went on without pause.

"The Holy War has started. With their latest atrocities in Puerto Rico . . . on the heels of their savage assault on our men in New York and in Rome, the forces of Satan in the world have once again shown that they cannot be permitted to live. Those responsible for these savage attacks upon Islam and upon civilized people everywhere will pay the supreme price for their satanic evil. That is the promise of Tenterallah, the Army of God, and we now warn all the nations of the world: You either stand with us or you stand with Satan. If you choose to do Satan's work, none of you shall be safe.

"From this moment on, we carry the fight into the enemy's heartland. Their lives are forfeit because justice is on our side. . . .

"God is great. That is Abu Beka's statement."

There was a metallic rattle as the man had replaced the receiver on the telephone wall unit, and then a squeak as the door to the phone booth opened.

Stanhope turned off the tape recorder, rewound it, and put it back in his pocket.

"No doubt now that this wog is our wog, is there?"

"None at all," Aziz said. "We're finally breaking through to Abu Beka."

"Good. Let's just get the silly bastard before the holy war starts," Stanhope said with a chuckle, and then slumped down into the seat. The wine he had spent the afternoon consuming had put a fresh glow into his stomach and his eyes felt a little tired. He hoped this would be a long ride. Perhaps he could even take a nap.

CHAPTER TWENTY-FOUR

"How much do you think she knows?"

Petrov lounged back in his chair, a cigarette dangling from his mouth, and watched Mark Donovan carefully. The big American seemed to be moving more slowly today, and Petrov suspected that the physical exertions of the weekend rescue had roughed up a body that Donovan had allowed to get a little soft. Or was it worry about Maggie Henson . . . or guilt . . . that caused Donovan to move gingerly forward in his chair?

"I don't know," Donovan said. "I hope you'll be able to find out tonight. But my best guess is that she saw something in the news about the mystery helicopter and she thought about Maxine. So maybe you can sort of deflect her," he suggested.

Petrov nodded. "I will tell her that you and I were together over the weekend. That you helped me with a personal family problem and that you're too much of a gentleman to talk about it. She'll believe that."

"That I'm a gentleman? I don't know."

"Everybody thinks you're a perfect gentleman,"

Petrov answered with a wry smile.

"You're in rare good spirits today," Donovan said.

"It's just pleasant to get out of the office once in a while," the Russian said. "And the sea air was good for my injury. I went to the physician today and he pronounced me miraculously healed." He turned his head and brushed aside his hair to show Donovan his scalp wound. Only a thin red line was still visible. "All in all, a good day," Petrov said. Suddenly he snapped his head toward the television set which was playing quietly atop the office's serving bar. "Shhhh," he hissed sharply.

The television newscaster, a Hispanic with a face that seemed to glisten under the studio lights, was reading a news bulletin.

"This just in from our overseas bureau. Abu Beka, the head of the terrorist Tenterallah group, has issued a statement promising reprisals against the people . . . and I quote . . . responsible for this savage attack upon Islam and civilized people everywhere.

"The statement was received, as is customary, by the head of the Paris bureau of the International Press Association this morning.

"It read:

" 'The Holy War has started. With their latest atrocities in Puerto Rico . . . on the heels of their savage assault on our men in New York and in Rome, the forces of Satan in the world have once again shown that they cannot be permitted to live.

Those responsible for these savage attacks upon Islam and upon civilized people everywhere will pay the supreme price for their satanic evil. That is the promise of Tenterallah, the Army of God, and we now warn all the nations of the world: You either stand with us or you stand with Satan. If you choose to do Satan's work, none of you shall be safe.

" 'From this moment on, we carry the fight into the enemy's heartland. Their lives are forfeit because justice is on our side.'

"The statement was reported to come directly from Abu Beka, the mystery man who has headed Tenterallah for the last ten years and made it the most feared secret terrorist organization in the world," the announcer said.

"In other news . . ."

"Well, we flushed him out," Donovan said. "You happy?"

But Petrov did not answer; he had risen from his chair and gone to look out the window.

After a few moments of silence he said, "Can we get a copy of that statement?"

Donovan shrugged. "You forget, this is the United States. It'll be in this afternoon's press."

"Quite right," Petrov said, his back still turned toward Donovan. He started to speak again, but was interrupted when the telephone rang.

"Mark Donovan."

Petrov turned, perched on the windowsill, and watched the American.

Donovan nodded his head toward him and said into the phone, "Yeah, Brian. What's up?"

He listened for a while, then said, "Great. Stay on it. How you feeling, by the way?" A pause and a smile. "Good. Petrov sends his love." Donovan grinned again as he replaced the receiver.

"Cole finally reached Aziz and Stanhope last night," he told Petrov. "They're in Paris and Aziz thought they might have a lead on Abu Beka's press statements. So with this statement just coming in, maybe we'll track down this bastard yet."

"That's what we're getting paid for," Petrov said. He came back and resumed his seat in the chair facing Donovan's desk. "He's made a mistake, Mark."

"Abu Beka?"

Petrov nodded. "His statement. He talked about the atrocities in Rome and Puerto Rico and New York."

"Yeah?"

"You know of any atrocities in New York?" Petrov said.

Donovan looked at him for a moment, then smiled as he understood.

"Right," Petrov said. "He's just confirmed that the two men I . . . those two mugging victims . . . were his men. That's something we didn't know for sure until now. That's a mistake."

"His first. Let's hope not his last. Christ, I'd love to nail this freak."

Petrov nodded. "One other thing . . . did you notice anything about that Tenterallah statement?"

"You mean the implied threat to the United Nations? All the nations of the world have to stand with them or with Satan?" He nodded.

Petrov was impressed; he had not thought Donovan subtle enough to recognize the threat in Abu Beka's statement. "If the U.N. decides to go ahead with some kind of antiterrorist proclamation, as your friend suggests, there may be trouble brewing. I think you should get hold of your police lieutenant and have him put some heat on Fazid at the restaurant."

"Why?" Donovan asked.

"Just to keep the pressure on. Abu Beka has made one mistake. Who knows? Maybe he cracks with tension. Maybe he'll make more. Let's find out. And Fazid is a liar. Maybe he knows something useful."

Even while he was speaking, Donovan was reaching for the telephone.

Lieutenant Robert Mendoza had not enjoyed a lunch this much in a long time—perhaps not since the luncheon party held after the christening of his son twenty years earlier when he got a chance to see all his relatives from Puerto Rico for the first time since he was a child.

After Donovan's call he went to El Fazid's with his partner, Gas Sullivan, and two health inspectors for the city. The proprietor had remembered the two policemen and had nervously seated them at a table right in front of the club's tiny dance floor, where a young girl from Guatemala was busily gyrating to mock middle-eastern music.

Mendoza ordered shish kebab, Sullivan the couscous, and the health inspectors had roast lamb with side dishes of humus and greens.

Fazid had hovered near the table during lunch, and when the plates had been cleared, hustled over. To him, so much time passing without trouble had been a good sign. He rubbed his hands together and rocked back and forth from his heels to his soles, and asked, "And how is everything over here at this table?" He tried to sound casual, as if it were a question he asked every diner every day.

Mendoza looked at the two health inspectors whose names were Bailey and Manidatta. "I give up," he said. "How is everything here?"

Manidatta, a slight East Indian with coal-black hair, silky brown skin, and a singsong accent, shook his head.

"Everything is not as it appears. Perhaps, I am not sure, you understand, but perhaps this lamb once pulled a cab in Central Park."

"What?" Fazid gasped, and stopped rocking. "The only connection that lamb ever had with Central Park is that its fleece was woolly as the snow that covers the park in winter. That lamb was never a horse. It was always a lamb."

He looked around at all the faces, searching for a hint of the joke, some expression of mouth or eye that would let him know it was okay to chuckle and join in the fun, but the four faces staring at him were as blank as fresh-painted gypsum board.

After an awkward silence Fazid chuckled anyway and said, "And besides, the city says you can sell horsemeat in restaurants. But that's a lamb."

Manidatta folded his arms across his chest. "Oh, yes," he warbled. "One may sell horsemeat. But only if it is labeled as such and the consumer is informed of same. On this greasy menu—" he pointed to the menus stacked on another table—"this consumer is not informed. Bailey, my dear girl. Do you have any comments? Did not that meal remind you of something you once bet on at Aqueduct?"

Bailey, who was fifty-two years old but still loved the way Manidatta called her "dear girl," snapped, "I wouldn't bet on anything that ran slow enough for this butcher to catch it."

She rose and removed her health inspector's badge from her purse and showed it to Fazid.

"Now, if you'll excuse me a moment, I have to look at the ladies' room. And then the men's. Perhaps, Manidatta, you will be kind enough to look at the kitchen. Check carefully for rat droppings. The humus was particularly pungent."

"My thoughts exactly," Manidatta said, and as Bailey strode away, he rose also. "There are problems with this job, I tell you," he said to Fazid. "Nobody likes to close restaurants, you understand? I'm sure you do. But someone must watch out for those who cannot tell a lamb from a horse." He wandered off in the direction of the kitchen, and Fazid slumped into his vacant chair, staring at Mendoza, then Sullivan, then Mendoza again.

"You can't mean this. Horsemeat? Never. I'll be ruined."

Mendoza leaned forward and spoke softly. "That's only the beginning. That so-called belly dancer. She's from Guatemala and she's only sixteen years old. She doesn't have a green card."

"She isn't. She does." Fazid was about to faint.

Sullivan leaned forward. "I hear she gives blow jobs in her dressing room too."

"And deals in crack," Mendoza said.

"No, no, no." Fazid wiped his brow. "This is all threats. I will call my lawyer. Sue you for false arrest."

"Who said anything about arrest? Did I?" Sullivan looked blankly at Mendoza. "Did I?"

"Nope," Mendoza said. "Me neither."

Sullivan leaned forward and his nose almost touched Fazid's. The restaurant owner blinked and Sullivan said, "Who's going to be arrested? You? That girl going down on customers in the back? Everyone in this place? Maybe a violent raid for trafficking in drugs and serving rat shit in your rice and having horsemeat in your freezer? An arrest like that might destroy the whole restaurant. So who said

287

anything about anything like that?"

Fazid's shrewd eyes noted that even though the conversation had been held at low sound levels, several customers had already gotten the gist of it and had signaled to the waiters for the checks. The fat man sighed and said, "Okay. What do you want from me?"

Mendoza smiled. "I knew you'd understand," he said.

CHAPTER TWENTY-FIVE

Maggie Henson had gone home to her quiet apartment after leaving the office. She had knocked on the door of Carol's room, got no answer, and opened the door just enough to see that her daughter was not in bed. Carol must have gone out, she thought.

She walked to her own room, climbed into her bed, and was asleep almost immediately. She woke up in a small panic, remembering that she had promised to have dinner with Tolly Peterson, but she was reassured when she saw by the clock that it was barely 6:30 P.M.

Plenty of time to shower and dress — if she didn't dawdle along the way.

She was just finishing her makeup, when the doorbell rang and she buzzed Tolly upstairs.

Petrov said, "Rest agrees with you. You look like a million dollars."

"I was hoping more for a million pounds sterling," Maggie said.

"That too," Tolly agreed casually, but reminding

289

himself that he had to be careful around this woman who might or might not suspect what they were up to. "Shall we off?"

Maggie nodded and walked toward the door, but then stopped.

"What's the matter?" Petrov said.

"Carol. I was just wondering if she might have left me a note before she went out. I'll just be a second."

She walked back down the hallway toward the living room, and Petrov watched appreciatively. Some women, he thought, just knew how to walk sexily, while others galumphed along. It was the difference between a sports car and a tractor; both got you there efficiently enough, but he had always had a weakness for sports cars in women.

He had very little time to pursue the pleasant idea because suddenly Maggie screamed and Petrov ran down the hall toward the open bedroom door on the far side of the living room.

Maggie was behind the bed, crouching over her daughter, who was unconscious on the floor. Carol was wearing only a thin satin nightgown, and Petrov noted, almost professionally, that one of her breasts was exposed and there were bruises around the nipple.

He pushed Maggie aside and took the young woman in his arms. Expertly, he felt for the pulse in her neck and then put his face close to hers to hear her breathe.

"She's breathing all right," he said, "and her pulse is strong. I wonder what . . ."

Before he could finish, Maggie snapped, "I know what." She picked up a medicine bottle from the floor. The empty lid lay alongside it.

"Tranquilizers," she said. "She's overdosed on tranquilizers." Her voice rose in pitch and Petrov reached out and touched her wrist.

"Don't worry. She'll be all right," he promised, then lifted her easily onto the bed and walked toward the telephone.

Mark Donovan snatched up the telephone at his apartment, expecting to hear Bobby Mendoza's voice but instead heard Tilda Matthews.

"I wanted to thank you for the flowers," she said.

"Oh, I'm glad you got them and I was really sorry that I had to run out like that. It was rotten but necessary."

There was a moment's pause as Tilda obviously was considering Mark's statement. Then she said, "Yeah, it was. Rotten, I mean. I was real upset until the flowers came. I thought that perhaps I'd made a mistake. The flowers made it all okay again."

"Good," Donovan said. "I'm sorry and I've just been swamped with work. How's Daniel?"

"Coming home after the movies tonight," she said. "Tell me, are you alone?"

"I'm so alone it hurts," Donovan said.

"I figure a cab from there to here might soothe the hurts," she said.

He thought for a moment of Bobby Mendoza, thought of missing the policeman's call, remembered that he had Mendoza's home number and could call himself, and said, "I'll be there in fifteen minutes."

Later, after they had made love, Mark Donovan slept like a well-fed dog. Tilda stayed awake, watching the male animal next to her by the dim light from the half-closed bathroom door. If she wasn't careful, she thought, she could get very possessive about this man.

Petrov sat with Maggie Henson in the visitor's lounge at St. Vincent's Hospital, waiting, even though she had told him that it was not his responsibility and she would not think worse of him if he left.

"Nonsense," he said.

"Why should you stay?"

He gave her what she had come to regard as his semi-amused look; it hit only his eyes, and his mouth was serious as he said, "Because you need me. And anyway, after I got mugged, didn't you give me soup?"

"Yeah. Soup and a hassle."

Petrov lit a cigarette, puffed it, and when he saw Maggie looking enviously at the smoke, lit another and handed it to her.

"You didn't hassle me," he said. "The way I like to remember it is that the lady wanted to sleep with me."

"So why didn't it happen?" she asked.

He took a long time answering. "I have a once-in-a-while sexual dysfunction. I wanted to have a chance to talk about it with you first."

Maggie considered that and said, "I thought perhaps that you were gay."

"I'm not. Trust me."

Maggie was silent for a moment. Since Carol's father, there had been many men in her sex life, all of them encounters that had left her emptier than before. Even without sex she did not feel that way with Tolly Peterson. "Things are going along pretty well," she said. "Why don't we just leave them alone?"

"Good idea."

"And where the hell is that doctor?"

As if he had been waiting for a cue, the doctor stepped out into the hall. He was a young intern with a name tag that read Dr. Koehler and the stance he took in front of them showed that he disapproved of them.

"You'd better do something about that daughter of yours. She almost killed herself tonight. Naturally, she says it wasn't on purpose. She says she doesn't do drugs often, but she's got a lot of pop marks on her skin that call her a liar. Have you two thought about treatment for her?"

293

"You tell me how to get her into treatment and I'll do it," Maggie said.

"I'm not in the counseling business," the intern said.

"I think that's about enough," Petrov said as he rose to his feet. "If you've got any concrete suggestions for Mrs. Henson, make them. But keep the badgering to yourself."

Dr. Koehler slumped. "Sorry. Had a couple of ODs tonight and I just never understand young people trying to kill themselves. There's some literature at the nurses' station. A good clinic out in Long Island. Check it out. And don't believe your daughter anymore. She's a heavy user, and users are liars."

"Can I see her?"

Koehler shook his head. "No, she's sleeping it off now and she'll have round-the-clock care. She won't wake up until morning. But, honestly, she'll be all right. Just go home and go to bed."

Maggie found her hand inside Petrov's and squeezed it intimately.

"I'll do just that, Doctor," she said.

Walking home from the hospital, Petrov told her that he had had some personal family problems over the weekend and that Donovan had thrown away his own weekend to help Petrov solve them. Then Petrov put his arm around her as if to shield her from the night air. "Forget my problems; they're minor. Is there anything I can do to help you?" he asked.

"I don't think so, Tolly. You've done a lot already." Maggie shivered despite the arm. "The doctor says not to believe Carol. Fat chance. I take one look at those baby blues and I think of her as a child. Her sixth birthday party, days at the beach, walks in the park, her first pomegranate, you know, those kid kind of things."

"I do know," Petrov said. "I feel the same way about my niece. She's blond, hazel-eyed and so smart her brain could start a fire. She's got an attachment to a stuffed rabbit I gave her five years ago. Every time I think of her, all I see is a baby holding that rabbit. When she's twenty five and in the space program, I'll still think of her with that rabbit."

"Space program?" Maggie murmured. "I didn't realized that England had one."

"None to speak of at the moment," Petrov answered immediately. "But if she has anything to say about it, they will when she's twenty-five or else she'll come to this country."

"What's her name?" Maggie asked.

"Ma—" Petrov was going to have to watch himself. What was there about this woman that made his defenses slacken? "Marsha," he said. There. That was a proper British name. Masha would have been hard to explain.

They were at her apartment building. "Would you like to come up for a drink?"

Petrov hesitated. "No. That is, I would, but I

295

think it's been a long enough night for you. It's after two in the morning."

"Would you like to come up and sleep with me?" she said boldly.

"Even more than I'd like a drink," Petrov said. "But same reason. Rain check?"

"For you, always," she said.

They stood on her stoop, looking at each other for a moment. Just before Petrov turned away, Maggie said, "Tolly, listen."

"Yes?"

"I don't know if you and Mark are up to something."

He opened his mouth to protest, but before he could, she said, "And I don't care what you may or may not be up to. It's none of my business and I know when to butt out. I just wanted to tell you that."

"Thank you," he said. "But we're not up to anything. Nothing at all."

She nodded at him, unconvinced, then smiled and let herself into her apartment building. When she turned and looked back, Petrov was still on the steps watching her.

Donovan felt himself shoved roughly in the bed. Tilda's voice crackled in his ear, "Hurry up. Wake up."

He groaned and stretched. "This is a fine how-do-you-do," he said. "Is this the way the rest of my life's going to be?"

"Only if you pick what's behind door number one," she said. She tickled his chest. "Come on, Daniel's coming home and I thought it would be better if you were in a vertical position when you met him the first time."

He grabbed her and pulled her down to him. "How long's he going to be?" he said.

"Twenty minutes."

"I can be done by then," he said.

"*I* can't," she giggled. "So get up."

Donovan showered and dressed quickly, then went into Tilda's small bedroom office to call Bobby Mendoza at home. When Jenny answered, he said cheerily, "Hi, big belly. Is Bobby home? Mark Donovan."

She chattered away for a couple of minutes about their son, Robert Junior, and how well he was doing at MIT, before giving her husband the phone.

"It's Mark. Sorry, I was out of touch."

"That's okay, gringo," the police officer said. "I just wanted to tell you we're making steady, if not spectacular, progress."

For a moment Donovan thought about telling Mendoza the truth that his investigation now was just an exercise in wheel-spinning. The two Arab bodyguards were dead and the man they had worked for, Hussein Ayoub, was dead too. There was nothing left for Mendoza to be investigating. Then he

297

remembered what Petrov had said about letting the cop keep stirring the pot and he decided to keep his own counsel, even if he did feel some guilt about it. Mendoza was an old friend and deserved better treatment.

But all Donovan said was, "Oh, really?"

"Yeah. We put some heat today on Fazid and so he finally remembered that maybe our two deceased friends had been in his restaurant earlier. And maybe he heard them talking once about being in the wheelchair business."

"The wheelchair business?" Donovan said. Of all the dead ends . . .

"Yeah. So, Gas and I are checking out wheelchair companies. If there's a fit, we'll find it. End of report. You got anything to tell me?"

Donovan heard the front door and then Tilda in the other room, squealing with delight. Daniel must be home.

"I don't think so," Donovan said cautiously. What was Mendoza driving at? It wasn't like him to ask questions just to make conversation.

"You told me once to check out Hussein Ayoub," Mendoza reminded him. "Well, I was doing that and now he's dead. He was killed in that ship hijacking over the weekend. That's what I told Fazid . . . his fucking around with me got a ship hijacked and six men killed, including Ayoub. You know about that, of course."

"I might have read something about it in the

298

papers, Bobby," Donovan said. He felt miserable, to be a good spy one had to enjoy lying, and it was a knack he had never picked up.

He could feel a chill in Mendoza's voice. "Well, I'm sure, Captain, that if there's anything to tell, you'll tell me."

"Count on it," Donovan said, and as the policeman grunted and hung up, Donovan thought, *Yeah, count on me to lie to you. Just like I've lied to Maggie and Tilda and now you. What the hell am I doing in this work? Yeah, you can count on me.*

Donovan's dark spirit fled when he walked out into the other room and saw young Daniel Matthews standing in front of his mother. The six-year-old had flaming red hair and looked like all the Dead End Kids rolled up into one.

He was emptying his pockets onto the table and Donovan paused in the doorway, thinking he had not seen such a marvelous collection of junk since his own childhood. There were two marbles, one of them broken in half, a silver police-style whistle, and the mirrored reflector cap from an old flashlight.

Tilda saw him in the doorway, grinning, and said, "Come on in, Mark, and meet my son. He's just showing me some of the treasures he's collected in the last couple of days. My boy, the pack rat."

Daniel looked embarrassed as he turned toward

299

Donovan, and Tilda said, "Daniel, this is Mr. Donovan."

"You can call me Mark," Donovan said.

"Okay," the boy said.

"If I can call you Champ."

"All right. That's a good name," the boy said. He advanced on Mark and seemed to reach almost straight up to shake the tall man's hand.

"Mark brought you a present," Tilda said, and brought from under the table the paper bag containing the Noah's ark that Donovan had purchased at the United Nations gift shop.

When Daniel saw all the small animals, he exclaimed, "Wow," and opened the box to spill them all on the floor. In two minutes he had forgotten that either his mother or the tall stranger were in the room.

Tilda looked at Donovan and said softly, "I think you've made a hit."

Donovan grinned, but thought sourly, *Yeah, until I start lying to him too.*

CHAPTER TWENTY-SIX

"In early today," Donovan said. "How's Carol? Tolly told me about it."

Maggie Henson was at her desk, looking at her boss standing in the doorway. When she answered, her voice was tired.

"I went back to the hospital this morning," she said. "I couldn't sleep. She's out of danger but in danger, if you know what I mean."

Donovan came around and sat on the edge of Maggie's desk. He put his hands on her shoulders and squeezed them in a friendly way.

"Listen," he said. "I know your mind's not going to be into work today. Why don't you take off? Go home or back to the hospital or whatever? We'll get somebody to fill in here. You take your time about coming back. We'll get along."

She searched his face and saw there only the concern and warmth that came from real friendship, and then suddenly her body was racked with sobs as all the tension of the past weeks slipped by her guard. She began to weep.

301

"Oh, Mark. I don't know what to do. Carol's on drugs bad."

"First things first," Donovan said. He was not used to seeing Maggie cry and had always regarded her somehow as strong beyond tears. "Let's get Carol well, and then I think you ought to put her in a place to get her dried out good and proper."

"The doctor mentioned a clinic on Long Island."

Donovan nodded. "Right. Well, send her there. Get her straightened out. It goes without saying that you don't have to think about the cost."

She reached her hands up and squeezed his, even as they rested on her shoulders.

"Every working girl should have one like you," she said. She paused. "You think it would help?"

He shrugged. "It's your best chance. You can't go on this way, and you have to give Carol a chance to straighten herself out." A thought popped unbidden into his mind. "And you too. You need a rest. I had this idea about taking everybody, my kids, Tolly, Tilda and her boy, up to the Pittsburgh house at the end of this week. I want you to come. You'll have Carol in the clinic and you can use the change of scenery. It'll be good to get away for a few days."

"Mark, I don't know . . ." she started.

"Well, I do. Jeff and Christine would hate Pittsburgh if Aunt Maggie wasn't there. You're coming and that's that. Now, go on, get out of here and stop worrying. We'll talk tomorrow. Don't worry about anything except Carol getting well."

302

Carol smiled sweetly at Rafjan Hassan. As soon as her mother had left that morning and Carol no longer had to look her worst, she had sweet-talked a male orderly into buying makeup for her at the hospital gift shop, then fixed her face as best she could before calling Hassan at home to tell him where she was.

Now he was here, standing alongside her bed, and she knew she did not look her best, but she had tried. She wanted him to like her, to want her, and she studied her fingertips, then showed them to him.

"Look, they're all chipped. I can't wait to get out of here and get to a manicurist. These fingers are good for nothing," she said, but as she sat on the edge of the bed, she reached over and stroked him through his gray woven silk slacks and said, "Well, maybe not for nothing."

Hassan smiled. "Ah, Carol. You're beautiful as always. Exquisite. I have never felt like this before about anyone. You must believe me."

She did not like his voice. It was soft and oily, just like his body, and she did not like that much either. But he had other qualities, foremost among which was an unending supply of drugs.

"I do believe you," she said. "I know you want what's best for me. And what would be best for me right now would be something to relieve the tension."

Hassan bent forward. He smiled and showed Carol

a Quaalude that was nipped between his teeth.

"Give me a kiss," he said. He leaned over, put his lips on hers, and Carol slid her tongue into his mouth, found the capsule, and lapped it back into her own mouth, then lay back and swallowed.

She rubbed his groin again. "I can't wait till I get out of here," she said. "I'll do more than rub you."

"You always do," he said. "Tell me. When we were talking yesterday, you told me something about a magazine or something? You were not really coherent. I did not understand."

"Not a magazine." Carol snuggled back in her pillow. "Maxine. It's a helicopter that Donovan's been working on. My mother's boss. It sounded like the one that was used the other day with the ship hijacking. A powerful helicopter, you know."

She felt the drug start to take effect. She knew her eyelids were beginning to droop, but she felt alive, vibrant, warm, and comfortable. "It's one that my mother told me about once and we were watching the news Sunday night and heard about the helicopter and she said 'Maxine.' Donovan is real proud of it, like the plane can do dishes and everything, and . . . I'm sorry, I'm starting to feel real sleepy."

Hassan kissed her full on the lips, tongued her mouth but then realized that she was asleep because there was no response. He did not care much. In fact, he liked it that way. And sometimes the other way, with a naked body squirming and squealing under him because he had inflicted too much pain. He especially liked it when he had inflicted the pain and they had passed out. Maxine? An experimental helicopter owned by that rich man, Mark Donovan? And maybe being lent to some government agency to fight hijackers? He thought that this thing about Maxine might be important information.

He stood up and looked at Carol. She looked angelic now, asleep, a faint smile on her lips. But there was nothing angelic about her. She was a devil in bed, as depraved as Hassan was, wanting hurt as much as he liked to give it. He had some new games to play with her, and he wanted her out of the hospital soon.

He reached down, touched her nipple through her thin hospital nightgown, and squeezed it as hard as he could. Her only response was to lick her lips sensuously. He smiled. She loved pain.

"Hi, Tilda." Donovan was grateful he had not gotten her answering machine.

"Did you really mean it about this weekend?" she said breathlessly, her husky voice teasing Donovan's ears. "Daniel's packing already. He's crazy about you, you know, especially now that he knows you're a pilot. He wonders if your kids would think he's a sissy if he wore his Doctor Dentons with ducks on them."

"No, you know young teenagers. They'd like to wear them themselves, and they think it's cute when

305

somebody gets away with it. Hell, I think I'd look real cute in them too. My feet always get cold in bed."

"I noticed," she said.

"Ha. You're the only warm-footed woman I know."

"I'll take that as a compliment."

"Dinner tonight?"

"No," she said. "The vice president's coming to town and I want to go to the press conference and then the dinner where he's speaking. It's a bore, but I want to do a cartoon on it by tomorrow." She sounded suddenly impatient to get off the phone. "Look. How about tomorrow night? I've got cartoons camera-ready now for the rest of the week and all I've got to worry about is next Monday. I think I'll do something about Kaddafi getting his ears pierced by the Ayatollah. What do you think?"

"That's political?" he said. The more he talked to her, the less he understood what political cartoons today were supposed to mean.

"It's like jazz, baby," she said. "If you don't know, I can't tell you. Talk tomorrow. I can't think and talk at the same time."

She hung up before Donovan could. He sat, thinking about her, then shuffled papers around on his desk until he got a paper cut. None of the phones in his office had rung since he had gotten back from lunch, and then he remembered telling Maggie's replacement that he did not want any calls. Donovan depressed the buzzer to the outer office.

Maggie Henson answered. "Yes, boss."

"You're back. What are you doing here?"

She clicked off the phone and came inside with a pad in her hand. She looked tired; there were huge circles under her saucer eyes that had always reminded Donovan of a brown velvet gown his mother used to wear. Her hair was raked as if her fingers had walked through it. She slumped in the chair opposite his desk.

"Tell me about it. You go to the hospital?"

"Yeah. Business first. Pittsburgh called. There's some problem with a load of wheels not fitting right and Sadie Longshore called with an invite to a dinner tonight where the vice president is speaking. Nothing else I can't handle."

"Why do I feel like I'm listening to a computerized voice?" he said.

"Just running on memory," she said.

"And Carol?"

"I saw her at the hospital. She seems to be getting better. I think this time she may go to the clinic," Maggie said.

"When will she be out?"

"Tomorrow. With luck."

"Then you make those clinic arrangements and that's that. And pack for the weekend in Pittsburgh."

"I'll think about it," she said.

CHAPTER TWENTY-SEVEN

It had been more than an hour earlier that Bobby Mendoza had first noticed the man sitting on a hard-backed chair in the small waiting area outside the detectives' offices and now, after an hour's hunting and pecking to typewrite a report, he looked up and saw the man still sitting there.

The man was slight, with darkly tanned vacationers' skin and restless eyes that were long-lashed and looked almost as if the man wore eyeliner.

Mendoza walked to the doorway and nodded to the man.

"Are you waiting for someone?" he asked.

"Lieutenant Mendoza?"

The policeman nodded and the man said softly, "I wanted to talk to you. If you had a moment."

Mendoza shrugged. "Sorry, nobody told me you were waiting." He gestured the man inside his office and quickly pushed aside the scraps of food from the meal he had just eaten at his desk. The first thing to go when you worked hard on a case was your diet.

He had grumbled about that to his wife the night

before and wondered out loud why he was working so hard on this, just because Donovan had asked him to. "Vietnam is over," he had said.

But Jenny had said, "Friendship is never over, Bobby. Stop acting like an idiot."

He had looked up at her in surprise and she said, "I see through you like a pane of glass, Mr. Lieutenant. First of all, you're feeling guilty because you're not spending any time at home here with me and me being preggers and all. And you're wondering how much longer I'm going to stand for it. So you come in grumbling because you want me to say that if it's for Mark Donovan, you should keep doing what you're doing and then you won't feel guilty anymore. So consider it said. Donovan is a special friend and so what if I don't get enough of your powerful virile body for a while. I'll make up for it later on."

"Sometimes I thank God you're not a criminal," Mendoza had said. "I'd never outsmart you."

"Remember that," she giggled, and plumped down onto his lap with her big pregnant body and they sat there, feeling the movement of life inside her belly.

"So what can I do for you?" Mendoza asked the man.

The man seemed shy and now he shrugged. "I don't know if it's important."

"Well, sit down and tell me. Let's start at the beginning. Try your name."

"My name is Castelnuevo. Gaspar Castelnuevo." He saw the food scraps on the desk and said, "You

309

were eating. Perhaps I should wait?"

"No, Mr. Castelnuevo, you've waited long enough. Go ahead, please."

Mendoza sat down again behind the desk.

"I run a wheelchair factory in the Bronx named Wheels. A family business. I read today in the *News* that you are investigating two murders last week and that you thought the men might have been in the wheelchair business?"

"That's right. Did you know them?"

"I don't know." He paused a moment. "Today's paper did not carry the men's names, and I was away on vacation when this happened . . . when was it, last week?" Mendoza nodded. "But I had two men working as salesmen for me for a while and . . . I don't know . . . maybe I'm wasting your time being here."

Mendoza went to a file folder on his desk and opened it. "The two dead men's names were Jacques Boule and Ferdinand Deladier. They ring a bell?"

At the mention of the two names, the little man crossed himself fervently and closed his eyes a moment as if speaking a prayer. Then he nodded.

"Those were their names," he said.

Mendoza sat down and looked at Castelnuevo. "What can you tell me about them?" he asked.

"Not very much, I'm afraid," the man said with a sigh. "They came to my plant in the Bronx about two months ago and asked me for work. I put them on as salesmen on commission. They were in for a couple

310

of days and then they never showed up again. They never sold a wheelchair and I never paid them anything," he said.

"Is that ordinary?" Mendoza asked. "To hire people without recommendations or references?"

The manufacturer shrugged his narrow shoulders. "Sometimes. Salesmen are hard to come by. You know, it depends on the economy. So if people come in and say they can sell your product and that they have contacts and will work on commission, who is hurt by giving them a chance?"

"And that's what happened here?"

Castelnuevo nodded.

"These contacts they said they had. What kind of contacts were they?" Mendoza asked.

"Maybe it was just talk. They said they were close to French organizations in the city. As I say, I didn't know . . . I thought . . . maybe I should not have hired them."

Mendoza saw perspiration start to bead on the man's forehead and said, "No, no, Mr. Castelnuevo. No one's implying you did anything wrong. I'm just trying to check out everything. Did these men strike you as actual Frenchmen? I'm beginning to get the impression that maybe they were Arabs."

"I don't know. Their names were French and when they spoke to each other, they spoke French," Castelnuevo said.

"Would you recognize Arabic if you heard it spoken?" Mendoza asked.

311

"In New York, you hear every language sooner or later. Yes, I think I would have recognized Arabic." The man wiped his forehead with a handkerchief, then reached into his pocket. "I checked my files at the office and I had their addresses written down. Here it is." He handed Mendoza a piece of paper with an address on East Ninety-eighth Street in Manhattan.

"Thank you. I appreciate that. We'll check it out."

"I just want to say, Lieutenant, that I'm impressed at all the effort the police department is going through in this case. We hear so much about tax money wasted, but . . . well, it's nice to know that our police department is on the job." He seemed embarrassed at his display of civic affection and said almost offhandedly, "Well, I just wanted to say that."

"And you say the men were at your plant for just a couple of days and then left and never came back?"

"That's right."

"And that was two months ago?"

Gaspar Castelnuevo nodded.

"I want to thank you for coming forward," Mendoza said. "Perhaps you've made our job easier."

"I hope so," the man said, and rose quickly from his chair, as if eager to get out of the police station.

Donovan was watching the television in his office when the phone rang. There had been no further word from Abu Beka and the Tenterallah, and news commentators were now beginning to speculate on what the radical group might be planning.

"Donovan," he said.

"Mark, this is Bobby. I may have a little lead on our two dead friends."

"Oh? What's that?"

"I heard from some guy today, some wheelchair manufacturer in the Bronx. He said they worked for him for a while as salesmen. But he didn't know anything about their being Arabs. Anyway, he gave me their home address. I'm going to check it out and I'll keep you posted."

While he still had the phone in his hand, Donovan called Sadie Longshore, whose secretary answered the phone with a pinched-nose upper-upper accent. But then Sadie came on the line with her usual blowsy rat-catching voice. "Mark!" she screamed. "Where have you been? Are you going to that dinner with me?"

"I don't know. I think I may have to work."

"Not the way I hear it, Chuckles. I hear from Tilda that you asked her out and she said no. And now she's going to be at this dinner and I thought you could surprise her. What the hell, Mark, you going to let the first nice lady you were ever with get away from you?"

Donovan chuckled. From his desk he could see the closet where he knew a tuxedo and dress accessories were hanging.

"It's tempting," he said. "Tell me, are they going to

313

have those orange and red cheese balls with nuts stuck in them?"

"You'd better believe it. And Ritz crackers too."

"I'll see you there, Sadie."

Mendoza decided to stop by the address on East Ninety-eighth Street on his way home.

With his luck, the place the two "French" salesmen said they lived was probably a fleabag hotel, he thought, but he reached Ninety-eighth Street and followed the street all the way to the end, looking out the window, searching for numbers on the old brownstones that had been carved into apartments. Kids played in the street in the warm night and the evening was racked by the shrieks from their game playing.

He reached the end of the block, where the street dead-ended up against the East Side Highway.

No such number. It was a fake. The two salesmen had given Castelnuevo a phony address. To go with their obviously phony names, he thought.

He turned around the block and started home. He was disappointed; he at last had thought that he would have some information for Mark Donovan, something worthwhile, and he had come up empty again. And he didn't know how many other leads he had to follow before everything in this case had dried up.

As he turned back onto First Avenue and headed north, he was filled with his thoughts and did not notice the car that had parked on First Avenue pull out into traffic and follow him.

Sadie Longshore had gone to the ladies' room and Mark Donovan was standing alone when he heard a familiar voice alongside him whispering.

"I'm so glad," the woman said. "I told my boy-friend I had to work tonight but I was so horny I had to come out. And now I've met you. How lucky I am."

Mark turned to look at Tilda. She was wearing a deep-plunging purple dress. Her red hair was piled in light spilling curls on the top of her head and the freckles around her brownish-red-lipsticked mouth stood out like an invitation. Donovan said, "Boy, the same thing happened to me with this creepy woman I'm hanging around with. Do you think this meeting was arranged in heaven?"

She leaned close to him and said, "Come home with me, sailor boy, and you'll think it's heaven."

"Where's Daniel?" he asked.

"I pressed the family into baby-sitting duty again. The place is ours . . . all ours."

"And I think that's my cue to leave." They both turned and saw Sadie Longshore standing behind them; she winked at them and left them both laughing.

315

Mendoza parked his car in the driveway alongside his house and, as he always did as he got out of the car, he paused to look around. He saw a dark green Ford going down the street past his house. The car looked familiar. Had he seen it while he was driving home?

The car did not slow up, and when Mendoza got into the middle of the street to look after the car, it was already turning the corner a block away, too far for him to notice its license plate.

When the dinner was over and they had tried not to snore through the vice president's speech, Tilda and Mark let Sadie off at the entrance to her Park Avenue apartment.

They went back to Tilda's place and were barely in the door when both of them were naked and on the floor.

"I'm glad you came tonight," she said.

"Not yet, not yet," Donovan joked as he pulled her into his arms.

There was only one message with his answering service and Donovan called Mendoza's number in the Bronx. Through the open door he could see Tilda sleeping, still naked, on the sofa.

"Bobby, Mark. What's up?"

"Sorry, boss. Just wanted to tell you that the

address I had on those two stiffs turned out to be a fake. Thought you'd want to know."

"Whoever said a policeman's lot was not a happy one wasn't just talking out his ass," Donovan said.

CHAPTER TWENTY-EIGHT

"You're going to have to get some help."

Maggie Henson stood with her daughter at curbside in front of St. Vincent's Hospital, waiting to catch a cab.

"The hospital told me about a clinic on Long Island that's had a tremendous success rate," she went on.

"Long Island? But that's so far away from—" Carol was about to say her friends and Rafjan Hassan, but she paused a moment and said, "From you."

"Perhaps that's just as well," Maggie snapped as they stepped into a cab. The vehicle smelled of cigar smoke. "I baby you too much. I let you pretend you're working at this modeling business, but I know you're not."

Tears welled up in Carol's eyes and she sniffed. She saw her reflection in the driver's rearview mirror and thought she looked properly repentant. She waited to speak until her mother had given the driver their home address.

"I don't want to be away from you," Carol finally said. She dabbed at her eyes with the back of her hand, careful not to smear her makeup.

"Please don't do that," Maggie said softly. Carol's eyes were lined with red and she had strain marks around her mouth. If Maggie had not known Carol was a stinking actress, she would not have believed it for a moment. Carol kept crying and finally Maggie said, "Listen, darling. There's a day clinic in the Village that I think I can get you into. But you have to go there every single day and talk to a counselor."

"Oh, Mommy, thank you. I promise. Just don't send me away."

The two women were silent until they were at the door of the apartment, where a large wicker basket of lilies, Gerber daisies, irises, and baby's breath was propped against the door. Carol snatched off the cellophane and rooted roughly around in the flowers for the card. Rafjan Hassan was very extravagant, she thought. And generous. She did not immediately find the card, and when Maggie got the door open Carol carried the basket inside, popped it onto a table, and searched through the baby's breath while Maggie poured herself a drink. For a moment she thought it was probably not a good idea to be drinking in front of Carol, but then she knew she was not addicted to alcohol and anyway, she would prefer a drinking problem in herself to what Carol suffered from.

Her daughter found the card finally, read it swiftly, and her face reddened. "These aren't for me, Mommy. They're for you. Who is this person?" Maggie realized that the flush on her daughter's cheeks was not from embarrassment, but from anger. Carol's eyes seemed to flash a brighter blue as she demanded, "Who is this Tolly person?"

"Tolly Peterson, not person." Maggie made the effort of a small joke but Carol did not seem to find it humorous. She dropped the card onto the coffee table and as Maggie went to pick it up, she wondered why her daughter was so selfish. Was it the illegitimacy of her birth that made her want to grasp on to more and more tangible objects? To rate her life by her possessions? She stared at Carol for a moment, annoyed with her insensitivity, but wordlessly assessing her. She saw a beautiful young woman with incredibly smooth and shiny peach skin that contrasted so well with her dark hair and bright blue eyes. Cornflower blue.

Maggie picked up the card. It read, "Dear Maggie. Always thinking of you. Tolly."

"So who is he?"

Maggie shrugged. "He works at my office and we've had dinner together." She saw an accusation in her daughter's eyes and added sharply, "And he found you when you were drugged out the night before last like a common street junkie and he picked you up and carried you to a cab and into the hospital, so maybe you can take that smart-ass snot

320

look off your face."

Carol backed off right away. "I was just wondering, Mommy. That's all. He works with Mark. Is he a nice man?"

"Yes."

"And are you serious about him?" Carol said, and tried what she hoped was a winsome, just-between-us-girls kind of smile.

"He's not going to give me his fraternity pin, if that's what you mean," Maggie said.

"Oh, Mommy. You're always joking." Carol picked up her purse. "I'm going to my room to lie down for a while."

"What about some lunch."

"I'm not really hungry and I have to check my service. Lester promised me a bathing suit layout."

Maggie nodded. "Sure. Fine. And after you do that, then call this number and make your first appointment." Maggie approached her with a business card in her hand. "Today."

Carol took it but didn't even glance at it. "Sure," she said.

"So Cole has heard nothing from Aziz and Stanhope?" Petrov asked. He and Donovan were having lunch in a small neighborhood restaurant around the corner from the office of Whirlaway.

"Not a word," Donovan said. "I'm thinking that maybe Brian ought to go to Paris and see if he can find out anything there."

Petrov nodded. "We're not getting very far," he said. "The wheelchair manufacturer's lead to the dead men was useless and now our two men in Europe are missing. It's damned frustrating."

"You've been spoiled," Donovan said lightly. "You're used to KGB operations with manpower tripping over itself. This is just you and me and I don't think we're doing so badly."

"How do you figure that?"

"We've put a hurting on Abu Beka with our two field operations and we've got him making a lot of wild threats. And you yourself said he made a mistake with the 'New York atrocities.' I don't know . . . I think things are plugging away all right."

"I hope you're correct," Petrov said as he pushed his plate away from him, hardly touched.

There was salami in the refrigerator but Maggie didn't have any taste for it. She called her office and spoke to the prissy young girl who was filling in for her and found out that Donovan and Peterson had gone out for an early lunch.

"I'll be in in a half hour," she said, knowing it probably wasn't wise to leave Carol alone, but knowing also that she couldn't spend her life as a baby-sitter.

Without knocking, she went into Carol's room to tell her she was leaving the house.

Carol had the telephone in her hand but hung it up quickly.

"Did you call the clinic?" Maggie asked.

"Mommy, you didn't knock." Carol's lower lip quivered petulantly.

"No, I didn't and I don't think I'm going to from now on. And if you try to lock the door, I'll get a locksmith in here to remove the lock. There are going to be a few changes around here. Since you need to be policed, I'll do it. And I want you to know—count this as a warning—that I'll search your room whenever I feel like it. And since you haven't called the clinic, I'll call them from the office when I get there. If you have not by then made an appointment, you are going to the Long Island sanatarium. Or else you're just leaving here. The choice is yours. And every day I'm going to call the Village clinic just to make sure that you've been there. Is it all very clear?"

Carol rose from the bed and strolled over to her dresser. She grabbed a wooden-handled brush and began to stroke her hair with it gently.

"Perfectly clear, Mommy. Have a nice day and give my love to Mark and your friend Tolly."

She waited until she heard the hall door close behind Maggie. Then she called Rafjan Hassan.

"Hi, darling. I'm starving. How about some lunch? Yes, I'm hungry for that too. Your place in an hour. Wonderful."

The remnants of a two-slice order of pizza sat in front of Maggie Henson when Donovan and Petrov returned from lunch.

"How's Carol?" Petrov asked. Donovan lingered for a moment to hear the answer, then vanished inside his office.

"Well, she's home. Now we'll see," she said. After Donovan left, she told Petrov, "Thanks for the flowers, Tolly. It was sweet."

"Sweet? I thought if I plied you with flowers, we might have dinner tonight. Sort of got short-circuited the other evening."

"Sure," Maggie said. "But tonight I cook. It might be good for Carol to meet you and vice versa. And anyway, I make a mean roast chicken."

Petrov nodded. "Seven o'clock?" he said. He looked forward to meeting Carol Henson.

CHAPTER TWENTY-NINE

Petrov hopped a cab from his apartment to the Arab section downtown near Lexington and strolled the street looking for a good Arab market.

He finally found one with a tempting window display and went inside. The smells immediately assailed his nostrils, reminding him of the time he had spent in the Middle East. The store was crammed with shelves of canned goods and sleeves of goat cheese and the pungent aroma of desert spices almost clouded the air.

Petrov saw no clerk, and then a man came out from a large walk-in freezer in the back of the store and stood behind the counter. He was middle-aged with light beige skin that shone like satin as it stretched across his high cheekbones. His eyebrows were thick and black above hooded black eyes and his hair was pomaded and plastered to his large head. There was a slight pot belly apparent under the white butcher's coat which he wore carefully over a pair of soft denim jeans with decorative stitching down the sides.

Petrov walked to the counter and spoke Arabic. He told himself that it was unnecessary and probably showing off, but some other part of his brain said that it was important to keep in practice.

"Ah, I see you have lavash," he said. "Where do you get it? Do you make it here?"

"In California it is made and flown here, where we freeze it," the man said back in Arabic, his eyes smiling at encountering another lover of the hard-to-find middle-eastern bread. "We also have this Afghanistan corded bread. Very good when toasted."

Petrov ordered a loaf of each, and then asked for rum balls and honey pastries. "I bet you made those yourself," he said.

"I have them made by an American woman. But I taught her myself. It is the next best thing to real. Me? I am just a busy old butcher and spend most of my time in the freezer cutting up meat."

As the man was shuffling his order, Petrov asked, "Have you been in this country long? Is business good?"

"You speak Arabic well," the man said, turning aside the questions. "It is rare to see an American speak Arabic."

"Not an American," Petrov said. "A European, and I spent much time in Saudi Arabia."

He paused, and as he expected, the man answered his questions. "I've been here nine years now. And business comes and goes. If there is terrorism anywhere, Americans stay away. If it is peaceful, they buy bread. The only thing sure is that it will pass."

"Terrorism? Oh, you mean those men in the pigskins? Many were outraged by that," Petrov said.

The man's nimble fingers pressed the cash register buttons. He mumbled, "Sew them all in pigskins for all I care. I'll provide the pigskins." He pointed in the general direction of his freezer locker and smiled at Petrov. "All Arabs are not Muslims, you know. Some of us eat pork. But I'll deny I ever said that." He smiled conspiratorially.

Petrov smiled back. "Your opinions are safe with me. Mr. . . . ?"

"Mossadegh," the grocer said. "And you?"

"Peterson. Tolly Peterson," Petrov said, surprised at how easily the name came to him now. He paid for his purchase and left, reminding himself to check up on Mr. Mossadegh and find out if he was active in Arab-American groups. One never knew; he might be a contact someday.

The man sat in the small green car in front of the small house on Long Island. The husband had gone to work as he did every day at three-twenty P.M. Only the mother and the young girl were still inside the house. He looked at his watch. It was just after six P.M.; dinner should be over—he knew the husband did not come home for dinner—and wondered what his next step was. He wanted the woman; he did not want the girl.

While he was making up his mind what to do, a station wagon filled with children pulled into the driveway of the house across the street and honked the horn. The little brunette girl ran out from the house and clambered into the backseat. She waved to her mother, who was standing in the doorway of the house.

The mother was young and pretty with blond hair and an open face and larger eyes than blond women generally had. The station wagon pulled away.

The door to the house closed.

It was getting dark.

The street was empty.

The man got out of the car and walked across the street to the house.

He gently tested the doorknob. The door was unlocked, and he pushed the door open and walked inside.

He already knew there was no dog. Earlier, when he was sure the house had been empty, he had walked up and knocked on the door. A dog would certainly have barked.

He could hear the clink of dishes and the woman singing softly from the kitchen in the rear of the house. He smiled to himself, certain that this would be a more productive evening than he had spent last night tailing that New York policeman around Manhattan and learning exactly nothing. He took a large knife from his inside jacket pocket and walked to the kitchen.

"What's all this?" Maggie asked Petrov as she unloaded the shopping bag. "Lavash bread. . . ." She read the label. "Ah, three thousand years old. Yes. I can see the burn spots." She pointed to the brown spots on the surface of the bread. "And feta cheese. I love it. And rum balls. And pastry . . . listen, I invited *you* and . . ."

"No gentleman arrives for dinner without bringing something, and I am a gentleman." Petrov, by now familiar with the apartment, went across to the bar and poured himself a vodka.

"Where's Carol?"

Maggie had turned away, concentrating on unpacking the rest of the food from the shopping bag. Petrov could see her from where he stood as she crumpled the bag and stowed it away in a drawer. American women were just like Russian women in that respect, he thought. They saved everything that might be usable again.

The oven was giving off good mixed scents, chicken and sage and tarragon, and he mixed a drink for Maggie, who came in and took it from his hand and said, "She's not here. She left a note saying that her agent, Lester, got her an appointment with a bathing suit manufacturer and she might go to dinner with them."

Maggie took a deep sip, then told Petrov about the Village drug clinic nearby, and how she had laid the law down to Carol. "But I called the clinic when I got home and they said she had been there and seemed to like her counselor." She hesitated. "I guess that doesn't mean much, but I'd like to think it did."

Petrov smiled. "She went and that's a start." He felt disappointed. He had wanted to meet Carol and judge her himself. The girl was causing her mother pain and he would like to understand if she did that by choice or by necessity.

"So, it's just the two of us for dinner? I like that."

"I'm sorry," Maggie said. "I did want you to meet her."

"Some other time perhaps," Petrov said.

Maggie took her drink into the kitchen to make appetizers from the bread and cheese Petrov had brought and the Russian sat on the living room sofa, and turned the television to an all-news channel. He caught the headlines, but there was no new follow-up on the rescue at sea. Already the story had started to fade.

From the kitchen Maggie called out, "I hear you're going to Pittsburgh this weekend. You'll love Mark's house. It's like a museum of Americana."

"Sounds nice," Petrov called back, but he thought it did not sound nice at all. "But aren't you going?"

"I don't know yet," Maggie said. "Mark's invited me but . . . well, I just don't know. I don't know if I should leave Carol just now."

"I can understand that," Petrov said, talking softly now as he came to the doorway of the kitchen.

Maggie looked up and smiled at him. "Somehow, Tolly, I knew that you would," she said.

A knife was at her throat and a hand slapped roughly over her mouth.

"Don't make a sound if you want to live," a man's voice croaked roughly in her ear. "Is that the door to the basement?" She could not see his face, but he waved with his knife toward one of the doors in the kitchen.

Frantically, she nodded, and he pushed her ahead of him toward the door. She could feel his body pressing against the back of hers as they walked in lockstep.

She glanced over to see his face as he walked down the steps side by side with her, the knife still at her throat, his hand still on her mouth as he reached awkwardly around her neck with his arm.

It was the kind of face that she knew well, a coarse middle-eastern face with dark-ringed eyes and a mouth that looked as if it had never smiled. There was a dark red birthmark on his cheek. But she did not think it was a face she had ever seen before.

Oh, God, what did he want of her?

The chicken was a mass of skeleton on the serving platter. Petrov had eaten more than he thought possible; he still was not used to the quantity and quality of food available in the United States.

Maggie was more mellow now, the result of the two bottles of wine they had consumed during the meal. She got up and wafted into the kitchen to make coffee along with the dessert that Petrov had bought.

He was sitting alone at the dining room table in the corner of the living room when Carol came in the apartment door.

She called out, "Mommy?" then saw Petrov and snapped, "Who the hell are you?"

Maggie came out of the kitchen, a paper towel in her hands. "Hi, dear. You're just in time for coffee, and this is Tolly Peterson, whom I told you about this morning."

"You mean Tolly Fucking Peterson who works with Mark Fucking Donovan." Carol's eyes were glittering blue, and Petrov could tell that the girl had done more drugs. She snapped at her mother, "I suppose you know by now that I went to your fucking clinic with the rest of the weirdos."

"Carol, please." Maggie sighed.

"For Christ's sake. Go ahead, act the martyr part. You do it so well."

Petrov had risen to his feet. Into the awkwardness he said, "Why don't you join us for coffee, Miss Henson? We can get acquainted."

"You work with Mark Donovan, I don't want to get acquainted." She licked her lips in a manner that Petrov thought was meant to be erotic. "I can't stand him, and one of these days he'll be sorry for not being nicer to me."

Carol could feel the fog of cocaine still surrounding her body, almost like a second, looser skin. She had visited Hassan for sex, had gone to the clinic, and then gone back to Hassan for drugs. He had kept her in the bedroom, pushing cocaine at her and kept asking her about Mark Donovan's work. The newspapers from the past week were spread across the bed in his elaborate bedroom suite and Carol had finally connected why he might be so interested in Donovan's helicopter business. It was a small price to pay for the best noseful in town.

"I suppose I'd better go," Petrov said apologetically to Maggie.

"Don't leave on my account. I'm going to my room." Carol slid through the living room like a sensuous cat. She paused at the hall doorway, turned, and leaned one hand above her head on the door frame. It was a model's pose, designed to pull the fabric taught over her bustline and show off her soft figure. "Excuse my temper," she said, and tried a smile, "but I've had a lousy day. I didn't get the bathing suit layout and my head just wasn't into meeting people. I'm going to sleep. Good night." A moment later Petrov heard the bedroom door slam.

Maggie threw up her hands. "I don't know what to do," she said. Tears started welling in her eyes.

"I know what to do," Petrov said. "Let's go for a walk. I could use the air and I know you could too."

Carol was listening from behind the bedroom door.

333

A minute later she went into the living room and found that they had gone. She ran quickly to the telephone and dialed a number.

"Hello, darling. There was this guy here who works for Donovan. An English guy, Tolly Peterson or something. Sure, darling, I'll find out everything I can about him. Just for you." She paused and said, "I'm not interested in money. I'm interested in other things. I love you, you know. I know you love me. I'll call later."

When she hung up the phone, her face relaxed into a pensive smile. Now that she knew what Hassan was really up to, she was pleased. Mark Donovan would get his; she would see to that. Whether or not he was really involved in antiterrorist activities meant nothing to her; all that counted was that he had rejected her again. And this would be the last time.

But first she was going to have to make nice with "Mommy." She ran hot water into the tub and poured a cup of strong black coffee in the kitchen. That would start it; a glass of wine would mellow her out and when Maggie and Tolly Peterson came back home, she would apologize for the temper tantrum and spend some time pumping the slight, thin Englishman.

It would work. It always did.

He had done things like this before and he ordered the woman to take her clothes off.

"All of them," he growled.

The man sat on the steps in front of the woman, the knife at the ready in front of him. Screaming would not help her; no one would hear. And there was no other exit.

Nakedness always worked. There was something about being naked in front of a stranger that broke down a woman's ego, shamed her, made her willing to do almost anything, to agree to anything, if only she would be allowed to cover her body.

For a split second, after his order, there was a look of fright on this woman's face. And then she began taking off her clothes. She did it economically, almost swiftly, without embarrassment, and her attitude took the pleasure out of it for him. When she was done and her clothing lay in a pile on the floor, she stood before him, naked, shoulders back, head straight up. There was no shame in her. There was even the tiny little hint in her eye of pleasure, of glee that she was flaunting it, and the man remembered that she was a dancer; she was used to displaying her body; and she was a brazen American with wicked American attitudes.

It was clear in her eyes that she thought she was as good as he was. As if any American could be as good as he; as if any woman could be as good as a man. He promised himself that he would take that gloating look off her face in a moment. There were other ways besides just nakedness.

He stood up and waved the knife in her direction.

"On the floor," he snapped harshly. "Lie down."

The smile vanished from her face now, and the rapidity with which she had disrobed was replaced by a reluctant slowness. At last the bitch was beginning to understand that this was not a game.

Maggie shivered as she and Petrov walked through the quiet late-summer night. It was nine o'clock and the streetlights made bright puddles in the fog above their heads.

"It's almost cold," Maggie said. "Not even Labor Day and it's chilly."

"Yes, an early fall. But nothing compared to where I come from," Petrov said absently, wishing he could put an arm around her, wishing to soothe her.

"Yes. I've never been there but I've heard about England's damp. Where are you from anyway? I don't believe you've ever told me."

"Rothbury. That's in Northumberland, near the Scottish border."

"And your family? Your parents are gone, aren't they."

"Yes. I haven't been back in twenty years." He mused a moment, then remembered she was there and said, "Yes, my parents are gone, God rest them." He doubted very sincerely if his father was resting in God's hands. He had been a vicious beast, but the wasted, sweet face of his mother deserved God's love and protection. If there *was* a God, which he

336

doubted. "And yours?"

"I don't know." Maggie shoved her hands into the pockets of her light coat. "It sounds strange, I know, to admit that, but when I left it was because they kicked me out. I was carrying Carol."

"Who is Carol's father?" They had come to Sixth Avenue and stood watching the traffic streak by. The question hung between them for a moment.

"There's a small bar over there that I know," Maggie said. "I'd offer to buy you a drink, but I left my purse back at the apartment."

"I can afford the price." Petrov tucked an arm through Maggie's. "We didn't get our coffee after all. A brandy might fill the bill right now."

They were settled at a wooden table in the center of the small pub's restaurant floor, their coffee in front of them, their drinks coming when Maggie finally said, "I wish I could explain to you about Carol's father. He was really nothing in my life. Just an attractive older man that I used to see around the small town I lived in. Then one day, I remember it was a rainstorm, and he picked me up in his car as I walked home from school. He talked to me. He treated me like an adult. He held my hand while he was driving. I was thrilled. A bank president had held my hand. That's what he was, an important man in our town. And I had come from a family with no affection, always believing that I wasn't wanted. It was a typical thing, I guess. I felt deprived and I was an easy mark for a grown man who wanted

337

to cuddle a young thing. He was, naturally, married with children as old as I was. When I think of it now, I just can't imagine why it happened between us, how he seduced me. Or maybe I seduced him. I don't really remember anymore. I've wanted to tell Carol about it a thousand times, but I can't."

"Maybe you should," Petrov said quietly. "It could well be that there's something in there that's the cause of Carol's problems. Why don't you call her counselor tomorrow and discuss it with him? Or her, as the case may be."

"Her. A woman, her name is Miss Oliphant and I keep thinking she might be fat, you know, like an elephant and I'm not sure I want to see for myself." She giggled and sipped at her drink, an Irish Cream on the rocks. "It does sound like a good idea, though, to talk to her. Enough about that. I want to forget Carol for a few minutes. What about you? No marriages? No serious love affairs? No mistress waiting for you back in Northumberland?"

"No, no, and no to all three questions," he said immediately. "As I told you last night, I have a problem. It came about in an odd way. I was fascinated by a woman who, as it turned out, was a paranoid schizophrenic. . . ."

He went on to describe a fictional love affair that ended in mutilation and disaster when the woman pulled a knife while he was sleeping and deballed him.

He had learned early on in his career that it was

338

always better to tell a full, flagrant story when you finally reach the point where silence would no longer do. If the story was bizarre enough and sounded painful enough, it ended the questioning for good. This was, he told himself, just good tactics now with Maggie. But he still felt like a swallowed rat for doing it to her.

By the end of the story, which he made up as he went along, Maggie was appalled. Her big brown eyes had not turned away from his, however, and he finally turned his head to break the stare. She mistook the action for embarrassment, took his hand and caressed it softly. "I'm so sorry," she said.

Petrov was drinking aquavit. He downed it and signaled the waitress for another round. Maggie said, "No, I don't pity you. We all have some kinds of scars or mutilations, physical or emotional or whatever. What I'm sorry about is that my problem with Carol must seem minor to you. I've been prattling on about it, using your shoulder to cry on."

"It doesn't matter." Petrov stroked her hand. The waitress put their drinks on the table. Petrov lit a cigarette and passed it to Maggie, who inhaled deeply. They were quiet as he lit one for himself. The bistro was an old one, wooden floors, wooden booths, wooden tables. For a moment they were alone on a wooden island, neither knowing what to say.

A crowd of five came in noisily, claiming a scarred table nearby. They were chatting and laughing as they chose chairs, and the two men strove to sit next to the prettiest of the three women. She had auburn hair the color of polished mahogany and teased the men with a throaty, heavily accented voice. "Boys will be boys," she said with a tinkly laugh, and Petrov heard her, sat up straight, and said to Maggie, "Perhaps we'd better be getting back."

Maggie had seen the quick look that he had given the woman and that, somehow, it had upset him. She downed her drink in a gulp, slurped her coffee, and said, "I feel like walking again. I know another place on Barrow Street. It used to be a speakeasy."

"Certainly," Petrov said abruptly. But as they rose to go, the redheaded woman saw him.

"Petrov, my darling," she called out, and hurried over to them, throwing her arms around Petrov and hugging him. She began to speak in Russian. "I never thought to see you again. How is your sister? Ah, those days in Moscow. And to think, here I find you in New York. Have you defected too? I had to. I found that—"

Petrov pulled away from the woman and interrupted her in cold, precise English. "I'm terribly sorry, madam. I think you have made a mistake."

Stricken as though her face had been slapped, the woman drew back. She looked hard at Petrov and then said in English, "Oh, my God. Yes. I can see that now. I am so desperately agonized with myself. It's just that you look like him, a man I knew in Moscow. I've offended. Please let me buy you and

340

your friend a drink to apologize."

"No," Petrov said. "That won't be necessary. We were just leaving."

The woman retreated to her own table and said loudly to her friends, "How stupid of me. I thought I knew that man. He looks just like Anatoly Petrov from the old days. When the KGB thought highly of me." She laughed her tinkling laugh again.

Maggie had almost to run after Petrov, he was so quick to leave. On the sidewalk she took his arm once more. "They say everyone has a double. I guess now you learned about yours. Come on. Barrow Street is this way."

She said no more about it, but each knew the other knew the truth. Maggie would never forget that "Tolly Peterson," when injured, had cried out in his sleep. In Russian.

In Russian.

The woman had told him she knew nothing . . . less than nothing.

But she had known something very important— she had known that she had seen many people when she danced in El Fazid's, and the only one who did not seem to belong there was an Englishman named Tolly Peterson.

But she knew nothing more about this Peterson except that he had gone back to England to his wife and, yes, Tolly Peterson was there in El Fazid's having lunch with her the day the two dead heroes had eaten there with Pierre Dubois.

Dubois had mentioned that his two bodyguards had gone off to check somebody out. He did not know who it was. And then their bodies had been found.

So, it was a very strong possibility that this Tolly Peterson, whoever he was, was responsible. The next step would be to try to run down somebody named Tolly Peterson.

The woman was still lying naked on the recreation room floor. A recreation room, he thought to himself. The place might be very well named.

He stood up from his place on the stairs and walked toward her, unzipping his trousers as he approached.

"I'll scream," she said.

"I'll like it better if you scream," he said. "And it'll give me a reason to cut your tongue out." He felt very noble about what he was doing. Sometimes Satan and the women of Satan had to be given doses of their own medicine, and this woman who accepted money to let strangers look at her body was no exception.

It was hard for Petrov to forget that he had hurt a dear old friend. It had been a necessity, he knew, but when he had first seen Tanya enter the restaurant, laughing with her friends, he remembered the days as students in Moscow. He must be getting old, he thought. People in his line of work were not supposed to have memories, not supposed to have feelings.

Maggie was a little tipsy as he walked her home. Inside the front door of her building he kissed her, exploring her mouth with his tongue, and she kissed him back. He was the one to pull away and she said, "Thank you for being here tonight. You seem always to be here when I need you." He squeezed her hand in response and she said, "I don't feel so bad now. I think I will try to go with all of you to Pittsburgh. We can borrow one of Mark's cars and I can show you around."

"Good," he said. The worry was gradually lessening. Maggie had suspicions about him, about his meeting with Tanya, but at least she would not pry and she would keep them to herself.

He was wrong.

Maggie let herself into the apartment and saw Carol sitting in front of the television in a white terry-cloth robe.

She jumped up and said, "Let me get you a drink, Mommy." She could see that Maggie already had had enough, but had not quite reached the point where she would quit. It was funny, Carol thought. Her mother worried about her being a drug addict, but Carol knew she could drop the drugs whenever she wanted to. Her mother with alcohol was something else; once she started on heavy drinking, she never

343

wanted to stop and usually did only when sleep intervened.

Of the two of them, Carol was sure that her mother had the bigger problem.

Carol poured a straight vodka over the rocks and came back to Maggie, sitting on the couch.

"I'm so awfully sorry. I hope I didn't scare Mr. Peterson off. I was just so upset about not getting that bathing suit layout, and you know why? They said I was too old. Me. I'm only twenty-two and they said I was too old." Carol forgot that she had used that story the previous week, that she was too old for some sort of commercial work, but it had been a cereal commercial she had auditioned for.

Maggie put an arm around her daughter. "It's okay, baby. You're not too old for anything. But you have to stop using the drugs though. It wasn't a good impression that you made on my friend."

"I know that, Mommy," Carol said, and snuggled closer. She said, "And I didn't even try to find drugs. It's just that after the audition for the swimsuit layout, there were a lot of girls around who didn't get the job either and one of them had some tranquilizer pills and I took one because my nerves were shot and it must have been stronger than I thought. I'm sorry. I hope your Mr. Peterson will forgive me."

"He will."

"He seems like a very nice man," Carol said. "Tell me about him. He has a very funny British accent, don't you know?" She spoke the last phrase in an

344

imitation of Petrov's British mannerism and her mother laughed and sipped her vodka, then took a large gulp of it.

"I'll freshen that for you," Carol said. Maggie did not agree or disagree. She was getting smashed and Carol was taking care of her for a change. It was a welcome change. She took the new drink and sipped it, wanting a cigarette.

"There are some Marlboros in my coat pocket, baby."

"I'll get them." Carol hopped up, retrieved the pack, and stood over Maggie, lighting the cigarette and handing it to her. "Although I wish you wouldn't smoke."

"I wish you wouldn't do drugs."

"I know." Carol sighed and sat again. "Come on. Something better than that. Tell me about Tolly Peterson. I don't want you getting involved with someone I don't know anything about. I was almost jealous tonight. I came home and I wanted to talk to you and tell you my troubles and then I couldn't because here was some stranger in our living room. Do you understand, Mommy?"

Maggie was tired; the alcohol was getting to her. "Yes, I understand," she said. "I asked him for dinner so he could meet you."

"I cleaned up the dishes," Carol said. "Is Tolly important? What does he do for Mark?"

"I'm not sure," Maggie said, and puffed on the cigarette.

"You're not sure? You know every single thing that happens there. I can't imagine what Mark would do without you."

"About Tolly, I don't know." Maggie's words were becoming a little slurred. "He's supposed to be on assignment from the British government to work out helicopter plans with Mark. But I don't know."

"What do you mean?"

"He doesn't seem to know anything about helicopters. And sometimes, I . . . well, I think he's Russian."

"Russian?" That was exciting, Carol thought to herself, and perhaps just the kind of thing Rafjan Hassan would like to know. "What makes you think that?"

Maggie sipped her drink, opened her mouth, and the words spilled out. She told Carol about the mugging, about her own Russian boyfriend and the way she recognized Tolly's Russian curses in his sleep, about the woman they had met in the bar that night. Carol kept nodding agreement and, being a dutiful daughter, kept refilling her mother's glass.

When she helped Maggie to bed an hour later, Carol felt she had some real news to give Hassan. Maggie went to sleep in her clothes, without a murmur. She would not remember any of it in the morning, Carol knew. It was a pattern she had gotten used to.

CHAPTER THIRTY

As the weather reports had promised, the next day was a cloudless, blue-skied wonder with smells of crisp autumn air. Donovan had arranged for a car to take Tilda and Daniel to Teterboro Airport, and his own children had arrived at his apartment in time for a late breakfast.

They were full of high spirits, and as he did every time he saw them, he believed that they had grown a great deal in the last two weeks. Christine, especially. She had her mother's blond good looks, but her blue eyes held more warmth than Ancie's cold, calculating ones. She was long-legged, too, and at thirteen, had the coltish look of the young horses that she loved being with.

"Daddy," she said, "I can't wait to see Bitsy again and the two colts."

Jeff Donovan at fifteen was already six feet tall, more practical than his sister, and Donovan saw in him a lot of his own father, the senator, who was a man inclined to listen to all the facts before making up his mind. The boy was sitting at his father's right at the table, his arms crossed over his chest, and he asked, "So who is this Tilda person we're taking with us?"

Donovan spread some imported marmalade across his toast but didn't bite into it. "She is a very good friend," he said. He eyed Jeff, man to man, and was pleased that his son neither blinked nor turned away. "She has a son, Daniel, and I hope you like him."

"How old is Daniel, Daddy?" Christine asked with the enthusiasm of a teenybopper hearing about a new boy on the block. There was a full plate of waffles, eggs, and bacon in front of her that she had only picked at. She was very fearful of gaining weight, especially since her mother had told her that it was better to be dead than to be fat.

"Only six, honey." Donovan forked up some of her eggs and shoved them at her mouth. "Not old enough yet to be interested in you women, and if you don't eat, we're not going."

"Oh, Daddy." Christine laughed even as she took the forkful delicately in her mouth and turned to her older brother. "He's always afraid," she told Jeff, "that I'm going to get some disease of the week that he saw in a TV movie. What is it this time, Daddy? Anorexia or bulimia?"

Jeff grinned and Donovan mock-growled to his daughter, "All right, smart guy."

Christine chewed and swallowed, then decided another bite of eggs wouldn't be likely to make her fat that very day. She had it down her throat when she asked, "Is this Tilda person a serious affair of the heart or is it a passing thing?"

Jeff groaned. "Honestly, Chrissie. There are times when you are such a nit."

"Oh, crap. You know you're just as curious as I am."

"Crap?" Donovan sat up sternly straight in his chair. "Since when do you use that word?"

"Daddy, don't be obtuse." Christine shoveled in more food and talked with her mouth full. "Since I started mucking out the stables when I was five years old. Most of you men called it horseshit, but I preferred to call it crap."

Jeff put his hand over his mouth to stifle his laugh, then told his father, "She also says she glistens instead of sweats. You've got one weird daughter."

Christine giggled and said, "I can't get away with anything here. Daddy, just tell us. Are we hearing wedding bells? Should Jeff get his ring-bearer suit out. Should I get a flower-girl costume?"

Jeff explained, "Christine thought if she acted coy and pretended not to eat and batted her thousand eyelashes at you, then you'd tell us the truth. I told her I trusted you to tell us." Jeff still had his arms crossed, his plate untouched in front of him. He was dark-haired like his father, and his eyes were as blue and his tone was teasing, but Mark knew somehow something was important here in his relationship with his kids, and he said, "Yes, I'll tell you the truth. But first this." He speared some waffle and bacon from Jeff's plate, leaned forward, and popped it into Jeff's mouth.

"Okay," he said. "I think this might be serious. In case you're really interested, we'll probably be spending the night in one room, Tilda and me, but that's up to her and how her son Daniel sleeps. I was going to give her another room, and then there would be sneaking around in the halls and you two would be up all night waiting for it. If it makes you feel any better, Tilda is worried about her parents in Pittsburgh, too, what they might think of her if they find out she was sharing a room with me."

"What about Daniel?" Christine already had a proprietary sense about the six-year-old. But then, she always did about anything small—children, kittens, puppies, colts.

"I thought we could put him in the old nursery. Maybe you guys could look after him."

"That spooky old place?" Christine said. "No way. Nobody's been up there for eons and it's probably got bats, big giant vampire bats. No. It's settled. Daniel will take my room and we can leave the door open between it and Jeff's room and I'll sleep in the spare room across the hall and keep my door opened too."

"Chrissie," Donovan said as he took her hand. "You are so loved."

"And Daddy, you are so sentimental."

350

Maggie was at breakfast when Carol swirled into the kitchen.

"Good news," she said. "Lester just called and he got me a different swimsuit layout. It's not as glamorous as the other one . . . strictly catalog work, so they don't mind that I'm too old." Carol rolled her blue eyes extravagantly, catching Maggie's gaze and giggling as if she had made a tremendous joke. "And it's not a week in Jamaica, just a weekend in Palm Beach. But I have to get my act together and be ready to leave from LaGuardia at noon."

"And when did Lester call?" Maggie asked sharply. "I didn't hear the phone ringing." Her head was splitting with a hangover.

"While you were in the shower," Carol said blithely. "He was already on his way to the airport. He said they had another girl lined up but they found out she's preg and the bosses are afraid it'll show already. Three months. Can you imagine how stupid men are sometimes? I know her and she won't show until she's in her seventh month, I bet. We're the same type though, and she's had a steady gig with them for four years. She's older than I am too . . . twenty-six or something awful like that." Carol knew that she was babbling like a twit, but she also knew that when she was excited, she always acted that way.

Maggie sipped at her strong black coffee. "Don't you think you should have asked me first? After all, the clinic . . ."

"Mommy, I'll call Miss Oliphant first thing, as

351

soon as it's nine o'clock, and tell her. If I get this steady job, I can help pay for the clinic."

Maggie bit her lip; she could not tell any longer whether or not Carol was lying to her.

"And I'll be back Monday. Mommy, don't give me a hard time about this. I need the work and you keep saying I'm not serious enough about modeling and I told Lester it was A-affirmative. You don't want me to break my word, do you?"

Putting her hands to her face to smooth out the worry lines she had begun to notice around her eyes, Maggie said, "I guess not. All right. The sun will probably do you good. And I think I'll go off to Pittsburgh with Mark Donovan and his kids."

"Is that other man going? Tolly?" Carol inquired, an edge of jealousy in her tone. It was the first time she had heard of the proposed trip.

"Yes. And so is Mark's new girlfriend."

"His what? He has a new girlfriend? Who is she?"

It was important to Maggie that Carol know about Tilda so that she would stop alternating between her crush on Donovan and her wild desire to treat him like her father. "Her name is Tilda Matthews," Maggie said. "I haven't met her yet, but I hear she's very nice."

"Tilda Matthews?" Carol thought hard. "That name is so familiar to me for some reason."

"It might be more familiar if you picked up a newspaper once in a while. She's a political cartoonist."

352

Carol ignored the dig. "Wait. Flame-red hair. I know her. I met her the night of the fund-raiser. I guess I'd better get packed." She hurried off to her room before her mother had a chance to dredge up the memories of Carol's behavior at the fund-raiser.

Her mother actually tried to be very sweet, Carol thought, but she could be stifling too. Everything was stifling, even the air in her bedroom. Well, things would be okay as soon as she got in a cab to Hassan's apartment. The first thing they would do is smoke some grass to relax and then get into bed. As Carol was plucking her eyebrows, she thought of how Raffi—her nickname for him—liked to tie her to the bed. She didn't like that part of the sex with him very much, but everything else was terrific and maybe she could break him of that habit.

She tried to remember Mark Donovan's redheaded girlfriend, but all she could think of was that she always thought redheads were trashy. Well, anyway, it was just another piece of information for Rafjan Hassan. He seemed so interested in knowing everything about Donovan and all his friends.

As the group gathered in a waiting room at Teterboro Airport, Tilda told Donovan, "I thought a private airport would be more glamorous than this."

"The galley slaves don't come on until noon," Donovan said. He rumpled Daniel's hair and said, "Time to board, champ."

Daniel pointed at Mark and explained to Jeff and Christine, "He always calls me that." They just smiled; when they were younger, that was what he had always called them too.

To Tilda, the private jet looked small and puny, parked outside the hangar, but it was the newest top of the line, and the inside was luxurious with room for everybody and space to spare. There was even a small bathroom which Jeff showed to Daniel right away.

"Mom," Daniel yelled. "We can go potty even when we're up high."

"Yes, Daniel," she said. "I bet that'll be the highlight of the trip."

Maggie and Petrov had already taken side-by-side seats in the rear of the plane after Petrov had mixed them drinks from the plane's small utility galley.

Mark leaned out of the cockpit to Tilda, who was in the front row. "How about being my copilot?" he asked.

"Up front? Listen, I'm not scared or anything, but don't you think you should have a real copilot?"

"Nonsense," he said. "Tolly is a pilot; Maggie has soloed; both Jeff and Christine could have their licenses if they were old enough, and pretty soon we'll be sending Daniel to flying school."

His face was so close to hers that she almost flung her arms around his neck. He was too close in many ways, she thought; he was almost under her skin and much more frightening than the plane, for he could take control of her soon and take control of the careful, safe exclusionary life that she had built for herself and her son.

"After the takeoff," she said. "Then I'll come up front. For a split second before I barf. But I know Daniel will love it."

"Well, then, once we get up, he can be my copilot." He looked around the plane and yelled to get their attention, "Okay, everybody. Buckle up."

He went back into the cockpit and got on the microphone to the control tower. His voice sounded different as he spoke into it; softer, lower, laconically professional. Tilda liked the sound of it; its confidence was reassuring.

Christine fussed to make sure that Daniel was buckled in properly, but he squirmed so much that as soon as they were airborne, she let him loose so that he could stare out the window. He watched the crazy quilt of land below with fascination. "Why are some trees green and some of them red and some of them yellow?"

"And the sky blue and the plane flying," Jeff said with a grin.

"The green ones are probably evergreens," Christine said. "They're probably always green. The others have leaves that are dying and before they die they change colors."

"Why?"

"I think they want to tell us that life was worth living," Christine said.

355

"Do we change colors before we die?" Daniel asked her.

"Maybe," Christine said seriously. She had never seen a person die, except on television, and they were usually splashed bright red with blood or purple from being choked.

"What color?" Daniel insisted.

"What's your favorite color?" Christine asked.

"Blue."

"That's the color, then. We all turn blue before we die," she said.

Daniel appeared satisfied by the logic of that explanation and sat back in his seat with a warming smile at his mother. She knew that he felt he was a very grown young man to be flying in this plane. And later, if Mark let him into the cockpit, it would be the thrill of a lifetime.

From their seats behind the children Maggie and Petrov could hear the conversation, and the two of them smiled at each other. Maggie knew Christine and Jeff well, and it did not surprise her that they would be solicitous and thoughtful of young Daniel's feelings. But Tolly, she thought, watched everything as if it were a big surprise to him. She wondered what he could be thinking about.

What Petrov was thinking about was decadence and the lack of it. He had almost declined to go on the trip because he had been very positive that he would hate Donovan's two children. He was certain they would have that hothouse quality of overripe

356

fruit—spoiled and selfish, and he found it hard to believe Christine's apparent immediate concern for the young boy. Jeff, of course, was still basically a cipher in Petrov's mind . . . sprawled in his seat and maybe even a little condescending toward his younger sister and the boy. But at least the boy had manners.

Petrov thought of his own sister's two children. These Donovan kids resembled them. He thought about that for a moment and decided no. He was sure now that once they got to Donovan's house in Pittsburgh, the two teenagers would put on those stupid rock videos and gyrate around the house to them. And the house would probably have thin walls so that Petrov would have to hear the noise and try to restrain himself from garroting the two young animals.

He should have gone to Paris with Brian Cole to look for Aziz and Stanhope. This was going to be an awful weekend, he decided. The whole thing was a mistake, and he slumped in his seat and worked over the vodka again.

When Tilda saw the home, she stifled a gasp. It was a mansion, of gray stone pillars and porticos and balconies, on a hill surrounded by acres and acres of tended grounds and woods. There were stables in the back, a swimming pool, tennis courts, and two friendly servants who ran from the house to hug Jeff and Christine, and then dropped into a crouch to

357

pamper young Daniel.

The maid, Marie, said, "Look at him. I'm so glad I baked the chocolate chip cookies now."

"Me too," Daniel said solemnly. "Can I have one? I didn't have to go potty on the plane, but I could go now."

Petrov, standing off to the side with Maggie, said, "I didn't expect this."

"It is sort of impressive, isn't it?" Maggie said. The house had no surprises for her; she had often stayed there when business brought her to Donovan's nearby Pittsburgh assembly plant.

"I guess I just assumed that Mark was passing well off," Petrov said.

"You missed that one, Tolly," Maggie said. "Not well off . . . stinking filthy capitalist rich."

Petrov squeezed her arm. "Let's try not to embarrass ourselves."

The two servants, Antoine and Marie, obviously were skilled at the business of handling guests. Marie showed everyone to their rooms while Antoine efficiently deposited the light weekend luggage where it was supposed to be.

Inside the house Petrov gawked at a Modigliani at the head of a staircase, and wondered about Donovan. He was already successful and rich; was it just possible that he was truly a patriot, in the battle against terrorism because it was the right thing to do? It had been a long time since Petrov had run into true idealists; even he himself had in the back of his mind the idea that if he handled this job successfully, it would probably bring a promotion, and might just move him one step higher up the ladder to the political power which was the only worthwhile currency in the Soviet Union.

Donovan announced that everyone should take their time checking in; they were on free time until the evening when there'd be a light dinner in the main dining room. "Don't dress," he said jokingly.

Petrov unpacked his single change of clothing in his room and rested on the bed for a half hour before going downstairs. He prowled the open rooms of the house, then found Maggie sipping coffee and eating a light salad on one of the side porches.

"Afternoon," he said. "Where is everybody?"

"Riding, like in a good English movie," Maggie said. She wiped her mouth daintily. "Or at least Tilda and Mark are. The kids are down at the paddock, trying to entice Daniel onto a horse. Want to see how they're doing?"

"Sure," Petrov said, and followed Maggie across the large open lawn to some stable buildings a few hundred yards away.

"Do you ride?" she asked him.

"No," Petrov said crisply.

"I thought all you Englishmen were born in a saddle."

"Not this one. My family was into shoes, not a blacksmith in the crowd."

They came up on the paddock and watched, unnoticed, from behind a fence as Jeff was holding Daniel in place atop a small, very gentle-looking mare.

"Now, hold on, Daniel. We're just going to go once around the block," Jeff said. Daniel clutched the horn on the western-style saddle; his face was white with fear as he dug his stirrups into the mare's sides.

"Not yet for that," Jeff said gently. "Keep your feet away from her until you know how to command her. Here, I'll lead you."

But Daniel was too nervous, and as Jeff took the reins and started the mare forward, the small boy dug his feet in once more and the mare began to trot off. The reins were almost pulled from Jeff's hands, but he held on tight and ran alongside the horse calling, "Whoa, Bitsy, whoa." As he stopped the horse, Daniel slid from the saddle and Jeff caught him, but the young boy vomited his breakfast and lunch all over Jeff's sparkling white T-shirt.

Jeff, unconcerned about the mess, squatted down and held Daniel in his arms and soothed him by rubbing the small of his back.

Petrov heard him say, "Well, Daniel, now you're a real cowboy."

"I am?"

"Sure you are. You only get to be a real cowboy by throwing up all your cookies the first time you get on a horse. It happened to me too, champ. And to my dad. You're going to be a terrific rider."

Daniel whimpered. "I don't have to stop now?"

"Nope. First thing you and I got to do, pardner, is

go over to the trough there and wash our faces. And then you get back up on Bitsy right away."

He led the young boy by the hand to the trough, splashed his shirtfront with water, and helped him wash out his mouth. Then he brought Daniel back and showed him how to use the stirrups to get back on the mare.

Petrov could see from Daniel's face that the kid was no longer so scared, and this time, with less of a show of nerves, he followed Jeff's instructions to the letter and in a few moments Jeff was leading the horse and Daniel around the big exercise yard. When they came abreast of Maggie and Petrov, who had climbed onto the fence, Jeff grinned and said, "This here buckaroo is on his way to being a real cowboy."

"Can he ride already?" Maggie said.

"Sure can," Jeff said. "And he's going to be the best rider in all of New York City. You wait and see."

Christine came out of the stable and waited for them as they continued around the yard.

Petrov said softly to Maggie, "Jeff's very gentle with the boy."

"That's Jeff," Maggie said. "He's always been like that. When he was Daniel's age, he used to take care of Christine when she was sick. Their mother . . . well, their mother does not like illness of any kind, so it always seemed to be Jeff's job to take care of things. Watch Christine now."

The long-legged blond girl joined the two boys and walked alongside them, manipulating Daniel's feet to show him how to command the horse with them. The mare, Bitsy, put up with it, trotting slowly, then cantering, but not with any speed. Jeff handed the reins up to Daniel.

"We're right here, champ. Chrissie there and me here. Now, you just ride her by yourself. Remember, pull right to go right, pull left to go left, and if you want to stop just pull up toward you. That's it. You've got it."

"You've got it," Christine said, her enthusiastic excitement patently honest and well meant.

Daniel looked as if he were in heaven. His face shone and his wet red hair curled wildly around his freckled face.

"I'm doing it! I'm doing it!"

"You sure are, champ," Jeff said.

Petrov looked at Maggie and she said, "That's how they taught me. I didn't throw up but I sure thought I was going to. Then suddenly they made it all right. They're special kids. I'm going to get a horse. Want to come along?"

"No thanks." Petrov lit a cigarette. "I'll watch, maybe take a walk. I haven't been in the country in a long time."

"There's a brook that meanders all through the property. It's very peaceful. Just head off in that direction," she said, waving up toward the hillside.

"The room we're in?" Tilda pulled her horse up

and let him lap at the brook's cool water.

Donovan, alongside her on a big stallion, turned in his saddle to see the sunlight playing in her flaming hair. "No, for your information, it isn't the one I shared with my ex-wife. As a matter of fact, the kids used to be up in the nursery and we had separate bedrooms in the east wing. We keep the wing closed now."

"Separate?"

"Yeah. Separate bedrooms. Then we moved to New York, then we got divorced, and then Jeff and Chrissie were old enough to move into rooms downstairs and I moved down the hall. The only woman ever in that bed was . . . Martha Washington?"

Donovan grinned and Tilda said, "Well, as long as she wasn't sleeping with you, I guess it's all right. I should stop in to see my parents while I'm here."

Donovan said, "I thought you would. Maybe you'd like to invite them out for a barbecue tomorrow?"

"It's a big family," she warned.

"This is a big house," he said.

The sunlight was dappled now, coming through the branches of the trees that formed a bridge over the stream. The strange mixed lights struck Tilda's face, making her seem hot and cold, peach and blue, dark and light, all at the same time.

They ambled on down the streambed, their horses side by side, holding hands like young sweethearts.

Petrov clambered to the top of a rock just in time to see them ride away from him.

363

He watched them silently for a long time, until they disappeared around a bend in the stream.

It was peaceful here, idyllic, and he sat and let himself muse about someday, perhaps, living like this. Surrounded by family and friends, in a place at peace.

But was there ever a place truly at peace?

Petrov was not a fool; he did not regard the Soviet Union as some kind of moral crusader determined to make the world a better place for mankind.

It was, in his mind, just another imperialist state, no better perhaps and certainly no worse than any other. But it was his country and he didn't know if he would ever have the ability . . . maybe the courage, to up and leave it. My country, right or wrong, but my country . . . was that the way the old western saying went?

No, he would never live in a place like this; he would probably never know a period of true peace in his life. He was a soldier for Russia; he had lived his life that way and someday he would probably die that way, in some alley somewhere with a knife stuck between his ribs.

Or worse. The thought of Afghanistan crept unbidden into his mind, and without being aware of it, Petrov's hand reached down to touch his scarred genitals.

He had been sent there by the KGB to find out why the Afghan war was going so badly. He had been out talking to troops in the field when their position was overrun by the Afghan rebels.

The rebels had decided the other Russian soldiers knew nothing and killed them quickly. But they had tortured Petrov, culminating in cutting off his testicle with a knife heated red in a campfire. A helicopter squad of Russian commandos rescued him only minutes later. He closed his eyes tight to blot out the memory; he didn't want to think of how he had taken his revenge. And that was a long time ago, in a faraway place, and this was now, here, near this brook in a land made for dreaming of impossible futures.

He was so deep in his mood that he did not hear Maggie's horse approaching and knew she was there only when he heard her scrambling up on top of the flat rock next to him.

"That water looks inviting," she said.

He looked at her and said, "No more inviting than you are."

"Tolly, you always say the nicest things," Maggie responded. She lay back alongside him on the rock and looked up at the sky spotted through the trees.

She reached down and took his hand in hers. "It's peaceful, isn't it?"

"I was just thinking that," he said.

They were silent for long minutes until Maggie said, "Tolly, do you ever think about me? About us?"

Petrov bit his lip before answering, "Only always," and then he turned his head to her, but her lips were already on his and she pulled him onto his back and the flat rock. Her mouth was glued to his; her hand was fumbling with the zipper of his trousers, and then her hand was around his already swollen penis and she pulled her mouth from his and moved down to take him in her mouth.

He ejaculated immediately and she held him for a long time inside her mouth, humming soft comforting noises to him while he looked up through the overhead branches at the painfully blue sky beyond.

She came back up and lay in the fold of his arm, then giggled in his ear.

"I guess you could call this being between a rock and a hard place," she said lightly.

"I'm sorry," he said.

"I'm not. Here, all this while, I was worried that you were impotent. It's so nice to find out that you're not. And tonight, in bed, we'll put that English lance to good use."

Their lips met again and they lay atop the rock, holding each other, until the sun turned down and the air began to chill.

Donovan had his face resting on Tilda's breast in the big bed that they shared when Tilda said, "Your friend Tolly is interesting."

"Oh? How so?" Donovan said casually.

"He never says much, but he's always watching. Somebody once called them house-counting eyes. He's like that."

366

"And you don't like him?" Donovan said.

"No. Just the opposite. I think I like him a lot, even if he is hard to get close to. He just gives you that impression that he'd be a good guy to have on your side if you were in trouble."

"That's the truth," Donovan said. "And he's quiet because . . . well, from what I know, he's had a tough life."

"Maybe Maggie will make it better for him," she said.

"You noticed, huh?"

"I notice everything," Tilda said.

Maggie's room was done in tones of burgundy and green and beige with a large Persian rug across the front of the room. She lay under the covers and waited for the visitor she knew would come.

It was after midnight when Petrov let himself into the room, locking the door behind him. He was wearing silk pajamas and carrying a bottle of champagne and two glasses, and when he sat down on the edge of the bed next to her, she said, "Anybody see you? I'd hate for my reputation to be ruined."

"What about mine?" he said.

"Oh, you dog."

Petrov said, "You pour the wine." He found some old half-burned logs in the fireplace and managed to get a fire going with the help of an old newspaper he found in a magazine rack.

As he joined Maggie in bed, she got up, turned out the room lamp, and lit a candle inside a hurricane glass. Then she slid off her robe and stood naked in front of him. Her body was full and tempting and reminded him of a vivid painting of a nude he had seen once in the Kremlin art museum.

She came to him and he spoke her name hoarsely and took her in his arms.

The first hint of dawn came too soon for them. They had made love all night and finished the bottle of champagne and then they came together, one last time, in a shivering climax.

Petrov leaned on his elbows above Maggie and stared into her eyes.

After a while he said, "Maybe I should go back to my room before the household is up?"

"No," she said, and caressed the back of his head. "You're better-looking this morning. Isn't that strange?"

"It must have been a visit from my fairy god-mother. Your Mother Goose stories, who was it, Cinderella?"

"Oh. Yes. I keep forgetting you had a Russian mother. She must have told you Russian fairy tales."

"Yes, she did." Petrov lowered himself to nuzzle her neck. He had forgotten that Mother Goose was a British product.

Maggie arched her back, almost ready to have him enter her again. "That was the first time I spent any time with you. When you were injured and you were swearing in Russian in your sleep."

"I never asked. How did you know it was Russian swearing?"

"I know how to swear in many languages," Maggie said, running her hands over his back, not telling him the complete truth. If she told him about her one-time Russian lover and then her other ex-lovers, he might talk about his and that was the worst thing that could happen at the start of a romance.

He lay alongside her and she handed him a glass with the dregs of the champagne in it. "I hope it's not too flat."

"Nothing about this night could be flat," he said.

She reached down outside the light sheet and touched his erection through the fabric.

"You are really a marvel," she said.

"And my . . . my injury does not repel you?"

"Sure," she said, putting her head on his shoulder. "You can tell how distasteful I've found this whole night."

He drained the glass, put it on an end table, and kissed her again.

"And now I take my leave," he said.

"I wish you didn't have to."

"I know. But we are guests and we must observe the proprieties."

As he stood up, Maggie put her hand around his erection and giggled, "I like observing *this* propriety."

"Unhand me, wench," Petrov said. He slipped away and put on the tops and bottoms of his pajamas.

Then he came back and leaned over the bed and kissed her again. Maggie responded and said simply, "I'm glad."

"And I."

After he left, Maggie finished the last bit of champagne, feeling decadent, still smiling to herself. Who cared if the man was a Russian or not? She would believe anything he told her.

Back in New York City, Lieutenant Mendoza was trying to avoid going to bed with someone. He had wanted to talk to Manda Esteban, the secretary at Castelnuevo's wheelchair company, so he had found out her address, but when he had gotten there, the woman was just coming down the front steps of her apartment building.

For a split second Mendoza had the idea that Manda Esteban was supplementing her income by turning tricks on the side, then decided that, no, she was togged up in this season's version of what the beautiful people, Latino branch, were wearing. She wore a short red miniskirt and four-inch-high red shoes, with straps wrapping around her ankles. Her midriff was bare and her top was a red sequined halter that fit like a tube she had slithered into. Her hair was piled high on her head and her makeup seemed to have been put on with a spoon. Still, she was a good-looking woman and the way she sashayed down the street proved that she knew it.

He wondered whether to follow her on foot or take his car but got out and walked after her for about a block. She turned into a small run-down–looking tavern that billed itself as the Salsa Dance Club, and even from the street Mendoza could hear the tooth-rattling rhythms played at a sound level that he knew exceeded all city ordinances.

He waited awhile, then walked across the street and inside the place. It was wall-to-wall people, but it was easy to see Manda because she was out on the dance floor, being swirled around by a young man her own age, and Mendoza sat at the bar and ordered a Corona beer.

The music came—as it always seemed to these days—from a disc jockey playing records at the far end of the small, packed dance floor, and Mendoza was in luck because when Manda came off the floor with the young man, she sat down at a table only a few feet from him. Mendoza considered himself a rarity among New York detectives: he had never cheated on his wife, but before their marriage he had been pretty competent at the singles' bar scene. Now it turned out to be child's play to catch Manda's roving eye, buy her a drink, and remind her that he was the policeman she had talked to a few days before and wasn't it all a wonderful surprise that they should bump into each other here in this glorious music club?

She must not have cared much for the young man

she had been dancing with because she dropped him like a lead pellet, joined Mendoza at the bar, and later wound up with him in a back booth in a far corner of the room.

And over the next couple of hours, a time period punctuated by her insistence that Mendoza "spin her around" once in a while on the dance floor, he learned from her that she had been working at Wheels for four years, that she knew the two "Frenchmen" who had been mugging victims, and that she had seen them around the company a couple of times a week for the last two months, but that she knew nothing about them personally and she would like Mendoza to come back to her apartment with her and "do the do."

In turn, Mendoza told her that he wondered why Mr. Castelnuevo had said the men were working there only a couple of days and that he thought Manda Esteban was just a gorgeous woman that any man would be honored to sleep with, but he had offered up his sexuality to God until the health of his mother back in Mexico improved, and he would be in to see her Monday morning at the office because he would like to talk to Mr. Castelnuevo.

"Hey, you not going to get me in any trouble, are you?" she asked.

"Your name will never come up," Mendoza said, and meant it. "I'll just say that neighbors saw the men around a lot. Don't worry about a thing."

He stood up, left some money on the table for her

bill and his, and said that he had to go.

She smiled at him and said, "I hope your mother's health improves quickly."

"So do I," he said, then left before he weakened.

CHAPTER THIRTY-ONE

Young Daniel was subdued on the Sunday evening plane flight back to Teterboro. While Tilda's family had come out to the Donovan spread for a barbecue, young Daniel had spent most of the day with Jeff and Christine, riding on Bitsy. The two older children had taken more than a dozen Polaroid photos of him on horseback, and during the flight Daniel studied each picture aggressively, totally ignoring the ground below which had so excited him on the trip out.

Maggie and Petrov napped in the back of the plane while Christine and Jeff talked to each other about the workload they expected to face in school when it started a short week away.

Tilda watched the ground from the front passenger's seat, fascinated by the patterns the fog made. Lights were coming on and she strained her eyes to see.

When they landed smoothly at Teterboro, there was a message waiting for Donovan at the flight control center. Tilda saw him read it, then crumple it angrily.

"Bad news?" she said.

"No," he growled. "Just Ancie. She's gone off somewhere for the week and she asked me to mind the kids. She's so goddamn thoughtless and inconsiderate. And I've got a week of what looks like hellish work ahead."

Tilda nodded, then said brightly, "Hey. No big deal. I've got the week off and Jeff and Christine can hang out with me. We'll do some of the grand touring of New York. And then every night when you're home from work, they can come back over and stay with you."

"I wouldn't put you through that," Donovan said.

"What through? Daniel loves your kids; they'll all have a blast. Don't worry about a thing."

Donovan thought of it for a moment, even as he watched the children. Daniel had hugged Christine, then offered his hand to Jeff, wanting to seem more grown-up.

As Donovan and Tilda approached, Jeff kneeled down and hugged Daniel.

"Hey, what's that?" Jeff said. Something was poking him from the pocket of Daniel's coveralls. Daniel pulled it out sheepishly. It was a small horseshoe.

Daniel looked nervously at his mother. He had been trying hard not to pick up things, but the horseshoe and the photos were all he had to remember the weekend with.

"It was on the floor of the stable," he gulped, looking first at Jeff, then at his mother, then at Donovan. "Does some horse need it?"

"No, champ," Jeff said. "It's yours. Maybe it'll bring you good luck. They're supposed to, you know." He hugged Daniel again and that made up Donovan's mind.

"Okay," he told Tilda. "Jeff and Chrissie will come home with me tonight, and we'll talk in the morning about how I'll pack them over to you."

"Good deal," she said. "They'll all love it."

"And me too. It gives me more chances to see you," he said.

"I've already thought of that," Tilda said.

When the limousine let Petrov off in front of his building, the Russian stood on the street for a while, smoking a cigarette, reluctant to go inside just yet. He had nothing specific on his mind, but he was not satisfied with the work he and Donovan had yet done and he felt he should be doing more.

They were no closer to finding where Abu Beka hid out; and the continued silence from Aziz and Stanhope, and now Brian Cole, in Paris was growing ominous. There must be a way to rattle Tenterallah's cage and get the animals on their feet. He thought about it for a moment, then walked to the corner and hailed a cab to take him to El Fazid's restaurant.

Not that he thought Fazid was a major player in this terrorist game — far from it. In Petrov's view, the man was just a merchant who heard a lot and saw a lot and, as a normal business practice, said very little. It had taken some heavy threats by Lieutenant Mendoza to get Fazid even to admit that the two dead Arab bodyguards and Ayoub had been in his restaurant more than once and that he had heard the men describe themselves as being in the wheelchair business. It was just possible, though, that Fazid knew that keeping quiet was not just the means to maintaining a good business but to maintaining good health. It was possible that he knew of someone a step up in the terrorists' organization, and if Petrov could get that name, perhaps he could start up the line until . . . until what?

Until he found somebody to kill, he told himself grimly.

But he was disappointed when he entered the restaurant and Fazid was not there. It was late on a Sunday night and there were only a few people in the main dining room, where a redheaded woman did a bored, desultory belly dance to recorded music.

He sat at the small four-seat bar, ordered a coffee, and engaged the bartender in conversation.

"No," the young man said, "Mr. Fazid takes off every Sunday night. His only day off." The bartender was young and blond and talked with a thick accent that Petrov had come to recognize as New

Jersey.

Annoyed with himself for running out on a wild goose chase, Petrov hunkered over his coffee and tried to shut the sound of the tinny music out of his mind.

He had almost finished his drink when a young waiter who usually served the lunch shift came to the service bar, saw him, and did a double-take. He came up to the Russian and said, "Mr. Peterson, can I talk to you for a moment?"

"Certainly," Petrov said, slipping back easily into his thick British accent.

The two men stepped off to the corner of the service area near the door and the waiter said, "Geraldine. You know, the dancer?"

Petrov nodded.

"Well, she called me a couple of nights ago." The waiter was whispering, and he looked over his shoulder to make sure that no one was trying to eavesdrop on their conversation. "She and I are pretty good friends. Anyway, she told me that if I saw you, I was to ask you to call her."

Petrov essayed a small smile. "I am back with my wife, I'm afraid."

The waiter shook his head. "It wasn't like that," he said. "She said it was real important, a matter of life and death." He moved his face closer to Petrov's ear, so close that Petrov could smell the spices from the young man's dinner, and said, "And she told me to make sure that Mr. Fazid didn't know." He shrugged. "I think it's important."

"And she didn't tell you what it was about?" Petrov asked.

"Sorry, no. You want her phone number?"

"Yes, please."

"I'll slip it to you at the bar. And remember, you didn't hear it from me."

Carol was sitting in a chair in front of the television when Maggie returned home.

"So how were things in Donovan's paradise?" she asked. Sarcasm steamed up from her voice and Maggie saw, with dismay, that there was a drink on the table next to her and the ashtray held the remnants of two joints.

"Everything was fine," Maggie said. "How come you're home? I thought you'd be on the shoot."

"It fell through. I don't want to talk about it." Carol slumped down deeper in her seat, not even bothering to close the robe that had slipped open and exposed the front of her body. Maggie could recognize the signs; her daughter was spoiling for a fight.

It had been a nice weekend; she didn't want to spoil it with a fight now.

"New bracelet?" she said lightly, nodding toward the three-inch-wide woven bracelet Carol was wearing on her upper arm.

"Yeah," Carol said sullenly. The bracelet had

379

come from Hassan; he had gone overboard this weekend and gone past the slapping and—he called it—"discipline" that she was used to. Instead, she had found herself naked on his bed with her wrists and ankles locked to the posts of the bed with iron cuffs. He had given her some drugs then, and she had begun to drift off into a never-never land and she expected Raffi to take her then, to make love to her, but instead he had flung open the bedroom door and invited men in to look at her naked body.

Even with the drugs in her system, Carol was afraid and embarrassed and three men—young ones—walked around the bed and spoke about her as if she were a piece of beef at a specialty butcher's. They made gross, lewd, evil suggestions about what they would like to do to her, and Raffi encouraged them, smiling, telling them that soon Carol would do anything they wanted her to because she was meant to be a slave.

"She was born for slavery," he had said. Finally, he had cleared the other men out of the room and while she was still chained, had done painful, violent sex with her, hitting her body, punching her about the legs. Often, in the past, he had teased and spanked her, but this went beyond that, into sharp pain, and it took more drugs to numb it and she passed out with Hassan inside her body.

When she awoke, she was still chained, and Hassan had dangled the gold bracelet in front of her eyes and told her it was hers because "you're my slave now. Say it. Call me master." And it really was a beautiful gold bracelet and she called "Master, master," and then the sex and the punishment had started all over again.

On Sunday afternoon he said that he had to go out on business, and soon after she showered and decided to go home. Let Raffi worry for a while about where she was. It hadn't really been such a bad experience, she had told herself. And the bracelet was real.

"Where'd you get it, baby?" Her mother's voice brought her back. She was talking about the bracelet.

"They gave one to me for canceling the shoot," she said. "Sort of a consolation prize."

"Expensive prize," Maggie said.

"Are you accusing me of something, Mother?" Carol snapped.

As Maggie shook her head, Carol stood up and her robe slid open. There were massive black and blue bruises on each thigh, as if somebody had been squeezing them.

"Oh, baby. What happened to your legs?"

"I was posing on some rocks by the sea and I slipped," Carol said, snapping the robe shut around her.

"I thought you didn't go on the shoot," Maggie said.

"I don't know what you want from me," Carol yelled, and snapped off the television. "You and your boyfriend go off to play house with Donovan and his latest floozie and you come home here all charged up with accusations. Maybe you should accuse yourself of something."

"I've done nothing to be ashamed of," Maggie said lamely.

"I'll bet. And Mark too. I bet all four of you slept at a monastery, didn't you? Especially the wonderful Mark Donovan."

"Mark's love life is none of your business," Maggie said, the temper starting to rise in her, despite her effort to control it. "Floozie? You talk about floozie? You're the real thing. Tilda Matthews is as good a woman as you can find, and I only hope it works for Mark. And as for his life, you butt out of it. And as for mine, well, I don't come home battered and bruised like somebody from a cheap whorehouse." She started to say more, then snapped, "Forget it, I'm tired and I'm going to bed."

For once she walked out on her daughter without saying good night, without begging for a kiss. She banged her bedroom door behind her. A few moments later, dressed in a warm robe, she wanted to take back the words she said, but thought it would be wrong. Let Carol stew. It was about time she got a dose of her own nasty medicine. She had been too pampered for too long.

Carol fumed. She fumed herself in a fury, her mother's insults adding flames to her drug-boiled brain.

She finally got up and went into her room. Fifteen minutes later she emerged in a lacy black dress cut tight below the bust to push her breasts up. An old-fashioned Spanish shawl with embroidered red roses caressed her shoulders. It had been hanging on a wall in her room, a gift from her mother years earlier, and she had never thought of wearing it, but now, with the shawl and the dress and very high-heeled red shoes, she felt like Ava Gardner. What was the movie? *The Barefoot Contessa*. The movie had turned out badly for Ava, but the evening, she was sure, would not turn out badly for her. Not tonight. Tonight was going to be hers and she was going to start getting even. She left her mother a note before slamming the apartment door.

CHAPTER THIRTY-TWO

"It's Aziz. He's dead." Brian Cole's voice over the telephone was low, guttural, and Donovan said, "Are you all right?"

"I'm okay," Cole said. "A little trouble, but I'm okay."

"Where are you?"

"I'm back in New York. At JFK. I'll be right up."

"Okay. The door'll be unlocked."

Jeff and Christine were asleep in the two guest bedrooms of Donovan's sprawling apartment. Donovan went into his study and dialed Petrov, but there was no answer.

Aziz dead. And Donovan realized with a touch of remorse that he had never even met the man. Hiring Aziz and Stanhope had been Brian Cole's job; neither of the two men ever knew whom they were working for. It was the way to build intelligence systems with cutouts all up and down the line.

And that was all good and it was all fine technique and it was all bullshit, he realized. When did the killing ever stop? He sat at his desk again, a wave of disgust flooding over him about the work he was involved with. He was just too old for this crap. He tried Petrov's phone number again, but again there was no answer.

Petrov had not wanted to call Geraldine from the telephone in El Fazid's, and he had long ago learned that public telephones in New York City never worked.

So he grabbed a cab back to his apartment and called from there the number the waiter had jotted on the inside of a matchbook. Petrov recognized the Long Island telephone exchange because the Russians had a lot of their spy operation in New York head-quartered out on the Island.

It was very late and he told himself that if a man answered, he was going to hang up. But Geraldine's voice picked up the call on the first ring.

"This is Tolly Peterson. If you can't talk now, just say 'wrong number' and hang up and I'll call tomorrow."

"Oh, no. Oh, Tolly. I'm glad you called. You were at the restaurant?"

"Yes. I got your message."

"I'll have to be quick. My husband's due home from work any minute."

"Yes, Miss Geraldine," Petrov said. He hoped this was not going to be another one of those interminable *Prisoner of Zenda* love stories.

385

"Tolly, I'm afraid you're in some trouble."

"Oh?"

"Friday night a man broke into my house and raped me."

Petrov sighed. "I don't know what to say. . . ."

"No, Tolly. He wanted information. About you."

"What kind of information?" Petrov asked.

"He wanted to know your name and I had to tell him because he had a knife on my throat, but then he wanted to know everything about you and I didn't know anything, so I couldn't tell him anything."

And thank God, Petrov thought, for being careful and telling no one any more than you had to.

"But he was very interested in you. I think it had something to do with those two greasers who were killed. Tolly, you're not in any kind of trouble, are you?"

"Not that I know of," Petrov said. "And I didn't even know those men. This man who . . . who came to you, what did he look like?"

"Like another fucking Arab," Geraldine said. "I hate those bastards. This one had one of those big red birthmarks, what do they call them, port-wine stains I think, on the side of his face. Bastard."

Petrov could hear her starting to sob on the other end of the phone. "I'm terribly sorry that you had to be put through this," he said. "Did you call the police?"

She paused and said, "No. Tolly, my husband wouldn't understand. He never wanted me to work for Fazid anyway and I'd just get a lot of I-told-you-so. I thought it was best not to say anything. But I had to let you know. You were always so nice to me."

"And you to me," Petrov said.

"I have to go now. I hear my husband," Geraldine said.

"Take care, dear heart. Take care."

Donovan heard a sound in the apartment outside his study and stood up and walked toward the door. He thought Brian Cole had made good time from the airport. But when he opened the door, he could hardly believe his eyes . . . for a half second the woman reminded him of Ava Gardner. It was Carol and she swung past him, turned, and said softly, huskily, "Hello, Mark. I thought you might be lonely."

And then, without hesitation, she was all over him, unbuttoning his shirt, running her hand gently over his nipples. He tried to push her away, but she just dropped down and unzipped his pants.

"No, dammit," he snapped. "Get out of here. Are you crazy?"

"My, don't we sound stuffy?" she said. "I'd like to be stuffed with you." She slapped his hands away as he tried to zipper his trousers and buried her face in him.

For a moment his resolve weakened. Just for a moment. Then he pushed her roughly by the shoulders, backed away from her, and zipped up his pants.

"What's the matter with you?" he demanded of her as she sat curled up on the floor.

"And what's the matter with you?" she snapped. "You just get so much pussy this weekend, you can't think of any more? This would be special, Mark. Trust me. It really would. And I don't know why you fight it. You know you want to do it to me. You always have."

"And you're so fucking drugged up, you make me sick. Get off the floor and get out of here."

Anger crossed her face for a moment, and then she smiled. "If you're not interested, Mark, maybe he is."

He followed Carol's gaze and saw Brian Cole standing in the doorway to the study. The big blond man looked as if he had been in a fight; his clothes were wrinkled and dirty and there was a gash across his left temple with dried blood crusted on it.

Mark saw him, then angrily turned to Carol, grabbed her by the shoulder, lifted her to her feet, and pushed her out of the study toward the apartment door.

"Get out of here," he said. "If you ever come back, I'll call the police on you."

She did not even make an effort to salvage her dignity. Instead, she ambled across the room in a hip-swinging parody of the cheapest of street hookers, and, at the door, turned and said, "I hate you, Mark. And you'll be sorry you did this to me. I've got friends, big friends, and they'll fix you. And all your

388

buddies."

Then she was out the door, slamming it behind her.

Donovan quickly went over and double-locked it. When he looked back at Cole, the big blond was grinning.

"So that's your new girlfriend," he said.

"Heaven forbid," Donovan said. He noticed Cole starting to waver a little on his feet and jumped forward to his side, steadied the man, and helped him into the study, where he put him on the big swivel chair behind Mark's desk.

"Sorry, Mark," Cole said. "It wasn't as easy as I thought. There was somebody waiting for me at the airport."

"You going to be all right?"

"Chip shot. I've gotten hurt worse in whorehouses," Cole said.

Donovan closed the study door and then dialed Petrov's number again. This time the Russian answered, and Donovan said, "There's trouble."

"More than you know," Petrov said.

"Brian is here. Aziz is dead."

"I'm on my way," Petrov answered.

Brian Cole's head wound had been more superficial than the amount of blood would have indicated, and Donovan had patched it up with a bandage from his medicine cabinet.

Now, sitting in Donovan's chair, Cole again went

389

over for Petrov what he had found in France.

"I couldn't find any trace of them at the apartment they had rented," he said. "But I did find some of Aziz's notes. He was working on a report I'd sent him about the phone calls from Abu Beka, and at the bottom of it, he wrote 'Les Fées Altérées' . . ."

" 'The Thirsty Fairies,' " Petrov translated.

Cole nodded. "Yeah. It's a café and, get this, it's right across the street from where the IPA bureau chief, the one who gets Abu Beka's phone calls, lives. I think Aziz figured out that that's where the telephone calls were made from, but that's just a guess."

Petrov nodded and Cole paused to sip from a steaming cup of coffee on the desk.

"The bartender at the café remembered seeing a guy in there who sounded like Stanhope to me, and it was the night the last message was telephoned in. But he didn't know anything about where Will might have gone when he left the tavern, and he didn't notice anybody else in there.

"What I figured, though, was that Will and Aziz hung around waiting for somebody to make the phone call and then they followed him."

"A reasonable guess," Donovan said.

"I had to figure the worst, so I checked with the Paris cops, but there weren't any unidentified bodies, so I started looking around. There's a town called Nogent about an hour from Paris. I found Aziz's body there. They had found it floating in the Seine. His head was shot off and the police couldn't identify him."

"You're sure it was Aziz?" Petrov said.

"Yeah. Of course I didn't let on to the cops that it was, but I could tell as soon as they opened the locker at the morgue. They had the 'unidentified' tag tied to his toe and Aziz had a deformed big toe, twisted almost sideways. It was him all right. The French cops are shit. They recovered an abandoned car, too, and just had it parked outside police headquarters, but they never thought to check it out. It was the car Aziz had rented. I know 'cause I found the rental slip back in their apartment."

"There was no sign of Stanhope though," Donovan told Petrov.

The Russian shook his head. "He's dead," he said flatly.

Donovan looked at him quizzically and Petrov said "Obviously both of them were together, trying to track down the phone caller. Aziz was killed and so, I'm afraid, was Stanhope. If he had escaped, we would have heard from him by now."

"I just wish you were wrong," Cole said.

"No more than I do," Petrov said.

"But I think you're right," the blond mercenary said. "There was something else that was important, I think. When I looked at Aziz's body, he had something cut into the inside of his arm. Two letters. It read 'U.N.' "

"As in United Nations," Donovan told Petrov.

"You could not have been mistaken?" Petrov asked

391

Cole. "The body had been in water. Could those just have been scratches?"

Cole seemed to bristle at that suggestion. "No," he snapped. "I looked carefully. The letters were carved, like with a penknife or something. But I couldn't figure it out. It was a strange kind of torture."

"I don't think it was torture," Petrov said. "I think it was a message from Aziz to us. Something is planned at the U.N. He wanted to let us know."

"My thought too," Donovan said.

"So when I was leaving this little town of Nogent, I got the feeling somebody was following me," Cole said. "I just hoped it was the bastards who got Aziz, so I tried to set a trap for them, but they were tricky and I couldn't nail them. So I wrote it off to my imagination and went right to Orly to get on the Concorde back here. But I don't think it was my imagination 'cause two guys jumped me when I got to JFK. Two wogs."

"Did one of them have a red birthmark on his face?" Petrov asked.

"How'd you know that?" Cole asked.

"Never mind. Just keep going," Petrov said gently.

"Well, they jumped me but I don't think they were trying to kill me 'cause they just got my wallet and then they split. I was a little too groggy then to chase them. When my head cleared up, I called Mark and came over here."

"Was there anything in your wallet?" Petrov asked.

"Just some money," Cole said. "I always keep my

passport and my ID in an ankle wrap." He patted the lower part of his leg.

Petrov did not bother to ask Cole if he was sure that he had not been followed. Cole was a good operative and would not have made such a mistake.

"So how'd you know about the guy with the red birthmark?" Donovan asked the Russian.

Quickly, economically, Petrov told the story about the rape of Geraldine, and how the assailant had seemed interested in one "Tolly Peterson."

"It's obvious," he said when he finished the recounting, "that they're on to us. They can recognize Brian, and they're trying to find out who Tolly Peterson is. I don't think they can trace anything yet to me . . . or to you," he said as he nodded to Donovan.

Donovan leaned against one of the bookshelves, tapping his lower lip with a ball-point pen.

"Well, screw 'em even if they do. Maybe it'll flush these bastards out into the sunlight. Meanwhile, we've got to assume that what was written on Aziz's arm was what we all believe, a message. So something's planned for the United Nations. But that doesn't tell us much. There's all those offices there, people working every day. Then there's the General Assembly."

"I'd bet on the General Assembly," Petrov said. "Whatever these people are going to do is going to be for show. Taking out some office clerks wouldn't do it. The Assembly is my guess."

"Mine too," Cole said.

"Well, one good thing about that," Donovan said. "We've got time. The General Assembly doesn't come back into session until next month some time. Usually around Columbus Day."

"Not this time," Petrov said.

"What do you mean?"

"I just heard it on the cab radio coming over. There's been a special session of the General Assembly called for Tuesday. Two days from now. To discuss terrorism."

It was not safe any longer for Brian Cole to return to his apartment in Greenwich Village. That was agreed upon, and since Donovan's guest bedrooms were already being used, Petrov insisted that Cole come and stay at his apartment.

"If they come after us, there'll be two of us for them to deal with," Petrov said.

"I hope they come," Cole said grimly.

After the two men had left, Donovan went back to the desk in his study. He had a gut instinct—and he had learned never to go against them—that whatever was planned for the United Nations would happen on Tuesday, at the special General Assembly session.

So little time, so much to do.

CHAPTER THIRTY-THREE

Lieutenant Bobby Mendoza was up early, cooking breakfast, when his wife came into the kitchen in the two-family house they owned in Queens.

As Jenny's pregnancy progressed, she was sleeping more and more; it had been that way with their first son, and now it was happening again. But Mendoza had no complaints. At least she had stopped all her foolish talk about an abortion.

She came up behind him as he was cooking bacon at the stove and put her arms around him and squeezed. He could feel the hard knot of her swollen belly pushing against his buttocks; he had always thought it was one of the best feelings he had ever experienced.

"Hey, wanna fool around?" she whispered in his ear.

"You're not pregnant enough yet?" he said without turning, then pushed the bacon to a back burner, turned, and embraced his wife.

Everything was wonderful and getting better. Now, if he could only find out something worthwhile in what he had come to regard as the "Donovan case." For all the guilt it had given him, spending some of Saturday night with Manda Esteban had not produced much of value. Still, there were a couple of questions worth asking Gaspar Castelnuevo — such as why did he tell Mendoza the two dead "Frenchmen" had been in his place for only a couple of days when Manda said they had hung around for weeks?

Even before asking the question, he knew Castelnuevo's response: "I'm sorry, I just didn't want to get involved." It was the answer policemen heard most, but the good ones still asked the question.

After breakfast he drove directly to the plant and office of Wheels.

He found the plant open, but the only person in sight was Manda Esteban, who was in the assembly room alone.

"Where is everybody?" Mendoza asked.

She shrugged. "Bobby, I don't know. I tried to call Mr. Castelnuevo and tell him I'd be late because I had to go to the dentist, but he didn't answer the phone and so I came in but there ain't nobody here. *Nada.* Nobody. Nothing. Everybody is gone. Like they took everything. Where is he? Is something going on?"

"I don't know," Mendoza said. "Do you have a home phone number for him?"

"In the office." Manda walked away, moving like a ghost, wispily and without human energy. Obviously she was not capable of having her known world made incoherent without an explanation. "Here," she said as she fingered a card in the Rolodex.

Mendoza pulled the card from the holder, dialed the number, and received a recorded message from an anonymous telephone company voice that the number had been disconnected.

"Dammit," he said, pounding the phone back on the base. "You ever call him on that number before?"

She slumped into her desk chair. "Only once," she said. "I hope nothing funny's going on here; he owes me a week's pay 'cause I wasn't in Friday. I don't have no money."

"You keep any petty cash around here?" Mendoza asked placidly, knowing that he would probably fork over some cash if she didn't.

Manda brightened and unlocked a drawer of the file cabinet and took out a cigar box. When she opened it, she whistled and riffled through some bills.

"There's more than a thousand dollars here," she told Mendoza, her face wide-eyed in confusion and surprise. "Last week there was only fifty."

"Well, you take it home with you for safekeeping. And if you don't ever get called again, maybe you just count it as severance pay."

Manda nodded and put the money in her purse. She went for her coat that was hanging on a hook inside the office door; she had brought no possessions with her when she took the job except a coffee cup, and she could leave that. It was an old one, a mug with her sister's name on it. If she wound up being able to keep the thousand dollars, she could get one with her own name on it.

She turned at the door and said to Mendoza, "He is a strange man, Mr. Castelnuevo."

"I know, but listen, if you hear from him, tell him to call me. I want to talk to him," Mendoza said.

"For you, Bobby, anything," she said, and gave him a large smile. It was small enough reward for anyone who put a thousand dollars within her grasp.

Driving back to Manhattan in his car, Mendoza got a radio message to call home. Worried immediately about Jenny having a problem with her pregnancy, he stopped at a stationery store and called her.

"Don't get upset," she said. "Nothing's wrong. It's just that Mark called and wanted you to stop in and see him after lunch. At his office. I told him I'd reach out for you."

"Okay, Jenny. I'll be there. You go to bed and rest, hear me?"

"And I'll dream of you."

Well, if it had been Tilda's plan to take the three kids to see all the New York City sights, the United Nations was as good a place to start as any, Mark Donovan thought as he rode with Jeff and Christine in a cab down to U.N. Plaza.

The two children were still filled with chitchat about the weekend, and Donovan, distracted by his thoughts of impending trouble at the United Nations, answered in monosyllables until Jeff said, "Dad, your friend, Tolly?"

"Yes?" Donovan said.

"Is he gay?"

"No. Why do you ask?"

Jeff shrugged in the manner of teenage boys for whom awkward was an understatement. "I don't know. He's just kind of . . . well, you know, quiet and doesn't join in with anybody."

"He's a loner," Donovan said, "but he's not gay. Take my word for it."

When they got out of the cab they saw Tilda and Daniel near the ornamental flower beds in the middle of U.N. Plaza and Jeff grinned. Daniel was bent down, extricating something from the dirt, and Jeff said, "Looks like the pack rat found himself another trinket."

"Tilda was saying he just can't resist shiny things," Mark said.

"Don't get huffy, Daddy," Christine said. "We both think it's cute."

Mark and Tilda embraced and there were formal handshakes from Daniel all around. The thing he had found on the ground was a combination beer-can-and-bottle opener and Tilda said, "Throw that junk away."

Daniel looked glum, and when he was sure his mother wasn't looking, he stuck it in his trousers pocket.

399

Mark took them inside and showed them where they signed up for the visitor's tour.

"You're not going with us?" Tilda said.

"I have to wait for Tolly," Donovan said, "and we have to see somebody. Then we'll catch up with you. If we don't get to you before the end of the tour, we'll meet you in the bookstore. Wait there for us."

He left them when he saw Petrov coming through the big open doors at the front of the building.

Dennis Hastings, deputy U.N. ambassador, was behind his desk, his sleeves rolled up above his elbows, when Mark and Petrov were escorted into his office.

Papers were strewn around the desk in front of him.

He rose politely, even though it was obvious that the last thing he wanted to see in his office was visitors.

"Mark," he said, and glanced questioningly at Petrov.

"Good of you to see us, Dennis. I know you're busy; we'll get out of your hair as quickly as possible. This is my associate, Tolly Peterson."

The two men nodded and shook hands.

"Sorry for the chaos. But an unscheduled meeting of the General Assembly . . . well, it's never happened before," Hastings said. "The logistics are a grade-A pain in the ass."

"Not to mention the subject matter," Petrov said.

"Beg your pardon?" said Hastings.

"He means terrorism," Donovan said smoothly. "It would seem that there would be some people around who'd just as soon not have the U.N. say anything bad about terrorism."

"Thank Jesus that that's not my problem," Hastings said.

"Remember when I was here last week, Dennis. I said that I'd heard that there might be trouble planned for the U.N.? Well, we think that's going to happen."

"Because of this resolution?"

"That's my guess," Donovan said.

Hastings was silent for a moment, a clear signal that he wanted the two men to state their business and clear out.

"Dennis, I need you to make a phone call for me. We have to talk to the top guy in U.N. Security, and we don't have time to go through normal channels."

Hastings shook his head; Petrov noticed that not one strand of his gray hair deviated from its original position.

"It'll be tough, Mark. For the reasons you said. The security arrangements here for a sudden meeting like this are a nightmare. I don't know what I can do."

"Is the security chief an American?"

"The security chief is away on medical leave. There's an assistant handling things."

"An American?"

"Yes," Hastings said. "A retired FBI man. But he works for the U.N. now and he's become a freaking internationalist."

Donovan grinned. "We'll talk to anybody. Can you tell him to see us? It's important." When Hastings did not immediately respond, Donovan said, "Dennis, I can have the President call you about this if you want."

"That important, Mark?"

"That important."

"Wait here," Hastings said, and walked rapidly from the office. He was back in less than ninety seconds.

"You're in luck," he said. "The security man is Ken Reynolds; he's got ten minutes between meetings and he's waiting for you right now. Two floors down." He gave them the room number and still another pair of visitor's badges to pin over the ones already on their jackets.

"These'll get you there with no problem."

"Thanks, Dennis," Donovan said as he pinned the badge on his coat. Petrov did the same, and the two men walked to the door.

"The President, huh?" Hastings said.

Donovan paused and nodded.

"Welcome back," Hastings said with a grin.

"Go to hell, you nasty old **man**," Donovan responded. As they left the office, they could hear Hastings's sharp laugh resounding in the room behind them.

The meeting with Kenneth Reynolds did not go well, and Donovan knew that the man had never been a working FBI agent. He had always been an administrator, in charge of moving personnel from one place to another.

He and Petrov had agreed they would tell the security chief as little as possible, since there was no point in getting anyone panicked. Donovan tried to get away with just telling the man that they had heard rumors from good sources that trouble was planned at the U.N. tomorrow.

"Demonstrations?" Reynolds asked.

"Or worse," Donovan said.

"Well, we hear those kind of rumors every day, Mr. Donovan. I wouldn't worry about it if I were you. We've got things in good order here."

"The security down below is abysmal," Petrov said. "The metal detectors don't even work."

"A little glitch but they'll be working by tomorrow," Reynolds said peevishly. "As I said, don't worry. These rumors never turn out to be anything. And I don't mind telling you, since you're a friend of Ambassador Hastings, that it's a good thing too. Sure, the security's not as tight as we'd like it to be, but it's a public building. We get girl scouts and nuns visiting from India, and you just can't screen everybody and give them a body cavity search. So we do the best we can and I'll tell you, I think it's pretty damned good. Some of our equipment is down right now, but there's a lot more that you civilians don't really know anything about, or even see. Detectors for explosives, for weapons, hidden cameras, specially trained guards looking for people who match psychological profiles, we've got it all, fellows. I tell you, our record is top-notch by any standards."

Donovan thought the man sounded like a public relations brochure, and Petrov said dryly, "I hope your record continues that way," but Donovan could recognize the disgust in the Russian's voice.

"These rumors we're talking about, Mr. Reynolds, are more than just your usual rumors," Donovan tried again. "They may be substantial."

"But you don't have a name or anything to give me. Just a suspicion that there might be trouble. So what is it you'd like me to do?" He took an obvious glance at his watch.

"I'd like you to bend every effort to tighten up security for tomorrow," Donovan said. "If we come up with anything more specific, we'll give it to you."

"I'm going to be very busy," Reynolds said. It was not an apology; it was a brush-off, and suddenly Donovan lost his temper, looking at the smirk on Reynolds's face.

"And I'd like you to make sure you're available this afternoon," Donovan added as he rose from his chair.

"Oh? Why's that?"

"Because the President of the United States is going to call and tell you again what I just told you. I didn't think you'd want to miss his call. I know you don't work for him, but you live in his fucking country and you don't know heat until it comes from the White House. We'll be talking, Mr. Reynolds."

Reynolds rose quickly to his feet behind his desk. "Now, wait just a second. Anything you've got, you can tell me. You can be sure I'll act on it. You don't have to hurry out of here."

Petrov looked at his watch and shook his head. "Sorry, we've got important business elsewhere," he said, and led Donovan to the door.

But before exiting, the Russian turned and fished into his jacket pocket. He pulled out a gray lump of a clayish substance and tossed it underhand across the room to Reynolds, who caught it with surprising facility.

"What's this?" he said.

"C-4 plastic explosive," Petrov said. "I walked right through your lobby with it in my pocket. You might want to recheck your explosives detectors."

"Was that really plastic?" Donovan asked.

"Of course," Petrov said.

"Where'd it come from?"

"I brought it into the country with me. It's no fucking wonder the world is plagued by terrorists when you have bureaucratic numbskulls like that one

405

in charge of security. I even tried to look suspicious when I came into this building."

"You can't look suspicious anymore," Donovan said. "You're too average-looking. Especially in that suit. You look like an American tourist from Podunk."

"Where is Podunk?"

"I don't know. Middle America somewhere. It's a saying, sort of."

"I will never understand you cowboys," Petrov said.

Their visitors' badges were supposed to be good to get them to only certain offices, but no one tried to stop them and they caught up with Tilda and the children as the tour had reached the General Assembly hall. Petrov was happy to see that Maggie had joined the group.

Donovan grinned at her. "Goofing off from work again, huh?"

"Sorry, boss. I wanted to talk to you and I thought this was the best chance I'd have."

"When we're done here," Donovan said.

The tour guide was a young, pretty girl whose travelogue was short, smart, and so well-rehearsed that she might have been loaded with a cassette, but Donovan had heard it all the previous week so he just spent the time admiring the mosaics on the meeting room walls.

They all rode down in one of the building's huge elevators to stop in the bookstore for souvenirs. Daniel was delighted at the thought; somewhere, Donovan decided, the young man had picked up a gene for shopping. As they left the elevator, Daniel was jabbering to his mother about some global map he wanted to buy, when a man in an electric wheelchair came out of the bookstore and made a sharp turn into the pedestrian traffic.

Daniel was in his path, his eyes glued to the colorful collection of toys in the gift shop window across the way. The man in the wheelchair yelled, "Get out of my way!" and Daniel turned, frightened and frozen in place.

The wheelchair grazed him, pushing him off to one side, and before Donovan could react, Jeff was at Daniel's side, holding him. "What are you, some kind of maniac?" Jeff demanded. "He's a little kid."

"He can walk," the man said ominously. "And I can't. Now, all of you get out of my way."

"With great pleasure," Jeff said. He had his arm protectively on Daniel's shoulders, and he squatted down and asked, "You all right, champ?"

"Yeah," Daniel said.

"Good. Let's go see what kind of toys they've got inside."

"Good work, Jeff," Donovan said.

Petrov must have seen the expression on Donovan's face because he came alongside the taller man and said, "You look very proud of your son."

407

"I am," Donovan said.

"You have every right to be," Petrov answered.

While Petrov went to the men's room, Mark took Maggie aside and said, "So what's so important that you had to leave the office."

She handed him a note. It read simply, printed in big block letters: FUCK YOU. I'M NOT PUTTING UP WITH THIS ANYMORE.

He looked at Maggie questioningly as he handed the note back.

"From Carol," she said. "I came home last night and we had a row and she must have walked out and left this behind. Mark, I'm worried sick."

Donovan put his arm around her. "She came by my place last night too," he said. "And I'm afraid I tossed her out."

"It was bad?" Maggie asked.

"Yeah." He shrugged. "But she left telling me she didn't need me, that she had lots of friends. I think that's where she went. She's probably staying with friends until she cools off."

"Mark, what can I do?"

"You won't take my advice but I'll give it anyway," Donovan said. "She's a woman now, not a baby. And you can't live her life for her. You've done everything you could do and if she still wants to act like a fool, I don't know how you can stop her."

"You think I've done everything?" Maggie said.

408

"I don't think, I *know*. That kid's had everything. You've gone without to make sure that she hasn't. And if she's got a chip on her shoulder, it's not because of anything you . . . or I, for that matter, had anything to do with. You can't go beating up on yourself because Carol . . . well, dammit, because Carol is a shit. It's not your fault."

She looked at him for a while before answering, then said, "Thanks, Mark. I guess I needed that. But what's going to happen to her?"

"Whatever she wants to have happen," Donovan said.

They were interrupted by the three children and Tilda coming out of the gift shop and Donovan said, "Look, you're not going to be any good to me in the office today. Why don't you hang out with Tilda and the gang?" He smiled in their direction. "I think she could use the help."

"I can work," Maggie said stubbornly.

"Good. Then you can follow orders too. Go with Tilda and the kids." He squeezed her hand. "Please. Do me this favor."

"How could I resist you anything?" she said.

CHAPTER THIRTY-FOUR

Bobby Mendoza stopped by Donovan's office. It was not what he expected at all. He had figured on Technology Modern and instead the outer office was filled with wicker étagères, rubber plants, large Chinese pottery, and couches covered with white cotton. The only thing that hinted at what kind of business might go on there was huge artsy-fartsy photographs of helicopters all over the walls.

The receptionist eyed him suspiciously, her long nails scratching near the phone beside her as if she were ready to punch the call button for security. Mendoza had to admit he didn't look like someone in the market for a fleet of helicopters.

"I'd like to see Mr. Donovan," he said.

The receptionist looked at him as if he had just belched at a state dinner. She seemed to have been carved from ice, with her platinum hair and cool blue gaze and Mendoza wondered idly if Donovan were banging the young woman. It would be a waste if he weren't, but he doubted it. If she was getting shtupped regularly, her manners wouldn't be so bad.

"Do you have an appointment?" she said, seeming to know the answer very well. This kind of person in his ill-fitting suit and his greaseball background would never have an appointment to see Mark Donovan.

He took out his wallet and flashed his badge at her.

"Just tell him Lieutenant Mendoza is here."

She seemed befuddled for a moment, and he resisted the urge to say *And tell him if he isn't out here in ten seconds, I'm coming in with both guns blasting.*

Instead, he waited and she called Donovan's office and said to tell Mr. Donovan that a Lieutenant Mendoza was there to see him and just the faintest trace of surprise tickled her face and she nodded and hung up and said, "You can go right in. His office is down the hall there, last one on the left." She even favored him with a small, timid smile.

There was another man with Donovan inside his big, window-wrapped office. He was not exceptionally tall, but he had a wiry look to his body and a hard face that gave the impression the man was not to be messed with.

"Bobby, I don't think you've ever met Tolly Peterson."

The two men shook hands as Mendoza said, "Right. The guy on the telephone."

"What's that?" Donovan asked.

"Your friend here was on the telephone one day while I was in El Fazid's. I thought you looked familiar."

Petrov nodded. "You have a good memory."

Donovan said, "Tolly's working with me on everything. Repeat—everything. So you can talk freely. Any leads?"

"Not a thing. I can't find out anything about the two dead guys. I even went up to Wheels, where they were supposed to work, and romanced one of the secretaries a little, but nothing's checked out."

"What is Wheels?" Petrov asked.

"A wheelchair factory in the Bronx. I told you, Mark, the owner, Castelnuevo, came in to see me and identified the guys, but he didn't know anything about them. Said they'd been into his place only one or two times. But then I talked to his secretary and she said she saw the guys around there a lot more than that so I went to see Castelnuevo and ask him about that." He chuckled. "I guess they weren't much in the way of wheelchair salesmen at that 'cause today it looks like the company went out of business. So I'm still trying to run down the owner, but so far nothing. Is that what you wanted me to stop in for?"

Donovan was silent for a few moments and Mendoza could tell that his old captain was wrestling with the thought of telling him something.

Finally Donovan said, "Listen, amigo. This is for

your ears only."

"Naturally."

"There's a chance that terrorists might try something at the United Nations tomorrow."

"Shit. Just what we need to make New York City perfect," Mendoza said.

"Anyway, we're still trying to check it out, but I need your advice. What could the New York City police do if there was some kind of unofficial word that there was going to be trouble?"

Mendoza walked to the bar and said, "Mind if I help myself?"

"No, go ahead."

The policeman poured himself a weak bourbon in a very tall glass filled with water. He sipped at it, then turned around and said, "Probably the most we could do would be to limit access to the building. You know, ring it with cops, seal it off, and allow in only authorized personnel. It'd be a big pain in the ass with a lot of screaming and yelling going on, but it'd be something anyway."

"But the U.N. is international property. Would you men have any authority or jurisdiction there?"

"Inside the building is U.N. property," Mendoza said quickly. "The streets outside belong to the city and we've got the right to do anything we want on the streets to preserve law and order."

"I was hoping the answer was something like that," Donovan said. "And who'd make the decision to take that kind of action?"

"The chief inspector. You'd have to go right to the top."

"You got any pull in his office?"

"None at all," Mendoza said. "I'm just a street cop. This'd be a case where you'd need your influential friends to grease the way."

"Okay," Donovan said. "You going to be around today?"

"In and out of my office all day. I'm going to have to start letting up on these two deaths and get to work on the rest of the stuff in the pile," Mendoza said. "My captain's starting to look at me like I'm a guy with a drinking problem."

"I'll be in touch," Mark said as he rose from his chair. "Let you know what's going on."

Mendoza drained his drink quickly and said, "No clues. You can't hint who might be causing trouble? Somebody I could chase through the files for you?"

"Not yet. Maybe later," Donovan said.

Mendoza looked at the other man, Tolly Peterson, and the Brit said, "The only possibility is Fazid at the restaurant. You leaned into him once, Lieutenant, and got him to open up a little. Maybe if you lean again, some more will come tumbling out of our fat friend."

Mendoza nodded and said, "Well, why not? I haven't had lunch yet today, and I do fancy his food." He grinned.

The three children had had a good time in Bloomingdale's. Both Jeff and Christine considered themselves too grown-up to be interested in the toy department, but they spent a lot of time helping Daniel find exactly the right toy. Without much encouragement he finally settled on a helicopter whose rotor spun with accompanying sound effects and had a lot of flashing lights and was able to roll across the floor by battery power.

When Tilda and Maggie followed the three children out the side exit of the store, neither noticed the van that was stopped in the no-parking zone.

The three kids were strolling on ahead and were snatched off the sidewalk first. Maggie and Tilda were deep in conversation, talking about Mark's family and their background, and it was only when strong arms grabbed at them and a gruff voice said to be quiet that they snapped awake. They looked into the back of the van, where the seats had been ripped out, and saw the three children sitting on the floor. Daniel was crying and Christine seemed near tears. Only Jeff had managed to maintain some composure, even though a pistol was being held near his head by a man with a red port-wine stain across the right side of his face.

"Get in without any noise," the man behind Tilda and Maggie said. "Or there'll be shooting."

The women let him push them into the van; the man clambered in and drove the vehicle away from the curb. In minutes both women and the three children had been bound and gagged by the man in back.

Only Maggie could guess why they had been kidnapped; it was because of Donovan's work, and she wondered with a sinking feeling if she had been in any way responsible for this awful act.

"Mark Donovan."

"Bobby, Mark. I thought you'd like to know. I stopped off at El Fazid's for lunch but it was closed."

"Oh? Why?"

"Shopkeeper next door told me. Fazid's dead. Shot at his home last night. Sounds like somebody else thought he might know too much."

"Thanks, Bobby."

They were probably still in New York because the ride had been less than a half hour and there had been none of the echoing sounds they would have heard had they been driven out of New York City through one of the tunnels to New Jersey.

Tilda had an idea they were near the river, and if she had to bet, she would have said the Hudson, because she could smell the oiliness in the air.

They heard an automatic garage door open and then felt the van back up, obviously into a building. Then, still blindfolded, they were herded into an elevator. When the door closed behind them, they were searched. The shoulder bags of the two women were taken away. Christine was not carrying a bag. Jeff's pockets were turned inside out and two male voices seemed dismayed when they discovered his Swiss Army knife. Jeff, hearing them, said, "Hey, lighten up. It's only a pocket knife."

"Quiet or you die," one of the voices snapped back in rough-hewn English.

Daniel, the only one not searched, was terrified. He didn't want to be dead. Dead was like his great-uncle Paul, his grandfather's brother who had a train set that Daniel had loved. He had lived in Brooklyn and he and his mom had gone to visit him lots of times. And then suddenly Uncle Paul was gone and so were his trains. Mom had said that Uncle Paul had died and gone to heaven. She had told him that being dead meant that you just didn't live anymore. He wanted to live till next Christmas, at least, because Mom had promised to get him a Nintendo TV game.

And then the elevator started up.

"Let's face it, we're dead-ended." Donovan looked at Petrov as if wishing to find in his face some proof that he was wrong, but all he saw was a bland sort of agreement. "If we had even an inkling of where to start, it was Fazid. And now he's belly-up. We're screwed."

"Sorry, Mark. I'm no help," Petrov said. "It may be time to call in the big guns. Get Washington to have the New York police seal off the building tomorrow. If we're right, at least we can give them a run for their money."

"I don't know if we can justify it," Donovan said.

"Hell, that's the easy part," Petrov said. "We make a dozen anonymous phone calls all over the city; call the police, call the press, threaten to blow up the place. It's simple. And everybody would be saying, 'protect our United Nations,' and Washington would be expected to act."

"Think it'll work?"

"I don't know," Petrov said with a sigh. "It's hard to shut a terrorist out if he's really wound up. And we don't know who we're dealing with. For all we know, there may be people inside the U.N., members of delegations who might be ready to carry out some weird suicide mission. But at least this way we've got a chance."

"Okay," Donovan said, the reluctance obvious in his voice. "I guess there's nothing better." He looked at Petrov and said, "We've been at this a couple of months now. I think I've come around to your way of thinking . . . we don't have a lot to show for our efforts, do we?"

"Don't get down on the operation, Mark," Petrov said. "Maybe we've got more to show than we think. First, we got rid of those savages from the airport massacre. And we saved a shipload of people from

God knows what. And we came real close to getting Abu Beka, through Aziz. But we've forced his hand. Even tomorrow at the United Nations . . . we've forced that out of him and who knows, maybe the son of a bitch will show up himself and we'll be able to silence him once and for all."

"You put a good face on it, Petrov. But we were set up in business to get rid of him and he's still calling the shots."

"Yes, that's true. But you said it yourself. We've been in business for only two months and we had only you and me and Cole and two hired hands who didn't know who they were working for. Maybe, if we can head this all off tomorrow, we'll get some more manpower. Some muscle. Go ahead, call Washington."

Donovan nodded unenthusiastically, but before he could reach for the telephone, his private line rang.

He picked it up and said, "Mark Donovan here."

Then he listened. As Petrov watched, the big American seemed to go white.

Then he hung up the phone and looked at Petrov with an expression of total horror.

"It was Abu Beka," he said, his voice low and somber. "They've got the kids. And Tilda. And Maggie."

CHAPTER THIRTY-FIVE

They had heard a man speaking on the telephone. He spoke a language they did not understand, but the message was only a few words, and even if he had been speaking English, they might have missed it.

They were in a room somewhere, where mattresses had been placed on the floor. Their hands were tied behind them and their ankles had been tied also. The ropes were very tight, and trying to slip the bonds was out of the question.

They wore blindfolds and they were gagged.

Maggie and Tilda had been placed on the same mattress; it was big enough to allow them to stretch out on their sides if they wanted to rest, but neither of them did that.

Tilda could hear Daniel whimpering, but it seemed far off and she could only hope that he was near enough to Christine and Jeff to be comforted. The reason she knew she was with Maggie was that Joy perfume was redolent in the room. She tried to talk to Maggie but all she made were muffled grunts. The blindfold itched, too, and for some reason she thought of that stupid commercial where a kid misses his mother because his clothes were no longer treated with the fabric softener he favored.

She mumbled again and heard Maggie respond with an identical grunt. It was hardly anything, but it was at least some kind of communication.

Maggie found herself oddly delighted to hear Tilda. The rag in her mouth was making her so dry that she felt as if she were in a dentist's office with that little tool they used sucking away all the moisture from her mouth. She thought of Carol. Was this her punishment for bringing into the world a child who might have been better unborn? *If I ever get out of this, things will be different,* she vowed to herself.

Jeff was sitting on the edge of a mattress, too, his mind sharp, trying to think carefully. They were not going to get him with this kind of treatment, no way. This was sort of a mind-bending, brainwashing experience, trying to deprive them environmentally, but he was going to reject it. He had read all about it once in a spy novel by Bill DeAndrea. He didn't know why they might be trying to brainwash him, but they weren't going to do it. And sooner or later they'd make a mistake, and he would stay sharp and be ready for that moment.

He felt a movement behind him, then realized a person was crawling next to him. The small body leaned against his, and he realized it was Daniel and the little boy was crying. Stop it, Jeff wanted to call out. You'll drown yourself in your own tears. And, almost as if he had heard Jeff's thoughts, Daniel's sobbing lessened. Good, Jeff said to himself. Together, maybe he and Daniel could get themselves free later on. At least after these gorillas who snatched them left them alone. He wondered where Christine was. *If those bastards have so much as touched her, I'll kill them,* he thought.

Christine was on a small mattress by herself. She had heard Daniel's whimpering and had rolled from one end to the other of the mattress, trying to figure out exactly where she was located. She finally managed to roll off onto a splintery wooden floor. She was wearing jeans and she managed to crawl and hop forward toward the sound of the whimpering and then the whimpering stopped. She hoped Daniel was with Jeff.

And then she heard a guttural voice that said, "Look, one of them got out of bed." The voice sounded as if it were making a big joke and another person guffawed as if appreciating the humor. Then rough hands grabbed her and felt her body as she was tossed back onto the mattress.

"Everybody stay where they are," the guttural voice said. "And that way, nobody gets hurt."

Carol had been free all afternoon—at least, free to walk around the bedroom of Hassan's apartment. But the telephone had been removed from atop the desk in the room and when she tried the door, she found that she was locked in. A prisoner. Who did Hassan think he was anyway? This was America, not Iran or some backwater country where women were supposed to stay home, under a veil and just breed for their masters. She steamed for a moment, then began to calm down.

It was all right. He had left a supply of cocaine on a dressing table and a few lines helped her get through the long afternoon and into the evening.

She found some tranquilizers in a medicine cabinet in the bathroom and took those and finally lay down to sleep.

When she awoke, she was tied up in the bed. The same bonds that she had gotten used to were holding her wrists and ankles to the four posts of the king-size bed.

Rafjan Hassan was sitting on the side of the bed next to her. He was fully dressed. His hand rested on her bare breast as casually as if it were a part of his body and not hers.

She realized that however it had happened, this man now owned her. She was his chattel and, for the first time since she had met him, she thought that perhaps she did not want to be owned by anybody. Or anything. Maybe her mother was right; maybe she was doing a little too much in the way of drugs. She would stop that. Tomorrow. Tomorrow she would start a new life, turn a new leaf.

She looked up at Hassan and tried to smile.

"Darling," she said. "I'm very hungry. Can I have something to eat?"

"You deserve it. You have done us all a great service. You may never know what it is, but it is a very great service." He smiled at her.

"Please. Some food," she said again.

"Beg for it," he said, his smile turning sour. "Let me hear you beg. It is how I want to remember you."

He squeezed her nipple viciously and the pain made her cry out. His smile only widened.

"Absolutely not." It was the first time Donovan had ever heard Petrov raise his voice; he blinked and looked puzzled.

"Petrov, we can't let the U.N. get blown up, or whatever else these people have planned. I've got to call Washington; I've got to get the New York cops on the job."

"And kill your children? And Maggie and Tilda?" Petrov shook his head. "No. I say no. Look. The man said he was Abu Beka. Did he say he'd release the kids?"

"He said if I stopped my activities against 'freedom-loving people' I'd see my family again this weekend. Otherwise their lives are forfeit."

"I think we should take him at his word," Petrov said.

Donovan sat at the desk, his head buried in his hands. "I just can't let it go like that. I can't let the U.N. get butchered. I can't, Petrov. I can't. I've got to call Washington. I've got to."

"Then, Captain Donovan, I think I have to remind you of the commission under which we work," Petrov said coldly. "The agreement that put us in operation said clearly that nothing is to be done unless both of us agree. I do not agree with calling Washington at this time."

His eyes were steely and his lips a thin line in his pale face. He had always thought Donovan was soft; but what the American wanted to do now was not the decision of a soft man; it was the judgment of a man who rated duty above all, even above family.

But it was unnecessary. At least for now.

"Dammit, Petrov. What the hell do you want of me?"

"Good. You're finally ready to talk. What I need, what we both need, is some time."

"What are you talking about?" Donovan asked.

"Look at it, Mark, look at the facts. There's been a leak in our operation. How was anybody able to trace anything to you? No way that we can think of and yet, Abu Beka's men are able to snatch up your kids and the women. How?"

"A leak." Donovan thought hard. "Not you, not me. Mendoza doesn't know anything and neither did Aziz or Stanhope. Brian Cole was the only other one who knew anything. Unless the leak came from your boss or mine in Moscow or Washington."

"A leak from our superiors would make no sense," Petrov said. "And even though he does not like me, I would stake my life on Brian Cole."

A voice behind Petrov said, "Well, thanks for the endorsement, Russky," and both men looked around to see Brian Cole standing there.

"Brian. You know what happened?" Donovan said.

He nodded and Petrov said, "I called Brian here. Now, we were talking about leaks. I think it was Maggie."

"Maggie?" Donovan snapped. "That's preposterous. She's been with me . . ."

"I don't mean that she did anything directly. But indirectly. Through her daughter. I've been thinking about this. You said Carol was with some Iranian diplomat at a charity ball."

"That's right," Donovan said.

"Do you know his name?"

Donovan thought for a moment. "Maybe she called him Raffi, or something like that. I'm not sure."

Petrov nodded. "Lately, I heard from Maggie that Carol was still seeing him. It's just possible that Maggie said something in an unguarded moment that Carol may have passed along. You remember, you know, that she was suspicious when she heard the news reports about the helicopter involved in the rescue. And I know she knows I'm a Russian, not an Englishman. Maybe she let one fact too many slip."

"It's just conjecture. How do we prove anything? How do we find out anything?"

"What you do is you sit there. You man the phones in case Abu Beka calls again. Brian, I want you here to make sure that Donovan doesn't try to call Washington to roll out the troops tomorrow to protect the United Nations. You give me time to try to track down Carol and see if we can get anything that way. Do it my way, Mark. If nothing else, we can still call Washington in the early morning. This is New York. They can muster their entire police department with an hour's notice. If we have to go your route, we will. But first my way."

Donovan sat silently for long seconds. "I'm heartbroken over this," he said.

"I know you are. We all are. And that's why we have to try it my way first."

Finally Donovan nodded. "Okay," he said. "It's seven-thirty. You've got till midnight."

"Six A.M.," Petrov said.

Donovan started to protest, then shook his head. "Fair enough," he said. "And you don't need to leave Brian here. You've got my word."

"I know that, but let him stay. Something may come up; Abu Beka may call again; you may need an extra pair of legs. And I work best on my own," Petrov said, trying to exude a confidence that in his heart he did not feel. "Later you may want to call Mendoza in. Have Washington assign him to you if you have to. He may know the best ways to cut the red tape with the police department if we have to go that way."

Without any more conversation Petrov headed for the door. So much to do, so many lives at stake, so little time.

Before he left, though, Donovan called out, "Petrov. You need a weapon? I have a gun in the desk."

The Russian shook his head. "I have my own weapons," he said.

Cole looked at him and said, "Go get them, Tolly."

Petrov nodded.

CHAPTER THIRTY-SIX

Petrov took a cab to the Russian Embassy, housed in an old brownstone on New York's fashionable Upper East Side.

He rang the night bell and counted off the ninety seconds it took for someone to answer. The man spoke to Petrov through a loudspeaker rigged up alongside the door.

"What can I do for you?" the voice said in English.

Petrov replied in Russian. "You can open the door. I am Colonel Anatoly Petrov, the Committee for State Security."

He took the KGB card from a secret pocket in his well-worn leather wallet and slid it through a slot in the door. The person on the other side looked at it, then examined Petrov carefully.

"Hurry, man," Petrov snapped, again in Russian. "There's a great deal to be done."

"Certainly, Colonel." The door was opened and Petrov slipped inside. The man behind the door was barely twenty-five years old, with already thinning light hair and a faint blond mustache on his long upper lip.

"What can I do for you, Colonel?" he said in Russian.

"You're the acting officer in charge?" Petrov said.

"Yes, sir."

"The first thing you can do is contact Moscow immediately to confirm my authority here. And then round up whatever staff we have available. We have to find a needle in a haystack."

The blindfolds had been left in place and all five kidnap victims had been spoon-fed some sort of tough stew and water. As soon as her mouth was free, Tilda had cried out, "Daniel, are you all right?"

"He's fine," Jeff responded, and Tilda realized that if his gag had been removed, too, at least two men were handling their feeding.

"Quiet," snapped the man next to her. "We have no intention of harming anybody at this time. As long as you obey our orders."

"But why were we taken like this?" Tilda said. "What do you want of us?"

Her answer was a hard slap across the face. "You will get your answers in due time. Now eat and be silent."

Tilda forced herself to eat, her mind rollicked

with confusion. Jeff was silent also; he had listened to her voice carefully. He estimated that Tilda was thirty feet away from him. It was just a fact he stashed away in his mind. Their time would come.

It was almost midnight when Donovan called Bobby Mendoza at home.

Jenny picked up the telephone and Donovan disguised his voice because he could not face up to useless small talk.

"Lieutenant Mendoza, please," he said.

Mendoza got on the telephone immediately and Donovan said in his natural voice, "This is Mark, Bobby. My kids and a couple of other people have been kidnapped. I need you here."

"Are you at the office?"

"Yes," Donovan said.

"Have you called the FBI yet?"

"No, and I can't. I'll explain when you get here. Can you make it?"

"I'm on my way," Mendoza said.

When he hung up the phone, Jenny said, "Mark Donovan?"

"Yes. He's got trouble," Mendoza said as he slid from the bed and began slipping into a pair of trousers.

"I thought it was him. He was trying to disguise his voice but I recognized him."

"I guess he didn't want you to worry," Mendoza said.

"What's going on? Can you help him? Will it be dangerous?"

"Would it matter?" Mendoza said.

"No." She shook her head. "Just be careful."

The Russians had, Petrov knew, no facility for building cars or computers or typewriters or telephones. But they were unmatched in the world at spy work.

He looked at the report that was placed before him in the desk he had commandeered in one of the embassy offices.

"Rafjan Hassan. Thirty-nine years old. Member of Iran's delegation to the United Nations for the past five years. His father was a wealthy landowner under the shah but somehow seemed to have made his peace with Khomeini and the other mullahs who took over the country because he still has a position in the government in charge of oil pipeline production.

"Rafjan Hassan has been involved in several altercations with police in the three years he has been assigned to the United Nations. Each case, which was dismissed because of payments made to the complaining witnesses, involved his beating of women. None of the incidents were ever reported in the United States media. Hassan lives in an expensive condominium, owned by his father, on East 60 st. While he lives alone, he is often visited by Iranians living in the United States. It has long been believed that he acts as a point man for the Iranian government in attempting to stir up trouble in the United States and coordinates activities with guerrilla groups. He is a known drug user and has a reputation as a playboy, often frequenting expensive New York restaurants and clubs. He had been seen occasionally at El Fazid's on West 29 Street." Another link, Petrov thought.

Attached to the report was a Xeroxed reproduction of a newspaper clipping that showed Rafjan Hassan and three other men talking to one another at some sort of charity fund-raiser. The image in the photograph was of a softish face with the petulant mouth that often characterized the spoiled brat.

Petrov stood up and handed the manila file folder containing the report and photograph back to the thin, blond-haired youth.

"I won't need to take this with me," Petrov said. "I want to thank you and your men for excellent speedy work."

"It was a pleasure to help, Colonel. Is there anything else we can do?"

"No," Petrov said. "I'll do this on my own. Should I need help, I'll call on the private night line. It's Yevgeny, isn't it?"

"Yessir."

Petrov headed from the office. "Thank you again, Yevgeny."

The food had been drugged. Jeff Donovan could feel it as the medication took over his body. He fought it as long as he could, even after he could hear the soft snoring of the others in the room and feel the regular breathing of Daniel, who still cuddled against him. Jeff could feel dampness, and he knew Daniel had wet his pants.

He fought the drug with all the energy in his fifteen-year-old body, but then it was too much for him and he curled over on his side to sleep.

But he stayed awake long enough to hear a door open, and footsteps going through, and one of the men calling out with a rough laugh, "Good night, sweethearts. Sleep tight. See you all in the morning."

Another man laughed, too, and then the door, heavy metal by its sound, slammed shut behind them. *See us in the morning. At least it's not poison.* And then Jeff Donovan went to sleep.

Carol Henson thought this had gone too far. There were welts on her body from a small whip Hassan had used, and looking at them, she feared they might leave permanent scars. She didn't want to be there anymore. She wanted to go home; she wanted her mother the way she had wanted her when she was a child and had the flu.

"I want my mother," she said softly over and over again.

Hassan laughed cruelly and used his coarse, hairy fingers to push white powder into her nostrils. "This is better than Mother, isn't it, my dear little junkie?" he said.

And it *was* for a few moments, and the pain seemed to go away, but then Hassan resumed whipping her and finally she passed out.

Petrov had waited across the street from the address on East Sixtieth Street until an old man, who had been in the lobby talking to the doorman, left the building and walked down the block.

Then he ran across the sparsely traveled street and into the lobby of the building.

The doorman looked up from behind his security desk.

"Mr. Hassan, please," Petrov said.

"It's very late. Is he expecting you?"

"Yes."

"I'll ring up there, then. What is the name, sir?"

"Mr. Johnson," Petrov said, and when the doorman turned his back to call up on the intercom, Petrov stepped close and hit the man over the back of the head with the small handgun he carried inside his jacket pocket.

He slid the man under the desk, obscuring him from view, saw the number of Hassan's apartment on the master list, took an envelope from the tenant's mail pile on the desk, and then walked swiftly to the elevators.

He rehearsed what he was going to say — some of his languages were rusty — and when someone inside Hassan's apartment answered his vigorous ringing on the doorbell with a curt "Who is it?" Petrov answered in Farsi, "I have a message from Abu Beka."

He held an envelope in his hand.

"Slip it under the door," was the answer in Farsi.

"No. My leader's instructions were to deliver it directly into Hassan's hands."

"I'm sorry. That's not possible," the man answered.

"Ruhi babat sag rid." Petrov snapped off the Farsi curse with vehement anger. "Abu Beka will speak to you of this, you imbecile."

He started to turn and the man called, "Wait."

Petrov heard the door unlock and then open. A young man stood there, his hand in his pocket, as if holding a gun. He was not Hassan, and as he began to speak to Petrov, the Russian kicked him in the groin and jumped inside the apartment, pushing the door closed behind him.

The man groaned, but before he could shout there was a pistol pointing at the tip of his nose.

"Where is Hassan?" Petrov hissed.

"In the back. In the bedroom," the man said.

"Thank you," Petrov said, and slapped the man across the temple with the barrel of his pistol. The man groaned again and fell unconscious.

"We've got to call in the FBI," Mendoza said. He was in Donovan's office, holding a container of coffee he had brought up with him and staring hard at his former army commander.

Donovan shook his head. "No," he said. "I gave Petrov till six A.M. I'll stick with that."

"Who the hell's Petrov?" Mendoza said.

Donovan looked at him, then at Brian Cole, and shrugged. "That's Tolly Peterson's real name. The guy you met. He's a Russian. And now that you know, Bobby, welcome to the team."

"I was always on the team," Mendoza said. "And now this team member says let's call the FBI."

"No," Donovan said flatly, and across the room Cole smacked his big hand on the counter of the built-in bar.

"Dammit, Mark," he said. "We're sitting here. We can get the whole New York police department if we need them. You can pick up that phone and have the President of the United States do what you tell him. We can get the FBI and the CIA here inside of five minutes. And what are we doing? We're waiting around for some goddamn Russian to do something for us."

"Petrov isn't just any ordinary Russian," Donovan said. "Trust me, he's our best shot. He knows these animals and how they think."

"Knowing and doing is something else," Cole said, not even trying to hide his disgust. "I think it's time to get tough—get out there and dredge up some of these bastards, whoever they are, and put a gun in their mouths and make them talk."

"And you don't think Petrov would do that?" Donovan said.

"All I know about this guy is he minces around and talks like Terry-Thomas," Cole said.

"When we were all back in Vietnam, do you remember Molina?"

Cole and Mendoza looked at each other. Molina, the Russian operative who organized counter-insurgency strikes behind the American lines, who had a price on his head like Al Capone; three times American intelligence had gone into a village where he was supposed to be holed up to capture him; three times they had come away empty. Molina had been the Communists' secret weapon in Vietnam.

"Not him," Cole said.

Donovan nodded. "Petrov is Molina. I know more about him than you do. You know when those bastards were busy taking all our hostages in Lebanon? You ever wonder why they didn't take

438

Russians as hostages?"

"Because they're all fucking Communists," Mendoza said. "Why would they take one of their own?"

"No, they're not," Donovan said. "Not Communists. Just crazy haters and they hate anybody who can read or write or do something more civilized than shit in the sand. They hate Moscow just as much as they hate Washington. So they tried once and they picked up a Russian professor as a hostage. They didn't even have time to get it in the press. Moscow sent in Petrov. He found out what group was responsible for the kidnapping and got the name of one of its leaders. Then he dug out that leader's brother, cut off his finger, and sent it in a box to the man with a note that read, 'Other parts to follow.' They released the Russian the same day, and that was the end of taking Russian hostages. Until these new assholes in Iran started busting everybody's balls."

Donovan was nervously drumming his knuckles on his desktop. "Don't either of you get the idea that Petrov's some pansy paper-pusher that Moscow sent over here; if my kids' lives have to depend on one savage human being, I'll take Petrov. So we don't call the FBI. We wait."

"Why are you doing this to me?" Carol moaned. "Let me go. I want to go home. I won't tell anybody anything. Not even my mother."

"Your mother's not around to tell anything *to*," Hassan said. He looked at her searchingly as she lay naked, tied, on the bed. An expression of disgust crossed his face. "You know, you're not pretty anymore."

Carol cried. Through her tears she saw a flash of movement across the room. She heard a thud. She squinted her eyes to clear them.

Tolly Peterson.

He was standing there, a gun in his hand. Hassan was sprawled out on the bedroom carpet, moaning.

Peterson spoke to her. "Are you all right?" he said. There was something wrong, she thought. It was his accent. Where was his British accent? He sounded different somehow.

"I think so," she said. He was at the ropes binding her wrists, untying them; he did the same for the bonds around her ankles.

"Can you walk?"

She nodded.

"Get your clothes on," he said. "Hurry. We're getting out of here. Dress in the bathroom. I want privacy."

He turned his back on her and squatted down next to Hassan, then began slapping his face back and forth, hard. Carol wanted to stay to watch, to see Hassan be hurt, too, but she did not want to make Peterson angry. He seemed to be on a short

440

fuse. So she went into the bathroom, where her clothes were hanging, and began dressing.

She heard only snatches of sound from the bedroom.

"Where are they?" she heard Peterson demand.

There was a mumbled response and then she heard another series of hard slaps.

Then she heard Hassan begging, "Stop, stop, stop." And then in a softer voice he was talking again.

She heard Peterson's voice again, this time speaking in a language she did not understand, although it was the same language that Hassan and the other men in the apartment often spoke.

What Petrov had said in Farsi to Hassan was: "You have ten seconds, you pile of jackass dung, to answer me. Or I will cut your throat out."

And then Hassan was babbling, babbling, talking like a flood in that strange language. And then there was a gurgling sound, almost like an underwater scream, and then there was silence.

Carol pulled her dress over her head and came back out into the bedroom. Tolly Peterson was at the large desk that occupied one corner of the bedroom, tearing through loose papers on the desk. Finally he took a notepad with writing on it and pushed it into his pocket.

She looked at Hassan on the floor. He was not moving and, oddly, Peterson had pulled the sheet off the bed and covered the top of Hassan with it,

441

so she could not see his face. As she watched, though, a red stain began to seep through the sheet. He was bleeding.

"I'm ready to go," she told Peterson, and he turned from the desk. Then she looked down at Hassan. "He's bleeding," she told Peterson.

He did not bother to glance down. He said, "He won't bleed for long."

There was another man lying on the floor in front of the hallway door as they ran across the big living room to leave the apartment.

And then the man was turning and she saw a gun in his hand and evil on his face and she saw, almost in slow motion, his finger squeezing on the trigger.

Carol never saw the bullet that slammed into her forehead and took off a large part of the back of her skull.

And she never saw Tolly Peterson dive across the floor atop the fallen man and drive an already-bloody knife that he took from his jacket pocket into the man's chest, then twist it as if he were trying to ream out a hole in a piece of soft wood.

Petrov ran back to where Carol had fallen; just a glance told him that she was dead; and without hesitation he strode to the front door and out into the hall.

He stopped the elevator on the second floor and listened for a moment. He could hear police sirens; they seemed to be outside the building. He stepped out into the hall and punched the button to send the elevator back upstairs. Then he went to the fire stairs at the back of the building, ran down until he came to a locked fire door that led to the basement. He kicked the door open, raced through the dark basement to an outside exit, and came out in an alleyway that led him through to the next block, where he stepped casually into the street and hailed a cab.

CHAPTER THIRTY-SEVEN

The telephone on Donovan's desk rang and he snatched it up before the first ring was complete.

"Mark Donovan."

"Mark, it's Jenny," said the female voice. "I'm sorry to bother you, but I have to talk to Bobby. Is he there?"

"Sure." He handed the phone to Mendoza. "Your wife," he said.

"Yeah, honey," Mendoza said. It must be important if Jenny was calling him here. He listened and said only, "Okay. Thanks, honey. Get some sleep."

As he depressed the receiver button, he explained. "My partner's been trying to reach me. I don't know what it's all about."

He dialed another number and waited through four rings.

"Hey, Gas. It's Bobby. What's up?" he said.

Donovan and Cole could hear only Mendoza's side of the conversation, interspersed by long pauses.

Meanwhile, the lieutenant was making notes on

Donovan's desk pad.

"When was this?"

"Any ideas what happened?"

"They find the knife?"

"Thanks, Gas. You didn't talk to me, all right? Nobody knows where I am."

Mendoza hung up the telephone and looked at Donovan for a moment before glancing down at his notes.

"My partner, Gas, knows I've been interested in Iranians and Arabs and the like, and he just got rousted out of bed on a case. Thought I'd be interested in it." He started to lecture from his notes.

"They found three bodies in a luxury condo on East Sixtieth. One was Rafjan Hassan, who's some kind of low-level diplomat with Iran at the United Nations. Cops think the other guy was a bodyguard."

"You said there were three," Cole interjected.

"The third one was a woman. A . . . oh, shit." Mendoza looked at Donovan with an expression of pain on his face. "I'm sorry, Mark. A Carol Henson. Is that Maggie's daughter?"

Donovan squinted his eyes closed for a long second, then nodded his head. "She's dead, you say?"

"Yeah. She was shot, apparently by the bodyguard," Mendoza said.

"And the other two?"

445

"The bodyguard was stabbed in the heart. Hassan had his throat torn out with a knife. The knife wasn't in the apartment."

His glance moved from Donovan to Cole and back to Donovan again.

The big American sat behind his desk, his eyes still pressed tightly shut. Only one word escaped his lips.

"Molina."

Mendoza nodded. Russian Lightning had struck again.

All he wanted to do was to sleep, but Jeff Donovan forced himself to wake up. He could not tell if it was day or night or how long he had slept because of the drugs, but he had to be awake now. It was his responsibility, and his father said people should always live up to their responsibilities.

He still could not see, and the gag in his mouth tasted like dried vomit; his body felt like a Gumby doll; the drugs the kidnappers had given them must have been powerful. For a moment he worried that they might have given Daniel an overdose, but he bent his head down where he could feel the form of the sleeping six-year-old and heard his breathing strong and regular.

There were no sounds in the room except for the steady breathing from the other captives, and carefully, trying to be as quiet as possible, Jeff slipped away from Daniel, off his mattress, and moved across the floor in the direction where he thought Christine would be.

He found that with his hands tied behind his back he made faster and quieter progress by rolling than by trying to crawl, and he rolled across the floor until he hit the edge of another bare mattress on the floor. He used his head as a probe and finally felt a body. There was a little muffled sound, but even through the gag he could identify Christine's voice. He hoped she would be physically able to help him. He nudged her with his head until he felt her rise into a sitting position. Then he put his head behind her so that his face touched her hands.

She was slow to react; maybe she was sleeping in a sitting position, he thought. He punched her back with his forehead and got a soft answering groan, then pushed his face into her hands again. She understood. Quickly, she pulled the blindfold from his eyes, just down so that it hung loosely over his nose.

They were in some kind of large, empty warehouse room. His eyes needed no time to adjust to the darkness since he had been in darkness for hours. A window high above the floor let in a little reflected light from street lamps, but it was obviously nighttime. Jeff looked around the room but saw no sign of their captors. They were probably outside the big steel exit door in the corner of the room. It was the only door.

Jeff put his face behind Christine again and this time she used her fingers to twist the gag from his mouth, down onto his chin. It was tight, and the pressure hurt his face, but it was such a relief to be able to talk again that he almost felt like letting out a war whoop.

Instead, he put his mouth close to Christine's ears and said, "Listen, Chrissie. Don't be afraid. We're going to be all right. Now I'll take off your blindfold." He squatted on the floor and his sister rolled over until she pressed her face against his hands. Quickly he lifted her blindfold and then tugged to get the gag out of her mouth.

Tears came into her eyes as she looked at her big brother and he said softly, "Shhh, quiet. Everything's going to be all right. I've just got to figure out how to get us loose. My hands are numb and these knots are too damned tight to untie."

She whispered something back and he put his ears close to her mouth.

"The pack rat," she said.

Of course. Daniel was the only one who had not been searched. Maybe there would be something in his pockets, some object they could use as a tool to loosen the ropes.

Jeff looked around the room. Tilda and Maggie were on another mattress about twenty feet away, curled up back to back, like Siamese twins who didn't like each other. Daniel was still asleep on the mattress ten feet away in the other direction. Moving confidently now that he could see, Jeff rolled his way across the floor until he was next to Daniel's sleeping body.

Daniel had been wearing baggy jean-style corduroys and a thick sweater, and Jeff turned his back and with his tied hands began patting the young boy's pockets. He felt embarrassed doing it, as if he were a child molester. In one of the back pockets he felt something. A piece of metal of some kind with one sharpish point that was pushing through the corduroy. He tried to fit his fingers into the pocket, but his hands were too big, so he grabbed the point that stuck through the fabric and began to push it back and forth, trying to rip through the corduroy.

His hands were big and strong but it was still tough going and it gave one thread at a time, and then the metal thing popped out. It had one rounded end and the other sharp, curved end and Jeff remembered it was the kind of beer-can opener people used before they invented pop-up tops. Where did Daniel get it? No one used them anymore, did they? He put the questions out of his head and started to roll back to Chrissie, careful not to drop the tool. If it slipped away from him, he might have a tough time finding it again in the dark.

He sat back to back with his sister. With one hand he held one of her wrists. With his other hand he used the point on the end of the can opener and began to pick at the rope binding her. He was glad of one thing: the ropes they used were the old cotton kind that could be picked apart. He did not know if he would have had the strength to pick through one of the newer woven nylon cords.

He could feel the rope starting to fray under the point of the device; it heartened him and he worked faster, harder. Who knew how much time they had left before the men came back?

He leaned his head back toward Chrissie's and said in a whisper, "If they come back, drop back on my hands and I'll put your blindfold and gag back on. Then you sit up and do the same for me. With luck they might not even notice. Okay?"

"Okay, Jeff." She hesitated. "Jeff, are we going to be all right?" The terror in her voice, a fear he had refused to face up to, made his heart seem to twist in his chest.

"Count on it, sis. Don't worry about a thing."

The sky was getting lighter. It would not be long before the sun came up, and he was looking for a needle in a haystack. The street was filled with warehouses, old dilapidated buildings that in most major cities of the West would have been torn down.

And in one of them were two women and three children and he was their only hope.

He had hoped for more from Rafjan Hassan. All that Hassan knew was that the hostages were being held in a building someplace downtown, near the Hudson River. He had not known who or where Abu Beka was. He had not known anything that might have been planned to disrupt the United Nations' special meeting and in fact, he was planning on being in the Iranian delegation there that day. But he *had* been the source for the leaks on Petrov's and Donovan's involvement. The information had come from Carol Henson, and Hassan had sent it back to Iran to the head of the secret police. But what happened to it from there he did not know. Nor did he know who killed Fazid or even that the fat restaurant owner had been murdered. He insisted that he was a low-level aide at the U.N. for Iran, occupied mostly with people's visa problems and political woes. He helped with hotels and with airline reservations. But he did nothing else. He knew nothing else. He swore that was the truth. And then Petrov cut his throat.

And now, here Petrov was in a jungle of tired old worn-out buildings, any one of which was more than large enough to hold hostages, and he didn't know which one.

The sun was coming up.

He looked around him in distraction. Maybe it was time to call Donovan; tell him to guard the United Nations and get a contingent of New York City police down here to comb through every one of these buildings.

Then he saw a sign. It was a small sign, next to the door of a particularly ugly red brick building. It read:

WHEELS.
WAREHOUSE DEPARTMENT.

Christine was free, and quickly she untied Jeff's hands and feet. He stood and stretched; it felt good to be moving again. Better than good. It gave him a chance.

He ran first to the window, but it was ten feet off the floor and with three women and a child there did not seem to be any way he was going to get them all out. Then he started to walk softly, like a cat, around the perimeter of the loft. He needed a weapon, something that would give him a chance when and if these people came back.

The room had been stripped bare. There was not a tool, not a piece of equipment, nothing that could be used as a club or a weapon of any kind.

He held in his hands the insignificant little beer can opener that he had used to cut loose the ropes. It seemed as if that would be all he had.

He stopped again and looked around the room. Christine had untied the two women and Tilda was at her son's side, untying his ropes. The little boy was still sleeping. A thought came unbidden into his head: How could anybody drug such a young child? He tightened his grip on the can opener. If that was his only weapon, then that would just have to do. That was another lesson he had learned from his father. What-ifs don't count; you did the best you could with what you had in hand.

"It's six o'clock," Donovan said. "Time's run out. I have to call Washington."

"Are you sure?" Cole said. "We haven't heard from Petrov. He's still out there. Maybe there's still a chance."

"I can't take that chance," Donovan said. "Six o'clock was our deal. And now we have to worry about the United Nations."

"Shit on the United Nations," Mendoza said. "Worry about your kids."

"I am, Bobby. I am. And yours too. And everybody's," Donovan said, then picked up the phone to dial Washington.

CHAPTER THIRTY-EIGHT

Jeff had untied everyone. Tilda had been awake but Maggie seemed to be almost in a coma and had to be slapped into consciousness. Tilda untied Daniel, but he would not wake up and she held the sleeping boy in her arms, rocking back and forth on the mattress.

Meanwhile Jeff looked around the big storeroom in the growing daylight, but the room was totally empty.

The only alien objects in the room were the three big mattresses on the floor.

Think, Jeff, think, the teenager told himself as he looked around in desperation. The men had guns; there wasn't any way he could take the two of them down long enough for the women to escape with Daniel.

Eventually, he went to the window again. He pulled over one of the mattresses and found that by folding it against the wall he could climb on it and, on tiptoe, just reach the sill. His fingers touched the dried-out wood of the window frame, and he began using the heel of his hand as a hammer, trying to break it loose. Finally, with a muffled screech, the piece of wood came free and fell into Jeff's arms. It was a two-by-four, about two feet long, and as he hefted it in his hands like a baseball bat, he felt better. It wasn't much, but it was something, and at least he had a chance to go down swinging.

Softly, he told everyone to stay seated on the mattresses and to wait. He himself went to stand behind the door, the two-by-four in his hands.

He heard them talking as he came up the wide wooden stairs, careful to walk as close to the wall as possible to reduce the chance of the stairs squeaking underfoot.

It sounded like two of them, and he could recognize the sounds of Farsi, but he could not quite pick up what they were saying.

The staircase made a forty-five-degree left turn, and Petrov could see that it opened into a large room with bright lighting. He got near the top of the steps, then lay down on the stairs to look around the corner into the room at floor level. People were quicker to spot things at eye level than they were on the floor.

He heard one of them say, "Time to feed our little sweethearts."

The other said, "Maybe, before anything happens, we will have the women."

The first man laughed. "You have been like a stallion in heat ever since you visited that dancer in Long Island. But why not? Still . . . the young one belongs to me."

"You always liked the young ones."

Petrov looked around the corner into the room. The two men were standing in front of a metal door; from the rear they looked big and powerful. One was unlocking the door with a key; the other, a port-wine birthmark on his face, stood behind him holding a half-gallon container of milk in one hand, a pistol in the other.

As Petrov rose to his feet, his own gun in hand, the first man pushed the door open with a cry of "Time for breakfast, children," and then stepped inside.

Petrov saw something flash; the first man fell and the door slammed back toward the closed position. But the second man dropped the milk, put his shoulder against the door and forced it open, then jumped into the room, waving the gun in front of him. Petrov could see that the first man to enter was still lying in a heap on the floor. He groaned. Petrov moved toward the door as the man with the gun reached behind the door and pulled out Jeff Donovan. The boy was holding a piece of wood in his hand and the gunman shouted, "You little bastard," and raised his pistol even as Jeff tried again to lift the club over his head.

"I command you to stop," Petrov shouted in

Farsi.

The man let go of Jeff and turned toward the sound. From twenty feet away Petrov shot him in the face. The man slowly crumbled into a heap, as deliberately as sand dropping through an hourglass.

Before he stopped collapsing, Petrov was in the room.

"Tolly," Maggie Hanson called out.

"Is everyone all right?" Petrov said.

"We're all fine," answered Jeff Donovan. He was still standing inside the door, the length of two-by-four hanging in his hand.

Petrov squeezed the boy's shoulder. "I should have known they'd be all right with you here. Let's get them moving."

The man on the floor groaned, but Petrov seemed to ignore him as he herded the people toward the doorway and the front steps.

"Jeff," he said, "take them downstairs. I want to talk to our friend here for a moment."

"I gotta pee," Daniel said. "Mommy, can I pee soon? I wet my pants once already."

"Real soon, honey," Tilda said.

As Maggie passed Petrov, she leaned forward and kissed him on the cheek. "Thanks, Tolly." He only nodded; there would be time for talk later . . . time to tell Maggie that her daughter had been killed.

But first there were other killings to worry about.

Petrov waited until he saw them moving down the steps and then dropped to the floor next to the other man, who was stirring.

"What is planned for today?" he said in Farsi.

The man groaned, opened his eyes, and said, "What?"

"Today. What is planned for the United Nations?"

"I don't know anything. I don't know what you're talking about."

In English, Petrov said, "That's your tough luck," and drove his knife up through the man's throat into his brain.

As he turned to follow the hostages down to the street, the telephone on the wall rang. It was an old-fashioned business-style phone without a dial, the kind used only for incoming calls.

Petrov picked it up and grunted as if he had just been awakened.

The caller said simply, "Kill them. Kill them all," and then hung up.

Petrov knew he had just heard the voice of Abu Beka.

CHAPTER THIRTY-NINE

By 8 A.M., when New York City had become fully awake, the streets around the United Nations building were filled with uniformed policemen. Barricades had been set up to keep any crowds across the street, and the only visitors allowed into the building had to pass through a single checkpoint, where they were scrutinized by a team of city police antiterrorist experts and their identifications were checked carefully by plainclothes detectives.

The city police had groused after Donovan called Washington, and the White House, in turn, had roused the city's top brass.

But the agreed-on cover story — that Washington had received a number of anonymous terrorist threats against the U.N. — had been clear enough justification to act.

Even the media seemed to take it in stride, choosing to categorize it on the early news shows as preventive steps rather than another raw, naked exercise of unwarranted police interference.

The only sour note came from the secretary general of the U.N., a mildly leftist politician from South America, who complained that New York's police were infringing on the rights and property of the United Nations. But the city's mayor, himself no fan of the U.N., said simply, "Their responsibility is the building; but our responsibility is the streets around the building and we're living up to our responsibility. That's something the U.N. ought to try."

When the go-ahead came from Washington, Donovan had gotten Bobby Mendoza relieved from duty and assigned to temporary duty under his control. Now the city lieutenant was on the barricades, in front of the United Nations, in contact by walkie-talkie with Brian Cole. Cole, in turn, had commandeered a pay phone in a store a half block from the U.N. and kept reporting in to Donovan at the office every few minutes. A fifty-dollar bill placed in the store owner's hands had convinced him that it would be good business to let Cole monopolize the telephone

Donovan sat in his office, watching the scene outside the U.N. on one of the early morning local news shows. He knew his decision had probably doomed the people he loved most in the world. And yet he had had no choice. He did not believe for a moment that Abu Beka had any intention of letting the hostages go free. Petrov had known that too; he knew the minds of these animals.

Petrov.

Maybe Donovan had been wrong in putting all his faith in the Russian's attempt to find and free the kids . . . Tilda . . . Maggie. But there had been no alternative that Donovan could see. A month of police slogging had produced nothing that he could have hung his hat on. So he had trusted Petrov. And now the chances were that Petrov was dead too.

Brian Cole called in on one of the desk phones, but Donovan had trouble concentrating on what he was saying. Even if they were successful in heading off any violence at the U.N., Donovan had lost; everything that was precious in his life had been yanked from him.

He heard Cole's words but somehow could not connect them with any reality he cared about.

"Mendoza just radioed me. Everything looks good so far . . . they're just letting in the safe ones . . . schoolkids and girl scouts and cripples in wheelchairs . . . I think Abu Beka's blown this one. . . ."

The other phone on Donovan's desk rang and he said in a desultory manner, "Hold on, Brian. The other phone."

He lifted the receiver and said, "Mark Donovan."

"This is Petrov. Everyone is all right."

Donovan lowered his head and wept.

461

Petrov had snared a brace of taxicabs and taken everyone to Tilda's apartment. He would rather had gone straight to Donovan's office but he felt he had to insure that there was no danger waiting there for the two women and three children.

He kept one of the cabs waiting while he went upstairs and looked through the apartment, then told Tilda to make sure that everyone stayed inside for the rest of the day.

"Open the door for no one that you don't know," he said, then took Tilda aside and handed her a small automatic pistol. "I didn't want to frighten the children," he said. "Do you know how to use one of these?" he asked in a quiet voice.

She nodded.

"Use it if you must," he said.

Before he left, he took Maggie into the apartment's small bedroom and closed the door behind them.

"I . . . what can I say?" Maggie stammered.

Petrov shook his head. "I'm afraid there's bad news, Maggie," he said.

She looked at him, searching his face for a clue and then she asked, "Carol?"

He sighed and nodded. "She's dead, Maggie. I'm sorry."

462

The woman squeezed her dark eyes shut tightly. Without opening them she asked, "How?"

"She was shot by that Iranian she was seeing," he said. "He was the one who was supplying her with drugs. I'm sorry, but I thought it would be better if you heard it from me."

"What happened to the man?" she said. "Is this another one of those diplomatic immunity insults?"

"No," Petrov said. "No immunity this time. The man is dead. So is his bodyguard." He paused and said, "I don't really know a lot of the details."

She looked up at him, and there was a small pained smile on her face, and she said, "At least they're dead." She reached out and put her hand on his forearm. "Thank you, Tolly. Thank you for that."

He met her eyes. There was so much that she did not know, maybe would never know. Carol had been the person responsible for their kidnapping with her leaks to Abu Beka's organization about what Donovan and Petrov were doing, but maybe it would be best if Maggie never learned that. He squeezed her hand once and left. Time would sort it all out.

When Petrov walked into the office, Donovan came across the room and threw his arms around him.

Petrov tolerated it for just a moment, then said in his most British accent, "Here, here, old sport. Enough of that now."

Donovan stepped back and with a smile creasing his handsome face said, "God, you're a cold-blooded bastard."

"I've heard that said, yes," Petrov agreed.

"Yeah. And you and I both know it's bullshit," Donovan said. "But it'll be our secret."

Petrov nodded and walked across the room to the television set.

"What is happening?" he asked.

"We've got the place rung by cops." Donovan glanced at the large wall clock over the bar. "The meeting's supposed to start in two minutes or so, and that dopey bastard Ken Reynolds has been ordered to have a full security force in the visitors' gallery, so we should have things in order. But I don't see how anybody bent on trouble can get in there. The cops are chasing away everybody except the safest bets. And with all those metal detectors and bomb detectors, I don't see how anybody could get a weapon in there. I think we're home free."

Petrov nodded, then leaned forward toward the TV screen. The tension in his slim body was evident, even from behind, and Donovan said, "What is it?"

"Look at this," Petrov said, his husky Russian

accent more pronounced now than at any time since Donovan had met him. The American came forward to the TV screen, where Petrov was pointing at a spot in the police barricades.

"That's the checkpoint," Donovan said. "All visitors have to be cleared through there."

"Look, man, look," Petrov almost shouted. He pointed behind the barrier of policemen to where two people in wheelchairs were rolling toward the ramp entrance to the building.

"Cripples, school kids, girl scouts . . . that's all they're letting in."

"Mark, it's the wheelchairs. That's how they're getting the weapons in past the metal detectors. They're in the wheelchairs. Nobody looks at a goddamn wheelchair."

It all flashed through Donovan's head, even as he jumped toward his desk. The day before, when they had visited the U.N., that wheelchair had almost knocked Daniel down; Donovan had seen it and later could not recall what the man in the wheelchair had looked like. Petrov was right; nobody looked at a wheelchair. Or the person in it.

He dialed the phone and Brian Cole picked up on the first ring.

"Brian Cole."

"Brian, get hold of Mendoza on the radio. Tell him the wheelchair people."

"What?"

"The people in those wheelchairs. We think they've got guns and that's how they're getting them in. Tell him, for Christ's sake."

"Got it," Cole said, and the phone went dead in Donovan's hand.

They watched it on television. The camera was fixed on the police checkpoint and they saw Bobby Mendoza raise his walkie-talkie to his ear. Then he turned and ran toward the building.

It was all stupid, thought Ken Reynolds as he stood in the back of the packed visitors' gallery. Washington getting all bent out of shape over a couple of anonymous threats and forcing him to load this place up with security guards. He looked around at the gallery, filled with girl scouts and schoolkids and cripples in wheelchairs. Did anybody really think these people were going to blow up the place? Hell, the U.N. got threats every day and none of them amounted to anything. Washington and the New York City police were going to look like giant-size assholes when this day's work was done, and if no one else leaked the story, he certainly would.

The delegates were in their seats and the secretary general, looking like a sociology professor, was walking to the podium at the head of the room to call the meeting to order. Reynolds knew that the group was to discuss some sort of anti-terrorist action, and he was surprised that the press had not picked up on it. Maybe the story just had not been out long enough for the media to start beating the usual drums. That was another reason he knew there would be no trouble; trouble came only at times when the press was making a big deal out of things. Today's action would be quick, easy, over and done with.

The secretary general adjusted his glasses and looked at the notes on the podium in front of him. Reynolds noticed a half-dozen men in ill-fitting suits come into the gallery to stand at the rear. They were quiet but they were cops; Reynolds could tell the breed, and even though he had once been an FBI man, he acknowledged no spiritual kinship between himself and these pavement pounders. He would be happy when tomorrow came and all these troublemaking intruders would be gone. He stole a glance at the closest policeman to him. Hispanic, ill-fitting suit, looked like he perspired too much. Reynolds had liked the New York police better when they were all Irishmen. A spick was a spick, with or without a badge.

The secretary general rapped his gavel and intoned, "I call this meeting of the General Assembly of the United Nations to order."

The buzz in the room quieted. Just then, a

467

man sitting in a wheelchair at the back of the visitors' gallery bolted upright from his seat. There was an automatic weapon in his hand. He raised it over his head and shouted, "Freedom for all our people."

Two other men jumped up from wheelchairs. They, too, had weapons. As the first man lowered his weapon to fire, the Hispanic cop jumped forward and pressed the muzzle of his revolver into the gunman's face. Reynolds heard him say, "Put it down, wog, or you're wallpaper."

The other policemen from the rear of the room had already disarmed the two men in the other wheelchairs. Ken Reynolds ran forward to take over the operation.

"I'll take one of those," Donovan said.

Petrov looked up from the bar, where he was pouring himself a giant-size vodka in a water tumbler.

"Drinking? Is that wise?"

"Today it is," Donovan said. "Hey, don't worry. I'm no alcoholic. I just choose not to drink most of the time. But this isn't one of those times."

Petrov poured him a drink too; they clicked glasses and toasted each other.

"Here's to victory," Donovan said. "Do you think Abu Beka's one of the men they nabbed?"

"No," Petrov said flatly. "I know he's not."

"Then here's to defeat," Donovan said.

"How do you rate this a defeat?"

"Our mission was to get Abu Beka. So we did some good and we freed some people and we saved the U.N. from getting shot up, but if Abu Beka gets away, the first thing will be that he's in the papers and our cover is blown. He knows about us. You and I are going to be matinee idols, Petrov."

"I always wanted that," Petrov said dryly. "Maybe Hollywood will make a movie of my life and I can buy a surfboard and go to California to live."

"You're taking this pretty well for a guy who's about to be put out of work," Donovan said.

Petrov sipped his drink and smiled. "We'll see what time brings," he said.

CHAPTER FORTY

So it had not gone as well as it should have. The television sets in the lounge areas around Newark Airport had been blasting the news about the foiled "terrorist attack" on the United Nations and the three suspects who were captured.

But none of them knew his name, so he was not worried.

Despite today's setback, it had been going very well for him and for Tenterallah these past four years and now it was time to return to Iran, create a new cover identity, and start all over again somewhere else.

The man thought for a moment about the merger of forces by the Russians and the Americans to bring him down. That was one of the day's bright spots. When the bodies of the three children and two women were discovered in that warehouse in lower New York, they would all have serious second thoughts before coming after him again. And that was important, for they had come close this time, getting to Ayoub, getting to

Rafjan Hassan, getting close to his man in Paris. Fortunately, none of those men could lead directly to him. It was the way he had designed his organization. There were only a half-dozen people inside Iran who knew his real identity.

He glanced at the large digital clock on the wall. Forty minutes to plane time, forty minutes to leave this accursed country. He rose from his seat in the no-smoking lounge area and started for the passageway that led to the plane gates.

He stopped at the men's room first.

He was sitting on a toilet inside a locked stall, looking down at his shoes. He glanced up and saw a pale white hand reach over the top of the door, stretch down, and open the lock on the inside of the stall.

Then the door opened and a man entered. He was a thin man with a pale face and unsmiling eyes.

The man on the toilet sputtered, flustered, unsure whether or not to pull up his pants or keep sitting there.

"What do you want?" he finally stammered out.

"You, Mr. Castelnuevo," the man said in English, and then added in Farsi, *"Nufusit bund birih, tukhmi haram."* Die, you bastard.

Gaspar Castelnuevo sprang up from the toilet, his trousers still around his ankles, but even worse as he moved he knew it was too late . . .

the knife was already in the man's hand. He started to plead for mercy, but the man answered coldly in another Farsi curse: *"Zahri mar ham nimydam."* I wouldn't give you snake poison.

And then the knife was in Castelnuevo's throat, and there was only a moment of pain, but he could not cry out because the man's arm was around his mouth and then there was a flash of light as the knife twisted upward and it seemed as if there were bubbles rising in front of his eyes and his nose had been poured full of hot wax. And then there was nothing.

He was dead. And he was spared seeing what came next.

Donovan had taken Jeff and Christine aside at Tilda's apartment and given them a partial version of the truth.

"Truth is, guys, I've been doing some secret work for the government," he said.

"Spy work?" Jeff asked. "Are you a spy?"

Donovan shook his head slightly. "More like intelligence work," he said. "You know, keeping my eyes and ears open. Anyway, those guys nabbed you all because they were trying to put pressure on me. I just wanted you to know and I wanted to tell you that there's no way you can tell anybody about this. It's got to be kept a secret. No one, not your mother, not anybody."

Jeff nodded sagely and Christine said, "You told Tilda this too?"

"Yes."

"Well, she won't say anything either," Christine said. "The only problem might be with Daniel." She looked at her brother and as he nodded, she said. "And we know how to fix that."

When Petrov arrived, the two older children were playing with Daniel and already seemed to have him convinced that the events of the last twenty-four hours were just a stupid game that some people were playing and they didn't like the game either and nobody was going to play it with Daniel anymore.

Petrov noted that the young boy seemed happy to have some sensible explanation for the madness and he was quick to agree that he did not want to play that game anymore, ever again.

Donovan grinned at Petrov. "So there you are. You have a nice day?"

"Only fair," Petrov said. "My butcher shop was closed. It spoiled my plans."

Donovan shrugged in a small gesture of confusion. "Tilda's gone down for Chinese food. We didn't need anything else."

He went to Tilda's liquor cabinet and poured Petrov and himself drinks; the two men walked to the far side of the room, where the television set was playing softly.

"Well, here's to us," Donovan said. "We gave it

a good ride."

"We *are* giving it a good ride," Petrov said. Before Donovan could ask him what he meant, Petrov bent over and turned up the sound on the television. Bobby Mendoza's face had appeared, being interviewed at a press conference in police headquarters.

Petrov was impressed with how smoothly the police lieutenant handled himself. He told how after the first two men were killed, he had managed to find out through Interpol that they were associated with Iranian terrorist causes. Then he lightly traced his investigation through his contact with the Wheels wheelchair company and Fazid's restaurant, and said that the clue that there might be trouble at the United Nations had come from Fazid himself. No, he had not had assistance from any agency of the United States government. And, he added, there had just been a lot of luck involved in busting up the U.N. plot. He made no mention of Donovan or Petrov or Abu Beka, and when he was done after seven minutes, Donovan spoke aloud to the screen: "Good work, Bobby."

"He is much slicker than he appears to be," Petrov said. "He would be worth having with us."

"It's all hypothetical now," Donovan said. A bell suddenly started ringing over the television set, and the news channel's anchorman said:

"This just in. The body of a man, his throat

474

slashed, was found just moments ago in a lavatory at Newark Airport. Police said that a note was found with the body which read, and I am quoting: 'I am Abu Beka. The failure of the attack today upon the United Nations was my failure, since I was in charge of this operation for the government of Iran. I cannot live with this shame."

The anchorman cleared his throat. "We have crews right now on their way to Newark Airport, but police there said they had recovered the suicide knife. Airline tickets on the dead man identified him as Gaspar Castelnuevo, but nothing further is known about him. In a ghastly and bizarre postscript to the death, police said that Castelnuevo was wearing a rubber pig mask over his head when his body was found.

"Now the big question is . . . is this truly the body of Abu Beka, the legendary head of the feared Tenterallah terrorist organization? We'll have crews covering the rest of this story for you as it unfolds. And now this message."

Donovan turned the sound back down on the television.

"Castelnuevo. Wasn't that the wheelchair factory?"

"Yes, it was," Petrov said. He was watching the television with his hands in his pockets. He felt the piece of paper he had taken from Hassan's desk just after killing the Iranian. It had read:

"G.C. From Newark, Flight 353 to Paris, 4 P.M. Tuesday." It had told Petrov what he needed to know, and now he crumpled the paper and dropped it into an ashtray.

Donovan was grinning broadly as he turned back to Petrov. "Did you have to use a rubber mask?" he said.

"I told you, my butcher shop was closed," Petrov said softly.

"I'll be sure to buy you a new knife," Donovan said.

"Perhaps. We must see first what your government and mine think about our work today."

How many has he killed in the last twenty-four hours? Donovan could not help thinking. *Four? five? And yet here he is as cold as an iceberg wondering about what our governments will think. No wonder everyone in Vietnam feared Molina.*

Later, Maggie Henson returned from the funeral home, where she had made arrangements for Carol's funeral. Everyone had finished eating the Chinese food that Tilda had brought home and she and Mark were in the kitchen cleaning up the dishes.

Maggie and Petrov found themselves alone in a corner of the living room and in response to the look on her face, he said, "You know it all now,

I guess."

"Yes, Tolly. I can only thank you for trying to save Carol."

"I'm sorry I was not able to do it."

After a long pause Maggie said, "I guess you'll be going back to Russia now."

"I guess so," Petrov said. "But the final decision will be made by my government. They may not be pleased with our activities today."

"You did nothing wrong," she said.

"No? But many are dead. We will see what Moscow thinks."

They were interrupted by the ringing of the doorbell. Jeff was the first one to the door, but Petrov pushed him aside gently and opened the door himself.

A delivery man stood there, cradling a cardboard box in his arms.

"Are you Peterson?"

"Yes," Petrov said.

"This is for you. Don't worry about the tip, it's already taken care of."

He handed over the box which was surprisingly heavy and Petrov took it inside, placed it on the coffee table, and began to open it.

"What is it?" Donovan said as he walked from the kitchen, drying his hands on a towel.

Petrov looked at the tall American and answered, "A case of Stolichnaya vodka."

And both men grinned.

ESPIONAGE FICTION BY WARREN MURPHY AND MOLLY COCHRAN

GRANDMASTER (17-101, $4.50)

There are only two true powers in the world. One is goodness. One is evil. And one man knows them both. He knows the uses of pleasure, the secrets of pain. He understands the deadly forces that grip the world in treachery. He moves like a shadow, a promise of danger, from Moscow to Washington — from Havana to Tibet. In a game that may never be over, he is the grandmaster.

THE HAND OF LAZARUS (17-100, $4.50)

A grim spectre of death looms over the tiny County Kerry village of Ardath. The savage plague of urban violence has begun to weave its insidious way into the peaceful fabric of Irish country life. The IRA's most mysterious, elusive, and bloodthirsty murderer has chosen Ardath as his hunting ground, the site that will rock the world and plunge the beleaguered island nation into irreversible chaos: the brutal assassination of the Pope.

Available wherever paperbacks are sold, or order direct from the Publisher. Send cover price plus 50¢ per copy for mailing and handling to Pinnacle Books, Dept. 17-333, 475 Park Avenue South, New York, N.Y. 10016. Residents of New York, New Jersey and Pennsylvania must include sales tax. DO NOT SEND CASH.

PINNACLE'S FINEST IN SUSPENSE
AND ESPIONAGE

OPIUM   (17-077, $4.50)
by Tony Cohan

Opium! The most alluring and dangerous substance
known to man. The ultimate addiction, ensnaring all in its
lethal web. A nerve-shattering odyssey into the perilous
heart of the international narcotics trade, racing from the
beaches of Miami to the treacherous twisting alleyways of
the Casbah, from the slums of Paris to the teeming Hong
Kong streets to the war-torn jungles of Vietnam.

TRUK LAGOON   (17-121, $3.95)
by Mitchell Sam Rossi

Two bizarre destinies inseparably linked over forty years
unlease a savage storm of violence, treachery, and greed on
a tropic island paradise. The most incredible covert operation in military history is about to be uncovered — a lethal
mystery hidden for decades amid the wreckage of war far
beneath the Truk Lagoon.

LAST JUDGMENT   (17-114, $4.50)
by Richard Hugo

Seeking vengeance for the senseless murders of his brother,
sister-in-law, and their three children, former S.A.S. agent
James Ross plunges into the perilous world of fanatical terrorism to prevent a centuries-old vision of the Apocalypse
from becoming reality, as the approaching New Year
threatens to usher in mankind's dreaded Last Judgment.

THE JASMINE SLOOP   (17-113, $3.95)
by Frank J. Kenmore

A man of rare and lethal talents, Colin Smallpiece has
crammed ten lifetimes into his twenty-seven years. Now,
drawn from his peaceful academic life into a perilous web
of intrigue and assassination, the ex-intelligence operative
has set off to locate a U.S. senator who has vanished mys-
teriously from the face of the Earth.

*Available wherever paperbacks are sold, or order direct from the
Publisher. Send cover price plus 50¢ per copy for mailing and
handling to Pinnacle Books, Dept. 17-333, 475 Park Avenue
South, New York, N.Y. 10016. Residents of New York, New Jer-
sey and Pennsylvania must include sales tax. DO NOT SEND
CASH.*